book one of the ellderet series

The
Deadbringer

E. M. Markoff

Tomes
& Coffee
PRESS

The Deadbringer

The Deadbringer *is a work of fiction. Names, characters, places, and incidents
either are the product of the author's imagination or are used fictitiously. Any
resemblances to actual persons living or dead, events, or locales is entirely
coincidental.*

Cover art: Pink Pigeon Studio, www.gabriellaquiroz.com
Map, interior illustrations, and formatting: E. M. Markoff
Edited: G. Markoff
Body text set in book antiqua

ISBN 978-0-9971951-0-1 (pbk.)
ISBN 978-0-9971951-1-8 (ebook)

Printed in the United States of America

DEDICATION

To the two slave drivers in my life, Gabriel Markoff and Silva D. Frankian. Without you, I would not have been able to breathe life into Moenda and its people. They exist because you believed in me and in them.

This book is also for You, the reader, for taking a chance. I am truly grateful that you decided to pick up this book, and I look forward to hearing your thoughts. Enjoy, and let's meet again at the end of Kira's journey.

Contents

The Land of Moenda

Cities ★ Towns ●
Canals ═ Rivers ─
Roads ---

N

Opulancae ★   Silver River   Jané ★
Xulmé ●   The Great Knife   Idle Bay

The Gods'
Spears

The
Sink

Winged Serpents' Dirge

Labyrinth
of the
Cursed   Silent River   Silfria ●
Rhaemond ●

The
Ayotil

Forged River   Suelosa ★

The
Eastern
Sea

Laloc
Desert

● Kessrennt   Nhaleri ●

The
Hidden
Sea

Foreign Hills

Lerpour ★   River of Veins   Ulivi ●
South
Basin

Kataru
Highlands   Trader's Road   Crescent
Bay   Ilvra ●

Western Mountains   Florinia ★

©E. M. Markoff 2016

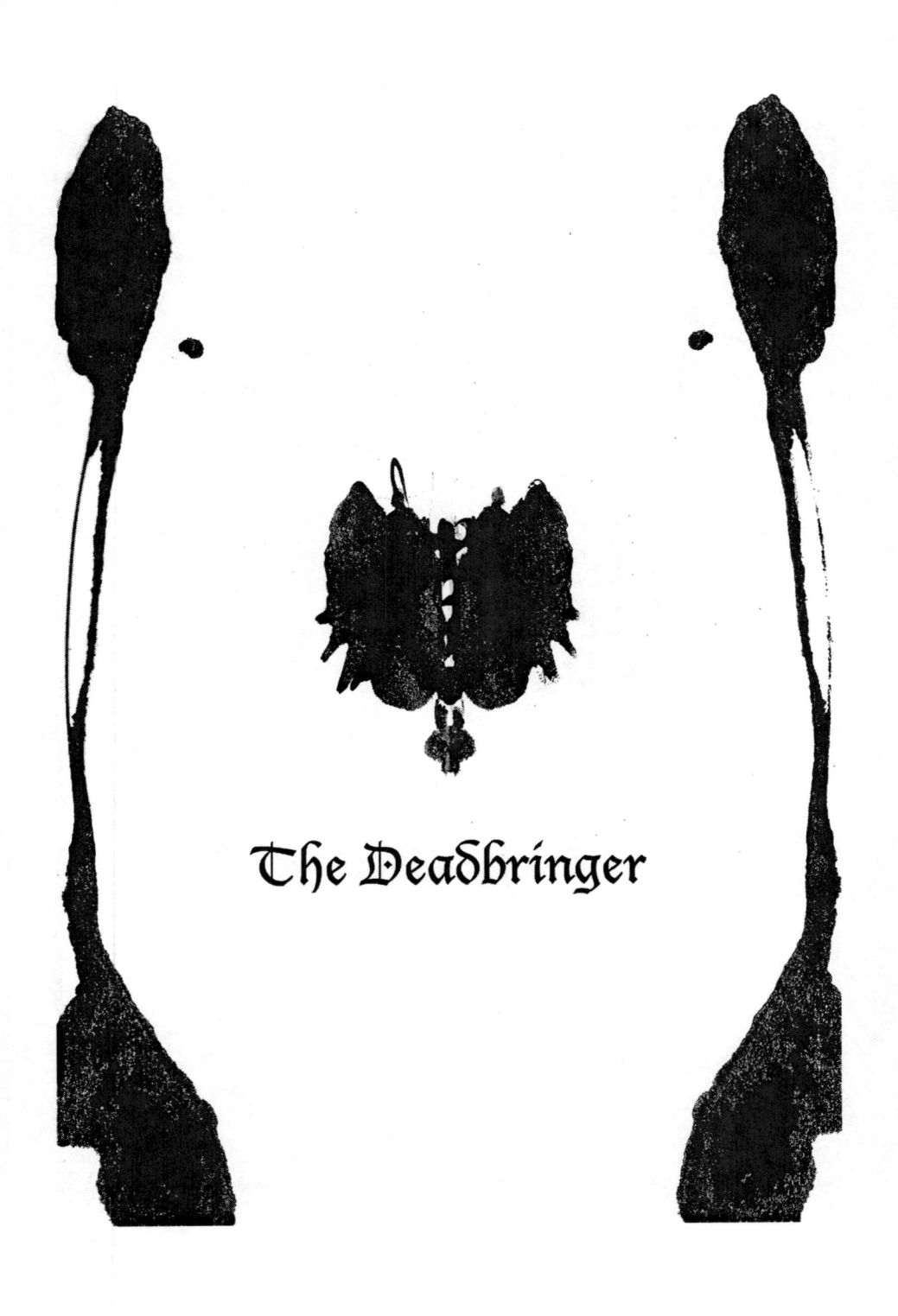

The Deadbringer

THE SHINING CITY

THE DAY HAD dawned gray, as it had for the past week, thick with storm clouds barring the sun. The gentle rains of summer had been late. Now, well into the fall, as if seeking to make amends for its tardiness, the rain turned dirt into mud that splattered onto everything, turned streets into shallow streams that carried away the filth that had piled up over the long, dry summer. But the dreary weather did not deter the bustle of Opulancae.

Kira Vidal looked up at the midmorning sky with slightly uptilted, emerald-gold eyes and let the rain briefly wash his pale face. It felt cold and refreshing, just like the touch of the dead. Laughing softly, the tall youth turned his attention back to the bustle of the city and resumed his trek against the human current, his dapple gelding following close behind. He pulled forward the hood of his woolen traveling cloak, revealing long gloves that followed the length of his arms. Aside from the cloak, his clothing was entirely of supple black leather: long boots that climbed to his knees, sturdy pants, and a loose vest with ivory buttons.

He was eager to be done with his errands in the newer part of Opulancae so he could ride to the Old Town to visit Elia. And he was growing tired of seeing the long-worn signs nailed throughout the city warning that Ro'Erden and Deadbringers were not welcome. He continued on, placing an order for slate and fieldstone at one shop and an order for rough lumber at another. As was customary, he paid half of the cost up front and would pay the other half when the materials were delivered.

"How's your uncle?" asked the second shopkeeper, as he gathered the gold from the counter.

"He's well," Kira replied cordially. Though young, his voice was rich, with just the slightest rasp. Lowering his hood, he took a leather tie from an inside pocket and began securing a cascade of raven hair that fell to his waist. It was damp and beginning to feel unpleasant resting against his back.

"Say, by any chance, was your parlor the one that buried Mrs. Stone?"

"No."

The shopkeeper continued as if Kira had added a *why* after the *no*. "Rumor's been going around saying that she was murdered and that it was her daughter who did it. Thought maybe the body passed through your parlor and that you could say whether it looked like a murder." He leaned over the counter. "I hear she looked like animals had torn her apart, and that the city authorities might petition the Bastion for aid."

"No, I know nothing of it," said Kira, repressing a sigh. He hated gossip.

He had indeed heard others whispering terrible rumors as he went about his errands, though it was the truth that their parlor had tended no one by that name. But he had learned that it was best to feign complete ignorance, as it kept his name and his uncle's out of the rumors. He doubted the Bastion — the ruling power in the North — would intervene in local affairs for something as common as murder. Taking his leave before the shopkeeper had a chance to ask anything else, he swiftly mounted his horse and rode off toward the river road and the Old Town.

HAD KIRA WALKED that day, he would have been able to reach the Old Town by descending the narrow flight of stairs that had been carved from the side of the high bluff that lined the river, upon which the newer sections of Opulancae had been built. But he had ridden and, since his horse could not sprout wings and fly like a bird or the long-dead winged serpents, he had been forced to take the river road, which went by roundabout way down the bluff to the river's embankments.

The Silver River had reached out beyond those embankments, submerging the ancient flood plain where the Old Town had long ago risen. Murky waters reached up to the dapple's cannons and *sloshed* wildly as it trotted along. Kira's heart ached with sadness as he neared the Old Town, for it had suffered from the heavy assault of rain, and the runoff pouring down the bluff from the surrounding city had only served to augment the damage. The ground beneath the town was a sea of knee-high water, and the modest wooden dwellings propped up on wooden stilts were islands.

Despite their misfortune, the people waved upon seeing him and shouted out greetings. They had learned to endure the many changes that life by the river brought with it. What they had not learned to endure was the harsh nature of Opulancae itself—the city their river had helped foster. The Old Town was a poor, largely ignored place.

Kira dismounted and offered to help where he could, but there was little he could do that the people had not already taken care of. Still, he helped carry a bale of wool from a home that had sprung a leak, and then helped sort out the damaged material from the undamaged. For the people of the Old Town, it was vital to take care of the few goods they had.

"Here to see Elia?" asked one of the townsmen.

Kira smiled. "Yes. Was her home damaged by the rain?"

"No, but we checked it ourselves. Just to make sure, you know?"

"Oh, yes! She will never admit to needing help."

The other man laughed heartily. "That she won't! Go on, boy, we've kept you long enough. I'm sure she's heard you're here and is waiting for you to arrive. Say hello to your uncle for me."

Bidding them farewell, Kira *sloshed* along with his horse in tow until he reached a wooden house built upon thick wooden stilts, surrounded by hanging baskets filled with aromatic herbs. Thankful that his height and long boots had kept him mostly dry, he stepped out of the water and onto the steps that led to the porch surrounding the house. His uncle had built the porch so Elia could hang her baskets to keep them from being damaged or washed away.

He approached the door and was about to knock when it suddenly swung open. A slightly hunched, elderly woman barely reaching his chest looked up at him with pursed lips. Soft gray curls crowned her head. She motioned for him to enter.

"Foolish boy, coming here with the rain. That uncle of yours knows full well that the river tends to overflow during the rainy season. Next time I see him, we're going to have a long talk." She waved her frail-looking hands in the air, displeased.

Kira had spent a few years as a child in the Old Town, and its people, in particular Elia, the old herbalist, held a special place in his heart. She had always been very kind to him and had taken it upon herself to be a very active part of his upbringing—much to his uncle's dismay.

"Though late this year, it is indeed the rainy season. Regardless, I wanted to see you." He placed a gloved hand over her head and gave her a kiss through it.

She brushed his hand away. "Don't give me that 'coming to see me' business. You young folk already have enough on your shoulders without wasting your time on a bag of bones like me."

There was a heavy weight to her brow that he had never seen before. "Did something happen?" She dismissed his question with a *humph* and took a seat at the dining table. Elia was rather proud, and he knew better than to press her. When she was ready, she would tell him what ailed her.

Opening the oiled-leather bag slung around his shoulder, Kira pulled out two square-shaped bundles wrapped in waxed paper. He placed them on the table and unwrapped them, revealing two small cakes. "I baked them myself. I used a bit more sugar than I would have liked—which means they are very sweet—but coffee should help wash them down." He returned his hand to the bag and pulled out an assortment of glass containers. "I also brought more coffee and spices to replenish your stores, since I saw that you were running low."

"It's appreciated, but I've told you not to bring me such expensive things. I don't like feeling like I'm a leech."

"You're not, and besides, I bought these with my money, not my uncle's, so it's my call how I decide to spend it." She mumbled under her breath but said nothing more. Kira removed his damp traveling cloak, hung it on a hook near the door, and set about to making coffee. It was something he always did when he visited her.

Elia called to him from where she sat at the table. "Well, just make sure you make enough. No sense in just wetting your lips and then being left wanting more."

He laughed warmly. Her sharp tongue was one of the reasons he adored her so much. His uncle, on the other hand, often commented that instead of age having claimed her posture, it should have claimed her tongue.

Once the coffee was brewed, he brought it over and laid out everything they would need to share the small meal. Elia took a bite of her cake. "Not bad. I wouldn't advise dropping your trade as a mortician for that of a baker, but"—she closed her eyes and sipped her coffee—"your skill at brewing flavorful coffee is quite impressive. I'd like to think I had a hand in this, but I'm sure your uncle would say otherwise."

"I'm sure he would if he could, but he's more a tea drinker, so he would have to keep his opinions to himself."

"As best he should." She soaked a piece of cake in the coffee and idly nibbled it. Her words were slow and weighted. "Kira, do you ever think of your parents?"

"Every now and again. But honestly, I don't—and can't—imagine my life without my uncle. Although, I know he thinks of my mother, his sister. Every year, during the weeks leading up to my name day, he becomes very morose and tends to stare at me when he thinks I'm not watching."

She frowned. "You don't bear much of a resemblance to your uncle, except in height. He confessed to me that your mother died giving birth to you. But, I'm pretty sure he told you that?"

"Yeah, he did. But he simply refuses to speak of her. And of my father—my uncle never knew who he was."

"Unsurprising. Many children born during the Purging don't know their fathers."

Kira quickly devoured his bit of cake and chased it down with a few sips of hot coffee. "My uncle does say that I didn't get my eyes from his side of the family, so my father must have been from the Western Mountains. But he doesn't ever talk about those years, though I have tried asking. I have to admit, I've always been curious to know what the Land was like during that time."

"The Nightmare Lords damn those years. Nobody wants to remember them."

A question came to Kira, one that he could not resist asking. "Elia, have you ever seen a Doll?"

She shot him a mischievous grin. "So, when you're curious, this bag of bones is finally good for something, hmm?"

Kira felt the heat rise to his face. "That is not what I meant!"

She laughed, obviously satisfied with his reaction. Then, flatly, she said, "I have seen a Doll."

"Really?"

"Should I say 'no,' instead?"

"No, no, no," said Kira, rushed. "It's just that I *know* my uncle has seen a Doll, but he won't tell me. Or at least I think he has. Actually, I'm not sure."

"Awfully curious, aren't you?"

"Of course! I mean, it is a part of the history of the Land. I guess my problem is that I'm not sure if I believe what I've read concerning Deadbringers and their Dolls—that Dolls were no different from the soulless, reanimated Risen. That they were monstrous corpses."

"If the Ascendancy heard what you thought of the printed words they spread as truth, you would not be sitting here. We may not be in the

South, but watch that tongue of yours. I wouldn't put it past the people of Opulancae to cry to the Bastion that you are a traitor."

"The Bastion is not the Ascendancy."

"*Humph.* A horse is a horse even if you dress it in silks."

"Fine, fine. Now tell me what Dolls looked like."

Elia took a curt sip from her cup before speaking. "A Deadbringer's Doll had fake eyes that never blinked and were vacant and glassy. Their skin was lusterless, and their lower arms and hands were often discolored, as if they had been dipped in a deep red dye. Not surprising, considering they were once alive. But no, the ones I saw were not 'monstrous.'"

"And?" asked Kira, almost unable to hide his excitement.

"And what?" Elia said tartly. "I can only tell you what a Doll looked like, not how one was made."

"Sorry. I let my curiosity get the better of me." Elia took a deep breath, failing to repress a shuddering sigh. He eyed her quizzically. "What's the matter? And don't tell me 'nothing.'"

She sighed heavily once more. "Must something be wrong? Can't an old woman sigh if she wants to?" Rising from the table, she walked over to an ornate cabinet and retrieved a red lacquer box. Taking her seat once more, she opened the box and held out a blue amber comb.

"This was given to me by my partner when we first started seeing each other. When my daughter came of age I gave it to her. She left it behind." Wetting her lips, she continued. "I'm old. I don't have anyone to leave my belongings to, and of the little I own this is the most precious. I know you'll take good care of it."

He took the comb from her. Though delicate in appearance, it was firm and heavy. "Thank you. I'll take good care of it."

"Then it's settled. Next time you visit me I want to see your hair set with that comb. Gods know you have more than enough hair to play around with. It might even help you find a pretty girl."

Kira sighed, vexed. He was glad to see Elia back to her sharp self but wished she had chosen another topic. "It's not that easy. You know that. Besides, I don't want to fall in love and then wind up accidentally killing them. I'm not very skilled at controlling this ability of mine."

"Nonsense! You're here, after all. Assuming that touching problem of yours was passed down from your father—because your uncle surely doesn't suffer from it—it didn't stop him from seeking out and bedding your mother." He winced, and she added, "Eutau wasn't very pleased when I discovered what your touch could do."

"No, he wasn't. I think it was one of the reasons we moved away from the Old Town. He was afraid that other people would become aware of it and that my life would be in danger."

Elia's mouth twisted. "Your uncle can have a cruel tongue and a violent temper when he chooses to, especially when he believes your life is in danger. He's very passionate about keeping you safe, but you can't hide behind those parlor doors forever, even though I'm sure Eutau wishes you would."

"He's the only living person I can interact with normally without having to wear these gloves for fear that I might hurt him. I love him dearly and will be content with my life as long as he's with me."

"A sweet sentiment to have, but also a dangerous one. We are not gods, but mortals whose lives quickly dwindle. One day he will die, and you will find yourself all alone in that grand house surrounded by the dead. That is not life."

Despite his better judgment, Kira smiled. "If my fate is to be surrounded by the dead, then so be it. As for my uncle, I'll make sure he never dies." Elia looked at him through narrowed eyes. "A joke, my dear lady," he teased. "Besides, happiness isn't dependent on finding a partner, and the people of Opulancae are not really my type."

She laughed heartily. "By the gods, now that is something I can agree with."

Kira would have liked to spend more time with Elia, but the afternoon was passing and his uncle would be waiting. He rose and bent down to kiss her farewell, but he was stopped by her wrinkled hand.

"None of this glove nonsense," she said, protesting. "Either kiss me proper or don't kiss me at all." He concentrated and kissed a bed of gray curls. Her hair was soft and smelled like lavender.

He would leave money with the candlemaker's son and see to it that she wanted for nothing and had plenty of everything, as he always did. Bidding her farewell, he took his cloak, mounted his horse, and rode away from the shallow sea that was the Old Town.

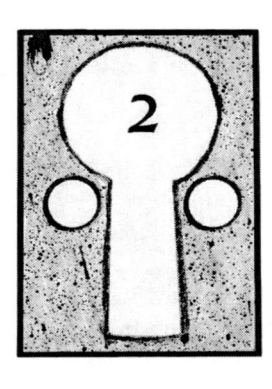

2

LOCKED DOORS

SHE HAS BEEN washed, clothed, and made up. Have you decided whether or not to have a viewing?"

The man sitting opposite him looked up in anguish. The cup of tea he had received sat untouched and cold. "I don't want people to see her as she is. I know she would've hated having people gawk at her." His body trembled as he spoke. "I won't let them laugh at her. I won't! I won't!"

Eutau leaned forward, arms resting on his knees. He was an austere-looking man with dark hair and pupil-less eyes the color of an oncoming storm. The softness in his voice seemed out of place. "She had been sick for quite some time?"

"Yes. But it wasn't her fault! She was a good and caring person and it wasn't right that she should've been stricken so ill."

"Indeed, she must have been a kind woman. Even in death, the gentleness of her spirit is evident."

"Your words are kind. But her body is wasted, her beautiful black hair thinned and balding. She is a shell; the last days of her life ensured as much." The man paused, shoulders slumping, head bowed low. "It's so awfully quiet without her. A part of me is grateful to the gods that she's no longer suffering, but the other part is stricken with grief, for I will never see her again. And, especially, not the way she was. Is it evil for me to feel this way?"

"No. The conflict you feel is testament to the love between the two of you." The man smiled weakly. It was the first time Eutau had seen him smile since he had come seeking their services. "I know this is hard for you, but would you like to see her?"

The man's smile vanished, and he drew a trembling breath. "Yes."

They rose and exited the spacious sitting room. As they entered the hallway, three small creatures scurried past. The smallest of the three, having trouble keeping up, ran back toward Eutau and went up on tiny hind legs. Eutau bent down and held out his hand. It climbed up his arm happily, swishing its bushy tail to and fro, and settled around his neck under an uneven mess of dark hair, where it proceeded to wash its short brown snout and the fluffy white tufts that adorned the tips of its pointed ears.

"Such odd looking kittens," the man said, his voice uncertain, questioning.

"Kittens? No. They are pointed-ear woodrats. This one is named Belle."

"Rats! Are such creatures not diseased?"

Eutau concealed his annoyance with a smile. "You are thinking of city rats. But, you are correct—many are diseased. Sadly, Opulancae suffers from quite a plague of them. Some worse than others." The man said nothing more and quietly followed Eutau to the viewing room that was directly across from the sitting room. In the center, propped upon a worked-metal table, was a pine casket with dainty lilies carved into the sides.

Eutau cautioned the man. "I beg that you do not touch the lilies, for the stain has not yet cured. The weather has not been cooperative."

Nodding, the man approached the casket and peered in. He wheeled about, outrage marring his face. "What cruel joke is this? This woman is not my partner!"

Eutau took the man's outburst in stride. "Is she not? Look closer."

"Do you take me for a fool not to recognize my partner of so many years?"

"What your eyes sought was the wasted body she passed away in. My nephew was able to restore a bit of her dignity by fashioning a wig from his own hair. A small thing it may seem, but, I agree, the change is shocking."

The pained man looked back at the body lying in the casket and, after a brief moment, broke into uncontrolled sobs. "It is her! Forgive me, my beloved, for not having recognized you! This must be a dream, ah yes, it must be. If so, let me never awaken."

Eutau went back to the sitting room to indulge in a cup of tea while the man wept to his heart's content. He drank slowly. The way the man was carrying on, there was no need to rush.

The sitting room had always been his favorite spot in the house. Large stained glass windows generously lined one wall from ceiling to floor. Even on dreary days like today, enough light still managed to pour in. It saved him from having to ignite the oil lanterns for their clients. The other walls were a deep shade of red with white trimming, while the floor was covered with woven wool carpets inlaid with intricate scrolling designs. The carpets, along with many of the other furnishings, had been imported from Florinia, a city in the South.

Recalling the man's expression upon seeing his partner, Eutau smiled. *It was more than a wig Kira fashioned for her, but that you need not know.*

Belle had abandoned his neck in favor of seeking shelter underneath his high-collared shirt. Her efforts had burst open many of the buttons, exposing his chest and stomach. She pressed her tiny body up against his waist, shivering. Keeping one hand cupped around his shirt so she would not slip out—which she was precariously close to doing—and holding the teacup with the other, he took a seat on a wooden, scroll-worked recamier. He then carefully set his tea down on the green medallion upholstery to better focus on Belle.

Coaxing her out of his shirt and onto his lap, he grabbed a nearby blanket, gently swaddled her in it, and laid her down near the headrest. He then began to refasten the buttons of his shirt, but paused. Starting at the base of his neck and running all the way down to his waist were numerous thick, uneven, red-black scars that marred his muscled body. His strong fingers settled on a scar over his heart, tracing the length of it. He then pulled up a long sleeve, revealing more scars on his arm. He sneered bitterly and began refastening the buttons.

The soft pitter-patter of rain rapped against the stained glass windows, blurring the world beyond. It was getting late, and Kira had not yet returned from his errands. Eutau had no doubt that he had gone to visit Elia in the Old Town. If so, Kira would return soaked from head to toe, especially if the river had overflowed. *Stew was the correct choice, after all.* Having finished his tea, Eutau went back to the viewing room and knocked on the door.

"Can I come in?" he asked.

A stuffy-nosed "Yes" answered him. Eutau entered. The distraught man had pulled up one of the chairs and positioned it next to the casket. His face was swollen, his eyes raw, but there was a peace about him that had not been present before. "I've decided to have a viewing. This way people will remember her as she was."

"Tomorrow, then. The viewing shall be held in the morning and, in the afternoon, the burial."

Peacefully, the man looked back at his partner. "Will the headstone be ready also? I requested quite a bit of work."

Eutau took a contemplative breath. The man had indeed commissioned an intricate headstone: a broken column, three feet high, partially draped by a veil and lightly entwined with broken rosebuds. "Stonework is my nephew's talent, not mine. Since he is not here, I can give no sure answer."

The man waved a hand. "I'm sorry. Please don't worry. Your parlor has been too kind to both me and my partner. I'm sure the fine wig the young sir fashioned must have taken time. The headstone can wait. Besides, this foul weather would hinder the placement of the headstone, correct?"

"Yes, it could shift. Your understanding is much appreciated." Eutau inwardly counted his blessings. Some clients could be very demanding when it came to having intricate headstones done on such short notice.

The man eventually left and, at last alone and with the day's affairs finally settled, Eutau made a mental list of what he would need for tomorrow while he tidied up the parlor. He wrinkled his nose as he closed the doors to the viewing room. The faintest smell of rot lingered in the air. He took a handful of incense sticks out from the drawer of a writing desk in the sitting room, lit them, and placed them all about the first floor. Scented smoke quickly filled the air. *Unlike you, my dear nephew, I am not fond of the smell of rot.* The thought put an unpleasant frown on his face, for it reminded him of the growing friction between them.

Eutau had dismissed it as concern over Kira's growing abilities but, in truth, the answer was simple. Kira's physical resemblance to his father as he aged was growing uncanny, as was his ever-increasing infatuation with interacting with the dead. But, above all else, it was his insistence in wanting to create a Doll that irked Eutau the most. Eutau snorted disgustedly. He hated Dolls. Yet, despite resembling *that* man, Kira was nothing like him. Kira's personality was more akin to his mother's, as were his eyes. For Eutau, the eyes were what kept him from becoming lost in memories he fought desperately to keep buried.

The doorbell rang.

Brought out of his morose contemplation, Eutau abandoned the sitting room and went out to the foyer. He opened the front door. Before him stood a tall, portly man who nervously wrung his hands as he spoke.

"Uh, yes. I'm sorry to be calling at such a late hour."

Eutau gave an exaggerated sigh. "The downside to being a mortician is that the living do not have a set schedule for dying. Please, come in." The man entered the foyer and looked about, eyes darting from one corner to another. "What can I d—"

"I need the service of a Deadbringer!"

"Deadbringer," Eutau said calmly. "Is that what they are calling morticians these days?"

"My mother was murdered. The local authorities believe my sister is to blame because all property was left to her. Also, it doesn't help that they found her unconscious in the same room as our mother. But she's innocent! I know she is!" The man took in a deep breath and steadied himself. "My sister is a strong woman, but the attack from all sides has been too much for her. Currently, she's living with my partner and me. She's in a pitiful and delirious state. I'm afraid of what she might do to herself." He looked down at the toes of his muddied boots, voice trailing off. "Please . . . please . . . I don't want to lose her as well."

"I am sorry for your plight, but you are in the wrong place. Also, a word of friendly advice, it is not wise to openly state your interest in a race that cannot be sought out or consorted with, on pain of a swift death from the authorities."

"Please, don't push me out! Please tell me I'm in the right place! I've already been to some of the other parlors in the city and they ran me out most viciously, assuring me I was mad."

Eutau was unsure what to do with the man, who seemed on the verge of having a seizure. "I am sorry that this is happening to you, but how you came to such a notion is absur—"

"Worthington!"

Eutau froze. "Excuse me?"

It took a few seconds for the man to realize that he had been asked a question. "Worthington is an old friend of the family's. He confided in me that the owners of a mortician's parlor were the ones responsible for bringing to justice the murderer of his youngest son. He said that the parlor worked in conjunction with the Bastion and that the Deadbringer was one of them. Worthington did not name the parlor or the Deadbringer—he also mentioned something about a binding seal—but your parlor is famed for doing wonders with the dead. Please, sir, I'm not mad, nor do I mean any offense to your person if such an accusation offends you. But if I am mistaken, please tell me so!"

Eutau schooled his face to remain impassive, but inwardly he was a hard knot of anger and concern. Already the man was causing trouble by visiting the morticians' parlors in Opulancae and giving the same idiotic speech. It would not bode well for them if rumors spread of Deadbringers residing in Opulancae. Their only saving grace was that the man was aware that the Deadbringer he sought had ties to the Bastion, and thus that it was not a fugitive. He resisted the urge to grate his teeth.

As he thought how to respond, Eutau caught sight of Kira hiding in the shadows of the hallway adjacent to the foyer. He had come in through the kitchen. It would not do for the man to see him. Thinking quickly, Eutau asked, "If your need is so great, then why did you not go straight to the Bastion?"

A flash of something akin to triumph passed over the man's face. "I feared that if I went first to the Bastion they would bar me from seeking the Deadbringer or turn me away or lock me up. I realized that if I could find the Deadbringer on my own and explain my situation, maybe then the Deadbringer could intervene on my behalf."

"And the thought of coming face-to-face with a race so feared it was hunted to extinction was preferable? Your excuse is rather weak."

"It's all I have."

Eutau pinched the bridge of his nose and hoped he was making the right decision. He was about to give instructions when it suddenly dawned on him that they had not exchanged formalities.

"Do you also have no name?" he asked testily. "It is poor manners to propose business without introducing oneself."

"My sincere apologies," the man said, abashed. "I am Nathaniel Kirk Stone. But please, call me Nate."

Eutau forced a smile, trying to conceal the fury that he was sure was welling in his eyes. "I strongly suggest, *Nate*, that you make time to visit the Bastion and ask to see Agent Kim Lafont."

"But what if the Bastion or this Lafont don't believe my story and think I'm seeking a Deadbringer for some malevolent purpose? I don't want to be locked away or put to death!" Stone's voice had taken on an unattractive high pitch.

Now *he is concerned!* Eutau thought, frustrated with the man and greatly wanting him to leave so he could speak with Kira and then step outside for a much-needed smoke. He wrapped an arm around Stone's shoulder, shuffling him to the door. "I regretfully assure you that neither death nor eternal imprisonment await you. Although, make sure to ask *specifically* for Agent Lafont."

Stone's shoulders twitched as he spoke. "Does this mean that . . . are you the Deadbringer?"

Eutau did not answer, instead repeating his instructions and adding, "Do not fret, for I personally will inform the Bastion of your plight . . . in detail." The portly man went pale. It was the reaction Eutau had wanted to see. Eutau walked the man out of the parlor, waited until he had mounted his horse and galloped away, and then slammed the door shut and locked it.

Only then did Kira walk out from the shadows, his clothes sopping wet and his feet bare. Eutau examined him. *He left his boots in the kitchen. They must be a mess.*

"I made stew," said Eutau.

"I saw."

"I have to call on Kim. Tonight."

"I know. But we will eat together before you ride out, right?" Concern filled Kira's eyes. He was well-aware of the consequences that would result if word of his existence spread.

Eutau smiled reassuringly and pressed the palm of his hand against Kira's cold cheek. "Go change into dry clothes. I will warm up the food and we will eat together, as we always do." Kira nodded and vanished up a flight of stairs. Alone, Eutau ran his fingers through his uneven hair and cursed to himself. *Dammit, why now?* He turned down the hallway that led to the kitchen. As he passed the viewing room, the faint scent of rot caught his nose.

It was going to be a long night.

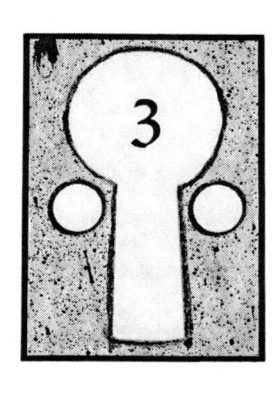

THE BASTION

WORTHINGTON'S GRATITUDE IS shallow and his loyalty poor. The Bastion, and Kim in particular, will not be pleased." Sal's face was somber, her voice stern.

"The binding seals used to silence tongues did not tighten in this case," spat Eutau. "They loosened."

"Your bitterness is merited, but talented spellcasters are difficult to come by these days, and seals are only as strong as their caster."

Eutau shot her an annoyed glance. "A lecture, Sal?"

Lean fingers ruffled a long mane of thick blond hair. "No. It's merely my way of saying 'sorry.' But you knew one day the moment would arrive when Kira's true nature would be discovered. Or have you been living in a fantasy?"

"I stopped living in a fantasy the moment Kira was born, and when I saw the Ascendancy's Sanctifiers publicly butcher the last Deadbringer. They proclaimed peace the second the woman's blood spilled onto the podium. And the Land cheered." He watched as pale blue eyes considered him. Sal's features were typical of northern women: narrow at the hips yet buxom in the chest, fair-haired, fair-eyed, and slender of face.

"You haven't asked why Kim isn't here. It is rather late."

Eutau's head perked up mockingly. "It slipped my mind, oh yes. Where is High Councilman Kim Lafont?"

Sal laughed softly. "Busy, but we'll see each other tomorrow, and I can relay the events then. Have you eaten? Kim brought back a wheel of goat cheese from further north. It's quite good, though a bit dry."

Faced with her kindness, Eutau felt childish, and he finally acceded to it. "Thank you, but I ate before riding out. Sal, did Kim tell you that he extended an invitation to Kira to become an agent of the Bastion?"

She furrowed her brow, interested. "He hadn't told me. I'm assuming you said no, but why would Kira reject the offer? As an agent, it would mean immunity for him against all of the Ascendancy, and the Sanctifiers in particular."

Eutau resisted the urge to laugh. "Our lives before belonged solely to us. We were unimportant, just two more people residing in Opulancae. Now the eyes of the Bastion are upon us and our lives are no longer ours. There is no such thing as immunity. Not anymore."

"The Bastion has never forced Kira to do anything. We have only turned to him when all our efforts have proven useless and the talent of a Deadbringer is the only solution."

"True, but how many times can Kira say 'no' before those in power decide to tighten the leash? He was spared death upon discovery because he proved useful to you, but what good is a tool if you cannot use it at will?"

"Kira is not a tool."

"And that is why Kim's offer was turned down. If Kira were to become an agent then he would truly become a tool." To himself, Eutau thought, *Not everyone in the Bastion feels as you and Kim do. To believe otherwise is a fantasy. And the simple truth is that the Bastion did little to protect the Deadbringers during the Purging. I have no doubt they would try just as hard to protect Kira.*

Sal pressed her lean fingers against the sides of her forehead. "Eutau. No one in the Bastion is a tool, we're not the Ascendancy."

"No, you are not," Eutau admitted. "But that is my point. The Bastion may be powerful in the North, but it is nothing compared to the Ascendancy, which holds full power over the South and even now has great sway in the North. And what has given the Ascendancy the upper hand all these years? The fact that its elite warriors—the Sanctifiers—are uniquely comprised of Katarus, Ro'Erden, lesser spellcasters, and others, all fiercely loyal to its cause. The Bastion arose during the Purging to counter the power of the Ascendancy, but it has never managed to be its equal. But what if a Deadbringer were to join its ranks? Kira would help shift the scales in favor of the Bastion—not much, but a little. I will not have him become a pawn in a petty power struggle."

"Nor would I, Eutau." Rising from her chair, she went over to the hearth and rested a hand on the mantle. The other arm she draped across her waist. "It's best if we put our views aside, at least for tonight."

"Forgive me, Sal. I did not mean to take out my frustrations on you."

"No, you meant that for my partner." She stared into the fire, fatigue slackening her face. "How does the remainder of your week look?"

"Tomorrow is booked, but thereafter we are available."

"I suggest turning down any new work that might come up, at least for this week. The Bastion will want this matter settled quickly."

Eutau rose, walked over to the hearth, and placed his hand over Sal's arm. "How is Kim? And you?" *Forgive me . . .*

"He's kept busy. As for me, I wish the healers had not limited my hours at work so needlessly. Kira's visited me a few times when I'm home. He brings me cakes that are a tad too sweet and chats about everything and anything."

"Yes, I know." *. . . I should have come sooner. But . . .*

Pale blue eyes looked sadly up at him. "You're always welcome, Eutau." He unconsciously squeezed her arm and looked away, into the fire. "The loss of my baby reminded you of your sister, didn't it?"

He continued staring at the fire but said nothing. The room seemed cramped, the air stifling.

"The healers told me that the grief will subside with time," said Sal. "But it doesn't, does it? It's been two months now, but this sense of loss is the one feeling that never truly leaves. With time it has become bearable, but it's always there." She took his hand in hers. She was trembling. "You have to pretend to be strong, to pretend that when you're alone the memory doesn't creep up, trying to drown you. And you don't want people to ask, 'What's wrong?' because if they do, you'll be swept away. So, you smile."

Eutau let out a shuddering sigh and looked at her. "Kira's name day was a few days before you lost the baby. I . . . I should have come to see you and offer my support. Forgive me."

"Grief has no prescribed way of behaving. It's an enigma." Sighing heavily, she pulled away from him. "Get the parlor's affairs in order and prepare for a Summoning before the week is out. Once a formal order is given, I will send word with Paten. Have you discussed with Kira whether or not he'll consent?"

"It is in the best interest of all that Stone's request be fulfilled. However, I would ask that, if possible, you find a more adept spellcaster."

"Very well. I know you don't have faith in the Bastion, but have faith in my partner and in me. We'll do whatever is in our power to keep Kira safe. It's the least I can do after what he sacrificed to help us bring to justice the murderer responsible for the death of Worthington's son and of so many other innocent children."

"Sadly, good intentions are not always rewarded. It is ironic that the very conscience that compelled him to reveal himself to you, his desire to secure the safety and freedom of others, is what compromised our own freedom."

"His actions were honorable. He should never regret that."

"Honorable? Oh, yes," he said harshly. "But if honorable people were themselves honored, then there would still be Deadbringers roaming the lands." Sal placed a hand on her cheek as if struck. Eutau ran his fingers through his hair. *Dammit.* "I should leave. My concern has rendered my mood dour and my tongue harsh, and you deserve none of it."

"Yes, it's late. I think we're all on edge and will continue to be so until all this is over. Afterward, you must promise to come and visit me as the friend that you are."

"Thank you." Eutau smiled, grateful that she had not taken offense to his rudeness. He was tired but still had work to do once he returned to the parlor, and he doubted he would get much sleep until the viewing and burial were over. He regretted having been so harsh to Sal and inwardly promised to make it up to her.

Word from the Bastion arrived the next day, a few hours after the burial, and with it came approval to grant Mr. Stone's request on the following night. As Eutau had predicted, he never managed to get more than a few hours of sleep.

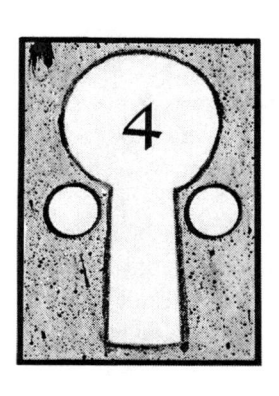

CORPSE ROAD

ON THE SOUTHWESTERN edge of Opulancae lay a ruined temple. What manner of temple it had been was unclear, and if gods had ever resided within its stone walls they were now no more than unrecognizable chunks of rock strewn across the cold floor. Vines strangled much of the stone and pierced through the cracked mortar, while ferns grew out of the walls and from rocky crevices. It was a garden of stone and plant.

In the center of the temple there was a round, shallow well. Its sides, just high enough to keep a curious child from falling in, were built of rocks the color of blood and bone. It was devoid of water yet, oddly enough, at the bottom there lay a mirror that gave it the illusion of being full. The mirror was tarnished and flaked with stones, but was intact.

Several miles south of the temple, curiously alone in the midst of the grassy plains that stretched for three days' hard ride south of Opulancae, rose a low, broad hill. A narrow, unpaved path wound from the temple door through the plains to end there. Perhaps because of its connection to the temple, the long-ago inhabitants of the Old Town had decided to use the hill as a burial site. Eventually, the path became known as Corpse Road, and the hill as Corpse Hill. For generations, the road felt the weighted feet of those carrying the burden of the dead in their hearts, until a series of unfortunate accidents led the people to believe that the path was cursed. The rumors of darkness and evil spread, and the cemetery fell into disuse.

It was where the late Mrs. Stone had requested she be buried.

The full moon hung overhead, illuminating a small group of people marching up Corpse Road in single file. Eutau led the way, hauling a wooden cart laden with a seven-foot mirror made of polished sardonyx, loosely covered with a thick tarp. He wore a simple coat with a wide-brimmed hood that concealed his face, a loose-fitting shirt that covered his scars, fitted breeches, and sturdy leather boots that climbed nearly to his knees.

Directly behind the cart was Kira, who helped steady it as they made their way up the pitted, stone-strewn path. He wore his normal black leathers with a traveling cloak, and like Eutau he too wore the hood of his cloak over his head. He took pains to make sure it concealed his face despite the occasional gusts of night wind that seemed determined to push it back.

Trailing close behind was Agent Paten, a muscular man with eternally red cheeks, a bushy mustache, and a wicked battle-axe. He wore an oilcloth duster over a dulled breastplate and dark blue agent's uniform. Behind him came Stone, his scared eyes seeming even larger in the light of the oil lantern he held out before him. He wore sturdy boots and several layers of clothing to keep warm throughout the long night.

In the rear were Sal and Tim, another agent. Tim was a sinewy man with oiled-back hair, a deep cleft in his chin, and droopy eyes that made him look like he was more asleep than awake. Sal and Tim were dressed similarly to Paten, save that they carried longswords as their weapons of choice. Oil lanterns in hand, they trailed close behind like a pair of glowbugs.

Before departing, Eutau had warned the party that the evil rumors concerning Corpse Road were indeed true. Only once had he and Kira ventured close, on a summer day several years before when Kira had been curious to have a look at the cemetery. They had only gone a few paces down the road before turning back after sensing something foul about the path and, even more so, about the fields that surrounded it.

Now, as the party slowly trundled along, the same foul feeling returned, and strongly. "No matter how troublesome the path may become, do not stray from it," said Eutau. "Your feet may thank you, but your soul will not."

Stone raised the lantern and looked out at the grassy fields on each side of the path. "I don't doubt your words. It was quite a hassle to convince the parlor within the city to bury my mother here. They too were wary of the path and begged that no one stray from it. But when I asked them why, they could not provide an explanation other than that the fields are cursed."

"So, how did you convince them to bury your mother at Corpse Hill?" asked Eutau, curious.

"Money."

"Maybe we should have brought some money to toss on the road," Tim jeered. "It seemed to work quite well for those fools."

"Not all the gold in the Land would have convinced me to accept such a request," Kira grumbled to no one in particular.

"And that's why I call them 'fools.' If *you* aren't comfortable here, then the gods help anyone else."

Sal studied the worn path and surrounding fields. The ground was smooth and bejeweled, with tall stalks of grass that swayed in the night wind like a silver veil. They looked warm and inviting. She shuddered. "I agree. There's something vile about this place."

Stone chuckled. "I'm glad I'm not the only one who is frightened by the superstition surrounding this area. Although, I must admit I had expected more courage from agents."

Eutau cleared his throat. "A courageous person does not ignore superstition, but acknowledges it and examines it. You would do well to heed our judgment, for this area is indeed dangerous."

"How so?"

Eutau steadied his grip on the cart. *The path is becoming more treacherous the further in we venture,* he thought. "This road—Corpse Road, Coffin Way, Procession Way, whatever name you choose to call it—was used solely for the purpose of transporting the dead. It became bad luck to use it for any other purpose than death.

"Depending on whether a path is Good or Bad, it can steal away the souls of the dead and trap them. These sharp rocks and holes are meant to trip the casket bearers and cause the corpse to fall onto the ground. When that happens, the soul of the departed is ripped away from the body and swallowed by the path—or at least, that is how I understand it." He looked down at the uneven terrain. "For whatever reason, this path is Bad, and it has swallowed many souls. As for why, I have no explanation."

Paten shook his head. "Ah, I must be a disappointment to this road, then, since my soul's already been collected."

"I didn't realize pleasure houses accepted souls as coin," jested Sal.

A mighty laugh poured from Paten's lips. "No need to worry. Come next payday, I'll have a bag full of 'souls' to part with."

Stone ignored them. "Returning to the topic of the road, why are we who still have blood pumping through our veins in peril?"

Eutau indulged Stone, not wanting to give Paten a chance to further inject himself into the conversation. "I have heard said that the Lurking Evil tainted this part of the land during the First War. In such a place, the living can become shadows that wander aimlessly until death takes mercy upon them. Others say that Deadbringers poisoned the land as a way to exact revenge."

"But if this area is tainted, then why is the path passable while the land beyond is not?"

"This path was laid long ago by the Ro'Erden. I suppose they wove some sort of enchantment into the stones as they were laid, but this path is like any other path in the sense that, if it is not maintained, it will degrade with time."

"You are a wealth of knowledge, aren't you? I see now why the Bastion holds you in such high esteem. After all, the Deadbringer is not you, but the boy. But both of you work together very closely, don't you?"

Eutau found the man's words odd, but he said nothing. Those words, however, had irked Tim. "His knowledge is our safe passage, and the boy's abilities your sister's freedom. And yes, they are under our protection. I suggest you commit that fact to heart."

Eutau felt a lurch in the cart and realized that Kira had stopped walking. Everyone stopped. Letting go of the cart, he clambered carefully across toward Kira, as the path was not wide enough to safely go around. He was grateful to see that Paten had bid Stone to stand clear so the obsequious man could not interfere.

Eutau leaned in and called softly. *"Dí'ame?"*

Kira looked out toward the tall grass, his eyes out of focus, his voice a distant whisper. *"U . . . ere . . . sangret."*

Eutau's storm-gray eyes grew wide, and he clenched his fists until his knuckles turned white. The words spoken were Ro'Erden, a language foreign to most people in the North, where almost everyone spoke only Moendan, the Land's common language. Eutau had taken pains to teach the Ro'Erden tongue to Kira so they could speak freely without eavesdroppers listening in. He looked up at the others. Paten and Tim had drawn their weapons and were busy scanning the area, while Stone's eyes were fixed on Kira like a hawk's. Everyone was on edge.

Sal marched up from the rear. "What's going on?" It was then that Kira turned to look down at her, and Sal's breath caught in her throat. His emerald-gold eyes were opaque, his skin ashen and marred by numerous blue veins that inched from his scalp toward his cheeks and eyes. She recovered quickly, and her voice showed no surprise or fear. "You know you're not supposed to call upon Death without first informing me. Explain."

Kira looked back at Eutau, who nodded his approval. "I didn't call upon Death willingly. This path is . . . evil. There are too many bitter souls trapped here and something has excited them. They are whispering that they long for blood."

Stone's eyes narrowed, and Paten and Tim muttered curses into the night.

Sal studied Kira closely. "Is it because you're a Deadbringer?"

He shook his head, frustrated. "No. I don't know. I feel like it's more than that, but I can't pinpoint what it is."

"Do you feel that you can continue forward?"

"I think so." Sal looked sternly at him. "Yes," he said, a little more confidently, "I can, but not at this pace. I don't want to linger on this path longer than necessary."

Sal turned to Eutau. "Do you believe it's safe for the rest of us to continue onward?"

"Yes, just do not err from the path, no matter what. If the cemetery is just as vile then it will probably be best to turn back. But I have never visited the grounds and cannot say if it is or is not."

"Understood." Turning, she instructed Paten to take Kira's place at the cart. She spoke firmly, making it clear that what she was about to say was not open for discussion. "Kira will go on ahead and make sure that the cemetery is safe for the rest of us. If so, then the Summoning will continue as planned. As you heard, there is evil lurking about on this path. Stay alert, keep close, and tread carefully."

The last she directed solely at Stone. "My respects to your late mother, but she had poor judgment in her choice of resting place." Stone simply shrugged his shoulders. "Kira, go! Once you feel better you have my permission to make any preparations necessary to carry out the Summoning. That includes calling on Death."

Kira half-laughed, as if amused that he had been granted permission to use his powers. He stepped up onto the cart and momentarily stood by his uncle. Storm-gray eyes pleaded for him to hurry and be careful. Nodding, he ran ahead, up the path to Corpse Hill.

CORPSE HILL

KIRA ARRIVED AT the base of Corpse Hill fifteen minutes later. His clothes and scalp were damp from running, but his skin had returned to its usual color and his eyes once again shone like emeralds. He stood on the last step of the path and studied the hill in front of him. It was wider than he had imagined, at least half a mile from end to end, and lower than Stone had described, rising only a couple dozen yards over the plain at its highest. There were no signs or walls to mark the cemetery, but the closely cramped, weathered headstones left no doubt as to the hill's function.

He looked back at the path behind him, arched brows knitting close together. *Even this far along, the path still has a vile sense to it, but it's nothing compared to what I felt back there.* He hoped that whatever had incited the trapped souls to thirst for blood remained confined to that area and stayed away from the cemetery itself.

Focusing on the task at hand, he left the path behind, took the first few steps onto the hill and felt . . . nothing. It was silent and peaceful. He let out a long-held breath and felt a tension he had not been aware of ease from him. The hill was covered with a low growth of lush grass that looked silver in the full moon's light. Taking a seat, Kira removed his traveling cloak and gloves and ran his fingers along his scalp, trying to get some of the sweat out.

After a short rest, he began scouting the surrounding area in search of Mrs. Stone's grave and, despite being pressed for time, took a few minutes to admire the intricately carved headstones, committing to memory several of the designs so he could try to copy them in his work at the parlor. He was awed by the many generations of families that lay buried together, but he also discovered that he was envious, for the line of his family started and ended with him and his uncle. *No doubt many of them have been broken apart now that Corpse Hill is avoided. It's a shame. This place is beautiful. So much history, so many memories.* He now understood why Mrs. Stone had wanted it to be her final resting place.

The late rains had packed down the upturned earth and ripped the petals off the withered bouquets laid over Mrs. Stone's grave. Her headstone was simple yet elegant. A sudden thrill of anticipation overtook Kira, for he was excited at the prospect of reanimating a corpse, a Risen, and about Summoning its soul back from beyond what he had coined the "Mirrorpall." In truth, he was not very skilled at dealing with souls — they could be such a nuisance and tended not to listen to him — but his dealings with the dead had been drastically limited since the Bastion had become involved, and he reveled in what he could.

He did not regret his decision to reveal himself to Sal. After all, his involvement had put an end to the string of child murders that had been plaguing Opulancae. A few of the bodies had found their way to his parlor, their souls broken, lost, unable to pass on. They had wept to him who the murderer was and, despite his uncle's pleas not to get involved, he could not stay silent. The choice had cost him and Eutau their freedom, but it had saved the lives of many children. He did not mind being collared by the Bastion, not really. What he did not like was that his uncle was collared as well. It made him feel guilty, as if he had destroyed everything his uncle had worked so hard for.

I'm getting distracted, Kira told himself, but it was difficult to avoid. *Sal will expect everything to be ready for the Summoning once she arrives.* He draped his cloak and gloves across a nearby headstone and unslung an oiled-leather bag. Gingerly, he emptied its contents onto the ground: three glass jars, a dagger with a twisted handle, and a thin, featureless porcelain mask. Taking one of the glass jars, he opened it and spread its clumpy brown contents around the grave's perimeter. *Salt infused with winged serpent's blood, to help keep any vile spirits contained.*

He clicked his tongue, distressed at having to use the precious substance instead of the plain salt he normally used for Summonings. Since winged serpents no longer roamed the lands, it was nearly impossible — and frightfully expensive — to obtain authentic winged serpent's blood. But something had been out there on the path and, despite the seeming safety of the cemetery grounds themselves, he did not want to take any risks.

After all, he told himself, *it's for this reason that I carry this special salt. I just never thought I would ever actually have to use it!* And his life was not the only one at stake. Thus far there had not been any mishaps, and he hoped it remained so. Kira enjoyed interacting with the dead, not causing death.

Taking the dagger from where he had placed it on the ground, he called on Death. It pushed out the warmth from his body and filled him with a coldness that intoxicated his every sense. Again, he took on a deathly pale, ashen appearance, and the veins that had marred his face before now spread to cover the rest of his body as well. Emerald-gold eyes were replaced with the milky white orbs of the dead.

Approaching the base of Mrs. Stone's grave, he went down on his knees, brushed aside the tattered bouquets, and dug the fingers of his left hand into the dirt, channeling his will to the corpse that lay resting within the coffin. A trembling sigh escaped his lips as he made contact. *It really has been too long since I truly interacted with the dead.* He held the dagger high in the air with his right hand and tightly squeezed the spiral hilt. The steel began to glow dimly with a strange light of its own. He forcefully drove the blade into the ground near the headstone and then sliced lengthwise through the dirt, down to the very foot of the grave. There was a muffled *crack* beneath the soil as the wooden coffin broke open.

The wind carried the sounds of voices, footfalls, and a protesting wooden cart. He would need to meet his uncle and the others at the base of the hill to give his report to Sal. Kira reached for the thin, featureless mask and secured the leather straps — he did not like having people look at him when he called upon Death. *I know uncle says I look fine, but that's only because he's used to me looking this way. But I have seen myself in the mirror and even I sometimes think I look unpleasant!*

The voices were getting closer. He looked down toward Mrs. Stone and called out to her. "The dead hold onto secrets better than do the living, but the dead cannot hold back secrets from their master."

He rose and went to greet his uncle, the agents, and Stone.

It was time to begin.

IT WAS ALWAYS strange having people watch him summon. Kira felt clumsy, especially since he had never properly learned how it should be done; instinct and his uncle had devised much of the ritual. And the only ones who could have told him if he was doing something wrong — or right — were long dead.

His knees had sunk slightly into the dirt as he knelt, facing the sardonyx mirror where it leaned against the headstone. *Before this is over,* he reflected, *the dirt underneath will shift further and I'll be covered.* He tugged at the mask on his face; it was secure. At his back were his uncle and Sal, their reflections distorted in the mirror's polished surface, while to his right were Paten, Tim, and Stone. The two agents smiled at him, their smiles weak and strained, and Stone was busy looking everywhere but at the grave. It made Kira feel embarrassed and angry.

He knew he should not be mad at Paten or Tim, but he could not help but feel a deep hurt and a smoldering anger when they looked at him in such a way, as if he should be ashamed of his actions. As a child, he had heard a rhyme about Deadbringers — a silly rhyme to scare children — that never failed to come to mind when he saw the agents' reactions:

> *One by one the Deadbringers came,*
> *bringing with them their Dolls to play.*
> *Will your strings be cut? Not on this day!*
> *The Dolls have found someone else to maim.*

Ignoring them as best he could, he took the dagger and dragged the edge across the length of his palm. Blood welled up within his cupped hand to fall to the ground, and he pressed his bleeding hand against the dirt, calling sternly to Mrs. Stone.

"Come to me."

He felt the sharp edges grab at her as she pushed her way through the fractured wood of the casket and the weight of the dirt crashed down all around her. He could feel the graininess of the dirt that found its way into the crevices of her body and pulled at her weak flesh, tearing bits away.

Their flesh was cold; their flesh was marred; but they would soon be whole again. He ran his fingers down his neck, reveling in the cold embrace that caressed every inch of him.

We've waited long enough.

Kira thrust his arm into the shifting dirt and grabbed onto Mrs. Stone, bringing her out of darkness and up into the moonlight. Vacant eye sockets and a face of rotted flesh greeted him. A white gown, sullied and tattered, clung to her body. Her flesh was discolored and bloated in many places where the moist, cold weather had kept her from desiccating, and her joints creaked and flesh protested as she knelt before him. The overwhelming smell of rot and wet dirt filled the air, as did the younger Stone's yelps and Paten and Tim's uncomfortable shuffling. Only Eutau and Sal remained impassive. It might have bothered Sal to see him look like a corpse, but for some reason it did not bother her to see him interacting with one. Kira admired and appreciated that about her above all.

He reached for one of the jars and opened it, revealing pasty, flesh-colored fiberclay. Tenderly drawing her close to him, he took the fiberclay and spread a portion of it on her face. Her skin wept with moisture at the pressure exerted upon it, and an inhuman guttural noise came from her throat. Gently, he began easing his fingers into her face, his touch decomposing flesh and clay alike, the thick liquid trailing down his arms. He was elated yet at the same time deeply saddened that it was only the dead that he could touch directly without fear. *If I ever lie with someone, will they rot beneath me?* It was a fear that kept him up on the restless nights when he longed to have someone to call his own.

A bony hand reached to touch him, and he smiled behind his mask at the skull staring up at him. Closing his eyes, he let his fingers slip further in and focused on molding the flesh-clay mixture by pouring some of his own life energy into her. He began at the temporal bone, running his hands down the mandible and expertly gathering the excess clumps of decaying flesh to mold elsewhere on her face. Normally, he relied on the shape and features of the skull to reveal the face's appearance, but Mrs. Stone's skull had been fractured, her face distorted. He would not expose her soul to even more suffering by confronting her with the brutality of her disfigurement.

He molded on instinct, feeling for the echo of her absent soul that he knew was imprinted in the very marrow of her bones. As her face began to take shape, he channeled more energy into her and watched as her body filled out, becoming supple, even curvy. A longing sigh escaped his lips. It had been long—far too long, he thought—since he had flexed this much power over the dead, and even longer since he had molded flesh.

It was done.

He stared down at the very image he had seen in his mind's eye made real: a woman of soft features and luscious lips, a far younger woman than Mrs. Stone had been. He cupped her face, ran his thumbs down to her dainty chin, and lifted her head slightly up. He lowered his face to hers until her heart-shaped lips touched the mask. Without it, their lips would have met.

His voice was deep, far deeper than anyone who knew him could have thought possible, as he whispered, "You are mine; I am your master. Regardless of the soul that inhabits this body, you belong to me. Your free will I will not take from you, but know that it is only so because I allow it. Engrave these words to your heart, mind, body, and make it known to the soul that enters."

Kira stood, helping her stand once again on her own two feet. He took her arm in his and guided her to the sardonyx mirror.

She faced her reflection.

Kira used the dagger to reopen the wound on his palm, which had already begun to knit, and pressed it against the surface of the mirror. Smooth stone phased from solid to liquid that undulated outward toward the vermeil-laced border like a pool of blood. He had begun moving Mrs. Stone closer to the mirror when she abruptly wheeled about, pressing her face against his chest. Her slender fingers pulled at his vest, popping off the ivory stick-pin that held the high collar together.

Surprised, he grabbed her by the neck, forcing her struggling body against the rippling mirror. Slowly, her struggling subsided. Soon, she would truly be Mrs. Stone, but until her soul was returned to her she was only a Risen, a mindless reanimated corpse. Or, at least, that was the little he thought he knew. No Risen had ever struggled against him like she had.

He ran his fingers up and down the small of her back, trying to decipher the emotions swarming him. Blood from his palm dripped down onto her gown, forming red blossoms. A strong desire to possess her, to care for her, flooded him, a feeling more akin to the need to cherish one's creation than a sexual one. He had never felt such a strong urge to keep a Risen from its own soul.

Reluctantly relinquishing his touch on her, he pressed his cut hand against the livid stone and peered intently into it. *The Mirrorpall – a maze of mirrors, and within some of these mirrors are traces of her soul. I need to focus.* His eyes darted from one direction to another on the mirror, but more than sight he used his connection to the Risen at his side to track what he sought. *Found them!* His hand slipped quickly into the mirror. With his blood, he cast threads into the labyrinth beyond the mirror and bound the pieces of Mrs. Stone's soul. Then, grabbing onto the threads of blood, he pulled them out and severed the link between the realm of the living and the Mirrorpall with his dagger. The mirror was once again nothing more than solid stone. He wrapped the threads around her body and faced her.

"It's time for you to return, Mrs. Stone." There was a sudden shift in her posture as her head jerked up toward Kira and then toward her reflection in the mirror. As he ran the last of the weaves around her, he bent down and whispered into her ear the reason she had been summoned.

Stone smiled. "She's finally here." Quietly, he pulled a small dagger from a hidden pocket and cut across his wrist, drawing blood.

There was a flash of silence as Mrs. Stone examined the faces surrounding her, then a terrified scream as she recognized her son.

RAIN OF BLOOD

IT HAPPENED SO fast, like a foul wind that had been lying in wait to attack at just the right moment. Tim lay on the ground, a sharp red lance lodged in his throat, another in his groin. Paten growled, "Kataru," and stepped just out of reach as a sword forged from the blood that had welled from Stone's wrist cut at him. Raising his battle-axe, Paten caught the downward strike with the axe head, stopping the blow.

The Kataru that had been Stone snickered, "You're in my way," and slipped the blood-sword's point down past the axe into Paten's neck. But even as Paten fell, he screamed the last of his strength into a wild swing that lodged the axe's bit deep into the Kataru's side.

Paten crumpled onto the ground. The Kataru stumbled but remained standing. He pulled the axe free and reached for the bleeding wound in his side, but Sal was upon him before he could touch it. Their blades clashed. The Kataru's strength was greater, his blows threatening to rip the longsword from her hands, but she held her own, keeping him from closing in. Eutau reached under his shirt, pulling a shortsword and a dagger from sheaths hidden on his back, and ran to join her.

She yelled to him, "Get Kira out of here!" but the Kataru was already ripping at one of the layers of his clothing, exposing a fine powder that tumbled out onto his hand. Before Sal could attack, he touched the powder to the blood seeping around his wound and then threw it at her. She flung up her arm to shield her eyes from the flecks that dug into her face like sharp glass.

The Kataru moved in to kill, but Eutau sprang forward, parrying the forceful blow with his shortsword. Without warning, Sal collapsed. Eutau cursed silently and thrust his dagger toward the Kataru's neck, but he withdrew, putting ample space between them. Eutau swiftly bent down and put a finger to Sal's neck, registering a weak pulse.

In that brief moment, the Kataru wheeled about and hurled a small object at Kira, who, after overcoming his initial shock, was making for Tim's sword. Kira winced as the thing penetrated his lower torso but continued onwards, determined. But his determination was cut short as his side ruptured obscenely and he went reeling to his knees, blood and entrails spilling onto the ground.

Eutau's agonized scream ripped through the night.

The Kataru drew another of the objects and took aim. *He means to fell me as he did Kira*, thought Eutau. His thoughts whirled. *Kira!* Then a small figure charged from behind the Kataru. It was Mrs. Stone. She flung herself onto the Kataru's back, clawing at his face, causing him to drop the object. It exploded at his feet, sending him flailing. Eutau ran to Kira, his boots splashing in the pool of blood building underneath Kira's body.

He still breathes, but is losing too much blood! Eutau looked behind him. The Kataru had peeled Mrs. Stone off of him and was cruelly beating her to the ground, smashing her skull and breaking her neck with his sword's pommel.

I need to end this. I cannot lose. Eutau stood and began moving swiftly away from Kira and the fallen bodies of the agents. The Kataru followed. He spoke, his voice sounding nothing like Stone's fawning tone from before. It was deep, guttural, forceful.

"You hate me. Good. Do me a favor and put up more of a challenge."

"You knew who we were," spat Eutau. "The Bastion has betrayed us to the Ascendancy and broken its oath to leave us be."

The Kataru laughed long and hard. "No, my clever Doll. It was Fortune who delivered you to me."

"I am no Doll." His eyes took in the great length of the Kataru's blood-sword. *His reach is longer, but if I can get close enough to him I can strike. But I need him to give me an opening, dammit!*

"If you say so." The Kataru grinned. "You're waiting for me to make the first move, my clever Doll." Eutau said nothing. "Very well. Let us make this a battle worthy of song." He moved forward, striking, and Eutau fell back, desperately trying to keep beyond his reach. In dismay, he realized that his opponent was being careful not to swing his sword into the ground or a headstone, and that he could not rely on the Kataru to give him an opening.

So he made his own.

He jumped back and stooped to pick up a rock bigger than his hand. The Kataru's sword swung past, and he darted toward a large, ornate statue, taking cover behind it. The Kataru stopped his advance, waiting for him to emerge. Eutau feigned exiting from the right side of the statue, then whirled back to the left side and threw the rock at the Kataru. It flew true, and, as the Kataru dodged, Eutau deftly leapt around the right side again and charged, closing the gap between them. He managed to thrust the dagger into the Kataru's shoulder, twisted it, and then brought forward the shortsword to cut at the wound made earlier by Paten. Eutau pulled the dagger out and whirled about, leaping away to avoid the Kataru's sword. But instead of the sword, a foot-long dart flew at him from nowhere, piercing his heart.

In agony, Eutau stumbled back and tried to pull it out, but the dart was barbed and tore at his palm. *I must push the dart clean through,* he thought distantly. *Cannot pull out . . . the dart . . . without tearing my heart.*

The Kataru laughed, though weakly. "My blood is my weapon. I hope you're enjoying the dart I fashioned just for you. You're quite the tenacious Doll." His voice was strained, and one arm hung limp from the shoulder that Eutau had stabbed. *"Pierce the heart, fell the Doll,* the old saying goes, but not you, oh, not you." He took a step forward, and Eutau took two staggering steps back.

"My heart is pierced, yet I stand. I am no Doll." *I will not lose him as I lost you. I will not!*

All mirth vanished from the Kataru. He brought his blood-sword forward with his good hand. "With the loss of your head, your strings will be cut and all that will be left is a broken Doll to play with. As for your master, all I want are the eyes. Like emerald flames with the burning gold of the sun dancing behind them." His face darkened. "Your head and his eyes will make exquisite trophies."

Their footing faltered as the ground beneath them erupted, and the dead emerged to dance under the full moon's light.

THINK. **IT WAS** becoming harder to form thoughts that did not trail off like the pool of blood steadily growing under him. *Move.* Kira slowly lifted his head and saw Paten, Tim, and Sal lying still. *Everyone's dead. Uncle!*

Ignoring the tearing pain, he lifted his head as high as he could and scanned the cemetery. The Kataru was alive and Eutau was alive, but his hand was bloodied and something was sticking out of his chest. Kira's vision blurred and his body gave out, his head crashing back to the moist, red ground. Bile spilled from his mouth and dripped down the side of his chin, spreading underneath his cheek. It smelled foul.

Alive . . . a . . . li . . . Breathe! His eyes shot open. The retching expulsion had nearly caused him to black out, but he needed to stay conscious. He tried to dig his fingers into the ground, but they would not respond. He wanted to laugh, but the muscles required to do so were no longer his.

Blood. So much. His lips twitched. *Mine . . . they're all mine. Come to me!*

The smell of fresh soil and rot engulfed him, and the cemetery came alive. Tim and Paten rose, but Sal did not. From afar he heard screams of rage and the sound of mournful laughter.

So sad. Please don't be . . . Kira felt something rest against his arm. Her face was crushed, unrecognizable, but he could feel that it was Mrs. Stone. She pressed against him and he knew that she was asking him to take back into himself the life he had given her. He did as she bid and felt his mind swim even as a little strength flowed back into him and her body fell, a mere corpse once again. He had brought her back only to suffer more. He had brought those he called friends to death.

Eye for an eye . . . The thoughts feverishly racing through his mind would have frightened him at any other time, but he was dancing the line between life and death, between sanity and insanity. He issued a silent command to the Risen of Corpse Hill. *I want his flesh, I want his life. I want him pinned down to the ground like a small, frightened animal. Take him. Make him yours. Kill him.*

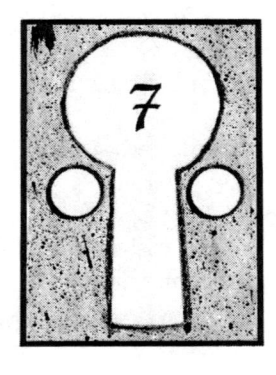

SLEEP

ῌOW IS SAL?" Eutau's voice was quiet as he changed the disintegrating bandages around Kira's torso. One by one, they found their way into a metal bin with a loud, wet *thunk!* He set a towel underneath the wound to catch the thick mixture of yellow-brown pus that was weeping onto the leather coverlet. *He is so still. All that moves is his chest, and even that is barely noticeable.* Kira's body was naked and uncovered, but even so sweat beaded all over it. *It has been three days now and the fever has not yet broken. I need more towels.*

Eutau turned and saw that Kim Lafont was shielding his nose from the pungent odor that emanated from the exposed wound. Behind Kim, numerous masks hung from the walls, staring at him with empty eyes. Distantly, he wished Kira had better taste in decoration.

Kim sighed, his voice muffled by the sleeve cuff he held in front of his nose and mouth. He was a short but strongly built man, not yet middle-aged, with swarthier skin than that commonly found in the North. Though he held the title of High Councilman, an important position in the Bastion, he wore the simple, dark blue uniform of a common soldier. "You weren't listening, were you?" he asked.

Storm-gray eyes were lost in an abyss of dark circles. "No, sorry. Please, tell me again."

"The healers say she is in a coma. But I have to think there is some poison at work."

Eutau placed some thin leaves in a mortar, covered them with moonwater, and began crushing them, forming a thick, foamy paste. He gently slathered it over Kira's wound and watched as it *sizzled* over the rawest parts. He kept his back to Kim, focusing on Kira. "What led you to that conclusion?" he asked.

"You told me that you saw Stone fling something at her, and she fell without explanation. My healers say that she must have been struck on the head, yet you said Stone never struck her. I've seen many wounded warriors before, but this is different somehow. The healers have tried everything, and still she lies with her eyes closed, her breathing slow. I don't know what to do anymore."

"That Kataru made fools of us all," said Eutau, his voice impassive.

"But Kira had the last laugh. What really happened at Corpse Hill?"

"I already told you."

"Part of Kira's torso was missing, yet he lies now with fresh skin sealing the gaping hole in his side. No Deadbringer would be able to heal that amount of damage, especially unconscious."

Even with his back to Kim, it was difficult for Eutau to keep his sarcasm and anger hidden, so he did not even try. "Oh, I did not realize you were such a learned source on Deadbringers? Sal sleeps, yet there is hope for her. Can you say as much for us? The Kataru claimed that he sought us of his own will, but he knew who we were. We were betrayed! And what will your noble Bastion think of its *pet* now that it has seen what *it* can do?"

"Kira summoned scores of Risen in that cemetery. Alone."

"He paid for it in blood, and almost—and maybe yet—with his life."

"He then directed the Risen to slaughter Stone."

"Who was a Kataru, who attacked him."

"And you are the only person alive to vouch for that fact."

"Sal knows."

"Gods damn you, Eutau! Do you think this has been easy for me? I lost my baby, and now my partner may never wake up. I lost good men, one of whom left behind a woman and children. The Bastion is in an uproar, the Ascendancy has learned of your existence and is threatening to send Sanctifiers, and I'm the one trying to keep shit from getting worse. If you haven't noticed, I'm on your side!"

Eutau had no doubt that his voice sounded as bitter as he felt. "How fortunate that we have such a champion."

Kim sneered. "I have always hated that word. It tends to conjure visions of grandeur and self-sacrifice, but no one sacrifices anything unless they can get something back in return." He sighed, exasperated. "The problem is Stone. To prove your story, you would have to show that the real Stone had been killed and his skin stolen. Katarus are common enough, but skinstealing is an incredibly rare ability even among the older clans, and only an elite warrior could have done the damage he did. Since there was not much left of his body, there is no way to tell what he was. Worse still, Stone's sister and partner claim that there was nothing abnormal about him. You have nothing to lend credence to your words." He briefly paused. "And you were the only one who was not injured."

"The Bastion does not trust me."

Kim's annoyance was clear. "You wouldn't be having this problem if you had accepted my offer to become an agent."

Eutau wanted to laugh, but he was too tired. His thoughts were wandering again and the ache in his heart where he had been stabbed by the Kataru's dart was beginning to creep up. He had lied to the Bastion, telling them that he had not been injured. He had lied to Kim, whom he was now certain had not believed him. *I feel like we are playing a game of cat and mouse, with neither of us wanting to be the mouse.* But instead of saying as much he simply asked, "Tell me, honestly. What is the Bastion planning to do with us?"

"Many are calling for Kira's death and your imprisonment. I'm trying to make them see that you would be more valuable alive, and as agents. Under my command, if possible. But I doubt my words carry much weight these days, not after all this."

The two men fell silent.

Eutau secured the last of the fresh bandages and cleaned his hands in the washbowl. His right hand was scarred where the dart had torn it, and he found himself with the sudden urge to peel off the scab and watch it bleed into the soiled water. *It has healed as much as it can,* he thought, *as has my heart.* He dried his hands, took a brush and ribbon, and began combing out Kira's long hair in sections, intending to braid it.

Finally, he spoke again. "Describe Sal's appearance to me."

Kim stepped forward, looking closely at Kira. "She lies as he lies. Never moving, hardly breathing." His thin brows were knitted, and his face—no longer covered by his sleeve, as his arms hung limp at his sides—was lost in despair. "Her skin is pale, almost gray. I move her body from side to side to avoid sores, but her skin is breaking down even so, and her limbs are becoming stiff. Her pink lips are almost black. I don't know what to do. I don't want to lose her."

Eutau did not answer for a time. He respected Sal, but, more importantly to him, he realized that Kim was right. Sal was the only one who could prove that Kira had been forced to defend himself, that he had not simply been the monster that Deadbringers were made out to be. *If Sal does not awaken, we will be forced to flee, and Kira is in no condition to do that.*

Eutau made up his mind. Speaking slowly, measuring each word, he said, "I have some skill in making healing potions."

Kim stirred. "Why didn't you mention this before?"

"Because my skill is nothing compared to that of a competent healer, and I am sure that you have the services of the best. But, who knows? I might be able to succeed where they have not. I see no reason not to try — for both your Sal and my Kira."

"And if Sal should awaken . . ."

"Then you will give all credit to the healers."

"Agreed."

Eutau pushed the finished braid aside and covered Kira's body with a thin sheet of cotton. *Come morning the sheet will be threadbare, but I can use nothing else until the fever subsides. Even the leather coverlet is deteriorating, and the wooden bedframe has begun to crack. In this state, you have control over nothing. Please come back to me. Please.*

He dimmed the lanterns and closely studied Kim's face. "Can you really guarantee that the Bastion will be placated by Sal's validation of my words?"

"No. I can guarantee nothing. But if she wakes, it will afford us time, maybe time enough to let tempers cool."

Eutau nodded, newly determined. "Then follow me, and do not trail behind."

Kim pointed to one of the lanterns. "You're forgetting that, unlike yours, my eyes aren't suited for darkness."

"Ah, yes." Eutau opened the door, and the three woodrats scampered past toward Kira. Eutau called sternly to them, "Sit," and they did as instructed, though the largest of the three kept taking small steps forward. "Leto. Sit." It stopped advancing and began bathing itself.

Kim bent down to get a better look. "These are woodrats, right?"

"Yes, they are my beauties. The smallest is Belle, the one closest to her is Pen, and the one looking innocent is Leto. I do not have to explain to you why I have been keeping them away from Kira."

Kim glanced back at the flaking leather coverlet. "No, you don't. I have never seen a woodrat this close. They are very secretive. But I see why you call them your beauties. Has Sal ever seen them?" A deep sadness filled his voice as her name crossed his lips.

"No, but when she wakes she can meet them."

"You sound so sure that she will wake."

"Do I have a choice?"

Kim laughed mirthlessly. "No."

Eutau called the woodrats to him, then grabbed a lantern and bid the other man to follow. They walked down a narrow hallway, one that

Kim was unfamiliar with. Finally, Eutau halted at a door that looked no different from the one they had just left, opened it, and stepped inside.

"This is my room. If you could, please help me light the lanterns. It will make the room more comfortable for you while you wait." He went over to a beautifully worked silver cage and placed all three woodrats inside. *Now I have one less thing to fret about,* he reflected. He turned about and saw that Kim had lit most of the lanterns but had stopped to examine the room, an amused smile on his face. Books lay scattered about and in mountainous piles, and neatly labeled jars of all shapes and sizes containing herbs and liquids were scattered about built-in bookshelves. The room was an organized mess.

"Yes," said Eutau, preempting the comment, "it is rather disorderly."

"You're always so well-dressed and downstairs is so overtly clean. It is refreshing to see that your room is not."

"I am as presentable as I need to be in my line of work. Enough. Where is Sal now?"

"At home. An agent is watching over her while I'm away."

"Good. There is mint water and wine on the nightstand. Help yourself. I will try to be brief." From the numerous bookshelves lining the walls, Eutau grabbed crystal flasks housing liquids that gave off an iridescent glow and jars containing herbs and roots that looked as if they would crumble if touched. He set to work meticulously measuring, crushing, and mixing the ingredients in a large bowl. As he did so, the mixture became a pearly white that dispelled all shadows around it. Last of all, he unsheathed a dagger from underneath his shirt and made a small cut in the palm of his scarred hand, letting the blood drip into the concoction.

"Blood?" Kim asked curiously.

"The potion is of moonwater, crushed *eilicht* bone and venom, dalora root, and various other things. I use my blood because all potions are at their strongest when the blood of the one making them is used. Your healers could tell you as much, if you asked. But, enough chatter." The potion had gone from a pearly white to an inky black. "Ride quickly and without stopping, for this potion must be administered within the hour or it loses its efficacy. If it begins to change color again, do not give it to her. It should work almost immediately, if not . . ." There was no need to finish the sentence.

Kim accepted the corked jar. "Thank you."

Eutau reached for the lantern and showed the other man out. "Make sure she drinks it all. If not, she may fall back to sleep."

Kim mounted his horse, nodded, and spurred back toward Opulancae.

A CHANCE ENCOUNTER

KIRA STOOD IN front of a plain white door. He blinked, and curls of white paint began slowly peeling away in jagged, disjointed patterns. His mind conjured images of someone trying desperately to claw a way out, and he tore his eyes away with a shudder.

Looking around, he saw that he stood in a narrow, misshapen hallway that seemed to have no end. He began to walk but after some time realized that, despite the feeling of motion, he was unable to move away from the white door. Standing in silence, a thought pierced his foggy mind.

This is a dream.

Desperate, he closed his eyes, pushed out the image of the door and hallway, and envisioned himself awake . . . and realized, with a start, that he did not know where "awake" *was*.

Uncle? Where am I? Where are you? Did we go somewhere?

Panicking, he opened his eyes and saw that he was no longer in the hallway. Instead, he found himself in a large, square room that was empty save for a single row of ornate, gilt-framed paintings and mirrors lining each of the four walls. He caught sight of his reflection in one of the mirrors and saw that he was masked and garbed in the attire he would typically wear to summon the dead.

A sudden sensation of familiarity, of something urgent, pricked at his mind, but was quickly replaced with an unwilling curiosity as he was pulled by an overwhelming need to look at the paintings. Morbid fascination took him from one to the next. The images were grotesque, debaucherous. And though each wall showcased a different focus, all were nonetheless joined by a common theme—torture. Torture of mind, torture of body, torture of soul.

Vaguely, he felt a cold numbness in his side and again found his mind wandering as if it were desperately trying to recall *something*. Then a gilt frame glinted, and Kira felt his mind pulled away from what it tried so hard to recall. He refocused his attention on the painting before him, a tableau of a bound naked man being pulled apart by two horses, and wondered if the gruesome image had brought about the unpleasant sensation in his side. The man's anguished look contrasted sharply with the ecstatic grins of the riders mounted atop the horses. To his horror, the skin around the naked man's waist and limbs slowly began to tear as the horses and their riders moved further apart.

The painting was alive.

"It won't be long now." A deep, powerful voice like velvet smoke cut through the fog in Kira's mind and echoed painfully throughout the room. "The man will soon be dead and the riders will have their fill."

Kira stiffened, his heart racing, and turned in the direction of the voice. He was surprised to discover that it belonged to a woman taller than him.

Her body was draped from neck to toe in a loose, strangely colorless garment. It was sleeveless and open in the front, revealing a polished corselet of some strange, lightweight material. Folds of dark cloth flowed from around the woman's waist beneath the corselet to sweep the floor. Aside from her armor, her clothing was plain and unadorned. But the simplicity of her clothing was in sharp contrast to the numerous filigree-worked silver and gold bracelets that covered her hands, forearms, neck, and even her hair, which was tightly braided halfway inward, allowing long, chestnut hair to flow loosely down her back.

Her voice pressed on his mind, hypnotizing him. "It has been a long time since I had a guest."

Kira tried to focus. For some reason, he could not make out her features, except for her intense, nearly black eyes. Yet, as a thrill of mixed desire and fear jolted his body, he knew somehow that she was beautiful—beautiful, but magnificent and terrifying.

"Is this a dream?" he asked.

"For most, yes, but for you—not quite." There was a slurred accent to the woman's speech that reminded Kira of someone, though of whom he could not recall.

"What does that mean, 'not quite?'"

The woman circled around Kira as she spoke, her eyes focusing intently on his side. "Individuals who harbor unfulfilled desires find their way to my hallway. Depending what they seek, they may be offered the opportunity to fulfill the impossibilities they crave."

Kira felt his cheeks flush underneath his mask. The woman's response seemed to see right into him, and he was grateful that his features were concealed. "But being fulfilled in dreams isn't the same as finding fulfillment in the waking world," he replied stoutly.

The woman arched a pierced brow. "True. Some—not all, but some—find reality disdainful and seek escape in dreams instead of embracing the waking world they live in. But, more to the point, this room is cut off from the hallway and belongs specifically to me. No one has ever entered this room, until now." She continued circling Kira, peering at him as if he was some oddity. Alarmed, Kira retreated to one of the walls, putting his back against it to prevent the woman from walking around him.

Amusement filled her voice. "The paintings on the wall are insights into some of the more . . . entertaining desires."

Kira wondered if he was being mocked. Refusing to look at the paintings, he angrily asked, "Do *these* kinds of desires entertain you?"

The woman—who, unable to walk fully around Kira, had taken to pacing back and forth in front of him—stopped and looked down at him with dark, contemplative eyes.

"Everyone, including you, restrains infinite longings they feel ashamed of. In some, those desires are violent, and mutual satisfaction through intimacy is nothing more than an illusion. Often, it escapes into their lives, destroying them. But it is an abyss to which they have willingly submitted, although"—she pointed with one claw-ringed finger to the picture of the man being torn apart by the horses—"it often drags in others not willing." The woman moved closer until she was only an arm's length away. Her dark eyes fell directly on Kira, who trembled beneath his mask.

"So now, I ask, what are *you* seeking?"

Her voice rang like black metal, and the question she posed echoed in Kira's ears while a sudden pain in his side, sharp and deep, caused his knees to buckle and his vision to go dark. Again, a memory prickled at the edge of his mind but disappeared before he could take hold of it. Finally, pain subsiding, he straightened up and found that the woman was gone and he was in front of another door, this one made of rusted metal. Shadows flickered madly across its surface.

Kira turned and found that the shadows came from a solitary candle burning brightly on a table in the middle of the room. In contrast to the last, this room was smaller and the walls were completely barren, but it was dim, and the floor was covered with strange, barely visible objects.

Kira stepped forward, but something crunched under his boot, causing him to jump back in alarm. He stooped to touch a long piece of what appeared to be porcelain. As his eyes traveled up its length, struggling to adjust to the dark, he realized that he was looking at joints, then a body, a face, and two shiny, glass-bead eyes.

"A Doll!" he exclaimed.

Eyes widening, he quickly removed his gloves, dropped to his knees, and eagerly reached out to touch the smooth, cold face looking lifelessly back at him. Even through the flickering shadows, he could make out the perfect ringlets, the delicate features of her face, and the strong curves of her naked, lifelike body. She was softly beautiful.

He blushed profusely as he examined her construction, but frustration soon trumped all other emotions. He could normally see so well in the dark, but the dim lighting seemed made of a living darkness that blinded him, making it difficult to determine how the Doll had been put together.

The woman's voice called out from the shadows, amused. "You know what she is, don't you?" Not receiving an answer, she rephrased the question, her impatience becoming clear. "Why are you so enthused with my pets?"

"Did you make her?" The words blurted out of Kira's mouth before he could stop them. He had never met anyone who knew how to make a Doll. At that moment, nothing else mattered.

Her voice seemed curious now, as she asked, "How important is that answer to you?"

Very! thought Kira, but he realized that the response would make him seem desperate and vulnerable. Instead, he asked the other question that was demanding to be heard.

"Are you a Deadbringer?"

Snide laughter erupted from the mouth of the porcelain Doll, followed quickly by mocking laughter from the woman herself. The sounds echoed from every corner of the room, seemingly coming from the very shadows themselves. Shocked, Kira dropped the Doll and stepped away, but then felt his back hit something. Before he could react, sharp metal tips from a claw-ringed hand were pressed against his throat.

Her deep voice whispered into his ear. "Would it please you if I was a Deadbringer?"

Kira's mind swam, and he wondered if the claw tips pressed against his neck were poisoned. He fought the fog that assailed his mind and looked down at the Doll. "Was she alive?" he asked desperately. "Did you kill her?"

"Everything that is dead once lived. And everything that lives came from nothingness."

"That isn't an answer." Kira had wanted his words to have more bite, but his eyes were becoming too heavy to keep open.

"But it is." The woman brought her face mere inches from Kira's own, intently studying the outline of his mask. Then the amusement went from her voice and was replaced by leaden gravity, gravity and a hint of anger. "You should not be here. What are you?"

What am I? Kira considered hazily. It seemed like the question he should have asked the moment the woman had first appeared. But fatigue claimed him before he could answer, and he collapsed.

Kira felt the woman catch him. Through nearly closed eyes, he watched as if from a distance as the porcelain mask concealing his face fell to the ground and fractured into two halves. Claw-ringed fingers brushed the hair away from his face and turned him over. Shock and bewilderment crossed the woman's face as she spoke. Unable to make out her words, Kira let sleep take him and woke up.

REVELATIONS

KIRA AWOKE, BUT fear kept him from opening his eyes. Fear that they would be waiting for him—the shadows, the Doll, the frightful woman. Panic gripped him, and he thought to scream, but his throat was painfully dry, and his lips cracked when he tried to form words. He felt damp and cold, and there was an overwhelming pain in his torso, and . . . he remembered. The Kataru, Corpse Hill, Paten, Tim, Sal, Mrs. Stone. And Eutau. Eutau!

Grief replaced panic, and he found that he did not want to open his eyes if his uncle was no longer in the same world as him. *I failed everyone!* Tears slid down his cheeks in the darkness, and he wondered where they could have come from, for he felt so parched. Yet there was a lingering taste in his mouth, a taste like the finest of wines. Then the memory of the dead tearing into Stone's body surfaced, and the urge to scream gripped him again. *Blood! It's the taste of his blood in my mouth!*

"Kira."

A familiar, worried voice called out to him, and he wondered if he was still dreaming or if it was a trick. But the voice called again, and again. Finally, he opened his eyes. The face that greeted him was his uncle's.

Eutau looked haggard, his voice hoarse. "I have waited so long to see your eyes open and remain open. To have you look at me and recognize me."

Kira focused on the feel of his uncle's fingers brushing his hair and touching his face. They were warm and smelled like tobacco and soap. A hint of a smile passed across Eutau's face. Then he stepped back, and Kira heard the sound of water being poured.

Eutau returned with a bowl of water and a sponge, which he moistened and pressed against Kira's lips. "Drink slowly," he said sternly.

Kira savored the crisp freshness of the water as it soothed his parched throat and washed away the taste of blood. *The blood was warm and thick, so unlike the water,* he thought. He gingerly touched the bandages on his side, but the simple movement fatigued him and caused the wound to throb. He let his hand fall to the covers and instead focused the little energy he had on talking.

"How long?" His voice was strained and weak.

"Two weeks."

Kira suddenly remembered that Sal had remained lying on the ground when Paten and Tim had risen at his command. "Is Sal alive?" he asked, overcome with guilt.

"Sal lives. She was in a coma, but Kim sent word several days ago that his healers were able to wake her. She is recovering, same as you. We can speak later. For now, you should rest."

But Kira did not want to wait. "I raised the dead in that cemetery. I used them to kill Stone," he whispered, his eyes wide with horror.

"You did what you had to. You were left with no other option. Now rest."

Kira pushed on, the memories overflowing. "They tore him apart . . . with their teeth, their hands. They feasted on his flesh and his blood and I felt every second of it as if it had been me doing it. And I reveled in it!"

Eutau tried to appear calm and reassuring, but he could not hide the desperation in his voice. "You had lost too much blood at that point. You were no longer in control."

"But I *was* in control! And when his blood coursed down my throat I felt his *life* flow into me, and I didn't tell them to stop because I knew in that moment that stealing his life would keep me alive! I didn't know I could do that . . . I didn't know . . ." His voice trailed off as the pain pulsed through his side.

"Kira, stop," said Eutau, "you are weak and know not what you are saying."

But Kira could not stop. "I don't regret stealing his life, and I don't regret directing the dead to slaughter him. What I regret is not having

acted sooner to save Paten and Tim. To protect Sal and you. I brought
Mrs. Stone back so she could relive her nightmare." There was a thought
dancing on the edge of his mind and tongue, but he admitted it only to
himself, horrified. *I enjoyed the taste of his blood! What am I?* He
remembered the woman in his dream asking him the same question and
felt a deep chill overtake him. *It was only a dream, nothing more.*

And then something else took hold of his mind and drove all other
thoughts and fears away. "Uncle, your chest!" he said, desperate,
panicking again. "I saw something pierce your chest!"

Eutau was stern, his face a cold mask. "Enough! You did what you
had to do to stay alive. I am alive. Sal is alive. Paten and Tim are dead,
but that is not your fault. They were agents and they knew the risks. You
were able to raise a cemetery of corpses because you almost paid with
your life! Such a feat cannot be repeated otherwise, do you understand?
As for what you experienced, speak of this to no one. Not your dear Elia,
not Sal, not Kim, not your shadow, *no one! Do you understand.*" It was not
a question.

Kira nodded, wincing. He was suddenly very tired again.

Eutau's features softened, and he took a seat on the edge of the bed.
"Sleep. I will stay here by your side. Come morning, I will change the
bandages and help you bathe and eat. I will kill one of the chickens and
make a broth from its bones. I am not sure if you can eat solid food at the
present but. . ."

Kira closed his eyes and listened to the sound of his uncle's voice,
and he felt safe. *Come what may, I will protect my uncle.* With that promise,
he drifted off into a dreamless sleep.

IT WAS JUST a simple bath. I smelled awful," said Kira.

"And you would have smelled worse if the wound had festered,"
Elia said sharply. She eyed him up and down. "What is he feeding you?
Air?"

Another two weeks had passed, and that morning Kim had arrived
at the parlor with Elia in tow. Kim had told Eutau that they had crossed
each other's path on the road and decided to travel together. Elia, for her
part, had stated, "He latched onto me like an unpleasant growth."

Eutau had not been pleased to see her, but her anger at not being
told of Kira's injury had been loud enough that Kira had heard her from
his room across the house where he lay resting. From what she said, or
yelled, it appeared that word had spread in Opulancae that he had fallen
ill and that the parlor had been forced to turn away clients. But once Elia
had heard, nothing could have kept her away from him.

She was still waiting for his answer, and her temper was obviously rising. "Broth," Kira said finally, knowing that she would disapprove, "and I've started eating meat."

"And to drink?"

"Mint water."

Elia was outraged. "Mint water! In your condition you need something more stout, like small beer." She pulled out a pint-sized bottle from her bag and handed it to him. "Drink it. It will help you relax and gain some weight."

Kira uncorked the bottle and poured its contents into a large mug. He sniffed it, then took a sip and repressed a resigned sigh. Eutau frowned on beer-drinking — though he himself was very fond of wine — but Kira had tried a dark, rich beer once, in Opulancae, and had liked it. Elia's small beer smelled like piss and tasted like sour water, but he knew her better than to complain.

She pulled two more bottles and a smaller flask out of her bag and handed them to him. "Drink one a day along with a helping of this."

"What is it?" he asked, with trepidation.

"Fish oil."

He groaned, "I thought you liked me!"

"I do. If fish oil didn't go bad so quick I would have brought a bigger bottle."

Kira shuddered. *I'd rather eat dirt,* he thought grimly. The small beer did not seem so bad by comparison. He put the bottles on the table, thinking the interrogation to be over, but when he turned back Elia was staring at him too closely. He wondered what she was thinking and felt awkward.

Finally she said, "Undo your shirt. I want to take a look at this 'knife wound' that your uncle claims you suffered."

Kira tried his best not to flinch. *That is the worst lie you have ever come up with, uncle! And to try it with Elia!* He removed his shirt.

Her brows knitted when she saw the dressings that covered the whole of his lower torso. "The bandages, too," she said severely. "Now." He was about to protest but thought better of it after seeing her glare. Reluctantly, he undid the bandages. Her eyes darkened. "Are you in pain?"

"Not much. It feels better than it looks, really. My uncle cleans and changes the dressing every day. He shovels as much food into me as I can hold without becoming sick and makes me walk in short spurts throughout the day so my muscles do not wither." He considered adding in something about the supposed "knife wound" but decided that it would only make the lie worse.

She scrutinized the wound for some time and then scoffed. "'Knife wound.' *Pfahh*. Your uncle is a bad liar. No wonder he told me nothing about this. He would have tripped over his own falsehoods. You should be in bed resting for at least another week, not walking around. Are you taking anything for when you do have pain?"

"*Nologis*, but I don't need it anymore." Her lips trembled and she averted her eyes. "Elia?"

"*Nologis* is a powerful root," she began, her voice unsteady. "It's stronger than poppy."

Kira was confused by her reaction, but he continued talking nonetheless. "Yes. I don't like it, but my uncle insisted I take it."

Elia took a deep breath. Then, quickly, quietly, she said, "It must be difficult for a Deadbringer to control his abilities under the influence of such a root."

Kira sat on the bed and took a shallow swallow from the mug of beer. He supposed he should have been shocked by the revelation that she knew what he was, but the shock never surfaced. Instead he asked, "Does the rest of Opulancae know? Do you hate me?"

Her gray hair shook side to side and she struggled to hold back her tears. She went to him. "Foolish boy, how could I?"

"How long have you known?"

"Since you were little. I was gathering herbs one day in the forest across the Silver River and I saw you bent down, talking to the remains of some poor forsaken child that had gotten lost and died of hunger and cold. I crouched behind a thicket and watched as you carried on a conversation with it. I could scarcely make out its words—but I heard it! You kept explaining to it how your uncle wouldn't allow you to be friends.

"Finally, Eutau arrived. I thought for sure he would realize that I was there, so I held my breath and prayed to the gods that he wouldn't see me, and he didn't. I expected him to be horrified, but instead he smiled sadly, and I knew then that my ears had not deceived me and that it had not been the first time you had spoken with the dead. He helped you dig a hole with that dagger he carries around with him like a third arm. You were quite distraught, which was my salvation because it kept his mind focused solely on you. I'm no fool. To this day I'm convinced that, had I confronted Eutau about what I saw, he would have been digging a hole for me."

"He'd never do that!" said Kira, horrified and indignant. He remembered that day, for Eutau had indeed scolded him later in the evening, and severely. He had warned Kira never to speak to a carcass again, and had revealed to him what exactly had happened to those like him. Until then, he had not fathomed that he was the only one of his kind left. He had suddenly felt quite alone.

"I'd expect that he'd forsake the Land to the Nightmare Lords themselves if it meant that you would be safe. That's the kind of man he is, though given the circumstances I can't fault him." Her voice was gentle now, but sad. "It's just . . ." she began forcefully, but then stopped with a trembling sigh.

"What's wrong?" he asked, worried. "And don't tell me 'nothing' and don't say it's because you learned that I'm a Deadbringer, because you already knew that. Please, tell me." *She looks so tiny and frail! What happened?*

She visibly gathered herself up and resumed talking, the words pouring from her. "I need to vent what I feel or I'm going to suffocate. The last time you came to visit me, you were right. Something *was* wrong. I had a dream, and last night I had that same dream again. I dreamed that my partner was alive. My heart was overjoyed to see him, but it was also pained because he looked ill and was very tired and weak. He looked at me with those drawn eyes and I told him . . ." She paused. "I told him that he just needed to rest. It was a lie and my mind knew it, but my heart begged me not to tell the truth."

She struggled to hold back the tears building around her eyes. "He was dead, but he wasn't aware of it. So he had come back to see me. It hurt so much because all I ever wanted was to see him and my children one more time, but alive and healthy. I'm grateful that only he appeared in my dream. If I had seen my children as well, in that state . . ." She brought up a hand to shield her eyes as the tears rolled down her cheeks.

Kira redid the buttons of his shirt and made sure that his powers were in check before going over to Elia and taking her in his arms. Never in his life had he seen her so vulnerable, and it hurt him. She sobbed into his shirt, and he shifted carefully to keep her weight from his wounded side.

Her voice was muffled by his shirt. "My partner was a Deadbringer. My children were Deadbringers too."

The sudden revelation caught Kira's breath, and the memory of their conversation about Dolls came back to him. Heart pounding in his throat, he struggled to find his voice. "I . . . I didn't know."

She pulled away from his embrace. Nostalgia filled her voice. "I was never good at riding. Always preferred my own two feet. But my partner was insistent that I should learn. Like a fool, I managed to get my foot stuck in the stirrup and spook the horse as well. For my efforts, I broke an ankle and scraped my arms and back pretty good." Her brow creased as she continued, now almost reluctantly. "A week later, news arrived that the Ascendancy's hounds had at last reached the north. My ankle hadn't yet healed, and despite all my partner's protests I managed to finally convince him to leave with the children. The eldest, our daughter, was sixteen, and our son was eight. They fled. I never knew where they went, for I refused to have any knowledge that could condemn them.

"Four days later soldiers from the Ascendancy arrived. They knew my partner was a Deadbringer and took me captive to gather information. I don't know how long I was in that windowless cell, but my hair had grown, and my nails even more so." She shuddered. "The pain I endured was nothing compared to the all-consuming dread that they would return with news that they had found my children and their father. I had managed to convince myself that as long as they returned to question me, my family was safe."

A bitter laugh escaped her lips. "Eventually, the Bastion secured my freedom on the ground that I myself was not a Deadbringer. The Purging had ended in Opulancae, all the Deadbringers were gone, and even the Ascendancy realized that I was useless to them. Thankfully, it was only their common soldiers who took me captive, and not their Sanctifiers, or I would have died in agony. Yet the day my eyes saw the light once more was also the day I knew in my heart that I would never see my family again."

Kira did not know what to say. Finally, just to say something, he said, "I'm sorry. I wish the Purging had never happened, but you're not alone. You will always have me. Thank you for sharing something so personal with me." He had hoped the words would comfort her, but fear was evident in her eyes.

"Kira, why is that man here?"

"Who?"

"That head agent, that Lafont."

"He's a friend. As is his partner, Sal."

"Promise me, that you're not lying to me! Promise me that the Bastion, the Ascendancy, the Sanctifiers, that they know nothing of you!"

Kira was startled. *If I don't affirm her words,* he thought, *she will live in fear that one day I too will be killed as her family was. My dear woman, that is no life for you.*

"To them I'm Kira Vidal, mortician and headstone carver," he said. "Only that, nothing more."

She smiled then, but it never reached her eyes. "Yes, you are Kira Vidal. Just Kira Vidal."

SAL IS AWAKE, and I have you to thank for that," said Kim as he took the tea Eutau offered him. They were in the sitting room, taking advantage of the bright sun and cloudless blue sky, unusual so late in the year. "How is Kira? You never sent word about his health."

Eutau smiled, and it was a grand smile indeed. He had finally managed to sleep to his heart's content. "I knew you would eventually come back, so I saw no need. It was good news to both of us to hear that Sal is recovering and that the coma did not have any lasting effects. As for Kira, he too is recovering, though he is still weak."

"Was it wise to let that old woman into your home?"

"She is an old friend and is aware of what Kira's touch can do, but she thinks him just some curious *moma* with an odd power. Of him being a Deadbringer she knows nothing. Besides, pushing her away would have made her suspicious and caused more trouble. She is quite stubborn concerning Kira." *And I trust her more than I trust you,* thought Eutau, *but that is not your concern.*

Kim looked skeptical. "A dangerous gamble. But I suppose you're no stranger to the concept. Anyone who would task themselves with the responsibility of raising a Deadbringer child as their own would have to be willing to risk all. Yet you've never struck me as the paternal type, though you would do anything to keep Kira safe. You must have loved his mother greatly."

"Of course I loved her," Eutau said calmly. "What would you have expected? She was my sister."

"I suppose Kira must look like her, then, or perhaps like his father? I have never been able to find much of a resemblance between the two of you."

"I presume that he resembles his father."

"You presume? She was your sister and you don't know who sired the child?"

"She was my sister. Not my property." *What game are you playing at?* Eutau wondered, his limbs tensing even as his face remained impassive. He sat across from the other man and saw that Kim was looking at him as if he were a stranger.

"Your blood is rather amazing."

"The blood was only one of the ingredients in the potion, and it was merely to bind it together. I am sure you confirmed with your healers that I spoke truthfully about the importance of using the maker's blood in a potion."

"Yes. I'm sure the other ingredients in the potion must have been first-rate, but it was your blood that woke her."

"Your point, Lafont?"

"Does Kira know? Or have you treated him as a fool, like you treated me?" Kim's voice was severe, accusing.

Eutau stood angrily, his tranquility shattered. "I know not what you are insinuating, but your *gratitude* for my saving your partner is so very much appreciated. Now, please leave. I can take Elia back to the Old Town myself."

"Is it so hard for you to admit what you are?"

"And what, pray tell, do you think I am?" asked Eutau, dreading the answer.

"A Doll."

Eutau laughed lightly. "Oh, is that it? I have never known you to jest, but you picked a poor one to start with."

Kim smiled, and his eyes glinted knowingly. "A jest, is it? Not according to my spellcaster—oh yes, Eutau—did you really think I would only have simple healers look at my precious Sal? As her life waned, I obtained the services of a spellcaster. And she told me that Sal was not in a true coma, but instead was in the grasp of a sleeping spell. And not any spell, but a very special type, one designed during the Purging to capture Dolls and Deadbringers. You know the one, I'm sure—the spell whose victims can only be revived by the blood of a Doll."

All mirth vanished, and the two men tensed, ready to spring. Eutau fought the urge to reach for his dagger. *You used Sal to trick me!* he screamed inwardly. *I could kill you! I should kill you! But . . . but your death would only bring more danger for Kira.*

He reined in his emotion. "What do you want?" he hissed, his words ice.

"You're different than any Doll I have ever seen—unique. I had, now and again, entertained the suspicion that you might be a Doll, but you are so lifelike that I did not believe it. And I did not truly believe your 'potion' would heal Sal. When she did open her eyes, my joy was mixed with shock. But Kira cannot possibly be your maker. He is far too young to craft something so . . . alive. Was his father your maker?"

"No."

"How did you come by Kira? Did you take him for yourself from some fallen Deadbringer's arms?" Kim's eyes glinted. "If you're alive, then your master must be as well. No Doll can survive long once its master is killed."

"Are you hoping for another pet Deadbringer?" spat Eutau. "I can *see* the greed in your eyes."

Kim ignored the mockery. "This isn't about me. You should tell Kira what you are before he figures out that his beloved uncle is nothing more than a puppet who is skilled at weaving tales."

Eutau swallowed his anger, but it was becoming increasingly difficult for him. "Like you once did, he believes I am just another odd *moma*. There are no more Deadbringers left. There are no more Dolls. All he has to go by is what scant literature remains that was not destroyed during the Purging." He laughed scornfully. "And in those pages the history of Deadbringers was distorted and rewritten to justify their genocide. Kira has no idea what a real Doll is, nor will he ever."

"Do you have so little faith in him?"

Eutau was stricken dumb. Kim's words pierced his heart deeper and more painfully than any Kataru's dart could have. "Get out," he rasped.

"For your sake and his, you need to tell him the truth. You need to trust him."

"Get out or I will gut you."

"Very well. But before I leave, you will want to know this." Kim pulled a letter from his jacket. "Sal has corroborated your story about what happened at Corpse Hill but, unlike me, our superiors remain skeptical. They insist on a hearing to listen to Kira's account of what happened before deciding whether to believe you."

"And if Kira fails to entertain, what then?" Eutau asked bitterly.

"Then he will be executed, or handed over to the Ascendancy as a gesture of our continued good faith." The words hung in the air like the death sentence they were.

"You will have to forgive my lack of gratitude," Eutau replied, finally. "Tell me, does the Bastion know about your great discovery of my true nature?"

"No, nor will they. That is my gratitude for what you did for Sal."

"When is this hearing?"

"Seven days from now. Until then, both of you are to remain under house arrest. Already, as we have spoken here, armed agents have taken their places to stand guard outside your house."

Eutau gritted his teeth, suppressing the rage that took him on learning that the trap had already been sprung. "And what tale have you woven to keep the good people of Opulancae from fretting?"

"It is well-known that before you took this house for your own it belonged to a rogue Ro'Erden. That Ro'Erden has returned and attacked Kira. Since this matter falls under our jurisdiction, we are sending agents to guard you from any further attacks."

Eutau was forced to acknowledge to himself that he was impressed, though it irked him to do so. "Very well," he said, and took the letter from Kim. "I do not appreciate having been deceived, nor do I like being bottled up inside my own house without warning. To make amends, you could at least confirm a suspicion. Does Sal know how you tricked me? That you used her sickness to discover what I am?"

For the first time, Kim looked uncomfortable. "Yes. She realized soon after waking that the healers were shocked at her recovery, and that something was amiss. It didn't take her long to wring the truth from me. She was . . . not very happy with me."

Eutau smiled softly, reveling in that small admission.

Kim continued. "Call that old woman here so we can leave together. I will tell her the story about the Ro'Erden myself. And then we must go. Additional agents will arrive before the sun sets."

Eutau watched as Kim and Elia set out, Kim on his mare and Elia on her mule. He then went upstairs to check on Kira and found him sleeping. *I need to show him this letter,* he thought briefly, and then crumpled it in his hand. He noticed the bottles on the table and sniffed the empty mug. *Small beer,* he thought, and wrinkled his nose in distaste. *I wonder what else she brought you.*

Leaving, he made his way to his own room, where he locked the door behind him. Walking over to the nightstand, Eutau poured himself a glass of wine and retrieved from his pocket a pea-sized nub of *nologis,* which he swallowed to quell the creeping pain in his heart. He then went over to the cage that held the woodrats. He was watching Belle and her friends when Kim's words overtook him.

Do you have so little faith in him?

Eutau covered his mouth to stifle a cry and let the tears he had been holding in stream down his face. In the silence of his room, he fell to his knees and wept.

TIME

THREE DAYS PASSED. Eutau wandered from one window to another in the sitting room, observing the agents who stood guard outside. One of the agents turned to look in his direction, and Eutau blew out a puff of smoke from his pipe, smiling warmly. The agent did not return his smile.

Eutau clicked his tongue, feigning annoyance. "Our guests are quite somber. But I suppose I would be as well if I had to spend my days walking in circles around a house." He abandoned prowling the windows to stretch out lazily over the headrest of the recamier.

Kira sat in a nearby chair, drinking coffee and watching the cloud of smoke that steadily grew over his uncle's head. "When are we leaving?" he asked. The question had been ever-present in his mind since Eutau told him of Kim's report that the Bastion might turn on them.

"Soon, when I have found a pattern to the agents' movements. They have been careful," said Eutau. He turned to look directly at Kira. "Do you have what you need packed and ready to go?"

"Yes. But can't we wait until the Bastion makes a decision? Kim has always been on our—"

"Everything is different now. We can no longer rely on Kim's status to keep us safe. I should have known better than to linger in one place for too long. It was an absurd thing to do."

"No, it wasn't," said Kira. "You just tried to give me a place to call home, and I ruined all your efforts. I'm sorry."

Eutau inhaled the last dregs of smoke from his pipe. A few seconds later he exhaled leisurely, but all the while he looked at his pipe regretfully. "Perhaps it is best this way."

"I don't see how this is better. But, is there any way to see Elia before we leave?"

"No," Eutau said sternly. "And for her sake you must never see her again." He went over to Kira, who was staring intently into his cup. "I know how much you love Elia, but you must let her go. Look at me." Kira looked up at him, and Eutau wished at that moment that he had not. Kira's grief was plainly visible on his face.

Eutau continued, and there was resentment in his voice, though he knew not why. "You must not be afraid of change, and you must not fail to act when your life is in danger. Make no mistake. If you wish to live, you must accept that you will have to kill. The Kataru at Corpse Hill will not be the last."

Irked by his uncle's callousness, Kira lashed back. "Why won't you tell me if what happened with the dead and the Kataru was something you have seen before?"

"Because I already told you that I have not," Eutau said irritably.

"Then why do I feel like you are hiding something from me?"

Eutau emptied the ash from his pipe into an empty cup and went back to sit on the recamier. "And why is it that you always try to find five legs on a cat when it has four?"

"Probably because whenever I ask you questions about Deadbringers or Dolls you get upset."

"And why are we in this mess?" Eutau asked condescendingly, as if he was lecturing a small child.

"Because I am a Deadbringer."

"No, you are Kira Vidal of Opulancae, son of my late sister. You are a mortician, a stone carver, and a boy who only half-listens to what I say. So, I ask again, why are we in this mess?"

"Because I insist on being recognized as a Deadbringer," Kira said heatedly, bracing himself for another lecture. But instead of berating him, Eutau instead seemed to shrink and leaned forward, his elbows resting heavily on his thighs.

"When I told you that you were a Deadbringer, I did not expect you to take it to heart, but you did. After that, I made a promise to myself that I would fill the need I had planted in your heart. I promised that I would make you forget that you were a Deadbringer so you would not feel alone." His voice, already quiet, faded as he brooded over his words. "I only ever wanted you to be Kira. Just Kira." The last was a whispered plea. "But, how do you love without being selfish? How?"

Kira looked on, startled and uncomfortable. He walked over to the recamier and placed his hands on his uncle's arms. Eutau looked up, dazed, and then turned away, embarrassed. He had become lost in his thoughts, forgetting that Kira was in the room.

Kira took a seat on the floor and rested his head on Eutau's thigh—it was a childhood habit he had never grown out of. Eutau's strong fingers began stroking Kira's hair, and Kira realized in that moment that his uncle also found comfort in that simple act. They sat in each other's company without saying a word. After some time, a sudden gust of wind rattled the stained glass windows. Outside, the agents could be overheard cursing the darkening sky.

"It's going to rain," Kira said finally. "I should start making dinner."

"Yes," agreed Eutau, as his fingers relinquished Kira's hair. "Afterward, we can retire to an empty room upstairs, where our 'friends' cannot spy on us. The sitting room is not as pleasant as it used to be."

Kira stood and was about to go to the kitchen when something caught his eye. "Uncle, I think Sal's outside," he said, surprised, "and her hair is cut!" He pointed at a newly arrived agent with short blond hair.

Eutau looked out. "Yes. She is," he said flatly.

"You don't sound pleased?"

"My displeasure is not directed at Sal, but at the Bastion."

The agent Sal was talking with waved her toward the house. "She's coming this way!" said Kira, excited. "I'll get the door."

"Wait! Quickly, gather your travel bags and go wait for me in my room."

"But we don't even know why she's here!" Kira protested.

"Please, do as I say. If all is well, I will fetch you."

"What about you?"

Eutau placed his hand on Kira's cheek. "Unlike you, I have no injury to worry about. Now, go, and get Belle and the others ready, just in case." Kira paused, then at last nodded and rushed upstairs.

There was a knock at the door. Eutau waited a few seconds before answering.

"Who is it?"

"Eutau, open up. It's important. I promise I'm not here to take Kira away."

Eutau hesitated. Then, with his hand on the hilt of the dagger he had strapped to his waist, he opened the door, quickly stepping back as Sal rushed in. She forcefully closed the door behind her. There were faint scars across her face where the Kataru's glassy shards had struck her. Her hair had indeed been cut short.

"There's not much time," she said, her voice a rush, "I think the Ascendancy is on its way. And not just regular soldiers. Sanctifiers."

The color drained from Eutau's face, and his hand fell from the dagger hilt. "Where are they? When will they arrive?" he asked urgently.

"There have been rumors of Sanctifiers roaming about the North for weeks now, but last night a group was spotted a day's ride away, heading toward Opulancae. Luckily, it was one of the agents under my command that spotted them, and I found out first. If the Sanctifiers demand Kira be handed over to them, I will send an escort to see you out of Opulancae. It is my shame to admit that there are too many in the Bastion who would rather see Kira dead than relinquish him to the Ascendancy."

"And should the Sanctifiers pay us a visit first?" Eutau asked dryly. Sal said nothing. "And Kim, what does he plan to do? Does he know you are here? *Why* are you here? I cannot believe he—or you—would just let us go free."

"As for *why*," she said, almost scornfully, "you saved my life, though it cost you dearly, and I don't forget such things. I will not see you or Kira killed, not by Sanctifiers or by the Bastion. But no, Kim doesn't know I'm here. He wants you safe in his grasp, but right now he is far more concerned with these Sanctifiers. The rest of the Bastion— even those that want Kira dead—will be in an uproar when they learn that the Ascendancy has butted into their territory without leave. Kim is busy gathering his troops, getting ready to send more guards, and arranging scouting parties to find where the Sanctifiers have gone to ground. Also," she continued, ignoring Eutau's distrustful stare, "for my sake, I need you to put on a good show."

"What kind of show?" he asked, his voice wary.

"The best kind," Sal replied flatly. She stepped quickly outside and called to one of the agents. When she returned with the agent behind her, her face was cold and angry, and her voice more so. "He is being insubordinate," she said. The agent shot Eutau a hostile look. "I'll ask you one more time," she continued. "The Bastion wants to hear your testimony about what happened that night at Corpse Hill. If you don't come with us it won't go well for you."

It was not difficult for Eutau to play along. "I will not leave Kira alone."

"You have been given an order!"

"And you have my answer."

"I'm not asking. I had hoped that you would be more cooperative. If I say that the Bastion wishes only to speak with you, then it is the truth. If I say that Kira will not be harmed while you are away, it is the truth. I had hoped that you would at least believe me."

Eutau sneered, and it was real, for her words had sparked a deep-seated anger within him. "A shame that the Kataru's sword did not find its way into that pretty mouth. You would have had no problem swallowing it, given that you are so adept at eating your own bullshit."

She took a step closer, her gaze unflinching. "We're both rather skilled in that respect. I wonder what Kira would say if we asked him, don't you?"

Eutau reached for his dagger without thinking, only stopping when he felt the material of his shirt brush against his hand. His face was a livid mask. Sal's own face was rigid, but this time the anger in her voice was genuine.

"You have your orders. I expect you to adhere to them." She turned to the agent. "I need everyone to stay vigilant this night. It looks like a storm is coming and I don't want our wards to believe they can do something foolish." She left with the agent and never once looked back at Eutau.

Alone, he punched the wall next to him until the wood cracked and blood ran down his knuckles. *Too many people know what I am. Too many!* The sound of rain lashed against the door, signaling that the storm had finally arrived. With any luck, it would delay the Sanctifiers. Eutau took hold of the lanterns in the foyer and began unlatching them from the wall. There was no remorse in his voice as he said, "This tale has come to an end," and began spilling the lantern oil onto the floor.

CURIOSITY HAD TEMPTED Kira to linger behind and eavesdrop, but he knew that he had to ensure that everything was ready to depart. He opened the armoire in his room and pulled out the two travel bags he had packed on Eutau's orders on the day the agents had first arrived. Among the few personal things he packed was the blue amber comb Elia had given him.

What I don't understand, he thought, *is why wait in* uncle's *room? Shouldn't it be the kitchen or someplace where we can easily get outside?*

Dismissing the thoughts, he changed out of the simple shirt he wore and into a thick, sleeveless leather vest with grommets at the shoulders to hold his long gloves in place. Then he slipped on a long jerkin and switched out his shoes for a pair of sturdy riding boots. Both the jerkin and the boots had sewn-in pockets to hold extra daggers, for Eutau was very fond of all kinds of knives and daggers and had long ago taught Kira how to use them.

He was ready. But before he went to Eutau's room, Kira went once more to the armoire and pulled back a plank from its wooden side, revealing a small hidden compartment. He reached in and pulled out a steel box, the seams of which had been sealed with wax, and pried it open. The familiar smell of rot greeted him as he pulled out four motionless, misshapen rats and laid them on the floor. After doing so, he cut his fingertip with one of his daggers and, one by one, pried open their snouts, filling each with his blood.

Even if nothing comes of Sal's visit, my rats will serve as my eyes and help me keep my uncle safe, Kira thought resolutely. He bent down and pressed his mouth against the rats' bloodied snouts, forcefully blowing air into each. Then he pulled one of his old shirts from the armoire and used it to wipe clean his mouth and the floorboards. He knew Eutau would not approve, and he wanted to avoid the inevitable confrontation as long as possible.

The sound of something brushing against wood drew his attention, and he found himself unable to hold back a satisfied smile. Tiny chests rising, tails twitching, the rats looked up at him through glass eyes. They listened intently as their master gave them their instructions.

A FEW MINUTES later, Eutau walked into his room and found Kira sitting on the bed. The smell of rot caught his nose, and he wondered what Kira had been doing before he arrived. He looked around but, seeing nothing, dismissed it as a trick of his imagination.

"Sanctifiers are heading our way," he said, cutting to the chase. "Did you do as I asked?"

Kira had begun to stand but stopped in a crouching position, shocked. He stared at Eutau in disbelief as he stammered, "Yes. Yes, I did. Belle and the others are in their travel cage and I pulled your bags out as well." Then, distressed, he added, "Why Sanctifiers? Why?"

Eutau ran his fingers through his hair and then shook his head. "My question exactly. To have *Sanctifiers* come to the Bastion's stronghold, and when they know we are in its custody. It makes no sense. But 'why' does not matter. We are leaving tonight. Neither of us stands a chance against them." He walked over to one of the bookcases and, grabbing onto a shelf, pulled. Books and glass jars toppled over onto the floor as the bookcase inched away from the wall, revealing a hidden passage. Once the opening was wide enough, he disappeared into it and reemerged seconds later with a large chest.

Kira bit his tongue. Despite the severity of the situation, it bothered him that Eutau had kept such a secret from him. "Why didn't you ever tell me about this?" he asked, irritated. Eutau ignored the question and flung open the chest, revealing an assortment of armor and weapons.

"That's a fortune's worth of armor in there! Where did you get it? Have you had it this whole time? You do realize you are ignoring me, right?"

Eutau rummaged through the chest and pulled out a mail shirt. "Here, put this on."

Kira rolled his eyes but obeyed. He removed the jerkin and slipped the mail over the leather vest. "It's so light!" he said in surprise. "What manner of metal is this? Or should I not expect an answer?"

Eutau was busy fastening a leather lamellar cuirass over his own shirt. "The metal is the kind that will keep you alive. If the need for combat arises, I want you to stay back. Your injury is still fresh and I will not risk you being killed. As it stands, the stress from the ride might be enough to reopen the wound."

"I am not going to stand back and watch you get hurt!" protested Kira.

Eutau looked at him, as if measuring him up, and then let out a long sigh. "Do what you can, but from afar. Understood?"

Kira nodded, satisfied, and then shuddered. "Are you still thinking of riding to the Gods' Spears?"

"Only as a last resort. With any luck, we will leave quickly and safely, and the Sanctifiers will not pick up our trail until we are through the Hanging Forest and far to the east, toward Jané. Now gather your things and hand me the cage." He took in the room one last time before setting his sights back on Kira. A sad smile formed on his lips. "Our time here has come to its end."

"What will happen to the house?"

"Even as we speak it is burning. This was our home, and I will not have anyone else use it. Come now, we have to hurry before the smoke and flames become visible." Eutau disappeared into the darkness of the passage, and Kira followed. They descended a series of steps that eventually leveled off into a tunnel. The ceiling was low, and they were forced to duck as they crept along. Water seeped through the stone-lined walls and filtered down onto the ground, forming small puddles.

"We're underground!" exclaimed Kira, amazed.

"Yes. This passageway leads directly to the stables. From what I was able to observe of the agents' activity, there is usually only one of them stationed in the stable itself. I hope I am not mistaken."

"Umm," began Kira. But it was now or never, and he blurted out without further pause, "I—*I sent a rat Doll to check on the stables!*"

Eutau immediately stopped in his tracks and wheeled about. Gray eyes bored into Kira, who wondered if the thunder he heard had come from the sky or from the storm brewing on his uncle's face. Not wanting to give Eutau a chance to be angry, he pushed on.

"I made four rat Dolls. One I sent to stand guard inside the stable. The other two I sent to chew on the agents' saddle belts once you told me we were leaving. The last I sent to the highest point of the house to keep watch and alert me the moment it saw anyone heading our way." He produced four magnifying lenses, each no bigger than a thumbnail. Each lens was housed in a silver loop strung on a silver chain that he wore around his neck. "Each lens corresponds to a rat," he began, but then stopped. Eutau was obviously not impressed.

"How many guards are in the stable?" Eutau asked coldly.

Kira held up one of the lenses to his eye. "Only one."

"Have your . . . *rat* . . . distract him so I can get through the trap door."

The guard, who had taken to resting against one of the beams, was not prepared for the rat that sprang at his face, biting and clawing. Shouting profanity, the agent peeled it off and threw it to the ground, spearing it with his sword. But as he did so, Eutau covered the agent's mouth with one hand and slit his throat. The man thrashed about, but Eutau held on firmly, not letting go until he ceased to move.

Kira came running up from behind. "You didn't have to kill him!" he whispered, aghast. "He was one of Kim's men!"

Eutau showed no remorse as he cleaned the blood from his blade. "Do you not remember that I told you killing might be necessary? That is one less agent to fret about." Then he went to their horses and fastened the saddles and bags.

Kira followed dully, his eyes wide as he stared at the agent's corpse. Eutau brought his horse over to the corpse, lifted it, and draped it across the saddle before mounting. Kira mounted and then rode over to the lanterns in the stable, throwing them into the hay. They moved away from the swelling flames and waited near the stable door.

Come sunrise, their home would be nothing more than a memory buried in ash.

FIRE!" **CRIED OUT** the agents, as first the house and then the stable began to burn. The agents pushed open the stable doors, then dashed aside to avoid being trampled as Eutau and Kira burst out at a gallop. One reached for his sword, but Eutau flung the dead agent's body at him, knocking him over.

Into a raging storm rode Kira and Eutau, the frigid rain pelting against them like tiny rocks. Lightning snaked wildly to the ground and thunder boomed as if to crack the very sky. Recovering from their initial confusion, the agents ran to their horses and mounted. Three succeeded and began the pursuit, but two others fell heavily to the muddy ground as their saddle straps broke. Amid the chaos, the two rat Dolls scurried away in the waterfall of rain.

The diversion allowed Kira and Eutau to break away from the perimeter, but the three agents still mounted were not far behind, whipping at their horses to ride faster. Suddenly, as Kira took a firmer hold of his horse's reins, he felt a painful stabbing in his chest. He took the lens for the rat Doll on post on top of the house and looked through it. Through thick smoke and approaching flames he saw a small group of horsemen clad in black riding to meet them from the east, the very direction in which they were fleeing.

"The Sanctifiers," he mouthed. Not wanting the rat Doll to suffer, he crushed the lens in his palm and felt the Doll's life disappear. He screamed to his uncle, "The Sanctifiers are in pursuit! They're in front of us!"

"Dammit!" roared Eutau. "They will track us!"

Kira looked over his shoulder, back at the three agents. Then he veered his horse to the right, back toward the southwestern edge of Opulancae.

"What are you doing?" Eutau called out, even as he changed direction to follow.

"Trust me!"

They rode, but after a minute Eutau caught sight of something hurtling toward him and ducked low over his horse's neck just as a crossbow bolt flew past. The change in direction had favored the agents and allowed them to gain ground. Seeing that they would soon be intercepted, Eutau brought his horse around, drew his shortsword and dagger, and waited.

One of the agents was riding a dozen yards in front of the others. As the agent closed in, Eutau hurled his dagger. Its thick blade wobbled through the air and connected with the agent's shoulder, throwing him off-balance. Before he could recover, Eutau kicked his horse into a gallop and was upon him, plunging the shortsword into the agent's chest. Then, lifting the skewered agent's body with his blade, he used it as a shield to block the downward stroke of the second agent's longsword. In that instant, Eutau grabbed the dead agent's belt knife, spurred his horse forward, and stabbed at his attacker's side and neck. Blood sprayed out, and the agent let go of his sword and toppled to the ground.

Eutau dropped his arm to let the first body slide off his blade, and then wheeled his horse about to find the third agent, the one with the crossbow, desperately reloading. But the crossbowman's movements suddenly ceased, his eyes went glassy, and he slumped forward and out of his saddle, a knife jutting from his neck. Directly behind was Kira, his long hair plastered across his face from the rain. He dismounted and retrieved not only his blade but the body as well, which he draped over the pommel of his saddle.

"Are you hurt?" asked Kira, his voice mechanical, impassive.

"No." Eutau eyed the body and then Kira, but said nothing more. As he reached for his dagger where it lay next to the first agent's corpse, a long flash of lightning lit up the night, revealing another band of horsemen not three hundred yards off, riding hard toward them.

Kira cursed in horror as he sprang for his horse. "Nightmare Lords take me! Are those the Sanctifiers? How are they so *fast*?"

Eutau wasted time on only one word. *"RIDE!"*

They rode south and west without looking back, afraid that the mere act would somehow bring their pursuers closer. Thunder boomed in time with the horses' stride, and the rain turned the land into an unrecognizable sea of darkness. Kira let out a sigh of relief as a low wall made of piled stones finally came into view. They were on the right path. Beyond the wall, tall stalks of grass swayed violently in the wind and blazed as lightning set the land afire in white heat. Kira and Eutau rode alongside the wall until they reached the old temple on the southwestern edge of Opulancae. They urged the horses through the temple grounds and onto their destination: Corpse Road.

The horses neighed and swung their heads, threatening to turn back, but they spurred them onward without mercy. They were only a few hundred yards along the road when suddenly Kira felt a sharp pain that caused him to nearly fall forward. A wave of nausea overtook him as the wailing screams of trapped souls demanding blood tore at him like whips lacerating his flesh. He turned in his seat to look back, horror filling his eyes as the lightning lit up the sky. The Sanctifiers had entered Corpse Road in single file, trotting slowly, apparently aware of its danger.

Eutau cursed. "Shit! Dammit. Shit. If your plan involved the Sanctifiers straying from the path . . ." His voice trailed off.

They charged forward in silence, their every sense focused on making sure their horses did not blunder off the paths to their deaths. They had reached the most dangerous stretch in the path, the very spot where Kira had been unwittingly stricken with the touch of Death the night he had summoned Mrs. Stone.

"Stop here, and don't do anything until I say so!" said Kira, coming to a sudden halt. Surprised, Eutau said nothing and instead stopped his horse and carefully brought it about.

Kira dismounted, grabbed the agent's corpse he had been carrying, and slammed it onto the path. There was a loud *crack* as the agent's skull collided with a sharp rock. Kira drew his dagger and called upon Death. Then his breath caught and he whispered, awestruck, "I can see them. A sea of malice." A web of arms with seeking fingers clawed along the edge of the path, desperately trying to reach further in. The terrain beyond was a mass of interlocked flesh and monstrous faces.

There was no time.

Nimbly, Kira began cutting into the man as if he was gutting an animal. He sliced through flesh, ripped through innards, and cracked the spine, severing it in two. All the while, with each cut he made, the damned of Corpse Road came closer, and he was forced to endure the feel of their cold tongues lapping away at the blood on his body. He took the portions of the man, the legs, the arms, the entrails, and spread them across the path until it was crossed with a thick line of blood and flesh. Kira heard a voice and thought that his uncle was calling to him. Then he realized that the voice was his own.

"It didn't have to be this way! It didn't have to be this way!" he screamed, over and over again.

There was no time.

He took the gore-stained dagger, cut his palm once more, deeply, and spread his blood across the terrible line he had created with the agent's body. The unseen walls keeping the souls away from the path crashed down, and the spirits smashed together from the sides of the path like roiling waves, forming an impenetrable barrier of malevolent souls.

He called out to his uncle. "Ride now, while the souls are distracted! GO!" Eutau nodded and wheeled his horse about, kicking it into a gallop down the path, toward Corpse Hill and the grasslands beyond. A swarm of ravenous souls writhed about Kira's legs as he stumbled to his horse and mounted. They called to him sweetly and dotingly as they made their way to the wall of flesh and blood and bone. Kira ignored them and rode out across the frenzied terrain, following his uncle.

His gelding neighed in fear, and he stroked its neck to keep it calm. He galloped down Corpse Road, resisting the urge to recoil as the stalks of grass that lined the path brushed against his legs, for intertwined with the stalks were the misshapen forms of the trapped souls. They were elated by him; they were proud of him; they were in love with him. Kira leaned over the saddle and threw up the hard knot he had been holding in from the moment his dagger had pierced the agent's neck.

Time was, at last, on their side.

THE SANCTIFIERS

THE STORM HAD ceased its assault, but the lightning that danced through the clouds promised that the respite would only be momentary. Four ominous riders halted their steeds paces away from the wall of meat and bone stretched across the path, silently looking on as Kira and Eutau fled down Corpse Road, making no attempt to pursue.

Moments later, the fugitives finally disappeared over a rise in the ground ahead, and the lead rider, a stern-looking woman seated atop a gray stallion, lowered the hood of her traveling cloak and cursed loudly in a strange tongue. Her garb consisted of a sturdy black vest, knee-length riding boots, and a dark riding skirt slit halfway up her hips. Every inch of her bronze body was well-defined and muscular. A disheveled mass of dark hair that might once have been a topknot before the rains came lay plastered over her ears, almost concealing their long points and numerous golden-hooped earrings. A wicked glint filled her eyes as she looked down at the wall of meat paces away from her. She pouted her thin, red lips in disappointment and began turning her steed to face her companions.

"Maintain your position, Marya," said the rider immediately behind her, in a voice like rolling thunder. He removed his traveling cloak and shook the water from it, revealing bold features and muscles that appeared to be carved from stone. He too had long, pointed ears, set with golden-hooped earrings like the woman's, and he wore his dark hair in a topknot that had somehow survived the rain. He wore a lamellar cuirass over a dark woolen shirt. The woman's eyes burned, and she appeared about to lash out at the man, but then she merely laughed and spat.

The third rider, a petite, scrawny figure as similar to the first two as a dove to a pair of eagles, slouched across the arched neck of a strong yet slender dun mare in silence, giving no hint that he had noticed the near-quarrel. There was a genderless quality to his body, though the curve of his pale jaw was male. His chestnut hair was long and braided, and it trailed out from under his cloak like a thick rope. A fringe of long bangs concealing his eyes made it impossible to determine if he was awake or asleep. He wore a black riding jacket over a dull, high-collared hauberk and leather shirt. Dark leather pants, sturdy lace-up boots, and riding gloves with silver buckles completed his look.

The last rider also sat silently but, unlike the third, he made his feelings known, favoring the first two riders with an ostentatious, mocking grin. That grin, frightening by itself, was rendered hideous by the boiled-leather mask that was molded to the upper half of his face, giving the illusion that his flesh was flaking off, or the impression of some strange reptile shedding its skin. He wore a thick headscarf that concealed his hair and neck. Otherwise, his attire was similar to that of the petite rider except that he also wore filigree-worked vambraces of hardened steel.

His horse, a golden buckskin stallion, dug its hoof into the path and nipped restlessly at the surrounding air. The masked rider made a series of clicking noises with his tongue and the golden switched from nipping the air to nipping the dun's rump. The dun swung its head in annoyance and stepped away from the stallion while its rider, who stayed slouched across its neck, remained oblivious to the commotion around him.

The grin spread wider across the masked man's face, but it was quickly replaced with severity as the woman called out the arrival of new faces — agents. A band of a dozen was trotting up the path from behind.

Dismounting, the rider with the stone-carved muscles strode back down the path to greet the approaching agents. Their leader was short but well-built and possessed a commanding aura — Kim Lafont.

"You have no jurisdiction here," Kim's voice boomed. "The Ascendancy agreed not to interfere unless petitioned to do so by the Bastion. No such petition has been issued."

The rider inclined his head in what seemed like respect, but his eyes never left Kim. "Councilman Lafont, my apologies," he said in a near-purr, a tone that was surprisingly gentle for so large a man but at the same time made clear that he was not sorry at all. "But the order has been given." He retrieved a rolled-up letter from his saddle and handed it to Kim, who opened it and read its contents in the light of a lantern held by one of his agents. The rider ran a gloved finger across one of his many hooped earrings and looked on with amusement at Kim's growing displeasure.

"As you have read," said the rider once again, "the order has been issued, and the task of apprehending the Deadbringer and his accomplice has been handed to my band. We are within our right to act as we see fit to execute this order."

Kim met the rider's amused eyes with utter disdain and barely suppressed rage. "That remains to be seen, Kristoff Herzmmen — *Kataru*." The last word was half spat, and for an instant it appeared as if the two men were about to leap at one another.

The sound of someone yawning loudly, as if stirring from a deep sleep, interrupted the tension, and both men turned to look at the source of the sound. The petite rider had at last awoken. He looked to the left and then to the right, seemingly uninterested. But upon seeing the terrible wall made by Kira he immediately enlivened and jumped down awkwardly from his dun, with the masked man following suit. Both began walking down the path toward Kristoff.

Kim looked up with hard, cold eyes at the line of flesh that Kira had strewn on the ground before focusing his attention on the two approaching Sanctifiers. A sudden, violent shudder assailed him. To his anger, he found that he could not suppress it.

Kristoff's voice rumbled in amusement. "Councilman Lafont, I bid you to stand behind me at all times. My companions are . . . impulsive. It would be unpleasant to all present if you were to be pushed over the path."

"I expect you to have a tighter rein on your band," Kim snapped, but nonetheless he was careful to keep the Kataru in front of him as the petite rider and the masked man approached.

"My rein is as tight as can be expected with such egocentric personalities."

The woman, Marya, snorted loudly. "And you, brother? Did you include yourself in that flattering description?"

Kristoff flashed a perverse smile. "But of course, sweet sister." Then, addressing the other two, "E'sinea. Amonos. How long before we can cross over the wall erected by the Deadbringer?"

It was the masked man who responded, in a harsh voice that grated obscenely. "The link connecting the two points must be severed."

Kristoff pondered the words for a moment before returning his attention to Kim. "Councilman Lafont, my fellow Sanctifiers are in need of volunteers to assist them in making this road safe to pass. They are asking for your permission to bid help from your men."

The petite rider tugged at his long braid heatedly and interjected. "*You* want his permission. Not us!" The voice was genderless—a child's voice.

"I could deny your request," Kim said flatly.

"Yes," agreed Kristoff, his voice again becoming amused.

"That *wall*"—Kim spat with disgust—"keeps you from crossing."

"Yes, it does. But this wall poses not only a hindrance, but a threat to us and to any fool who treads down this path."

"And why should I be put out by fools?" Kim asked irately. Once again, he looked out toward the wall as if measuring whether giving or withholding the requested assistance was more dangerous. After a brief pause, he stated sharply, "Very well, ask among my men for help. But if not one among them volunteers, you will resolve this problem on your own."

"Fair enough." Kristoff signaled to the petite rider. "E'sinea."

E'sinea tugged at his braid. "'Bout time!" He turned to the masked man, excitement filling his voice. "Amonos, let's go see who wants to play with us!"

"Play . . ." Kim's eyes grew wide with dread as the word slid off his tongue like a waking nightmare and a terrible recognition set in. The faintest of smiles formed on the lips of the masked man, Amonos, as he walked past Kim toward the other agents.

The masked man's voice, only moments before harsh and otherworldly, now came strong and clear and melodious, ringing through the night like a great rally cry. The agents looked on as if entranced as, standing tall before them, he spoke quickly of duty and justice, of bravery and unity. His words were few but eloquent, and—to Kim's obvious shock—two agents stepped forward to assist the Sanctifiers.

The two followed E'sinea and Amonos to the wall, never once meeting Kim's eyes as they walked past. Kim muttered furiously to himself. "Pray the gods show mercy for your ill judgment, for *they* will not."

Kristoff had overheard. "Troubled?" he asked offhandedly.

Kim shot daggers at Kristoff with his eyes. "Among you Sanctifiers there are two that even you loathe. I mistook you for a man of better judgme—" He froze as the ear-piercing wail of a child ripped through the night.

"Make them stop! STOP IT, *STOP IT, STOP IT!*"

Amonos nodded and rapidly drew a dagger from one of his vambraces, slitting the two agents' throats in a single terrible slash. The dying men fell to the ground, a brief moment passing before the terror of what had transpired registered on their faces as they clutched frantically at their throats. A veil of blood dyed their blue uniforms black.

The other agents roared in anger and drew their weapons but stopped as Kim's voice, ice-cold now, cut through the chaos. "Hold your ground! Those two chose to believe in the hollow words of a Sanctifier. Their deaths are on no ones' heads but their own. The fools should have known better." But as the men subsided, he whispered to himself, "*I* should have known better."

Amonos grabbed hold of the gasping, flailing bodies of the two agents and carefully positioned one along each side of the bloody wall Kira had made. A sudden gust of wind emanated from the tall stalks of grass beyond the road as the agents' bodies made contact with the wall. The horses panicked, and the surviving agents found themselves fighting to keep their steeds from rearing and bounding away, gasping as a stinking miasma enveloped Corpse Road. Kim too found himself struggling with the sudden onslaught of wind and decay.

"What is this smell and presence?"

Kristoff stood impassive. Neither he nor Marya nor their horses had moved an inch. "*That* is a fine vintage of countless souls entertained in everlasting malice. I have no doubt that you will understand the events unraveling before your eyes."

Kim looked on, unease creasing his brow, as E'sinea scrutinized the bodies of the murdered agents. Then a proud smile shaped his lips and he proceeded to remove his right riding glove. Unsheathing a small dagger, he stood between the bodies of the agents, slit his wrist, and let the blood drip down onto the road and over the two bodies. He pressed his hands against the ground of Corpse Road and, just as abruptly as the foul wind had begun, it ceased.

"It can't be!" Kim muttered in dread.

Kristoff's voice rumbled with satisfaction. "But it is. E'sinea and Amonos are Deadbringers." He moved in closer, close enough for only Kim to hear. "For one so young, this Deadbringer of yours is very talented, but he will be no match for my two companions."

Kim's shock was replaced with renewed determination. "The boy is no fool."

Kristoff pulled at one of his earrings, his gaze scrutinizing, penetrating. "Nor am I. We are strong and he may be young, but *I* would be a fool to underestimate someone who is willing to do what he must to survive." He beckoned Amonos to him, and the masked man wandered over idly. "How long before the path is returned to its prior state?"

"Once the sun rises." Without waiting for further instructions, Amonos turned and walked straight back to E'sinea.

Kim's eyes were taut yet unreadable. "I take my leave. Do as you please," he said curtly, as if he had come to a decision. He quickly mounted his horse and rode back toward Opulancae at a gallop, ignoring the many rocks and pitfalls of Corpse Road. His men followed, many daring hateful, fearful glances as they departed. The Sanctifiers were left alone.

Marya dismounted from her gray. "Traitorous worm," she grumbled. "You should have pushed him over the edge of the path and been done with him." Together they walked up the path to E'sinea and Amonos, who had each taken a seat atop the stilled agents.

"Can we pursue?" asked Kristoff, addressing E'sinea.

E'sinea looked up, his lips stained red from the blood he had been lapping from the wound on his wrist. "With the wall—or bridge, really!—connecting the two sides of the path cut off, the spirits' social gathering has been stopped. Mind you, they weren't pleased. They nearly began a revolt," he said, matter-of-factly. "After all, it's not every day they get to visit their neighbors across the path. But when you have two warm bodies to throw about, well, everything is forgiven!"

"E'sinea," Kristoff said impatiently.

"Yes, in another hour, two at most, we can cross the wall and ride all over the fields and the sprits will not bother us. But I wouldn't suggest anyone else try to use the path until these bodies have rotted away."

Amonos laughed, a horrible, guttural sound, and Kristoff rounded on him. "Explain yourself."

"Explain what, exactly?"

"You told me that we could not cross until the sun rose. A direct answer was expected, yet once again you lied to me."

"Lied?" Amonos laughed again, his voice mocking, grating. "No, for you only asked when the road would return to its normal state. Come sunrise tomorrow, the bodies will be fully consumed by the spirits, and the path will return to its normal state." Kristoff's brow hardened, yet he remained silent.

E'sinea whistled, impressed. "Ah, but we may *pass* sooner! Oh, that was very clever, Amonos. I do so love it when you use words in that manner."

Amonos smiled warmly and, taking a piece of cloth from his bag, began binding the wound on E'sinea's wrist, though it had already begun to heal. "What are your intentions now, Kristoff?" he asked.

"Marya and I will begin pursuit as soon as the path is safe—that is, in an *hour*, Amonos." Kristoff's eyes glinted, and not in a kindly way. "Most likely they are desperate and mean to enter the Gods' Spears if we pursue. If Fortune is kind, we will come upon them before they reach that place. However, there is always the possibility that they may use this delay of ours, short as it may be, to double back to Opulancae. You and E'sinea will remain behind to ensure that does not happen, and to gather information."

"And if the Deadbringer manages to cross over into the Spears, and you cannot follow, what then?"

"Regardless of the outcome, Marya and I will wait for you in Xulmé. Rendezvous with us once your business in Opulancae is finished. We shall meet in a fortnight at latest." Amonos looked at E'sinea, and E'sinea nodded his approval.

"So be it," said Amonos. "We will travel to Opulancae and join with you later in Xulmé."

Exactly one hour later, Kristoff and Marya mounted their horses, and together they began their pursuit of Kira and Eutau.

THE GREAT KNIFE

THE GREAT KNIFE was a steep ridge, a thousand yards high, which began at the foothills of the Western Mountains and traveled for many leagues eastward toward the sea in one long, continuous uplift. The Knife's reputation was poor, and travelers avoided it. But on this day, an observer would have seen two small figures struggling up its north slope, between the low shrubs and scattered pines that dotted the rocky soil — Kira and Eutau.

Kira's horse lay dead of exhaustion at the base of the slope far below them, sprawled out like a shattered branch. A few yards away lay Eutau's horse, also dead. Flies buzzed and crawled all about, busily depositing their eggs, while overhead a kettle of vultures circled, gradually riding the currents downward to partake in the grand feast. But a single vulture broke away and glided toward the top of the Great Knife, away from the savory meal.

The lone vulture inched downward, the bright midday sun beaming through the finger-like tips of its magnificent wings. Kira halted and gazed upward at the vulture with a deep longing to be able to fly as freely as it did so effortlessly. His legs visibly trembled, and for a moment it appeared as though his weariness would have its way, but he remained standing. His sight traveled further up until the skin of his neck stretched painfully, and he shuddered. For looming beyond the ridge of the Great Knife, like an unearthly vision dividing the sky, stood a dense collection of trees that seemed to touch the very sun itself—the Gods' Spears.

He turned to look behind him and his face contorted in horror, for down on the plains below, a mere mile from the foot of the Great Knife, were two horsemen that could only be the Sanctifiers. They had caught up at last. Fear gripped Kira, channeling strength back into his haggard body, and he resumed scaling the mountain. He frantically called out to his uncle, "They've caught up!"

Eutau, a few yards ahead and above, wheeled about, storm-gray eyes scanning the plains below. Urgency overtook him. "We must cross over the ridgeline and make our descent before the Sanctifiers reach the Knife."

"We have a good start. Surely, we'll make it before they do."

"Not if a Ro'Erden is among them."

"But how—"

"The 'how' does not matter. Now, climb!"

Kira clicked his tongue, but he redirected his annoyance at being silenced toward reaching the top of the Knife.

A steady trail of loose soil and small rocks dislodged by their feet followed in their wake, forming a pair of stone rivers that trickled down the side of the ridge. The sun blared overhead, but its heat could not penetrate Kira's growing tension. The ridgeline, which had seemed just within reach prior to spotting the Sanctifiers, now seemed to be moving further and further away as they climbed. Suddenly, a violent spasm shot through Kira's wounded side and he lost his balance, falling to his hands and knees.

"Kira!" cried out Eutau, and he turned, backtracking carefully down the steep slope.

"I'm fine."

"Nonsense!"

Kira yelled again, his voice tinged with frustration and anger. "I said I'm fine! I need only a moment, so keep going!" But Eutau continued his descent. *Heh, he's ignoring me, like he always does. But I'm fine. I have to be fine.*

The feel of the rocks digging into the palms of his hands and the sparse soil dancing around his fingers drew his attention away from his growing frustration. He looked past Eutau toward the ridge of the Great Knife and found it no longer beyond his reach. He stood tall and straight, his face betraying nothing of the pain he had felt moments ago, and reluctantly let the pebbles he had grasped in his hands slip down from his fingers.

Eutau halted paces away from Kira, looking him over from head to toe. "Speed will do us little good if you collapse from exhaustion."

"I can continue."

"Can you?"

"Yes, I can."

Kira began scaling the mountain once more, leaving a less-than-convinced Eutau standing still behind him. Seconds later, as he sped upward, Kira heard the sound of Eutau's movements, following. He smiled, pleased that he had proven his uncle wrong. *Although,* he thought grudgingly, *if the Sanctifiers continue their pursuit into the Gods' Spears, then I am going to pass out from exhaustion!*

Higher and higher they trekked, until the low shrubs and pines were replaced by barren stone and occasional patches of half-melted snow, remnants of the prior winter's storms that had survived the summer's heat. The wind whipped at their faces like ice, and the waning light of the sun was devoured by the looming wall of the Gods' Spears. But at last, after four arduous hours, Kira and Eutau arrived at the thin crest of the Great Knife.

Both stood, still and breathless. Kira glanced at his uncle and saw on his face the same building terror he felt, for the forest above, before and below them, on the southern side of the Knife, was not a mere collection of trees, but rather monstrous spears thrust into the ground by a god. The trees, barely a hundred feet away from the sheer southern edge of the ridgeline, rose from somewhere far below, yet they still reached upwards for hundreds of yards above their heads. Their trunks, thirty yards or more in diameter, dominated the landscape. Their bark appeared thick and hard, and it was deeply ridged, invoking images of gorges and their rocky walls.

Kira found his mind wandering to fables passed down throughout the ages that told that once the trees grew tall enough to ensnare the sun and the moon, the gods of old would return, plunging the land into darkness. But a fable is merely a fable, he reflected, and the gods of old nothing more than the monsters that inhabited it. Unlike the gods, the forest before him was no myth.

Eutau turned and looked back toward the northern plains and down to the base of the Knife, which Kira knew the pursuing Sanctifiers must have already reached. Eutau's brow furrowed, and Kira realized that even now his uncle was having second thoughts about proceeding further and was trying to decide whether the Sanctifiers or the Gods' Spears posed a greater threat. Almost reluctantly, Eutau refocused his attention on the looming forest, and Kira understood that they were to continue.

"The south face of the Knife is a sheer drop with very little outcrop to hold on to," muttered Eutau to himself. He ran his fingers through his hair and swore bitterly. "Shit! It is times like these that I fancy believing in the gods just so I could curse them. Scaling down this will be far more difficult than I had anticipated."

"Perhaps," Kira said pensively. Leaving his uncle behind, he walked along the crest of the Knife, carefully studying the outcrop. He went a good hundred yards before he stopped suddenly and called out to Eutau, who hurried over and looked over the edge, a satisfied smile shaping itself on his lips. Though still steep, this part of the face had more pronounced outcrops and ledges that promised a potential route down, not merely a fall to their deaths.

"It is still going to be a bitch to climb down," said Eutau, though with less pessimism.

"True, but at least this improves our chances."

They had dallied long enough. Each repositioned their travel bags, Eutau taking extra pains to make sure Belle, Leto, and Pen would be safe in their cage. Kira kept a lookout, anxiously scanning the slopes they had just climbed, expecting at any moment to see pursuing figures, but he saw no one. *No doubt they are already climbing after us. No matter, we've reached the Gods' Spears. I just hope we can lose them in the forest.* He felt a sharp pull in his chest and turned his gaze toward the north, where Opulancae lay hidden in the distance. *My dear Elia, how I will miss you.*

Eutau took hold of Kira's shoulder and pressed firmly. There was a sad yet determined look on his face. "We must go."

Kira nodded, and together he and Eutau began the grueling climb down the sheer south face of the Great Knife, down into the Gods' Spears. They descended quickly but carefully, trying to ignore the great fall below them. Time passed and, as the outside world receded to an ever-thinning ribbon of sky above them, Kira made a promise to himself.

Even if it costs me my life, I will protect my uncle.

SEVERAL HOURS PASSED, and night was upon the Land.

"I believe we have missed our chance," said Kristoff, holding a torch over the sheer drop of the Great Knife's south face. He studied the tracks, barely perceptible to any but a hunter, which indicated where their prey had begun descending the cliff. The jagged outcrop glimmered in the torch's light, and the trees beyond morphed its rays into an oily, impenetrable darkness. Kristoff turned to look at Marya, who stood at his left, staring ferociously at the brooding mass of the Gods' Spears. "Shall we pursue?" he asked flatly, as if anticipating her response.

Marya tore her sight away from the black wall and snorted. "Once in a lifetime within that wretched place is more than enough for me." An unpleasant frown overtook her lips and she pulled her thick Sanctifier's cloak tightly around her to keep out the wind.

"If they survive," she continued, almost bitterly, "they will have earned my respect."

"Fortune will not have blessed them this far only to abandon them now," said Kristoff, his voice contemplative. He absent-mindedly kicked a few rocks over the side of the Knife. The sound of them colliding against the outcrop echoed momentarily before being swallowed up by the silence. "Come. E'sinea and Amonos will be on their way to Xulmé soon. When we see them there we will hear what they have learned of the Deadbringer, and we can determine where he might ultimately be fleeing."

Turning about, he began retracing their steps down the north slope of the Great Knife. Marya followed, keeping in stride with him. Kristoff began pulling at one of the many hoops adorning his long ears. His voice rumbled, "Fortune favor us and we arrive before they do."

"E'sinea will keep Amonos in check until we arrive. I asked as much of him."

Kristoff's laugh was a harsh bark that could have cracked stone and would have caused any other person to flinch. "You spoke to our dear E'sinea without his well-trained yet spoiled dog present? I'm impressed, but it will be for naught. Amonos will do as he pleases, leaving his master to apologize for his actions. As he always does."

Marya merely shrugged at his cynicism. "But the dog is useful and hence indispensable." She leaned against her brother's arm for support as she crouched to all fours to descend a particularly difficult part of the slope. "Also, the dog is fair to look at." Kristoff shot her a threatening glare. Marya responded with a frigid smile before climbing further down. "But enough of our wayward friends. What of the Deadbringer? We shall continue the pursuit in Xulmé, you say, but what does that leave him free to do in the meantime?"

"In the meantime, let the Deadbringer and his kin enjoy their fictitious freedom within that accursed forest."

E'SINEA AND AMONOS

EVEN AS KRISTOFF and Marya climbed up the Knife in the last gasp of their pursuit, their companions were descending into the Old Town. E'sinea and Amonos had left their horses untethered to nibble the sparse grass growing on the edge of the bluff over the Silver River while they themselves entered the Old Town by means of the ancient stairs carved from the side of the bluff. The stairs were steep, narrow, and chipped in places, and while Amonos took pains to descend the stairs carefully, E'sinea, who seemed oblivious to the steep drop, did not.

"You should be careful," said Amonos, keeping his gloved hand pressed against the side of the bluff.

E'sinea turned to look at him, pouting. "*You* should be careful. Me, I'm always careful." He looked down at the ragged step beneath his feet. "Oh, but you've made me lose count!"

Amonos let out a resigned sigh and counted the number of steps separating them. "Eight, nine, thirty, one . . . You are on step one hundred and thirty-three."

E'sinea smiled and resumed his descent, boisterously calling out the count as he went. Finally, when they reached the last step, he turned on his heel and made a proclamation. "Four hundred and ten steps to reach this place, and I bet you that everyone here already knows about us and the Deadbringer."

"Gossip is the swiftest bird alive," Amonos said darkly.

"Yes," said E'sinea, turning to view his surroundings. "I should like one day to catch Gossip and wring its neck."

The inhabitants of Opulancae proper had been very cooperative, and some had even been eager to assist the Sanctifiers. Indeed, it had not taken long to find some freely willing to tell them that the Deadbringer frequented the Old Town and, in particular, an "old, foul-mouthed hag." But where the people of the newer portions of the city had been effusive in their assistance, the faces in the Old Town were guarded and suspicious as E'sinea and Amonos walked its paths in search of the herbalist's home. No one approached them, and some townsfolk even openly went out of their way to avoid passing near them. As the two walked slowly along, lingering here and there, the muddy paths and alleys gradually emptied and a blanket of silence fell over the Old Town, until only the eerie sound of river birds and the far-away buzz of Opulancae remained.

Amonos eyed the huts and shacks through his mask and mused quietly, "You can see the face, but you can't know the heart."

E'sinea tugged at the end of Amonos's headscarf. "I wonder how Mar Mar is doing?" he asked sharply, piercing the silence.

"I'm sure Marya and Kristoff are fine."

"I suppose," grumbled E'sinea.

Finally, as the sun began to drop toward new storm clouds that loomed over the bluff to the southwest, they came upon a house surrounded by hanging baskets overflowing with herbs. The herbs, having flourished from the constant assault of rain, filled the surrounding air with a pleasant array of fragrances. Amonos circled the porch, inspecting each basket until he came upon one with multiple clusters of mint leaves. Carefully, he pinched off a number of leaves, handed a few to E'sinea, and then knocked on the door. The two of them chewed on the leaves while they waited.

Several minutes passed, and then rusting hinges protested as the door opened, as if reluctantly. Elia stood in the doorway. She glanced at her basket of mint and then brazenly eyed her two guests, displeased.

"We seek Elia, the herbalist," said Amonos, still chewing on the mint leaves.

Elia showed little patience. "What do you want?"

"You know why we're here."

"Yes, I know. The people of Opulancae gossip more than they piss and shit."

E'sinea laughed openly, a high, tinkling sound, while Amonos ran his gloved thumb across his lips, seemingly amused.

"May we enter?" he asked. Elia snorted and waved offhandedly. They followed her inside, and she directed them to sit at the dining table. Three purple roses set in a simple vase at the center of the table quickly absorbed E'sinea's attention. Amonos glanced at the roses as well, but he kept his eyes focused on Elia, who had ventured into the kitchen to make coffee.

Age obliged her to use both hands, yet she expertly tended the fire and quickly filled the heavy cast-iron kettle with water. From the cabinet she pulled fine porcelain ware and arranged the table to her liking. Amonos looked on, watching her curiously, and once she turned back to the kitchen he reached for one of the cups and held it up to the light of the fast-vanishing sun. The faintest of smiles formed on his lips as the light passed through the cup. He gently placed it down and, looking up, saw that E'sinea was reaching across the table to grab the purple roses.

But E'sinea's conquest was interrupted as Elia returned with a decanter of fresh coffee that she brusquely placed on the table. He plopped back into his seat, puckering his lips at the steaming decanter as if blaming it for having come between him and the roses.

Elia took a seat across from the Sanctifiers and, blowing at the steam rising from her cup, eyed the two of them disdainfully. After some time, she addressed E'sinea.

"You have traveled far, but your hunt is without merit."

E'sinea smiled genuinely, for he knew that the herbalist had recognized him for what he was, and not what he appeared to be. "Of course it's merited," he said, spooning some sugar into his cup. "We've been tasked with hunting the Deadbringer and his kin."

"And what crime is he accused of?"

"Simply being a Deadbringer is punishable by death."

"Then his crime is his birth?"

E'sinea took a sip of his coffee and made a sour face. He began adding spoonful upon spoonful of sugar until the coffee became syrupy. Amonos chewed on his bottom lip, as if wanting to object, but said nothing. Finally, E'sinea took a sip of his ruined coffee and smiled, satisfied.

Again he spoke. "Oh, it's much more than that. He has committed a terrible sin—he's become powerful! Even if the crimes he is accused of didn't exist, those in power have secretly yearned for this moment to arrive, and they would have eventually made up something just to get at him. Each sits behind closed doors unable to sleep because of a feared threat that, left alone, would never even be a threat at all. For neither wants the other to lay claim to this Deadbringer. It's quite funny when you think about it."

"A person's fate is not a joke," Elia said curtly.

E'sinea shot to his feet, his chair crashing to the floor, and slammed his hands against the table. "But it is! I'm telling you it is! Why won't you believe me?" he pleaded desperately. He backed away from the table, looking all around him as if expecting someone to be near him. Elia looked on, scared and confused, unsure what was going on, while Amonos began to rise from his seat and stiffened as E'sinea spoke, his words now hushed, emotionless.

"We are the spirits of pandemonium, thrust into this world by the actions of one man. Before this journey ends, we will claw out our eyes and wander crazed, in pursuit of an illusion, so the Land may have its false, fragile peace of mind returned." He fell to his knees, clasping his gloved hands over his mouth.

Amonos stood to his full height, his mouth a grim line, but instead of focusing on E'sinea his eyes were set on the purple roses, or perhaps somewhere beyond them, far away. The sound of porcelain rattling echoed through the room, and Elia let go of her cup. She took a series of deep breaths to help steady the trembling in her hands and then looked at the crumpled boy on the floor. Her voice was firm, but the plea in it was evident.

"Abandon this pursuit. It is meaningless, for all your efforts will not satiate those in power. Nor will the Deadbringer's death restore the illusion of peace you speak of. With time, the people of this land will find someone else to blame. There will never be true peace. Why cause so much pain for a mere illusion of something that can never be?"

E'sinea let his hands fall to his side. "Is that what I said? My, so old, yet so feisty, but . . . I don't think I was referring to *this* journey . . . or maybe I was?" His voice trailed off, becoming a lost and distant whisper. "I don't know . . ."

For the first time since entering, Amonos spoke, his masked countenance still gazing down at the roses. His voice was harsh, deadly, with no trace of amusement for once. "This woman has no information to contribute. We should go."

"Yes, I suppose we should," said E'sinea, "but first . . ."

He jumped up from the floor and pounced on the vase, removing the purple roses. He handed one to Amonos, who wordlessly placed it in his bag, and one to Elia, who silently put it back in the vase. Then, taking a cloth from his own bag, he carefully wrapped the last rose and gently packed it away. He smiled. "This rose I shall give to your Deadbringer. Amonos, the game is over. We've been gone for a while and I want to get back before your horse does something to Pretty Mare."

"As you wish, but my golden knows better than to try to have his way with your mare. He still remembers what happened to him the last time he tried."

"Yes, but still. Let's go!" E'sinea ran out without waiting for Amonos, who did not follow but instead closed the door, locked it, and turned to face Elia.

"You have lived a long time," he began.

"Too long," she said curtly.

Amonos returned to the table and poured himself another cup of coffee, with no sugar. "I am sure you are aware that there is another rumor spreading rapidly in Opulancae." His voice was flat now, unreadable.

Elia laughed softly. "Let them say whatever damned well pleases them."

Amonos quickly emptied his cup. "They need someone to blame, and your past makes you an easy target."

"I'm not surprised. That lot has always had their noses too high in the air." She rose and began gathering the dishes, placing them in the wash bin. Amonos took his own cup and followed her to the little kitchen, placing his cup in the wash bin as well. He looked on as she rinsed the dishes and laid them out on a towel to dry. Elia shot him a sidelong glance. "I won't have the place being a mess. I'll be damned if I give them that satisfaction."

Amonos's mocking grin reappeared for the first time since E'sinea's outburst, and he ran his fingers across the brow of his mask. "Oh, there is nothing to fear, for they will get no satisfaction from you."

Elia went over to the cupboard and pulled out the jar of coffee. She held onto it tightly and let out a long-held sigh. "No. They will not."

"Will you not plead?" asked Amonos, taunting.

"Do the tears of a shriveled-up old woman amount to anything? I think not."

"You have no fear? Do you reassure yourself with some false hope that you will be reunited with your family soon?"

Elia grinned right back at him. "My partner was a Deadbringer. He told me what lies beyond Death. Get it over with."

The sound of steel sliding from its sheath filled the room. Elia glared defiantly and calmly took a seat at the dining table, placing the jar of coffee on her lap. She straightened her posture, as much as age would allow, and waited. Amonos tilted his head to one side, as if bewildered by her reaction. Then his grin vanished, replaced by a warm, genuine smile of admiration.

"My dear lady, the hour may be late, but I am glad we were able to speak, if only for a little while."

"I'm disappointed we had to meet at all."
Amonos took a firm hold of his sword. "I'm not."

THE GODS' SPEARS

THE DAY HAD dawned gray and wet, just as it had yesterday and the days before. Overhead, the harsh, scratchy sound of a jay or squirrel vibrated eerily through the dim, musty air. Below, the *buzzing* of biting flies accompanied Kira and Eutau. They trudged along in single file through sour, knee-deep waters covered by a thick layer of needles that had fallen from the trees over the untold years. Their boots *squelched* unpleasantly with each step they took.

A fly — thimble-sized, with large, dark compound eyes — landed on the brim of Eutau's hood, and he quickly swatted it down, hoping that the others would stay away. But the act only served to enrage the other flies, which now focused their attack around his hood. He muttered a few words and, in an instant, Pen was at his shoulder, swatting at the bothersome insects with his bushy tail. Seconds later, Belle and Leto surfaced from Eutau's bag — their cage had been left at the wayside long before — eager to assist as well. They crawled awkwardly about Eutau's cloak, swatting and pouncing and, occasionally, feasting on flies too slow to avoid their sharp teeth.

Kira lagged a few paces behind. Unlike his uncle, he was not wearing his travel cloak, and he paid no mind to the flies *buzzing* near him. His face was drawn, his hair damp and matted, and the leather vest he had worn since fleeing Opulancae had begun to flake, decomposing from the prolonged contact with his skin. The silver necklace hanging around his neck brushed against his chainmail as he walked, producing a faint, melodious *clink, clink, clink*. Of the four lenses for his rat Dolls, only one remained intact.

A single fly broke away from the swarm and landed on his bare forearm, settling greedily upon a vein. It moved a few inches up his arm, fluttered its wings, and then, quite abruptly, fell dead to be swallowed by the muddy waters. Thereafter, the flies kept their distance.

Rubbing the fatigue from his eyes, Kira looked upward, past the giant trees and toward the distant sky, nearly hidden behind an uneven ceiling of green. *The trees are even taller here, and their canopy more dense*, he thought. *It has been so long since we've properly seen the sun and the moon and the stars.* As he smiled longingly at the thought, a single drop of rain, large and cold, landed on his cheek. He let out a heavy sigh and called out to his uncle.

"It's going to rain. Again." As if to confirm his words, the rain began. The twisted canopy overhead swayed violently from the storm's heavy winds, and down below the rain fell in uneven sheets, hitting the rank water with thunderous *plops* that echoed like ominous drums. Kira watched listlessly as the flies scattered, vanishing back into the darkness that clung to the trees, and the woodrats darted back into the shelter of Eutau's bag. "Do we continue or should we try to find cover?"

Unexpectedly, Eutau stopped and turned around. Gray eyes, rendered almost black from the scant light, examined Kira. "Can you continue?"

"Yes." Kira felt as if he should say more to reassure his uncle but found that he could not muster the will to do so. As he stood, hesitating, Eutau walked quickly to him, removing his gloves as he approached. Kira closed his eyes at the feel of his uncle's hand, cold against his cheek and neck.

Eutau's voice was dire. "Your skin is burning to the touch!"

Not bothering to open his eyes, Kira leaned forward until his brow rested on his uncle's shoulder. "I hadn't noticed," he said, and braced himself for a lecture. Instead, a strong hand rested gently atop the back of his head.

"We will find a way out of this forest, and travel to a place where the Sanctifiers cannot follow," said Eutau, in a near-whisper.

Kira opened his eyes and smiled wearily. "That sounds nice." He wanted to echo his uncle's confidence, but as the days had passed within the endless bowels of the Gods' Spears he had begun to wonder if they would ever escape. He pushed away from Eutau and reached for his travel cloak.

"We should continue, but if we manage to find a safe place to take shelter it would be nice to rest for a few days," said Kira, donning the cloak. "It's been so long since we've had rest, since we could sleep without fear . . ."

"Agreed," Eutau said solemnly.

For some time the forest remained unchanged, but as the day progressed the water flooding the ground rose higher, and roots jutting out from the ground below began to appear in greater numbers. Often, Kira and Eutau would come around the trunk of a tree only to find their way barred by a wall of roots sewn together like an intricate web that reached several feet over their heads. Usually, they would duck under or climb over the roots, though with some difficulty. But sometimes the roots were impassible and would force them to backtrack, wasting time and energy as they sought an alternate route.

Eventually, after what had to have been several miles of onerous trekking, the rain stopped, and Kira and Eutau lowered their hoods. They stood in frozen silence atop a huge, serpentine root, a dozen feet above the water and ten feet in diameter. The rain had indeed stopped, but if the storm had cleared they had no way of knowing.

Kira could no longer mask his dread. "Where have we come to?" he whispered. "How can this place exist?"

What surrounded them were no longer trees, but monsters whose bodies were encased in a dense armor of bark the color of dried blood. Hundreds of feet overhead, misshapen branches reached out like grotesquely broken arms with long, twisted fingers, their ancient needles shrouding the forest in a darkness that light could scarcely pierce. For not the first time, Kira was grateful that he could see in the dark and wondered how anyone could live otherwise. He shivered at the dreadful stillness that possessed the air and found himself wishing that the flies would return, just so that he could hear the *buzzing* of their wings.

Eutau said nothing in return, and after a while they began walking again in silence, moving across an irregular lattice of roots woven together into a sort of causeway above the murky waters. Where before the roots had blocked their path, they now stretched and curved in a nearly solid, undulating surface that wound around the trunks of the trees, allowing them to avoid the water below. It was a welcome change. But they had gone only a few hundred yards when an unfamiliar sound ripped through the darkness.

Ska-trit ska-trit ska-trit. Ska-trit.

The sound, though distant and faint, echoed all around them in the terrible silence of the trees. Kira pulled his cloak closer to his body and reflexively began sliding his fingers across the grip of his dagger.

The sound quieted. Eutau spoke in a hushed voice, quiet but firm. "I know not what manner of creature could make such a noise, but I have no desire to linger here and find out." Kira nodded in agreement, and together they set out once again.

They traveled for several hours, making good speed now as they took advantage of the causeway of roots, and the disquieting sound did not return. As they traveled, mats of deep green moss began to appear, carpeting the roots, until at times they could nearly forget that they were not walking on solid ground. Large patches of lichen, ash-green with a black vein running through the center of each flake, appeared on the trunks.

From time to time, Eutau would halt, take his dagger, and carefully scrape bits of the lichen into a small wooden box. Kira was not sure exactly what Eutau planned to do with it, but his uncle had long ago taught him that certain lichens could be used as a poultice, while others could be eaten once thoroughly boiled. *Never eat lichen raw unless you long for an upset stomach,* Eutau had told him. *And reserve lichen that is flecked with orange or red as a gift for your enemies.* At each stop, Kira would sit, exhausted, darkly wondering whether Eutau was planning to make a poultice for his fever, or if instead his uncle was reserving the lichen to make *gifts* for the Sanctifiers or other enemies. But Eutau did not say.

During one such halt, Kira gazed listlessly at a nearby tree with a trunk that was splintered down the middle and charred, as if branded by some great fire. The tree seemed different somehow and held his attention. Unlike most of its fellows, the lattice of roots surrounding it climbed at least a dozen yards up its trunk in concentric rings that formed what almost seemed like a circular staircase.

Suddenly, Kira's eyes widened, for he realized that there was a hollow in the trunk, nearly hidden in the gloom at the top of the rings of roots. He blinked, initially unsure if what he was seeing was a delusion from his fever, and then called out to his uncle, pointing. "*Psst!*"

Eutau turned and looked, and his eyes lit up in hope. Hastily, he pushed back the flap of the bag holding the woodrats and scooped Belle out. He then pointed her in the direction of the hollow and whispered into her pointed ear: "safe."

Belle jumped out of his hand, landing deftly on her feet, and quickly scurried over to the charred tree, scaled the root rings, and entered the hollow. Eutau looked on, his mouth a grim line, and Kira knew that he was worried about her. Of the three woodrats, Belle was the eldest and his favorite. She had been a part of their lives for as long as Kira could remember.

A few minutes later, Belle emerged at the entrance of the hollow and quickly put her front paws together twice, as if clapping. A swell of relief visibly washed over Eutau, and he gestured for Kira to follow him.

The hollow was spacious, bigger than the tearoom back at the parlor, with high walls and a domed ceiling. Its floor was cushioned with bits of brittle wood and decayed needles. Though it had an unpleasantly musty smell, there was no indication that any creature was using it as a den. The only entrance was the one through which they had entered.

Belle, obviously pleased with herself, ran up to Eutau, who crouched down to stroke her back. In an instant, Leto and Pen jumped out of their bag and the three woodrats began chasing each other around the hollow. Eutau looked on with fond affection and laughed. Kira smiled as well, for it was the first time since fleeing Opulancae that he had seen a genuine smile grace his uncle's lips.

Kira unloaded his travel bags and laid his daggers out, meaning to oil their blades to prevent rust, and began stripping off the soiled, musty clothes and mail that clung to his skin. Then he felt a hand rest on his bare shoulder, and he turned to meet his uncle's eyes. They were drawn, and Eutau's skin was marred by sweat and dirt, but the rest of him remained unchanged. *Time never seems to pass for you, does it?* thought Kira. Idly, he ran his fingers through his uncle's dark hair, thinking to himself that it seemed lighter than he remembered.

"Your hair fared better than mine," he said.

"I have advised you to cut your hair. It is far too long."

Kira tried running his fingers through the mats in his hair and grimaced. "Before this journey ends I may not have a choice."

"*That* I will not believe until I see." A grim look settled on Eutau's face. "Let us change into fresh clothes. But, before you dress, I want to examine your wound."

Kira knew better than to argue, so he smiled ruefully and continued stripping down until he was wearing only his undergarments. Eutau approached, he too now in his undergarments, and crouched down to examine the wound. Kira focused on the feel of his uncle's fingers gingerly prodding the thick scars covering much of his torso, and suddenly he felt the full weight of his weariness hit him.

Eutau stood. "The wound and the surrounding skin are swollen but not infected." He opened the palm of his hand, revealing a small, nubby root. "The *nologis* will bring down the swelling and the fever. It will also help you sleep. But if you should start to hallucinate or have vivid dreams, inform me immediately. The root is not kind to all who consume it."

Kira's eyes traveled to what he was certain was a new scar over his uncle's heart, and he felt a deep sense of guilt overtake him. Since leaving Opulancae, Eutau had still refused to say whether he had indeed been hurt during his battle against the Kataru. Kira ached to ask, but he had learned long ago not to question Eutau about his scars.

Silently, Kira accepted the root and turned to rummage through his bag. He pulled out and put on a fresh pair of leather pants, and then set aside for later a high-collared, sleeveless leather vest with laces in front and grommets along the shoulders.

Dabbing a bit of oil onto his hands, he spread it over his mail, which he then stowed away in an oilcloth sack. He then shot a quick glance at his daggers and decided that he would tend to them later, upon waking. Finally, he sat, skillfully rolling the *nologis* across his fingers, as if it were a coin, all the while looking at it disdainfully. "Maybe I'll have a vision involving pretty girls?" he murmured to himself quietly.

Eutau had overheard nonetheless. "Wrong root. Now take it and get some sleep."

Resigned, Kira popped the *nologis* in his mouth and began chewing. It crunched between his teeth, scalding his tongue, and tasted foul. But, within minutes, as his lids became heavy and the world around him grew distant, the lingering pain in his side faded. Gradually, the hollow became a blurred mess, and then . . .

Kira opened his leaden eyes, startled and disoriented, but then a drowsy smile shaped his lips and his anxiety washed away. For lying next to him, fast asleep, was his uncle. Leto had curled behind the nook of his uncle's knee, while Pen lay sprawled out like a dead thing across Eutau's neck. Kira searched for Belle and found her perched at the entrance of the hollow, vigilantly keeping watch. He wanted to continue lying next to his uncle, but, after some time, the need to piss and eat proved too strong to ignore, and he rose.

From his bag he pulled out a ration of dried meat and some rock-hard bread that had begun to mold. Taking the wineskin, he poured a bit over the bread in an attempt to soften it. He ate and dressed quietly, trying his best not to disturb Eutau. Then he pulled the necklace out from under his vest and looked through the remaining lens for the last rat Doll.

"Get rid of that thing. Or *I* will get rid of it," Eutau said angrily.

Kira flinched. "No!" he said, hurt, turning to face his uncle. "Aren't you the slightest bit curious to know how I made them?"

"No."

Leto and Pen, sensing the growing tension in the air, ran toward Belle.

Kira took a deep breath, trying to suppress the sudden anger that had stirred at that single word. He tried to think of some profound explanation why the rat Dolls were important to him, but he knew he would be unable to come up with anything that would satisfy Eutau. Instead, he decided to go with defiance.

"I want to see how long it lasts."

"So, you care little if it suffers?"

"You are not turning this around on me," said Kira, raising his voice.

"Would you apply the same principle if your Doll was a person?"

"No!" cried Kira, enraged and shocked. "I can't believe you would even say that!"

Eutau stood, running his fingers through his hair and cursing bitterly, apparently realizing that he had gone too far. "Shit! Shit! I am sorry. I know how much it means to you to make a Doll, but look at the situation we are in. A Doll would only have complicated matters."

Kira went up to him, pleading. "Why can't I even *talk* about Dolls and Deadbringers without you getting upset?" He watched as Eutau's face became a smooth mask and knew that his uncle was on the verge of losing control of his temper.

"Because this romantic notion you have about Dolls is absurd."

"It's not a romantic notion. It's more of need."

"A need?" Eutau's brow hardened, shattering the mask. "Well then. Explain this 'need' to me. Tell me of your rats and what you did to them."

"You're patronizing me."

"Patronizing? *Nit!* More like *indulging.* Now, tell me, before I change my mind and forbid you from speaking."

Kira stared at his uncle for a moment. Then, taking a deep breath, he began. "Because they were small, I gutted and stuffed them. Their eyes and the lenses" — he held up the silver necklace — "came from one of the mirrors I used for Summoning — the one that shattered and that you instructed me to bury. Well, I did bury it, but I kept the glass." *I made a few other things with the glass,* he thought, *but I am not going to tell you about them, because you will probably want me to get rid of those as well.*

He continued. "I then used blood and air — and by air I mean that I breathed into them — to reanimate them. I didn't mold the bodies or channel my power to bind them to me — or at least I don't believe I did. Is any of this making sense? Do the rats even count as Dolls?"

"I suppose they count as Dolls," Eutau said grudgingly. After a moment's pause he asked, "How did the idea of using the agent's body as a wall to bar the path come to you?"

Suddenly uncomfortable, Kira shifted his weight. A part of him had hoped Eutau would not ask that question. "I had originally planned to use my blood to bar Corpse Road to our pursuers."

"That was a reckless and dangerous plan, especially with you wounded."

"That's why I decided instead to use the agent's body to do it."

Eutau's eyes lit up in realization. "And by doing so, you only had to use your blood to break down the barrier keeping the spirits from the path."

"Yes! At least, that's what I hoped would happen. I was never really sure."

"You 'hoped'! So your actions were based on what, instinct?"

". . . yes," Kira said slowly, and then, "you're surprised?"

"Of course! This is why I hate these conversations. You always believe that I somehow have the answers to your questions!"

"Then why do I always feel like you're holding something back from me?"

"This conversation is pointless," Eutau said dismissively. He tried walking past Kira to step outside the hollow, but Kira jumped in his way, cutting him off.

Kira feared he would see a furious storm brewing in his uncle's gray eyes, but to his surprise he found only a scared animal that had been cornered and was seeking a way to escape. It was not the reaction he had expected, and the anger he had felt earlier returned. For the first time in his life, Kira found himself yelling furiously at his uncle.

"LOOK AT ME! WHY WON'T YOU LOOK AT ME? You've been lying to me! That's it, isn't it? Fine. So be it, I don't care. Past is past, but now I want the truth!" Eutau remained silent and, unexpectedly, Kira felt his own anger turn into anxiety. "Please! Please say something! I promise I will listen and understand whatever it is you have been hiding from me. Just don't be quiet like this!"

Eutau backed away from him toward the wall of the hollow. Upon reaching it, he fell back against it with a loud *thump* and closed his eyes for several minutes. Finally, he opened his eyes, but still he avoided meeting Kira's gaze.

"There have been lies," said Eutau, his voice filled with sorrow and bitter resentment. "The reason I have what you would call an 'irrational hatred' of Dolls is because I am familiar with what a Doll is and how they are made. I . . ." His words trailed off, and he visibly struggled to continue. Then, taking a deep breath, he finally met Kira's gaze. "Before you were born, even before the Purging, I was a mercenary. I hunted Deadbringers and their Dolls."

"Hunted . . ." said Kira, shocked, as that single word struck his heart.

Eutau pushed on. "I was a mercenary, yes, but I did not kill indiscriminately. The Deadbringers I hunted deserved to die! They reanimated to fulfill their own selfish needs. Yes, *needs*, do you understand now? They killed anyone that caught their eye—women, men, even children—and would turn them into Dolls, just so they could *possess* them, *manipulate* them!" He lowered his voice to a furious whisper of disgust. "I believed I knew atrocities first-hand, but those *Deadbringers* gave the word new meaning."

Kira felt angry and confused but, above all, hurt. Hurt that the man he had spent his life admiring had contributed to his solitude as the last Deadbringer. He locked eyes with Eutau. "Deadbringers disgust you, don't they? Why then . . . why did you let me live when you seem unable to separate me from *them*? Or," he asked bitterly, "should I not expect an answer?"

Eutau flinched. It was something Kira had never seen him do, at least, never because of him. "She," Eutau said desperately, then stopped suddenly and started once again.

"My sister was all I had. She was my life, but when I found out that she was with child and that the father was a Deadbringer, I was less than compassionate." His voice trembled. "The peace I had found by her side was replaced by solitude and emptiness when she died giving birth to you. Your birth changed my life—my routine—and, because you were born during the Purging, I was forced to constantly be on the move. Those were terrible years. Housing and food were nearly impossible to come by." He pushed away from the wall, moving slowly toward Kira. "Then, I met a Florinian who offered us shelter for as long as we needed it."

"J'kara," said Kira, his voice faint.

Eutau nodded. "Yes. She saw your arrival as a gift from her god—an answer to her despair of being unable to bear children of her own. And, despite your abilities, she loved and accepted you unconditionally. You were safe and happy, and I saw her willingness to care for you as a chance to reclaim my freedom. So, one day, I walked out the door and never looked back.

"At first I was elated to be free, but, no matter where I went, no matter how many people I met and passed the time with, I could not stop thinking about you. I told myself that it was because I had become accustomed to you and that, with time, the feeling would pass. But I was wrong. The feeling never passed, and the joy of having my life belong to me alone faded quickly."

Eutau slowly took Kira's hand in his and squeezed it desperately. "When I walked back through J'kara's door, I was greeted by two things: her fist and your tears. Almost two years had passed, and I did not think you would remember me, but you did. And when I lifted you up and felt your small arms wrap around my neck, I finally felt complete. In that moment, I realized I had come home to my heart."

Kira let out the shuddering sigh he had been holding in and tightly embraced his uncle. Eutau tensed, as if afraid, and then engulfed Kira in his arms and began sobbing uncontrollably. Running his fingers through his uncle's hair, Kira wondered sadly, *Why can't I remember the day he returned? It seems like something I should remember, but I can't. I only remember when he left, when he walked out the door and never came back.* He pushed the thought aside.

"Do you think," Kira asked slowly, "if we were to travel to Florinia, J'kara would allow us to stay, if only for a few days? It is far to the south, but we are already heading in that direction."

Eutau's voice was hoarse and nasal, but his eyes, though red-rimmed, were thoughtful. "We have no safer place to go, so the further the better. I cannot believe that the Sanctifiers have been able to track us in this forest, even if they were brave enough to enter it at all, but they surely know we must leave it and go somewhere. And they know the entire North is looking for us. Most likely, they will resume their search in the towns on the southern border of the Spears. To do so at this time of year, they will have to travel east to the coast, and there either cross the Knife in the wilderness east of the Spears or board a ship in Jané and sail South, to land in Silfria or another port town."

"They will never give up, will they?" asked Kira.

"No." Eutau's face fell.

"Will we be able to cross the Spears and pass deep enough into the south before the Sanctifiers arrive?"

"We will have to. And if we are to have any chance of succeeding, we must both rest." Eutau began to pull away, but he stopped and nearly choked on a stifled cry as Kira whispered "Thank you," in his ear.

THEY SAID NOTHING else to each other that night and rested in silence, each alone in his own thoughts. The next day, they resumed their journey with as much haste as the forest allowed, determined to reach the South before the Sanctifiers. Eutau seemed driven as if he now viewed their journey as a race against time. He walked faster than before, almost jogging at times, but would stop every few minutes and cock his head to one side, as if listening to something that Kira could not hear. Kira, unused to the new pace, soon became winded again, but he trusted his uncle's woodcraft and purpose, and said nothing.

Two days passed like this, and the forest changed again. The trees became even bigger, though Kira had not thought it possible, but the causeway of roots they had marched upon dwindled, so that it was like they walked on a series of bridges between spindly platforms, with the murky water below visible once again. Sometimes they walked easily upon thick roots, other times they crept carefully across narrow roots, and sometimes they had no choice but to descend and wade through the dark waters.

At one point, while cautiously picking their way across an entwined mass of roots as thin as candles, Kira called out to his uncle, who was a few paces ahead. "Do you think we are going the right way?"

Eutau waited until they had crossed back onto wider and sturdier roots before responding. "I would have more confidence if we had not only the lodestone but also the sun or the moon as a guide." His voice was thick with frustration. "I have some woodcraft and knowledge of swamps, but this cursed place is beyond me."

"Well," said Kira, "Belle and the others seem to think we are going in the right direction." On some occasions when Eutau had seemed unsure, the woodrats had jumped from their bag and attempted to guide him, as if they knew more than their masters.

"True," said Eutau, "but they travel toward *an* exit, the shortest way as they sense it. But the shortest way for them is not always the easiest way for us." He frowned. "It is a bit tiring reminding them of this truth."

In spite of his weariness, Kira laughed, and then looked around. "I wonder how old some of these trees are?" he asked. Despite the hostile nature of the forest, he could not help but be curious. In the North, words such as "old," "evil," and "to be avoided" were used to describe the Gods' Spears. Nothing else was ever said beyond that.

Eutau scowled at the trees, unimpressed. "Too old to even be worth remembering."

Suddenly, the woodrats emerged from their bag and began sniffing the air frantically. Then, in unison, they lifted their snouts upward and let out a shrill howl. Kira and Eutau halted and drew their weapons, their eyes darting around them, looking for an enemy.

For a moment, nothing happened. Then the muddy waters beneath the roots they stood on began to ripple, the ripples gradually increasing in size and frequency. A stench different from any they had yet encountered in the forest filled the air, causing their eyes to sting and their throats to burn, and a noise, like water being sucked into a clogged pipe, echoed all around them, growing steadily louder. And then the sound they had heard the day they discovered the hollow rang through the air.

SKA-TRIT, SKA-TRIT. The sound quickened. *SKA-TRIT SKA-TRIT SKA-TRIT SKA-TRIT.*

"Do we run?" Kira asked nervously, resisting the urge to rub his stinging eyes.

"Where to? We have no idea where this noise is coming from or what is causing it!"

Yet still they saw nothing and so stood their ground, waiting and hoping that it would pass them by, whatever *it* was, as it had done before. But their hopes were lost as Pen howled mightily at the nearest tree, not ten feet from where they stood. They turned to look, their eyes scanning up the length of the trunk. Disbelief and shock drained the color from them.

A creature with a red-armored, segmented body over four yards long and a yard wide was descending the tree at an alarming rate. Its uniramous legs, long and skeletal with sharp brown claws at the tip, clattered against the trunk, creating the unnerving sound. Upon its rounded head was a grotesque collage of human faces.

Kira stood with his mouth open, horrified, but Eutau quickly dropped his sword and drew a pistol crossbow from his bag. In one smooth motion he loaded and cocked a bolt, aimed for the center of the creature's nightmarish head, and loosed. The bolt shot true and buried itself deep. Each of the human faces screamed in a chorus of agony and the creature writhed, released its grip on the trunk, and fell like a stone.

Eutau yelled, "*SHIT!*" and together he and Kira leapt to the side, desperately trying to avoid being crushed by the falling creature. But, as its thrashing body impacted the root, it knocked Eutau off his feet with one of its many legs, sending him and the woodrats into the rippling water below. Kira screamed, but his anguish was short-lived as the root he stood on cracked apart, sending him reeling into the water as well.

Kira had expected the muddy water to be shallow, no more than waist-deep. But when it closed in all around and he could feel no solid ground beneath him, he thrashed out in panic. He had not taken in enough air and was sinking, sinking into a body of water that seemed to have no end. He opened his eyes, searching for the surface, but found only darkness.

His lungs began protesting. He needed air.

He swam in a frenzy, all the while beating down the fact that he did not know where the surface was. His heart pounded loudly and his muscles began to cramp, threatening to betray him at any moment. Kira swam. He kicked and kicked and then, unable to hold his breath any longer, took in the foul water.

He thought of his uncle and kicked his legs one last time.

Kira's head broke through the surface, fallen needles and mud clinging to every inch of his body. With great effort, he pulled himself atop the nearest root and coughed as if to die. *Where's my uncle?* he thought frantically, as he forced himself upright so he could look all around him.

There was no sign of either the creature or Eutau.

Terror seized him. *The waters!* He removed his travel bag, placed it atop the root and then began digging through it. He quickly retrieved a long rope, tying one end to his waist and the other around a narrow but sturdy root. Finally, he took a deep breath and jumped back into the dark water, only to find it no more than ankle deep.

"N-. No. *No! NO!*" Kira snapped. He drew one of the daggers strapped to his boots, dropped down to his knees, and began stabbing furiously at the shallow water and the firm ground beneath.

"*GIVE HIM BACK! GIVE HIM BACK!*" he yelled, over and over. He stood and broke into a run, but a sharp pull from the rope tied around his waist sent him reeling back to the ground. Ignoring the searing pain in his side, he brought the dagger forward and cut the rope. *He's here! I just have to keep looking!*

He searched desperately for the deep waters from before, but found only solid ground. He scanned the trees and searched beneath their roots, crawling in places on all fours through the mud. Then he stood still, and the tears streamed down his flushed cheeks and into the treacherous water. He fell to his knees and screamed.

Time passed, but Kira saw and felt nothing. Finally, he glanced up at the looming trees and the amorphous shadows, and he sneered. *They're watching me*, he thought angrily. He wiped away the sweat trickling down his face, stood, and walked to the nearest tree.

Dully, he climbed atop its roots and pressed his hands against its bark. His eyes became milky white and his skin veined and ashen. *He's gone. I swore I would keep him safe, but I led him to death.* The bark of the tree began to grow brittle, crackling and flaking like a mess of swarming maggots. A sound like moaning rustled through the air, and then the tree and its roots pulsed like a beating heart. Kira smiled obscenely. *I will take its life for my own.* And he began doing so.

The tree was sentient. It had a soul.

Kira fought the urge to scream as Death tore into him in a way that he had never experienced. He felt as if the bones in his body were breaking and his flesh was peeling off. No longer certain of his actions, he tried to pull his hands free from the trunk but found that he could not. Unable to withstand the pain, Kira cried out and collapsed against the tree, just barely holding onto consciousness.

A series of images flooded his mind.

He saw a sky ablaze with lightning. He saw a land draped with countless bodies. He saw people: running, stumbling, crawling toward him, toward the tree. People scaled his body and climbed onto his branches, seeking protection from a shapeless fog that crept across the ground. The people clinging to him wept, and prayed, and pleaded to him. In a multitude of different languages, many of which he had learned during his youth, when the land was green and the sun shone and the people traveled through the forest, the people all asked for the same thing.

Save us.

Kira looked up at the frightful sky and willed himself to grow taller, as far away as possible from the vile fog. But there were many, far too many, who could not climb so far up. So he pulled his roots out from the soil, just out of reach of the fog. The air above the ground was bitterly dry and cold, and he wondered if he would ever feel the comforting embrace of the soil again.

But his efforts were in vain. All around him the Land was changing; all around him there was nothing but despair. Up until that moment, he had never understood what that word meant, for it was not an emotion that his kind felt. He called out to the many lives clinging to him, hoping that they would understand his words, and spoke in the tongue he knew best.

The Land is lost. She has closed her heart. Whisper to me the dreams of your life, for the end draws near.

From among the many people who had sought refuge there came a reply. Their call was sweet, but laced with deep sorrow.

Do not despair, for we have a secret — we have learned the ways of the dead.

Distantly, as if it were someone else's, he felt his body pulled. At the same time, the tree's memories collapsed, and Kira fell into darkness.

A STAFF THE color of aged bone crashed down on the tree's trunk, shattering it. His hands freed, Kira crumpled onto the root, his body flailing in uncontrolled convulsions. A strange woman approached and grabbed his hair, dragging him away from the damaged tree. She went a good ten yards before throwing Kira's still-convulsing body back onto a root. Blood had begun to trickle out the sides of his mouth.

The woman was tall, and she easily pinned Kira down with her own body. Forcing a strip of some strange material into his mouth, she held it there until the convulsions ceased. Yet, though Kira fell still, the woman did not rise. Instead, she swiped at the blood on the sides of Kira's chin and then smeared it in one quick motion across his neck. A dour, angry look settled across her face as she began slowly wrapping one claw-ringed finger at a time around Kira's throat. The veins on her hand bulged and the whites of her knuckles shone, but as her free hand entwined in Kira's black hair she abruptly let go of his throat and stood to her full height.

She strode over to the wounded tree and studied the rotted mess of brittle wood. After several minutes, she turned back to where Kira lay and stared at him with a ferocious intensity. There was a pronounced silence, and then a dreadful smile bloomed on the woman's face. She laughed, a deep, resonant laugh that caused the trees to shudder and the amorphous shadows to flee.

PURSUIT

THE SILVER RIVER ran eastward from Opulancae, winding its way to the sea. Its chill waters, which swelled each spring with the ice and snow of the Western Mountains, and each fall with the cold rains of autumn, were often treacherous. Even so, the river provided much of the North with drinking water, indispensable trading opportunities, and a rich, loamy floodplain, vital for farming.

It also provided transportation.

A riverboat, pulled along by the current, sailed east down the river toward the sea. To the north, another sea, this one of pine and fir, stretched on for miles across gently rolling hills, some of which were dusted with new snow. To the south, the forest changed, and the deep evergreens were exchanged for strange, leafy things with long, tentacle-like branches that swept the ground. Past that, the flat, grassy plains rolled away for long leagues out of sight to finally come to an abrupt end at the base of the Great Knife.

The river was empty this day, and the air was bitter with the hint of winter. The boat was a large craft for the river, wide-bodied with a shallow draft, built for heavy loads rather than agility. Boatmen clad in oiled cottons and leather boots as thin and taut as the skin on their faces moved about with purpose, staying the unwieldy vessel on its course.

Merchants clad in stout wool to conceal their stout bellies shuffled about, or huddled together at the stern for warmth, each with an opinion about the current state of the Land and the direction that the various trading guilds should take. Their politics were of the kind that E'sinea had very little patience for and cared less about. After all, the Land was forever in a state of flux, and to assume it would stand still long enough to chat about its "current state" only meant that you were being left behind.

Ignoring everyone around him, E'sinea strode the length of the boat, past bundles of goods and high stacks of lumber. The brisk wind nipped at his sturdy wool cloak, and he tightened the clasp around his neck to keep it in place. The chill in the air did not bother him, not really. But few were brave enough to bother him when he was wearing his cloak, for its rich black was embroidered with the emblem of the Ascendancy. And as for those foolish souls who might trouble a Sanctifier, Amonos trailed behind him like a shadow, and no one ever dared bother Amonos — cloak or no cloak! Boatmen and merchants alike scampered to remove themselves from *his* path.

E'sinea arrived at the bow and took a deep breath. The smell of wool, hides, and cut pine filled the surrounding air. Then he began pacing in circles around a carefully piled stack of lumber that lay nearby, loudly dragging the heels of his boots on the deck as he went. Boatmen twice his size shot him irritated sidelong glances, but they dared not approach. Suddenly, E'sinea halted next to the stack, at a spot where a rope secured it with a series of intricate knots. He reached up with a slender arm, tapping the bindings. The rope was thick and sturdy, meant to endure. A twitchy smile touched his lips. The riverboat was so quiet . . . so dull.

Reluctantly, E'sinea pulled his hand away. Then, turning abruptly on his heel, he broke into a run. His long braid whipped like a reed in the wind as he dodged and swerved around the people in his path. Not until he had run clear to the stern, past where the boatmen had set up a covered horseline on the deck as a sort of rudimentary stables, did he stop. He bowed his head, resting his hands on his knees. His breathing was labored and heavy.

A hand rested gently upon his back.

"That brisk walk did not knock the wind from you, so why are you breathing so hard?"

E'sinea stopped breathing loudly and turned pouting lips up toward Amonos. "I was trying to scare you."

Amonos let out a resigned sigh. "You can't scare me. You know that."

"You say that, but back in the Old Town you were scared. I know *that.*"

Amonos pulled his hand back and looked away at the river, up the stream from whence they had come. "Did you have a vision?" he asked.

"I guess so," E'sinea said lazily. He closed the distance between them. "I don't remember much of it. Did you see it?"

Amonos's grotesque leather mask gazed down at him, his eyes shaded and inscrutable. "No."

E'sinea took a step back in surprise, the heels of his boots *clicking* against the wooden deck. "Really! Really, really?"

"Really," replied Amonos, laughing softly.

"Then why have you been so quiet since we left the old woman in Opulancae? My Pretty Mare and your Goldie have more to say to me than you."

Amonos ran his tongue across his upper lip and half-laughed. "Because I have been thinking about fucking women."

"Oh," said E'sinea, in a tiny, deflated voice. "Yes, well, keep those thoughts to yourself."

Amonos choked on an involuntary snort and then buckled over, roaring with laughter. A few merchants who had wandered close by froze at the unpleasant sound. Then, with haste, they resumed their walk and quickly disappeared past the horseline and up the deck.

After what seemed like minutes, Amonos finally quieted and straightened to his full height, wiping away the tears that had streamed down his cheeks from under his mask. In a tone that was half-sincere and half-mocking, he said, "If you say so. But I still think you are missing out on the best part of the game."

E'sinea pursed his lips, aware that Amonos was laughing at his expense. He stomped his left boot against the deck in protest and winced reluctantly. Then he sat on the deck and began picking at the tattered laces of his worn leather boots. "No. I don't think so," he said, at last. "Now, let's move on to a pleasant topic. Such as, do you think Mar Mar and Kristoff were able to catch the Deadbringer before he entered the Spears?"

Amonos crossed his long legs and crouched down, across from E'sinea. He then reached for E'sinea's boot and unfastened the remainder of its laces while speaking. "No. Whether Kristoff realizes it or not, he's bored. The hunter has found a worthy prey, and to catch the Deadbringer too soon would bring no joy to Kristoff. Or to Marya." He tugged the boot off and shook it. Three tiny pebbles, each no bigger than a raven's claw, rolled out onto the deck. "I will never understand how you tolerate rocks in your boots," he said, annoyed.

E'sinea shrugged. "You get used to it."

"I haven't gotten used to it."

"That's because you think about it too much."

The two sat in silence. Amonos gathered the three pebbles and tossed them high in the air, deftly catching them one by one. He then shoved them into a pocket sewn on the inside of his coat, and afterward sat still and silent. The sound of boatmen shouting orders and merchants checking their cargo drifted past them, along with the occasional whinny of the horses. E'sinea smiled, for among the horses were his Pretty Mare and Goldie, though they were being kept separate from the others. Bringing forward his travel pack, he threw the flap back, exposing a surprisingly large pile of apples. Atop the red mountain lay the carefully folded scarf housing Elia's purple rose. He started to rise, eager to share the apples with the horses. Then he glanced over at Amonos and changed his mind.

"Something else," he began, "something irksome has been bothering you and, try as I might—and mind you I have tried!—I can't see what it is."

A wide grin stretched to the very corners of Amonos's full lips. "Perhaps we should turn this into a game? There are plenty of participants aboard."

E'sinea stretched out his skinny leg, resting his bare toes against his apprentice's knee. "No game. After all, we have to get to Xulmé, and neither of us knows how to steer a boat. Although," he said, in a considering tone, "it doesn't look too hard . . ."

Amonos bowed. "As you wish." He leaned forward then, and his amused grin faded. "You wish me to confess? I am upset at being sent out like a dog. I am no dog, especially not for the Ascendancy."

"But we're traveling with Kristoff and Mar Mar again. And it had been so long since we'd seen them."

"This is different. It is no ordinary hunt," sneered Amonos. "The order to pursue was given by the Ten. I follow only one master. You."

E'sinea beamed, his bare toes wiggling in excitement. Then, quite abruptly, he froze, an anxious look stealing his joy. Taking a firm hold of his braid, he asked sheepishly, "Does this mean that you're tired of the game?"

"I will never grow tired of our game. But *this* game has begun to grate on me."

E'sinea jerked his leg away, bringing his knees to his chest. "But not Kristoff and Mar Mar, right?" Amonos stood then, looking down at E'sinea, who seemed suddenly small and uncertain. To anyone observing, the unfolding scene was one of a pouting child being lectured by his elder.

"No. And yet we have both wondered what the game would become if the two of them played along."

E'sinea grabbed his boot and began shoving his foot back into it, his face grim. Amonos crouched close beside him. "Yes, I have," admitted E'sinea, finally, "but I don't think I would like that game very much."

"Why is that?"

"Oh, I don't know!" said E'sinea, fussing with the laces of his boot.

Amonos playfully nudged his master's shoulder with his own. "I feel the same. Though I am certain it would prove to be a most memorable game."

"Maybe. But I think they would wind up ruining it. After all, I doubt Kristoff really trusts us. And Mar Mar, well, Mar Mar." E'sinea's shoulders drooped. "I don't know what she thinks."

"Perhaps we should consider it. It would cure Kristoff's boredom," said Amonos, persisting.

E'sinea secured the last lace and then stood. "His boredom, or yours?" he asked levelly.

"My boredom will be eased the moment we arrive in Xulmé."

E'sinea suddenly recalled the conversation he and Marya had had before setting out to Opulancae, how she had whispered a request that he keep his apprentice restrained, the way her voice had been playful but her eyes so severe. Clearing his throat, he pointed a gloved finger at Amonos.

"*Ahem, ahem.* Don't forget we have to stay within the town, which means that it won't do us any good if the townsfolk start getting uppity. Oh, and then if Kristoff finds out, he'll get all somber and glare at you with that rock brow of his because he's good at glaring, and also because he can't say anything to us."

An ostentatious grin spread across Amonos's lips. "I know."

E'SINEA AND AMONOS arrived in Xulmé five days later to find Kristoff and Marya already there. E'sinea had seemed pleased. Amonos had not. Kristoff had taken note of that, while Marya merely dismissed it as "Amonos being Amonos."

Over much food and drink, the four relayed the events of the past days to each other. The master and apprentice sat together on one side of the drinking hall table, the brother and sister on the other. Eventually, as the hours and a number of pitchers of beer passed by, the Katarus declared that they found the Deadbringer to be a worthy foe and looked forward to seeing if he survived the journey through the Gods' Spears.

From behind a mug of beer, Amonos smiled knowingly at his master as if saying, "I told you so." E'sinea clasped his hands over his mouth in response, attempting to stifle a sudden laugh. Marya, her face dreary with drink, ignored them both as she chewed idly on a half-devoured turkey bone. But Kristoff quietly studied them with his hawk-like eyes. He began to ask something, but E'sinea waved him away, distracted as he was with a mouthful of food.

Kristoff turned to Amonos instead. "This Elia revealed nothing, then?"

"She did not, but this did." Amonos reached into his bag and pulled out the purple rose E'sinea had given him.

Kristoff raised a thick eyebrow in curiosity. "Explain how a dyed rose will lead us to locating the Deadbringer's whereabouts." Then, pointedly, he added, "Explain clearly, fully, and *without* any hidden meaning."

Amonos bit his lower lip as if complying with the order would be a difficult undertaking. He then let out a frustrated sigh and answered. "It is true purple, not dyed. This race of rose does not thrive in the cold North. Their stems are sensitive, and rot sets in if the slightest bit of frost grazes them. Elia was indeed an adept herbalist if it was she who managed to *fully* cultivate these roses so far from their origin—Florinia."

Kristoff was not impressed. "I have traveled often to Florinia and have seen such a rose. It grows everywhere there, and the Rose Market itself is named after it."

"But I doubt you have ever seen one in bloom? Or maybe you have," said Amonos, sneering.

"You enjoy prolonging things, don't you." It was not a question, and Kristoff did not say it kindly.

Amonos grinned until his lips appeared as if they would tear. "I take pleasure in prolonging *all* things."

"For once I agree with my dear brother," Marya said impatiently, her voice surprisingly clear for one who had so shortly before appeared so drunken. "Stop talking in riddles or this bone will find a place in your throat."

E'sinea giggled. Amonos smiled magnanimously and shifted his attention to Marya. "It was said that the God of the South enjoyed drinking the blood of the dead. As you might expect from such a deity, his own blood became as putrid and foul as that of a corpse." His smile grew. "It was also said that he kept a garden of wild red roses because he enjoyed not only their scent, but also and most of all the feel of their thorns ripping into his skin.

"One day, he found a single white flower growing in his garden of red roses. He stooped to remove the intruder but, as he reached to pick it, he pricked his hand upon its thorns. Instantly the stem became frail and blackened, and its snowy white petals darkened to an intense purple. Yet, despite the damage wrought to it, the rose endured and became a great favorite of the God, and gave rise to others like it. But it never managed to take root anywhere in the Land, save Florinia."

"You speak in riddles even despite our warnings, Amonos, but at least this riddle seems to have a point, if I am not mistaken." Kristoff grinned sourly. "And yes, I have not seen this rose in bloom. The buds never open and wither quickly, though I have heard the eldest Florinians say that the city was once awash with showy purple blooms. Why is that?" he asked, unable to mask his curiosity.

It was E'sinea who answered. "Because they turned their backs on their god." The Katarus looked on, expecting some further explanation, but E'sinea only crossed his arms over the table and laid his head down. He tried stifling a series of yawns but failed.

Marya sneered back at Amonos. "The Faceless God." She spit on the floor of the drinking hall. "Or, as his followers sometimes styled him, 'The God of the South.' An appropriately arrogant title for an even more arrogant god."

Amonos reached for the pitcher and refilled his mug. "Yes, styling yourself as *the* god of the South is rather pretentious." He drank deeply, wiping his mouth with the back of his gloved hand. "Especially since the homeland of you Katarus *is* located in the South, and you worship a completely different god. What is it you call him?" He waved a hand in the air and then snapped his fingers. "Ah, yes! The Absent God. The Forsaker. The God Who Turned His Back On His People."

Kristoff's brow hardened, and Marya's dark eyes grew cold and hard. "I would not speak of such matters so lightly," she hissed.

"Sweet Marya, I voice only what I have heard."

E'sinea slapped the table with surprising force, causing the mugs to shake. "Oh, enough already! Just tell them exactly why we decided on Florinia, so we can go to bed." He yawned again and then pressed the palms of his gloved hands against his hidden eyes, ruffling his fringe of bangs. "I'm tired," he said quietly.

Amonos seemed genuinely abashed. "Forgive me, Master." He turned to address the Katarus once again. "Despite the heavy rains, the Deadbringer's home was naught but ash and a stone shell, and we did not bother searching the ruins at first. Upon seeing the rose, however, we thought better of it. Eventually, patience—"

"More like frustration," snapped E'sinea.

"—guided us, and after hours of searching and picking through the rubble we found that the boy and his kin had a number of rare items specific to Florinia. Back in the city, we inquired—forcefully—if there was a merchant who dealt in such Florinian imports, but there was none."

"But the best part was this!" E'sinea said suddenly, and then pulled out the cloth holding the rose he had taken from Elia. He opened it, and inside now were five purple roses. "There were a number of jars among the rubble, but most of them were cracked and broken from the fire, save a few. And inside one of those jars were these purple roses."

"The point is," said Amonos, "that the herbalist must have obtained the rose from the Deadbringer and they, in turn, must have brought it with them from Florinia. It is a strong possibility."

Kristoff smiled then, and his voice was a deep purr. "Then our path is clear. The Deadbringer appears to have had a deep connection to the South and, more specifically, to the Ascendancy's own stronghold. We travel south, to Florinia." He delicately picked up one of the purple roses, handling it as if it were a venomous snake, and looked on it distastefully. "South, to the Faceless God and his purple roses."

A CONVERSATION

KIRA LAY ON the ground within the hollow of a tree. He looked up at the vast, dark cavity above him and thought, *There is no moon here. If I find the moon it will lead me to my uncle.* He started to rise but then stopped momentarily, realizing to his surprise that he had been lying in a puddle. He stood fully then, watching the water roll down from his body to the wet ground, the sound of it dripping echoing within the cavity like glass shattering. *It's so hot. I need to go outside.* He moved away from the rippling puddle and stepped out of the hollow.

Kira stood at the highest point of a towering tree. The hollow was nowhere in sight. He looked up at the turbulent night sky, howling with a freezing wind. *Even here there is no moon.* Another thought formed in his mind, one that was not his own. *If we could flee to another part of the Land we would do so. But here we took root, and here we will remain.*

A mighty rumble emanated out of the South, crackling the air, and a giant beast with wings akin to those of a bat soared into view. Its elongated body was covered with cream-colored scales; its wings, though cream as well, were veined and accented with scarlet. Another thought came to him as he watched the winged creature vanish South. *Our friends leave us — we will be alone. They seek to reclaim the Land from those who have hurt and scarred her.*

From below, a man's voice boomed out to the trees. Kira turned his gaze away from the winged creature and felt an uncontrollable knot of disgust and hate grip him. The man was tall. He wore a long, dark coat with a high, rigid collar over a strange breastplate molded to emulate a ribcage. Vambraces and greaves of neither metal nor leather crawled up the length of his forearms and legs like disembodied spines, while intricately pinned dark hair flowed down to his thighs like writhing snakes. A featureless onyx mask concealed his face. Red boulders surrounded him.

The man rested a pale hand atop one of the many boulders and said, "I have a gift for you." Then he rapped the boulder on which his hand had been resting. It twitched and began uncoiling, revealing a many-segmented creature with numerous insect legs. Atop the creature's insectoid head, like some badly sewn quilt, were human faces.

We should end you, called out Kira, seething with anger.

"Because I gave them what they wanted?" The man flashed a plain, narrow sword, his voice severe. "I gave *you* what you wanted. You did not want to be alone and they did not want to leave." He brought his arm up over his shoulder and placed the plain sword in a scabbard strapped to his back. "They will remain here, as guards. This way" — the tips of his fingers caressed the mesh of human faces on the creature closest to him as if he were bidding farewell to a lover — "they will be of use."

You take our friends to battle. You take them to death.

"They take themselves to death."

They will despair by your side.

"And yet they see me as their hope. They are truly wondrous creatures."

The sudden smell of smoke permeated the air, and Kira turned to look for its source.

This is . . . Kira's thought trailed off like the tears trickling down his cheeks. He was back in the parlor, standing in the hallway that led to the kitchen and staring directly at the closed doors of the sitting room. The smell of smoke grew stronger. From behind the door there came a rustle, like someone sliding against fabric, and then a voice.

It was his uncle's.

An inexplicable fear gripped Kira, but he knew not why. He reached for the handle of the door, turned it, and swung it open. A swell of relief washed over him.

It's the moon. I finally found it.

KIRA OPENED HIS eyes and found himself staring into the flames of a campfire, his vision unfocused and vague. *What was I dreaming? I can't remember now.* His fingers automatically squeezed the pelt covering his naked body. He tensed. *This isn't my coat! We haven't been carrying a pelt with us. And where are my clothes!* He stood, wrapping the pelt around his waist, looking around himself in panic.

He had been lying in the middle of a flat, grassy area near the edge of a shallow mound roughly ten yards across. It was dark, very dark, and for some reason his normally keen night vision could not penetrate the gloom. All he could see was what was illuminated by the queer, flickering light of the campfire. Dancing shadows slithered along the side of the mound, playing on the bare trunk of a thin, branchless dead tree that jutted haphazardly out of the ground.

The skin between Kira's shoulders tingled, as if someone's eyes were on him, and he shivered involuntarily, turning every which way to peer into the gloom. Then, as if a lantern had been unveiled, moonlight shone down upon him, and he gasped in surprise. He stood stock-still, gaping upward, his eyes growing wide with awe as he beheld a wavering silver ball, suddenly revealed from behind thick clouds. *The moon! It's been so long . . .*

But then Kira realized that the rest of the sky was still dark, as if he was looking at the moon through a black funnel. He looked around him, and saw in the moonlight that the grassy area lay in the middle of a small lake or pond, surrounded on all sides by towering trees that leered over him, blocking out the rest of the sky. He shuddered. *I'm still in the Gods' Spears,* he thought, and even as the words formed in his mind another cloud covered the moon and the blackness closed in again.

The fire crackled as a log crumbled into ashes. Again shadows danced on the mound. Kira nearly moaned in despair. Then, forcing down an overwhelming sense of hopelessness, he approached the campfire cautiously, squinting as he closely examined his immediate surroundings. His belongings were neatly placed near the fire, and the clothes he had been wearing were hung upon a series of branches that had been jabbed into the ground. His daggers were lined up from shortest to longest, their blades reflecting the orange glow of the fire as if they had been honed and oiled. He retrieved the longest and then reached for his clothes to begin dressing. He had just slipped into his pants when a voice spoke as if from all around him. It was deep yet unmistakably feminine, and it was strangely familiar.

"I asked you once, 'What are you?' and you did not answer. Now I ask, who are you?"

Kira's eyes darted from one side to the other, but the darkness was thicker than ever, and he saw no one. He held the dagger by his side, ready to throw or stab at the first sign of movement, and called back, trying to sound bold. "Show yourself!"

The voice laughed softly. "Very well."

Kira saw, or rather felt, something move in the darkness at the edge of his vision, and he turned quickly to meet it. A woman stepped soundlessly into the firelight as if gliding on shadow, and the light seemed to recede before her. Her impossibly tall outline was obscured as if by a haze, but her hair glowed as it reflected and magnified the light and heat of the fire, and her beautiful features were terribly clear. Kira flinched, nearly falling backward as if struck.

"T–this. I'm dreaming. You're not real! I dreamed you when I was ill!" he said in terror. Kira glanced all around, looking for the other images from his dream as if to support the assertion of falsity: the endless hallway, the door, the terrible portraits, the porcelain Doll with the perfect ringlets, laughing at him from the shadows once more. But there was nothing. Only darkness, the firelight, the Gods' Spears—and the terrible woman.

The woman began slowly walking around Kira, and though she kept her distance she seemed to become more visible, as if she was deigning to allow the light to touch her. The dark folds of cloth from beneath her corselet rustled across the dirt. Her face was expressionless.

"Denial does not become you," she said.

"Stop circling me!" said Kira, tightening his grip on the dagger.

"So many demands. And yet, you have not even answered my question. Nonetheless . . ."

The woman abruptly stopped and turned toward Kira, who backed away, holding the dagger up in front of him. The woman stopped her advance, the faintest of smiles shaping her lips.

"Had I wished to hurt you, I would have already done so. Instead, I freed you from the grasp of the tree, brought your body to this mound, and stripped you down to tend your wounds and fever. The list goes on"—she gestured with a jewelry-adorned hand to the campfire—"but it is not my habit to render aid and then expect something in return." Her dark eyes narrowed. "Nor is it my habit to repeat a question."

Kira worked moisture back into his dry mouth. He considered giving the woman a false name but somehow knew that, if he did, the mound would become his grave. "My name is Kira Vidal. I'm from the North. From Opulancae."

"Kira Vidal. From the North. From Opulancae. Who has never yet answered *what* he is." Darkness seemed to flow around her, as if it too was waiting for the answer.

She's already seen what I can do, thought Kira in desperation. *I can't lie to her.* "I'm a Deadbringer," he said at last.

"Is that so," said the woman. Her voice was suddenly tinged with clear amusement, and to Kira's surprise she laughed, a rich, pleasing laugh that somehow seemed to make the darkness creep back. "Well then, *Deadbringer*. I am Daemeon." She gestured at the campfire and then held up a hook with something bloody dangling from it. "Sit, and dine with me. Or, you could instead gather your belongings and be on your way. It matters not to me. But know, little one, that if you leave you will die in the Gods' Spears."

"Will you hunt me down?" asked Kira, fighting to keep his voice level.

The woman took a seat near the campfire and, using the tip of one of her clawed rings, began skinning and gutting the thing that hung from the hook. Without looking up, she said, "There would be no need. You would die of exposure or by murdering yourself in madness." She fell silent then, saying nothing more as she prepared her meal.

Kira turned and walked a few steps away, feeling ill. A few minutes passed, with no sound but that of the woman's work, skin pulling back, flesh yielding, innards *hissing* as she threw them into the fire. The moon appeared again from behind the clouds. He gazed up at it, but now it seemed to pulse like a beating heart, and he looked away, feeling sick. *It's only my imagination. It has to be! This. Is. Just. A. Dream!*

But the dream did not end, and he did not wake up.

Kira took a series of deep breaths to steady himself. Then, keeping his blade in hand, he walked back to the campfire and took a seat across from the woman. The meat was cooking now, and the sight and smell of it on the open flames caused his stomach to lurch painfully. His mouth watered on its own accord.

The fire was warm against his skin, and he drew his legs to his chest, wrapping his arms around them. Fat from the meat dripped into the open flames, *sizzling*. Kira found himself wishing fervently that his uncle had been the one sitting across from him. Then Eutau's face flashed before his eyes and he nearly choked on a stifled cry. *I couldn't keep him safe.*

He felt a hand touch his shoulder and turned, flinching, to see the woman standing next to him, holding out a skewered piece of the seared meat. Kira hesitated, and the woman responded by unceremoniously taking a bite of the meat.

"It's not poisoned," she said.

Kira accepted the meat and watched intently as the woman went back to her side of the campfire, the flames and the shadows enveloping her.

When did she move? When did she reach for the meat? I don't remember seeing her move! he thought, trying to beat down the anxiety squirming around the edges of his consciousness. Warily, he took a bite of the meat and soon found himself eagerly devouring it. It was tender and rich, with a strange yet savory taste unlike any meat he had ever tried.

The woman spoke. "Your touch rotted the tree. Your touch has marred the pelt I laid over you. And yet my flesh is intact."

Kira tried meeting the woman's eyes, but something—perhaps the flames and the smoke—prevented him from doing so. *I can't see her at all from here.* Curiosity outweighed caution, and he stood and moved around the fire, closer to her.

She sat leaning back, using her left hand to prop herself up. She had one leg crossed while the other was brought to her armored chest, exposing boots that went past her knees. The material appeared soft and flexible, but it caught the light like the iridescent shell of a beetle. With her right hand she held out a drinking skin.

"What is it?" Kira asked suspiciously.

The woman drank deeply. "Wine. I also have a gourd filled with blood, if that is what you seek to quench your thirst."

Kira felt his face blanch. The memory of tasting the Kataru's blood through the Risen of Corpse Hill came back to him in a rush of guilt and fear. *Can she know?* But instead he said, "No, the wine is fine," and sat just out of arm's reach from the woman. He drank from the skin, and his brows shot up in surprise.

"This wine is excellent."

The woman held up another skin to her amused lips. "Then drink."

Kira drank. He savored the taste of the wine in his mouth, and for a long moment he thought of nothing else. Finally, when he put the skin down, he recalled what he had meant to ask.

"Aside from my uncle, I have never met anyone else who could"—he paused, searching for the word—"*interact* with me without getting hurt. Especially when I am asleep."

"Then, when you are conscious, you have control over this ability of yours?"

"Somewhat."

The woman's face became pensive. "Then either your control is greater than mine, or your ability is weak."

Kira was taken aback. "Are you saying that your touch rots?"

"Shall I show you?"

Kira swallowed his fear and nodded, mentally preparing himself for some grotesque performance, but she merely pulled out one of the logs from the fire, wrapping her hand around it. He flinched, bracing himself for the smell of burning flesh, but the noxious odor never came. Instead, the log's embers grew dim and the wood began to rapidly flake in her hand. She opened her grip and let the log fall to the ground, where it shattered in a spray of dust and ash.

Kira looked on, amazed, leaning forward without thinking, and suddenly he was too close, and the woman had reached out and was running her fingers through his hair. Kira pulled away, a sudden swell of anger overtaking him. He screamed inwardly, *Only my uncle touched me in such a fashion and you are not him!*

The woman's voice was expressionless, her face impassive. "Tell me. What do you believe I am? What do you want me to be, Kira the *Deadbringer?*"

Want? The unexpected question beat at Kira, smothering his anger. *She's a Deadbringer like me, right? What else could she be?* He felt, rather than heard, the woman's strange emphasis on the word "Deadbringer" and found himself suddenly terrified. And yet . . . *I don't want to be the only one. I don't want to be alone.* Reluctantly, he forced himself to meet the woman's cold gaze. "I want you to be a Deadbringer."

The woman arched a pierced brow, and then she smiled. "Then, for you, I am a Deadbringer."

Kira moved back, away from and out of reach of the woman, more confused than ever. *This is only a dream. When I wake up none of this will matter.* But, instead of comforting him, the thought left him feeling embittered and lonely.

The woman drank again and let out a long sigh of satisfaction as she put down the wineskin. "You are being hunted, are you not?"

"Yes."

"You spoke of another, blood of your blood, yet I have seen no one but you."

"My uncle," Kira paused, his voice quivering. He continued, for there seemed no longer any reason not to speak the truth. "The Gods' Spears, this forest, it was the only place we could think of to escape the Sanctifiers. We were trying to get through it and reach Florinia."

"Sanctifiers. And they hunted you because they discovered that you are a Deadbringer?"

"Yes," Kira said bitterly, his voice heavy with resentment.

"Such fools. You would have lived out your life as merely another man among many. Or perhaps I am mistaken?"

"I always complained to my uncle about not being able to just be a Deadbringer. I hated having to watch everything I did. I hated always having to look behind my back. But now . . . now I would gladly accept the life I had before if it meant I could have my uncle back."

"So your uncle is dead. Is that why you lashed out at the tree?"

"It was a foolish thing to do. I realize that now. If it hadn't been for you, I would be dead."

"And would death be unwelcome?"

Kira looked away, drawing his knees to his chest.

The woman's voice echoed all around him. "What do you seek?"

"I don't know." His voice was muffled. "My life has been built on lies."

"Is that so? Well, here I sit as I truly am before your eyes. And, if it is what you desire, there do not have to be any more lies. Be what you yearn to be, and stop living for false ideals."

He peered at her. "Why are you telling me all of this? What are you trying to say?"

"I find you interesting, Kira the Deadbringer. You could learn many things from me."

"If I had been stronger I could have protected my uncle. Instead, I let him die."

"Strength alone would not give you what you seek. And much that I could teach you has little enough to do with what you think of as *strength*." The woman leaned forward and smiled. "Yet, if you were to recover his body, what would you do with it?"

Kira shuffled uncomfortably.

The woman's smile became knowing, perceptive. "A pet—no, that's not the correct word—a *Doll!*"

"He hated Dolls. Passionately. He would never forgive me if I did that to him."

"Then you have made a Doll before?"

"Not really. No."

"Of course you have not," said the woman in a low whisper. "But, consider my words an offer. If you choose, you may follow and learn from me." She pulled a leather bag from the shadows at her side and began rummaging through it. After a few seconds, she retrieved an evergreen branch covered with lance-shaped leaves and a small, square pouch with symbols stamped in the leather.

Kira squinted, trying to get a better look. A shadow moved across the woman's neck like a snake and he blinked, wondering if he had really seen it. *It is just my imagination again,* he told himself, and focused his attention on the objects, calling out their respective names. "Yew leaves and a *jaave*, though I don't recognize any of the symbols."

The woman's eyes narrowed. "Yes. A *jaave* is one word for it, one of many. *Jaave*, charmbag, *mirakor*, even, to some fools, a 'magic pouch.'" She tossed the *jaave* to Kira. "But, what kind of *jaave* is it? Perhaps you might recognize the symbols, if you take a closer look."

Kira picked up the *jaave* and examined it, to no avail. He shook his head and then tossed it back. "No, I have never seen one of these. But, I'm not very good with this kind of stuff." He smiled sadly. "It was my uncle who was skilled in all of this."

"Is that so," she said, removing a handful of the yew leaves and placing them in the pouch. "Tell me, now that the blood of your blood has left this Land, what are your intentions? I have made you an offer, but there is also your journey and its destination. Will you regret not seeing it through until the end? Think this through before you respond."

Kira's thoughts roiled. *If I had been as strong as this woman, this Daemeon, maybe I could have kept my uncle alive. Maybe I could have defeated the Sanctifiers. But she's frightening, maybe evil. The things I saw in those paintings in that white room, and the things I'm seeing now . . . And yet, another Deadbringer! One of my own!* He ran his fingers through his hair unthinkingly and, finally, let out a long-held sigh.

"I've decided," he said, "to see my journey through to the end."

"Very well." The woman handed Kira the *jaave*. "If, after you complete your journey, you realize that you cannot go back to living as you once were, take the yew leaves from within the *jaave* and eat them. They come from a special yew tree, one I have cultured over the years with some of my blood. Do not misplace them."

"But aren't yew leaves deadly poison?"

"To all except those who know the ways of the dead."

The woman stood suddenly, towering over Kira, who looked up at her in awe. *She's so tall! I wonder if this is how people feel around me?* He tensed as if to flee, but the woman turned and walked away from the campfire to where the dead tree stuck from the low mound. Resting her hand upon its bole, she looked out to where the lake and the Gods' Spears lay hidden in darkness.

For some reason he did not understand, Kira found his gaze drawn to the tree. He stood and walked to it, making sure to stay on the side away from the woman. The length of the tree sticking from the mound was a good four feet longer than he was tall. Up close, it darkly reflected the light of the fire like a dull gemstone. Kira placed his hand on it and frowned. *This isn't a tree, it's some sort of stone!*

"Kira of Opulancae. Should you decide to summon me, know that I may — or may not — answer your call. But should I decide to answer, if I still find you interesting I will become your master, and you my apprentice." A hint of severity tinged her words. "You will learn *all* that is within your abilities. And know that if you should die on your journey, or after, I will collect your body and fashion you into one of my pets."

"That's not a very endearing offer."

"Would you rather I lied to you about my intentions . . . Deadbringer?" said the woman, her voice now harsh as black ice.

Annoyed, Kira shot a quick glance back toward the campfire. "I'd rather you gave me a better offer."

"Is that so?"

Kira looked back and found her inches away, staring down at him. His mind screamed, *Back away! Back Away!* But instead he looked up, determined to meet the woman's dark gaze, and stood his ground.

The woman raised her right hand and began indolently tracing her finger around the shape of Kira's eyes. Her finger was calloused and rough, her presence oppressive and imposing. Kira fought not to flinch.

She laughed softly. "You are, indeed, *young*," she said, emphasizing the last word in a way that left no doubt she had meant "fool." Then she pulled away and, leaning her back along the stone tree, slid sinuously down along it until she was seated with her back against the mound. Kira remained rooted to the spot, his heart pounding, cursing himself for his bluster, for allowing himself to forget for a moment how dangerous the strange woman was.

"Night wanes," she said, as if dismissing him. "Sleep. You'll need your strength on your journey."

Kira worked moisture back into his mouth. Hoarsely, reluctant to antagonize her again, he asked, "My journey. I will go nowhere if I cannot find my way out of this forest. Can you help me escape it?"

"I told you once that you would die by yourself in the forest. And you still would. Do you believe I would offer you gifts if I were going to let you die? Do not be such a fool that I regret my offer. Now, *sleep*. No creature will harm you while you are by this mound."

Kira nodded, chastened, and made his way back to the campfire, half-relieved that he had been dismissed. He retrieved the pelt, laid down, and buried himself under it. Then he closed his eyes and waited for sleep to take him. It was a long wait. Memories of his uncle and Elia plagued him, and he turned restlessly. *Why do I feel like I've betrayed them both?* he thought, disquieted. It was not until hours later, as the seemingly endless night wore on, that Kira's mind gave him mercy, and he drifted off into a dreamless sleep.

KIRA AWOKE AS the first rays of dawn pierced the night sky. Rubbing the sleep from his eyes, he sat and, to his surprise, saw a figure crouched near the smoldering embers of the fire. *It wasn't a dream!* he thought, amazed and afraid. Then his eyes narrowed. *Something's not right.* Daemeon was a tall woman, her silhouette otherworldly and intimidating, but the figure before him was small and unobtrusive. Kira took hold of the dagger he had slept with. The figure stiffened, as if sensing him, and then turned to face him.

"Who are you?" he demanded, unsure who or what to expect.

The voice that responded was that of a young woman. "Daemeon sent me. I'm your guide," she said, and then tossed back her hood.

Kira felt his breath catch. The stranger was a beautiful young girl with deep-red hair that flowed in waves past her shoulders. Her large, purple eyes, lined heavily with *atche*, were set in a dark olive-skinned face, and they gazed upon him with an exciting, fiery look. At that moment, he felt very self-aware, but even so he would have done anything for her.

Then she spoke again. "I'm here to get you out of this reeking shithole. I've been made to understand that you are a fucking idiot, but if you don't do anything stupid and do follow everything I say, you might even survive. Now, let's go."

In the distance, Kira thought he heard Daemeon laugh.

ENDINGS AND BEGINNINGS

KRISTOFF DISMOUNTED AND motioned for his companions to do the same. From where they stood on the crest of a low, sandy hill a few miles west of the port city of Jané, he could gaze upon its rooftops and the masts of the ships docked in the Idle Bay. Further off, almost out of sight, flecks of shimmering white betrayed the spot where the Bay's calm waters collided with treacherous whitecaps rolling in, the endless waves of the Eastern Sea. A large gull flew overhead, as tranquil as the late afternoon sun's rays on the grass of the hilltop. Kristoff kneaded the deep knots in the muscles of his neck and frowned, as if considering something unpleasant.

"We will enter Jané on foot," he said, finally. "For—"

"Yes," said Marya, deepening her voice in a mockery of his own, "for the man who leads his horse unhurriedly is not to be remarked upon, while the man who rides with purpose is an object of curiosity and fear." She rolled her eyes and spat. "I have heard you say that often enough to know the words by heart, and still I think it a stupid saying, particularly for a Sanctifier. I would rather be feared than ignored, and I see no reason to go slowly now when we have spent the past days riding hard." Nonetheless, she dismounted and brought her gray alongside his black.

Endings and Beginnings

"And as always, dear sister," Kristoff responded, unfazed, "I say back to you that fear is not always useful. In any case, I doubt we could charter a ship to Florinia today even if we hurried."

E'sinea dismounted as the two sniped at each other, but not before steering his mare a few yards away. As they bickered, he fussed with his saddlebags, as if he was trying to avoid talking to them or perhaps trying to decide what to say. Finally, he turned to face them, a playful smile on his lips.

"Are we going to spend the night here? Oh please, let's spend the night! I'm tired of sleeping on the hard ground or on the bouncing back of Pretty Mare. And the horses are tired. And I'm sure Mar Mar is tired, and you are tired, and Amo—" Abruptly his voice cut off, and his smile vanished.

Not for the first time, Kristoff wished he could see the eyes behind E'sinea's fringe of hair, for the eyes often revealed more about a person than expressions alone. "E'sinea—"

"I know what you're going to ask and no—for the, oh, I don't know how many times now—I don't know where Amonos went!" His mouth twisted sourly. "I still can't believe he left me behind. *Humph.* I am his master, after all!"

To Kristoff's surprise, his sister whacked the back of his head with the flat of her hand. It was something she had not done since she came of age.

"Brother," she said, "relieve your frustrations with one of the many *pé'bos* in this town and let E'sinea be. I do not approve of Amonos having abandoned us in the dead of night like a coward, but he has never given cause for distrust. Most likely he has gone ahead to Florinia—though what path he could have taken only Fortune knows—and, if he is indeed in Florinia, I will give him an opportunity to explain his actions. If I like his explanation, then I will not gut him."

At that, E'sinea let out an agonized wail. The siblings whipped their heads around to him, and the horses danced nervously. "Oh Mar Mar, please don't kill Amonos! I'm sure he has a good reason, but even if he doesn't we've been together for so long that I would be quite lonely without him."

Kristoff studied his companion and wondered, as he had on several occasions since Amonos's unexpected departure, if the words were genuine or merely for show, especially since E'sinea had kept watch the night Amonos had vanished.

On that night, when the band had still been a week's ride from Jané, a whimpering noise had ripped the Katarus from their sleep. Swords in hand, he and Marya had sprung up, ready for an attack. But the attack never came and the noise had ceased. All they had found was E'sinea unconscious and crumpled on the ground, and Amonos and his golden stallion gone. Then the whimpering had begun once more, coming from E'sinea. Marya had tried rousing him and had even gone as far as kicking his shoulder, but he would not wake. The siblings had remained awake and watchful the rest of the night, but nothing else had happened.

The following day, E'sinea had guffawed at Kristoff for even mentioning the possibility that Amonos had abandoned their party, let alone done something harmful to him. Yet as the day waned and Amonos did not return, E'sinea had become sullen and distant. He had remained in that mood for the rest of the journey.

Kristoff took in a deep breath, blew it out through his nostrils, and decided that Marya's blow had been justified and that he would no longer question their companion. Instead, he strode over to E'sinea and placed a gloved hand atop his head, playfully mussing his hair. E'sinea froze at his touch as if unsure what to expect. Kristoff had no doubt that he had Amonos to blame for the mistrust. Once again, his thoughts turned dark. *If the apprentice has truly turned against us, can the master be far behind?*

But what he said was, "There is an inn within the town, near the docks, that I have stayed in. The rooms are small, but the beds are soft and filled with feathers instead of straw." E'sinea relaxed then, and an eager smile, an honest smile, shaped his lips. "Should we be on our way?" asked Kristoff, relaxing, confident that he knew the answer.

"Yes! I can't wait to plop onto a soft bed and stretch every which way. Are you excited as well, Mar Mar?"

"A soft bed is welcome, but what I desire most is an endless feast of meat and drink, especially before we set out to sea."

They started down the hill toward Jané. Marya and E'sinea went ahead, chattering together, while Kristoff walked behind, leading his black and watching them thoughtfully. A memory stirred, and he thought back, back to his first encounter with E'sinea and Amonos.

His band had consisted of himself, Marya, and two Ro'Erden. Kristoff had joined the Ascendancy soon after his coming of age. Like many other young Katarus during the years leading to the decade that came to be called the Purging, he had eagerly answered the Ascendancy's call to unite the Land against Death. For many of his brethren, that call had been a convenient excuse to seek glory, a prize hard to find in times of peace.

Kristoff had not been immune to that call but, for him, the goal of uniting the Land and saving its peoples was more than just a rallying cry. He believed in it. Marya, who had joined up years later during the Purging, after she had come of age, agreed with him—or, at least, she said she did when he had asked, though he rather suspected she was just humoring him and his more philosophical interests. But their two Ro'Erden companions had held no such pretentions.

To be sure, they had proclaimed similar views upon first joining the Ascendancy but, as the war progressed, it became apparent that their claim was a farce, and they soon gave up pretending. They had joined not because they believed in the Ascendancy's ideology but because they profoundly hated its enemies — the Deadbringers.

During his time riding and fighting with the two Ro'Erden, Kristoff had always remained wary of them. They were cruel and seemed to delight in causing their enemies pain, and more than once when angered they threatened Kristoff and Marya or accused them of treason or insufficient faith. But such things were to be expected in war, and they barely troubled him. Instead, most of his caution stemmed from old songs passed down through generations of his clan, sagas that told of the Great Dance of the Dead and the Land — or, as it was less lyrically known to all the races, the First War.

The sagas told of a foreign race of horned men and women that had arrived aboard strange ships in numbers that only the stars of the night could match. But just as quickly as they had appeared, they vanished. Shortly thereafter, diseases unfamiliar to all began to ravage the Kataru clans along with the other races of the Land, and it was not long before the dead outnumbered the living.

From the mass graves, a foul miasma came into existence. Though at first isolated to where the dead lay, it soon crept beyond the grave trenches and drifted across the Land, killing all in its path. And so fields sown with golden stalks of wheat would shrivel, orchards would blacken, and fowl would raise their beaks desperately toward the sky, collapse, and call no more. Not knowing what the miasma was, the people of the Land began to call it the Lurking Evil.

And then the foreign race that had vanished reemerged as conquerors. They called themselves the Ro'Erden.

Kristoff frowned. The stories and songs were consistent among the different Kataru clans regarding the emergence of the Ro'Erden. To his annoyance, the same could not be said about what had happened next. As a youth, Kristoff had tried to learn all the stories in his travels across the Land, and it seemed that no two of the stories about the First War told the same tale.

He looked over at his companions. Marya and E'sinea had lapsed into silence and seemed occupied with their own thoughts. *Good*, he thought. The sun still shone brightly, the wind was beginning to carry the smell of salt, and he was rather enjoying recalling the old sagas. They had always fascinated him, and the distraction was rather welcome after their hard journey. Amonos's disappearance had only added to the unease he had been feeling since leaving Opulancae.

Putting the present aside once more, Kristoff brought to mind the different variations of the story and settled on the one told to him by his grandfather. As the memory of his grandfather's sonorous voice enveloped his thoughts, he could see the story emerge before him.

The Sun was in dismay over the plight of our people and sought with its heat to dissipate the Lurking Evil. But the Sun's actions only served to bring further ruin. Ashamed, it traveled westward, vowing to return one day and make amends for its weakness. Neither the Moon nor the Stars ascended that night. Instead, in its place a thick blanket of black and yellow clouds covered the sky, plunging our land into a surreal union of day and night. What the Lurking Evil did not kill, the Earth Movers—or Ro'Erden, as they named themselves— did.

The land shook and parted where they set foot; plateaus became mountains or gorges, and mountains that were once dangerous but crossable became frozen wastelands and nightmarish landscapes. Our gods forsook us or fled to die, save one, the Twin God. Only He chose to abandon the eternal hunting fields and walk among us, leading us to glory. And when He marched He was not alone, for the North's Serpent Rider, angered at the destruction of the Land, joined with him. Yet neither our Twin God, nor the Serpent Rider, nor the strength of the clans would have prevailed had it not been for a new people that arose from the Voiceless Woods to oppose the Earth Movers. They were the Deadbringers.

The Deadbringers had broken down the veil separating Life from Death, and had learned the secrets of the Dead. Unaffected by the Lurking Evil, they marched across the Land, recalling the fallen bodies of all they encountered— many of them Kataru. Finally, when their army was equal to that of the Earth Movers, they struck at the Earth Movers' place of power, beyond the Western Mountains.

The battle raged for years, and blood on both sides was spilled. The battlefield, already saturated with gore, became a sea of blood. It is the reason the land beyond those mountains is now a vile swamp, the Ayotíl, where none may tread. It is also said to be where the Serpent Rider confined the Lurking Evil, though it cost him his life to do so. Finally, Fortune shone upon the Deadbringers and brought them forth to victory over the Earth Movers. Defeated, they scattered. The Sun returned, bringing with it a new age.

Kristoff furrowed his brow as he recalled the two Ro'Erden Sanctifiers and their hatred for the Deadbringers. Theirs was a hate that stemmed from a war fought and lost millennia before, a war that had doomed their proud race of conquerors to relative obscurity. But what of the other peoples of the Land, who had so willingly turned against the very race that had delivered them from the Ro'Erden? He pulled at one of his hooped earrings at the thought that crept into his mind.

The peoples of the Land, including his own, had turned their backs on the Deadbringers because of fear, a fear rooted in the unknown mysteries of Death, mysteries that the Deadbringers had an unnatural control over. Had it been right to exterminate an entire race based solely on the fear of what they *could* do, and not what they had actually done? It was a question he had often asked himself during the Purging, on dark nights by campfires that had long since smoldered to nothingness; it was a question he found himself asking now. Shaking his head, he looked again at E'sinea and finally brought to mind the memory that had sent his thoughts wandering to a past of stories.

One winter, during the height of the Purging, shortly after Marya had joined, the Ascendancy had received word that a fleeing party of Deadbringers was preparing to cross into the Western Mountains. The mountains were impassable in winter, but rumor whispered that the Deadbringers, driven by desperation and fear, were seeking a terrible weapon that could be unleashed in their struggle with the Ascendancy. Kristoff's band had been closest, and so they had received the order to pursue.

They hunted the Deadbringers to the very edge of the mountains, but Fortune had not been on their side and the Deadbringers had escaped. They followed. Had the Ro'Erden not been with them, the task of surmounting the snow and ice-covered spires of rock would have been impossible. Never before or since had he experienced such a cold. To remain still for even a moment meant to risk the very blood in his veins turning to ice. For eight days and eight nights they pursued the Deadbringers through wind-blasted passes and frigid valleys.

On the fifth day, as the Sanctifiers treaded through an icy canyon formed by the closely connecting walls of two mountains, a dreadful realization greeted them. They had reached the end of the Western Mountains and were at the cusp of the Ayotíl — the very swamp of his grandfather's stories. Fear gripped Kristoff and Marya then, as the terrible understanding came to them that it was the very same Lurking Evil of legend that the Deadbringers sought. Even their cruel Ro'Erden companions were not immune to this realization, and they spoke among themselves in their own language in an intonation that betrayed their fear.

Kristoff was unfamiliar with the intricacies of the Ro'Erden tongue, but he had learned enough of it over the years that he soon realized that their primary concern was not with the Lurking Evil or even with the swamp itself, but with something else entirely. As if to confirm his guess, the Ro'Erden became withdrawn, consumed in following the trail left behind by the Deadbringers. Every so often, they would halt in their tracking just long enough to exchange a few words. and then they would quickly resume the pursuit, oblivious to the Katarus following in their wake.

Hours later, the canyon suddenly came to an end, opening on a window high in the air over a steep cliff that dropped hundreds of yards down to lower foothills, and from there to the Ayotíl itself. Kristoff and Marya gazed tired and awestruck at the setting sun, the first they had seen in days, as it lit up the fogs that hung low over the ominous marshes.

Yet even as they did so, the Ro'Erden were already descending the icy cliffs. The Deadbringers' trail was fresh. He and Marya could only follow as best they were able, as the Ro'Erden, more agile in their descent, rushed on ahead to dispose of their prey. Kristoff had not protested for, even though he did not trust them, he had faith in their skills as warriors.

Quickly but carefully, the two Katarus dug their short daggers into the grooves of the icy rock wall, following the Ro'Erden, who had reached a ledge halfway down the cliff and vanished from sight. When Kristoff and Marya finally reached the ledge half an hour later, they were surprised to find that the trail led into a gaping cave that opened in the cliff wall itself. Even Marya had shrunk at the prospect of following their companions into that terrible opening, but the Deadbringers had gone there, and they were bound to follow.

After what had seemed like an eternity of scrambling through the dark, with torches their only light, they stumbled into a large cavern partially exposed through an overhead sinkhole to a gray, cloud-filled sky. The cavern floor was covered with numerous depressions of varying size. Kristoff at first believed them to be empty, but after stepping in one by chance he discovered they were filled with water. For a brief moment, the crystalline water rippled and then was still. He gazed into the depression and saw his reflection staring back at him.

The sound of a choked scream echoing from another part of the cavern pulled him out of a trance he had not been aware he was in. Swords at the ready, Kristoff and Marya ran along the cavern wall and around a corner leading to the chamber the noise had come from.

Kristoff had expected to see either the Deadbringers or the Ro'Erden dead, but not both. Yet both groups lay before him, their bodies mutilated beyond recognition. Behind the piles of gore stood two figures, one a scrawny child with a long braid, the other a tall man. Blood dripped from every inch of their bodies as if they had rolled around in the carnage in front of them.

E'sinea's appearance then had been the same as it ever was, but the boiled leather mask that Amonos wore like a second skin had not been present during that first encounter. In the years since, Kristoff had often found himself struggling to recall the face he had seen in that cave, but the image would not form. He could only recall an ostentatious grin — and the eyes, eyes like those of a rabid animal. It was a wonder that he could recall the exact conversation, but he did. E'sinea had spoken first.

"I'm bored, Amonos."

Kristoff's voice boomed in the cave. "Bored? You defeat a band of Ro'Erden and Deadbringers and you proclaim yourself to be bored? If such is the case then why do you not attack us?"

"Because we have no quarrel with you." A child's hand, stained red with blood, pointed to the pile of bodies. "Them, we didn't like. But we like Katarus because they have such pretty long ears that they make even prettier with all those golden hoops." Idly, swaying side to side, he said, "I wish I had a pretty golden hooped earring."

Marya laughed snidely. "Are we to believe that you are just going to let us be?"

"Oh yes, you can go if you like. But I do so wish I had a golden hooped earring." He stopped swaying. "Why don't you give me one?" Back then, Kristoff had dismissed E'sinea's request as a mere whim. It had only been after years of riding together that he had come to realize that E'sinea at that moment had meant to rip the earrings from their dead bodies.

Amonos spoke finally, softly, his eyes glimmering with madness. "Or, if you so wish, we can add you to this warm pile of fresh corpses. I'm not bored." He grinned. "At least, not yet."

Kristoff kept his sword ready. "It seems likely that death is our only option. The Western Mountains are not forgiving and I must humbly admit that my sister and I only succeeded in coming this far because of the Ro'Erden. Without them" — he grinned back — "well, without them we will be anything but bored as we attempt to cross back to the east." In truth, Kristoff did not lament the loss of the Ro'Erden. He regretted only the loss of their skills.

"Oh," said E'sinea, as he got down on his knees and began rummaging through the indistinct piles of meat. He took hold of a curved object and, though it was barely recognizable, the horn he held onto betrayed it as Ro'Erden. "*Hmmmm.* I think we got carried away." He paused and looked up at Amonos, pouting. "Had we known, we would've left them less squishy."

Amonos spoke again, his voice now a mockery of graciousness that left Kristoff's skin acrawl. "My master and I apologize for the inconvenience we have bestowed upon you. It was not our intention." He bowed low, low enough to clearly expose the nape of his neck. Kristoff's sword arm twitched, and had it not been for Marya quickly placing her hand over it to stop him, he would have struck the man down.

Amonos rose, unruffled. "If I may impose upon you further, why are you here? I doubt you seek to enter the swamps, but perhaps you do? As you so clearly pointed out, death at the moment appears to be your only option." His grin widened. "Although you have quite a few alternatives to choose from in that particular regard."

Kristoff snorted dismissively. "Fortune will decide whether we live or die. Our business is none of your concern."

"But we already know what you seek," said E'sinea, his voice coy. "The dead themselves told us."

At the limit of his patience, Kristoff brought his sword forward. "Enough. If you cannot speak clearly, then fight."

Neither E'sinea nor Amonos were impressed. "We have an offer to make you," said Amonos, ignoring the blade. "My master and I are bored. We find this 'Purging' to be . . . interesting. So, in reparation for your fallen men, we will aid you in your journey back to the east. In addition, if you so desire, my master and I will freely offer our services to your cause."

"Nothing is free. State your price."

Amonos cocked his head, the madness in his eyes subsiding so that he looked almost thoughtful. "You're very direct. Very well. My master and I freely offer our services to your cause, provided that we are allowed to enjoy our kills. And I have no intention of defining the word *enjoy* . . . although, I could show you."

Marya curled her thin lips into a smile. "Brother, I think they would get along with us quite well. The Ro'Erden bored me—they were far too serious. Never any room for *fun*." The last word was said with emphasis. It was an emphasis that had caught and retained E'sinea's and Amonos's attention. Later, after he and Marya had safely crossed the mountains and returned to the warmer lands, Kristoff had asked her why she had played along with their game. The words she gave in response had never left him.

Because I wanted us to live.

But back on that day in the cavern, she had continued. "But what skill have you in battle that would be of benefit to us? And, what are *you* doing here?"

Amonos smiled. "My master and I are Deadbringers, of course." Kristoff raised a brow in disbelief while Marya laughed until her eyes watered. Amonos continued to smile, seemingly amused, and waited until she had stopped laughing before continuing. "We were seeking a very old friend, but, alas, our friend is not to be found."

"Another Deadbringer?" Kristoff asked skeptically.

E'sinea pulled at his braid, irate. "*Humph!* No, anything but."

Kristoff realized then with some heat that Amonos was looking Marya up and down as if she were a particularly delectable slice of meat. But, just before he became angry, Amonos turned to him. "My master's name is E'sinea, and I am his apprentice, Amonos. So, may we occupy the positions once held by the Ro'Erden?"

KRISTOFF PULLED HIS thoughts back to the present as they entered Jané. The Katarus had accepted the Deadbringers' offer and, to date, they had not regretted the decision. He hoped it remained so.

He shook himself to awareness and looked around. The streets were bustling with life from the numerous vendors and people walking about. Suddenly, E'sinea made a loud proclamation.

"No Amonos around means I can eat all the sweets I want!" he shouted gleefully. In his eagerness, he dashed on ahead into the crowd, leaving a protesting Marya to care for his mare. Kristoff looked on with amusement as his sister hollered in vain after the departing fringe of hair and long braid. He had come to enjoy E'sinea's sudden exclamations. But his amusement soured quickly as an ostentatious grin gripped his thoughts.

Amonos's unexpected departure had added to the concerns nagging at him — the appearance of a young Deadbringer strong enough to escape them, the purple roses found in Opulancae, and now the unexplained mystery of their companion's sudden departure. It was, he considered, a very odd confluence of unlikely events. *Paranoia, perhaps.* But Kristoff was not merely one of the few Katarus who had joined the Ascendancy in its early years out of an honest desire to do good. He was also one of the few who remained alive.

FULL CIRCLE

€'SINEA SPRINTED DOWN the packed dirt street, ignoring Marya's calls. He turned a corner and slipped into a narrow alley just wide enough for him to squeeze through. He needed to be alone.

After waiting a minute, he stepped out the other end of the alley, onto a street that was similar to the last. He looked around but could not see far given his short stature and the number of people about. Still, the Katarus were nowhere in sight.

Good, he thought, yet he was not pleased. *I can't allow myself to trust that Mar Mar and Kristoff won't turn on me. And with you gone . . . I like them. A lot. And I want to continue liking them, but what if . . . I don't want to hate them. I don't want to . . . have to . . .*

E'sinea cried out in frustration and stamped his foot, earning himself mistrustful glances from the people in the street. Then, not wanting to draw any more attention, he removed his Sanctifier's cloak and began patting the dirt off of his clothing. He quickly decided that it was beyond hope.

Kristoff pushed us hard on that ride. I probably look like a thieving urchin. He sniffed his gloves and then wrinkled his nose. *An urchin that smells of horse sweat! Oh well.*

He sauntered down the street, taking in the scenery and thinking. Mostly, he tried to get his thoughts in order and wrestled with the question of whether to sail south with the Katarus or follow Amonos on his own. But he found no easy answers.

As he walked, he passed by a number of stalls, each displaying treasures from various parts of the Land. A gentle breeze blew in from the bay, bringing with it the smell of salt and fish, and he found himself reflecting how different the Jané of today was. For he had passed through Jané once long ago, when only huts of mud and clay dotted the sandy shores, and fishermen with their simple boats, poles, and nets fished the Idle Bay. Back then, wandering traders sought to sell pelts, remedies, and slaves to sailors from the merchant ships that occasionally dropped anchor in the bay.

But that had been a long time ago. That had been a different life. The Jané of today had buildings of stone and lumber that towered over him, and merchants who saw no need to pack their goods and wander between villages in order to survive. His eyes stung, and he rubbed at them with the back of his gloved hand, murmuring how he desperately needed to scrub the dust clinging to his face from the long ride.

A stall managed by a fat sugar merchant caught his attention. The merchant was haggling with a young man dressed in fine wools and supple, polished leather boots. But E'sinea found the man's dress, lavish though it was, to be nothing in comparison to the rich assortment of candied fruits and confections that adorned the stall. He inched closer, curious to hear the conversation, but not so close that the merchant would believe he was trying to steal something.

The young man was arguing that the price the merchant asked was far too high, though E'sinea knew it was actually quite fair. The bartering continued for several minutes. Then something happened that made E'sinea glad he had removed his Sanctifier's cloak.

The young man flashed an insolent smile. "Don't you know it is treason to defraud a Sanctifier such as myself?" The merchant balked, his eyes becoming as round as saucers, and the man's smile widened.

E'sinea sighed. He had seen this show before. Sanctifiers had a fearsome reputation, yet not so fearsome to scare the unscrupulous from using that reputation for their own ends. He spoke up. "I know it's treason to cheat a Sanctifier, but I also know that a Sanctifier always carries with him a seal with the mark of the Ascendancy. So, if you are what you claim to be, show us your seal."

Both the merchant and the man turned to look at him, seeing him for the first time. The merchant looked at him hopefully, though unsure whether to call the bluff, while the young man glared at him as if considering whether to crush E'sinea beneath his boot. Finally, the man guffawed.

"I have nothing to prove to a sea rat. Be off with you."

E'sinea had the grace to look embarrassed as he said, "Oh, I suppose you're right. But I did see some Sanctifiers—nasty looking, beefy Katarus—over on the next street. How about you try proving your worth to them?" He let a full-toothed smile blossom as the color drained from the man's face.

The merchant at last found his voice, and a strong, angry voice it was. "Off with you, thief! Lest I take this boy's advice and bring the very Nightmare Lords upon you." The young man's eyes narrowed petulantly at the merchant, but at E'sinea they dripped fury. He vanished into the noise of the street.

The merchant turned his attention back to E'sinea. "That was a foolish thing to do, boy, but brave. What if he *had* been a Sanctifier? But, tell you what, I'll let you pick any candy you like."

"Actually, I want half a pound of the candied squash, and another of the honey-glazed red beans."

The merchant's amusement soured. "I appreciate your help, boy, but it is not worth a pound of free goods."

E'sinea held out a closed fist, which he waved as if he were giving a performance, and then opened it, revealing numerous gold coins. The merchant's eyes glittered, but still he refused to accept the gold.

"Whose pocket did you steal that from, eh?"

E'sinea pulled his hand back, slowly. "Oh, darn! And I was so certain my quest for sweets was over. But I guess I'll just have to keep looking." The merchant frowned, apparently aware that he was being mocked, but nonetheless began weighing and packing the candy in a sturdy wooden box.

E'sinea happily paid him and then ran off down the street, seeking a place where he could sit and enjoy his prize. It was not until he was a good many yards from the hustle and bustle of the city center that he chanced on a calm and relatively empty side street. He was not familiar with this new Jané, but he knew that the bay was due east and he was not afraid of becoming lost.

He crouched, removed his gloves, and pulled a piece of candied squash from the box. Then he placed the box in the dirt of the street, next to his boot, and deepened his voice in a mockery of Amonos's.

"Sugary foulness. It sticks and makes sticky everything it touches, gets stuck in your teeth and, above all, makes you chatter non-stop—it's very draining."

He sucked on the candy for a moment or two, savoring its grainy texture against his tongue, and watched the few people moving up and down the street. The candy steadily disappeared, and for a moment, as he became lost in the sweetness, it seemed to him that the well-dressed townsfolk became ragged fishermen, and the city was gone, and a small child was gazing upon the bay in awe . . .

An angry voice, from behind. "How dare a sea rat make a fool of *me!*"

Before E'sinea could react, the man's boot crushed into the curve of his spine, sending him sprawling on the hard, unrelenting ground. He tried to rise, but the man stomped his boot into E'sinea's shoulders, pinning him to the street as a collector would pin a prized butterfly. A few inches from where E'sinea had fallen was the piece of candy he had been about to eat. He reached out to take hold of it, but as he did so the man's other boot came crashing down to crush the back of his hand. E'sinea clenched his teeth, determined not to cry out.

The man bent over and snatched the candy, wiped away a bit of dirt that had settled on it, and casually popped it into his mouth. He sneered as he chewed. "Consider this a *free* lesson in etiquette." Then he stepped off of E'sinea, picked up the box of candies, and strolled away, without a care in the Land.

E'sinea lay on the ground, not moving, hardly breathing, watching in silence as the man vanished. But his mind was racing. Why had he not fought back? Why had he allowed himself to be hurt? What was happening to him?

His fingers twitched as two pairs of worn black leather boots halted in front of him. "It is not like you to lie like a defeated animal," said Marya. "Tell us who is responsible, and I will polish my sword with their blood." E'sinea pushed himself up to a sitting position, but he avoided facing the Katarus.

"Let it be. It doesn't matter," he said bleakly, not rising from the ground.

"Fortune strike me blind if I am mistaken," said Marya, her voice rising, "but without Amonos at your side you feel lost."

E'sinea felt the little self-control he had left crumble. Was that why he had not fought back? It seemed like such a trivial reason, and yet he could not find it in him to deny her words. Pushing himself to his feet, he repressed a bitter laugh, wondering what the siblings thought of him now that they had seen him in such a pitiful state. *I'll leave. Tonight.* A low whinny drew his attention. His mare was at the entrance of the side street, eager to join him. He went to her and made ready to mount and ride off.

Kristoff called to him sternly. "Wait."

E'sinea stopped reluctantly, his thoughts turning gray. *Why can't they just let me be?* He spun around on the heel of his boot and faced Kristoff.

"What do you want?" he said shrilly, angrily.

Kristoff ignored his rudeness. "I know that neither Marya nor I can replace the void Amonos has left, but you are not alone, E'sinea. You have *us*, and there is no shame in relying on your friends."

"Oh, ok," E'sinea responded curtly.

Kristoff's eyes fell, fatigue casting deep shadows on his unshaven face. He seemed very tired. "I know that you do not trust us."

"I've never said anything to make you think one way or the other."

Marya inched closer to him and E'sinea looked up at her. There was a sadness in her dark eyes that he had never seen before, and it hurt him deeply to think that he, perhaps, was the cause of it. "No, you have not," she said. "Yet, since Amonos's disappearance you have been distancing yourself from us. Do you believe that we care so little for you that we have not noticed your pain?" She paused and then continued, her voice quiet. "Do you intend to betray us, as well?"

Damn caution! And damn Amonos! "I would never hurt you or Kristoff or anyone in your clan! But why should I trust you? Because we've *known* each other for so long?" E'sinea felt unbidden tears roll down his cheeks and desperately began wiping them away. *They can't see me cry. They can't!* But it was too late. He stared at his bare hand.

Black streaks, thick and oily, covered his hands like leeches. He watched in panic as a thick drop fell to the ground, where it sizzled in the dirt like boiling tar. The siblings had never before seen him cry. He waited for them to say something, but they were silent. They merely watched and waited for him to speak, and suddenly E'sinea felt angry, angry because he found it difficult to believe that they would simply accept, no, *trust* him without any sort of explanation.

He held out his hand toward the Katarus, brandishing his tears as if they were some strange shield. "You know nothing about me! Nothing! How can you trust someone like this? How can you accept me so blindly?" More drops fell from his hand, roiling the dirt.

Kristoff slowly drew his sword and prodded the dirt where the black tears had fallen. He then examined the blade. The tears had clung to the sword and seemed to pulse, as if trying to bore into the steel. Solemnly, he said, "A man exposes who he truly is in battle, and I have come to trust you with my life. If you wish to share your stories with us, we will listen. But only Fortune need know one's life from birth till death."

"Fortune!" E'sinea laughed as if he had heard the greatest joke in the Land, and perhaps he had. He reached out to take hold of Kristoff's sword and carefully wiped the black tears away with his hand, all the while grumbling under his breath. "Stupid Fortune doesn't even know himself."

"Will you stay with us, E'sinea?" asked Marya. He looked up at her and noticed that she too was very tired. He felt guilty.

"Yes, I'll stay."

"Will you trust us?" asked Kristoff. E'sinea studied their faces, something he had done many times before, but it seemed as if he were somehow looking at them for the first time. Kristoff was smiling warmly and, despite his rock-hard face and forever frowning brow, it somehow suited him.

And though it was only one word, to E'sinea it felt like a speech. "Yes."

THE THREE SOON found that it would be two days before a ship would sail south to Florinia, and after making arrangements to be on it they made their way to the Unbroken Spar. The inn was not difficult to find, for it was one of the largest buildings in Jané and one of the few that had brick walls covered with stucco in the southern fashion. A heavy wooden sign bearing a painting of two oars crossed against a mast hung near the door. Inside, the inn was warm and alive with a raucous gang of people eating, drinking, and talking.

The three looked around the common room as they entered. E'sinea immediately noticed a group sitting at a table far on the other side of the room near the hearth: Katarus and Ro'Erden dressed in the black cloaks of Sanctifiers. Kristoff's sturdy hand muffed his hair. It was something he was beginning to enjoy, but he knew it would have to stop if Amonos ever returned.

"It would appear that we are not alone," said Kristoff, as he inclined his head to acknowledge a Ro'Erden who had turned to look in his direction. The Ro'Erden turned to address another of his kin, a man with silver hair and ram-like horns, and then nodded at Kristoff.

Goats, thought E'sinea, as they made their way up three flights of stairs to their rooms, *the lot of them!*

E'sinea's room was small but clean and well-accommodated. A low fire burned in the hearth, filling the room with warm smoke. He thrust open the draperies, exposing a view of the harbor and the bay, and opened the windows to breathe in the salty sea air and the smell of gutted fish. Jané was very different now, but the smells—no matter how much time had passed—remained the same.

There was a knock at his door as the hot water arrived from the kitchen. He sat in a wooden chair and brushed his long hair as the servant girls filled the copper tub. When they were done, he thanked them and gave each a gold coin.

He sat in the tub, exulting in the steaming water and letting it soothe the pain all along the curve of his back and in his right hand. There was no bruise or welt to show he had been attacked, but the bones and muscles ached nonetheless.

He brought his hands out of the warm water, the skin bright red and wrinkled, and paused to look at his wrists. They should have been covered with a layer of thick scars from the countless times he had slit them, yet they were as smooth as porcelain. He muttered to himself, "It always hurts. Every time." Then he took hold of the sponge and soap and began scrubbing. When it came time to wash his back, his battered shoulders winced and he wished desperately that Amonos could be there to help him as usual.

That night he supped alone in his room, though the siblings had made him promise to sup with them and the other Sanctifiers in the common area at least once before they departed Jané. E'sinea crawled into bed, gloomy and exhausted, wrapped himself in a cocoon of blankets, and quickly drifted to sleep.

As Kristoff had promised, the bed was soft and stuffed with feathers.

THE UNBROKEN SPAR

THE UNBROKEN SPAR was bursting at the seams with people eager to find shelter from the late afternoon storm that had rolled in from the coast. Girls and boys ran about refreshing drinks and bringing food, or scurrying up and down the stairs tending to the guests in their rooms. It was a cold night, for the winter's chill had finally come to the coast. Now and again the main door would open, letting in a gust of damp wind, and the patrons nearest the door would cry out their displeasure, heckling the newcomers to "close that damn door!" But for Kristoff and Marya, such irritations were of little concern, given that none of the townsfolk had dared deny the two Sanctifiers a spot by the hearth.

Comfortably warm, Kristoff watched a woman hurry down the stairs with a basket of dirty linens. She was older than any of the other servant girls, perhaps in her late forties, and had a braid of white-blond hair that trailed down her back. Kristoff had seen her enter E'sinea's room many times since arriving and could not help but wonder why he tolerated the company of a stranger when he refused to open the door to either of the Katarus.

The woman reached the last step, turned a corner, and was out of sight. Marya leaned close to whisper into his ear. "It would appear that our dear E'sinea has a taste for the old."

Kristoff scratched his beard thoughtfully. "E'sinea has a taste for many things, but I do not believe pleasures of the flesh to be one of them. He is not Amonos. After all—"

He was interrupted by a sudden uproar of laughter that erupted from a nearby table, immediately followed by calls for more beer. Kristoff rolled his eyes and gave up. It was indeed a very busy night.

Marya fiddled with the laces of her corset, her generous breasts spilling over its top, the hard muscles in her shoulders and back glistening with sweat from the warmth of the fire. It was a corset that Amonos had had fashioned for her a few years back when he had last passed through Florinia. Its brocade was of a simple pattern with gold threading that complimented her bronze skin and the golden hoops she wore in her ears. To Amonos's discontent, Marya had never worn it in his presence, though she carried it in her saddlebags wherever she went, as if to taunt him. But she wore it now.

She joined in the laughter. "Agreed, so long as you do not count sweets among the 'pleasures of the flesh.' Do you believe he will finally come down this night? We set sail tomorrow, after all."

Unexpectedly, the cheer in the room dimmed. A tall man with large, dark horns that began at the base of his forehead and curled around his head stepped off the stairs and into the common room. Behind him followed two other Ro'Erden, just as tall as he, along with three Katarus who were of stronger build though not as tall. All were dressed in the Sanctifier's black and wore the insignia of the Ascendancy. The group halted directly in front of Kristoff.

"May we?" the leader asked, inclining his head toward the table.

Kristoff waved for them to sit. "Vas'tu, I did not believe you and yours would be down this night."

The man flashed him a smile, revealing sharp canines. He took a seat directly across from Kristoff. The other Ro'Erden followed, as did the Katarus, though they sat further down the table.

Marya smiled at the Ro'Erden, then turned to Kristoff and said, "I would not bet on it." Then she scooped up her drink and moved down the table to sit with their kin. Kristoff knew that she was referring to E'sinea's distaste for the Ro'Erden. Without Amonos present, he too suspected that E'sinea would remain holed up in his room. But E'sinea was not the only one who found the Ro'Erden distasteful. They were still in the North, after all. The sounds of benches being pushed out and the creaking of the main door's hinges signaled that at least a few people, though not too many, had decided their night was over.

Gradually, the noise in the tavern began to return, though the warmth that had been present did not, and the servers moving about the room kept their distance. Only a girl no older than twenty approached.

She was very beautiful and curvy, and Kristoff found himself eyeing her. But she seemed to only have eyes for one of Vas'tu's Ro'Erden—a woman with straight, deep blue hair, striking eyes, and sharp doe-like horns that complemented her even sharper features. The woman smiled sweetly at the girl, who blushed. She took their order and quickly scurried off.

In truth, it pleased Kristoff that Vas'tu had come down, for the recent events had made him eager to speak with another Sanctifier who had fought during the Purging. He had neither known Vas'tu well nor considered him a friend, but few enough of that old band remained, and Kristoff valued their counsel greatly.

Though it had been years since they had last seen each other, Vas'tu was little changed. He was a fearsome-looking man with long, dull silver hair scattered throughout with strands of black. Deep-set, uptilted jade eyes sharp as knife-edges stood starkly against ashen skin. His face was angular, his jaw squared, and his ears were scalloped along the edge and pointed, though still nowhere near as long and proud as those of a Kataru.

The serving girl returned with pitchers of beer, followed shortly thereafter by plates of different foods and sweets. Vas'tu reached out a talon-tipped hand and took hold of a braised fish head. Each finger was the color of black tea, from the base of the first knuckle down to the talon itself. "Dine with me," he said then, his voice smooth and rich.

Kristoff did not need to be told twice. He reached for a fish head of his own and took a bite, bone and all. "It seems that Fortune has been kind to you."

"I hear of this 'Fortune' often," said Vas'tu. He inclined a horn toward where Marya and the other Katarus sat playing a drinking game. "It is strange how one god can have two faces and multiple names, even among its own people."

"And I have often found it difficult to understand how your people can remember all the different gods you pray to," said Kristoff, wary. He silently counted off the number of Ro'Erden gods he had heard mentioned in his travels. "Ten, at least."

Vas'tu laughed, though coldly. "There are far more than that."

"One god. Two faces. That is more than enough for me."

"Fair enough."

The noise in the tavern became louder, and Kristoff seized the opportunity to speak without the fear of being overheard. He leaned in. "No doubt the rumors brought by the sailors who arrived from Nhaleri this day have reached your keen ears?"

"Yes. The people speak of nothing else on the streets. If not for our presence, this tavern would be afloat with these rumors as well." Vas'tu mulled over his words for a moment, as if deciding what to say. His knife-eyes fixed on Kristoff, as if dissecting him. At last he seemed to relax, and then continued.

"The Deadbringers seek vengeance against the Land. The second Purging is at hand. The Bastion kept the Deadbringers hidden, and now will use them as a weapon to overthrow the Ascendancy." He paused briefly. "And my personal favorite: Florinia has risen against the Ascendancy, leaving it aflame!" Both men laughed at the last.

"Yet—" began Kristoff, glancing briefly at his sister, who had abandoned her game and was now deep in conversation with a young, strongly built Kataru. He knew her well enough to sense that she was angered, though he could not tell why. He resumed his conversation with Vas'tu. "—both factions are indeed uneasy. The Deadbringers *have* reappeared."

He leaned further in, resting his arms on the table. "Many of these rumors are without merit. But I do not fault the people and their fancies, for not since the Purging and the years it took thereafter for the Ascendancy to secure its hold have we Sanctifiers ridden in force."

"True," said Vas'tu. "Many of our number have been given the duty of finding and silencing these newly surfaced Deadbringers. And now we ride far and wide in the North, in the Bastion's very homeland. That itself is worthy of talk in its own right, even if the Bastion does not dare oppose us." His voice hardened ever so slightly. "But your band is the one that has been tasked with hunting the Deadbringer from Opulancae, is that correct?"

Kristoff nodded. It had been a secret assignment to begin with, but the whole Land would by now know what had happened in Opulancae and would know that it had been Kristoff's band. E'sinea and Amonos had . . . a reputation.

"He managed to escape into the Gods' Spears. He has proven to be quite adept."

Vas'tu snorted, apparently unimpressed. "He will die within the Spears. But, I digress. A *boy* managed to elude the great Kristoff?"

Kristoff brushed aside the mockery. "A boy, perhaps, but he has shown great skill."

Vas'tu leaned back, his horns resting against the wall behind him. Slowly, he began moving his head side-to-side along the wall, taking away curls of wood with the tips of his horns. It reminded Kristoff of the rams near his village that would sharpen their horns on the rocks that dotted the mountain foothills. After a moment's pause, Vas'tu spoke, his jade eyes afire. "Skill? How so? You are a man who does not easily give praise."

"You surely have heard that he raised an entire cemetery on his own despite being gravely injured."

"The extent of his injury was never clear to our sources. But perhaps you have learned something of this during your pursuit?"

"Unfortunately not. But even if he had been uninjured it would not have lessened his accomplishments. No Deadbringer I encountered during the Purging could have managed such a feat. At least, not alone."

"What *else*, Kristoff?" Vas'tu asked touchily. The man was suddenly impatient, though Kristoff did not understand why.

"There is a dirt burial path on the outskirts of Opulancae. It is tainted ground, unclean. The Deadbringer fled there as we pursued him."

"*Corpse Road*, the locals quaintly call it. I am familiar with it."

"Well, that *boy* used a body to seal off the road by joining the trapped souls on either side of it to form a barrier. On our travel here, E'sinea commented to me that once the walls keeping the souls from the road were removed, an ordinary Deadbringer would have been rendered immobile by the vast number of souls present. This boy is unique. Just as E'sinea and Amonos are unique."

Vas'tu's face had become cold, unreadable. "Yes, E'sinea is indeed . . . *unique*. But, from your report, this boy may prove to be even more so."

Kristoff found himself at a loss for words. Far from providing reassurances, Vas'tu had further roiled his already troubled thoughts. Before he could demand that Vas'tu explain himself, the other two Ro'Erden at the table hissed like angry cats, their eyes fixed on something behind him.

Kristoff whirled about, ready for a fight, and found E'sinea standing quietly before him. He had at last come down from his room. His long bangs covered his eyes as ever, but his normally braided hair hung loose down his back, reflecting the light of the fire like a deep copper cape. His usual black leathers had been replaced by deep browns, and he wore nothing that identified him as a Sanctifier. A petulant sneer settled on his lips as he took a seat beside Kristoff.

Vas'tu emptied his mug and then placed it on the table, forcefully. "Take care that your companion does not one day decide to use you as its entertainment."

Kristoff chuckled coldly, and his eyes locked with Vas'tu's, who seemed to be measuring him. "We may have both worn the Sanctifier's black for many years, but for all that you are a stranger to me, while *he* is a friend. Who do you think I would trust to hold a blade to my throat?"

Vas'tu nodded slowly, as if satisfied by the response. E'sinea too seemed pleased by Kristoff's words, and he promptly snatched an entire apple pie and filled a bowl with fish-skin soup. His sneer was replaced with a mischievous smile.

"I see the serving girl forgot to bring out a bale of hay for the goats. Or perhaps you'd prefer mud pie? Being clots of dirt an' all."

One of the other Ro'Erden—as gray as Vas'tu, yet far younger and with horns that just swept back from his forehead over a mess of black hair—took the bait. "Corpse fucker!" he shouted, as if ready to fight, though he made no move to stand. The Ro'Erden with the blue hair shot E'sinea an angry glare, but she kept her temper in check.

E'sinea stabbed a piece of pie with his fork, appearing displeased, though Kristoff knew better. "Not even a choir of maggots would fuck your ugly corpse."

Kristoff decided that the fun had gone on long enough. "E'sinea," he said sternly.

"Oh, alright! I'll be good. The food's too yummy to let the goats have it all, anyways." And with that final jab, E'sinea ignored the Ro'Erden and instead focused his attention on eating the pies, cakes, and fried sugary breads on the table. His bowl of soup sat untouched, forgotten.

Vas'tu reached for the pitcher of beer and refilled not only his mug, but Kristoff's as well. "Your . . . friend has quite the stomach for sweets," he said mockingly. "I have never seen anyone eat with such determination. Does Amonos keep him on a tight leash?"

It was difficult for Kristoff to come to E'sinea's defense, for he was indeed laying waste to all the sweets in front of him. "E'sinea indulges his apprentice by *declining* to eat sweets." *And I think I'm beginning to understand why Amonos is so vocal about his master eating sweets.* Kristoff suppressed a frown. *It will do us little good if E'sinea suffers from an upset stomach while at sea.*

"And where is the apprentice?"

Kristoff hesitated. Vas'tu's questions were too probing for his liking. He caught the sound of his sister's voice, heated and ever rising, and looked over to see that she and the other Kataru were close to coming to blows. He suddenly remembered her words from back in Xulmé. "Amonos is being Amonos," he muttered reluctantly.

"Ah." Vas'tu swirled the beer in his mug, unaware of or simply uninterested by the brawl that was obviously brewing between Marya and one of his men. "Well, it's odd not seeing those two together. That is why some among my kin are finding it difficult to believe that you are not scheming with them to have a laugh at our expense." Kristoff turned his attention back to the man and found that the knife-eyes were measuring him again. "But you are not that kind of man, are you?"

"No," said Kristoff, his voice flat.

Vas'tu laughed then, a harsh, full-throated laughter that never reached his eyes and suddenly made him look very old. When he finally quieted, he asked simply, "When you find this boy, will you kill him?"

"For the good of the Land, I will do what must be done."

Vas'tu nodded slowly, as if mulling over the words. He began to open his mouth to speak again, when suddenly what Kristoff had feared came to pass. Marya and the other Kataru threw their benches back and rose shouting curses at each other, ready to fight. Their furious voices dripping with venom carried throughout the common room, casting it into an uncomfortable silence. Vas'tu made a chiding sound and began to rise, but Kristoff stopped him.

"Don't." His words were hushed yet urgent. "To intervene now would shame them both in the eyes of our kin." Kristoff nodded toward the remaining two Katarus from Vas'tu's band, who had stayed seated. Vas'tu shrugged and settled back on his seat. Kristoff then quickly turned his attention to E'sinea but found, much to his relief, that E'sinea had not so much as moved, though his hand was wrapped tightly around his fork. Thanking Fortune for that small favor, Kristoff turned his attention back to his sister and watched the scene unfold.

Marya was livid. "I will live my life as I see fit and *not* as custom dictates!"

"Then why continue living among us?" the other Kataru roared back. "Why not sever your ties to the clans and take up with an outsider?" He took a second to measure her up and then sneered, the derision in his voice clear. "You're a *moma*, after all."

A faint murmur passed through the tavern, and Kristoff's anger boiled over. *Coward! If we were among the clans he would not dare use our lineage against us.* He wanted to intervene, to ram the Kataru's face into the table until bones broke, but the argument was not his.

The interloper continued. "Yet you dare judge *my* actions when it is you, not I, who defies tradition. You've hidden behind an elder brother who shamefully supports your straying from the rightful path laid out for our women long ago. I say that it is *this* kind of action that will be the first step toward the destruction of our people."

Marya leaned across the table, her face inches away from that of the other Kataru, her nails digging into the wood. "The destruction of our people comes from those who carry daggers in the dark to use against enemy and family alike. That *treachery* is the true bane of our people. Tradition would have you face your rivals openly, as a warrior. But you only believe in tradition when it suits your needs, as a way to mask your cowardice." Her red lips sneered disdainfully, and Kristoff thought to himself that he had never seen her look so confident and beautiful. It made him proud.

The other Kataru's eyes narrowed, and then an odd glint filled them. It took Kristoff a moment to realize that the glint was one of adoration.

"They say that no one among the clans has claimed your hand, for they cannot best you in combat. I will change that." He stepped back from Marya and drew an ornate dagger from his belt. Then he wrapped his hand tightly around the blade and held it up high so all the Katarus present could see — so Kristoff could see.

"Marya of the Herzmmen clan," he began, "whether you like it or not, you will have to assume your role as Amistrite." He squeezed the blade, and blood trailed out of his palm and onto his wrist, where it began circling down his thick forearm like two coral snakes. The blood began to grow brighter and brighter, like metal in a forge, until his arm was wrapped in flames. Panicked cries filled the room, but Kristoff heard only the words that spilled from the man's mouth. "Such is your birthright, Marya. As it is my birthright, as Undolot of the Solbrennt clan, to challenge you to combat for the role of clan Amustrite." He grinned lustfully. "You will be my woman."

Marya's face was calm, her words cold. "I will enjoy killing you."

The fire vanished, and Undolot stabbed the dagger into the table, blood still dripping from his hand. "Fortune will decide the victor." With those parting words, he left the table and walked out of the Unbroken Spar. One of the other two Katarus in Vas'tu's band followed suit, never so much as looking at Marya or Kristoff. The other remained behind, his eyes fixated on the dagger as if it were a venomous snake.

The crowd in the common room quieted, and a few returned to their night, but most of the rest decided it was best to retire to their rooms or leave. Cold wind howled through the open door as groups of people left, causing the fire in the hearth to flicker wildly. Marya grudgingly pulled the dagger out from the table and then sat heavily down next to E'sinea, who scooted over to give her more room.

"I *will* kill him. I *will* kill him," she said to herself in a heated whisper, as if it were some chant.

The last of Vas'tu's Katarus who remained rose from where he sat and came closer, sitting next to the Ro'Erden with the blue hair. Finally, as if he had to work up his courage to do so, he spoke, his voice fast and high-pitched as if he was nervous.

"Do you know why that fool left the room so quickly after his speech? He needs to bandage his hand before he collapses. Undolot's fire is a deadly weapon, but like all Solbrennts he has no control over his blood. The last time he used fire in battle we had to strap him to his horse for a week afterward so he would not tumble off it. I, for one, would not welcome him into our clan."

"*Our* clan?" asked Kristoff, surprised.

Marya looked up, stopping her chant. "Yes, I see it now! Your face has pricked at me all night and now I know why. You're Meddo, Lucill's eldest."

"One of our own and us none the wiser," Kristoff said bitterly. "To meet you only now that Travail has visited us does not bode well." The sound of laughter once again crept up as the inn's remaining patrons resumed their night as if nothing had ever happened. Kristoff wished that he could do the same, but there was no going back, especially not for Marya.

Meddo shook his head and laughed sharply, as if in pain. "It seems you have no idea. The Twin God's face has turned. Fortune is gone. There is only Travail."

Kristoff watched as the color drained from his sister's face. He had no doubt he looked as she did. "Grandmother? Does she live?" asked Marya, visibly dreading the answer.

"Yes," said Meddo, and Marya let out a sigh of relief. He continued. "You rightly accuse Undolot of treachery, but you don't know the half of what happened this past summer. Back home far too many Amistrites have been slaughtered by the Solbrennt and their Amustrite. The clans are fractured and at each other's throats. Our clan has survived because your grandmother is strong, and support for her has never wavered. But she is old, and her Amustrite as well."

He took a deep breath and then spoke slowly, as if choosing his words with care. "Your father has swallowed his pride and sought the aid of your mother's people. I do not have to say more, save that her aid was the last gift Fortune sought worthy to grant us."

"How do we not know about this?" asked Marya, visibly shocked. "Father has forever kept us informed just so he could pester me about my duties."

"Your father has sent many hawks to the Ascendancy requesting your return. But, from what I am gathering, you have received no word."

Kristoff pulled at his earrings. "No." *And I wonder if we ever would have if Fortune had not put Meddo in our path.*

"If affairs are this wretched back home, and you knew of it, then why are you here?" asked Marya, pressing him.

"I am here because the Ascendancy has promised to help bring order to the clans, provided that a few of us could be spared, and they believed me strong enough to become a Sanctifier. In addition, as long as we have the backing of your mother's people, the other clans dare not attack."

Kristoff's thoughts were dark. *For father to have spoken with mother, the situation must indeed be dire.* Yet, as the memory of his mother's red-lipped, sharp-toothed smile came to mind, he found his thoughts wandering in a different direction. *I wonder what she thought upon seeing father after so many years?* He pushed aside the memory to look over at his sister and then at the dagger she had placed on the table. Until the day of the challenge, she would have to carry that dagger. He longed to see it thrust into Undolot's throat but . . .

"Meddo," he asked, "I think I have kept abreast of clan politics, but I had never heard of Undolot before this evening. He may be a fool as you say, but he carries himself with pride. Is he of status in the Solbrennt?"

Meddo stared at him with surprised eyes. "You *have* been away for too long! Yes, he is. He's the son of their Amistrite." Marya cursed heavily under her breath, and Kristoff and Meddo fell silent. The two younger Ro'Erden shifted in their seats, unsure what to say, while Vas'tu, who had been watching with silent interest, leaned back against the wall with his eyes closed.

E'sinea reached for the dagger and turned it in his hand. "Soollbrenn-tah? Solbrennt? Now I remember! Oh, I'm so proud of myself for remembering! Isn't that the clan that is said to have been favored by the Twin God, just because they can make their blood burst into flames, etcetera, etcetera? And that the Fortune aspect of the Twin God will always be on their side, blah, blah, blah?"

The Katarus all stared. Kristoff was shocked, for in their years together he had never realized that E'sinea was aware of the lore of the different clans, a lore that was closely guarded to ensure surprise in battle with outsiders.

Meddo opened and closed his mouth as if wanting to reproach E'sinea, but then thought better of it. Instead, he scolded Kristoff and Marya, though not without his voice trembling a bit with nervousness. "You know such knowledge is forbidden!"

A deep red tinged E'sinea's cheeks, and he shoved a large piece of pie into his mouth, as if trying to avoid having to speak. Marya calmly broke off a piece of piecrust for herself and then looked directly at Meddo. She pointed the crust at him.

"Don't be a fool. Neither of us has spoken of such matters with E'sinea. But he is long-lived and well-traveled and no doubt heard it from somewhere. Or have you forgotten that he can speak not only with the living, but also with the dead?" She flicked her wrist, hard, and the crust connected with Meddo's forehead in a shower of crumbs. Meddo winced as Marya continued chiding him. "You're not exactly the portrait of discretion yourself. Discussing everything so openly." She shot a glance at the Ro'Erden. "No offence."

"None taken," said the Ro'Erden with the blue hair, and smiled in amusement.

Vas'tu spoke up. "I cannot say that I have not found all this talk to be enlightening. But to make reason of what has been said is beyond me. Nor do I care to try. However, I will say this: Undolot is one of my men. He is prone to insubordination and, more often than not, I have wished the Land would swallow him. But he is a formidable warrior and has been of great use. If you are to fight to the death, do so when I no longer have need of him."

Kristoff sighed, his voice grim. "The moon has cast a heavy shadow this night."

"Well, then," said Vas'tu, "I suggest we cast some light on this shadow." He hailed the young serving girl from earlier. "More beer and wine. The night is still young, and I intend to drink my fill."

He turned to Marya, his jade eyes studying her, not knife-edges now but deep, contemplative. She held his gaze and stared back, unafraid. "Woman, Kataru, when the time comes, kill him slowly. Painfully. Can an old man be so bold to ask this of you?"

Marya flashed her best smile, and again Kristoff was reminded of their mother. "You honor me with such a request," she said, laughing. "Consider it done!"

Then Vas'tu laughed too and held his drink up in the air. Marya met it with her own, and the other Ro'Erden lifted their mugs, followed shortly by Kristoff, Meddo, and even E'sinea, though he made sure to grumble the entire time.

"*Ve'sau!*" said Vas'tu, leading the toast. The others echoed him and the night began anew. It was strange, for though Kristoff was surrounded by very few of his kin and his thoughts were heavy, in that moment he felt at ease.

E'SINEA SAT ALONE in his room. It was warm, for the fire burned strongly in the small hearth, but he felt cold. A bottle of wine sat on the dresser, nearly empty. He glanced at the mirror hung over the dresser and peered at his reflection — a pale figure surrounded by a halo of light and moving shadows. He poured the last of the wine into his glass and drained it.

He spoke to the shadows, his voice quiet and strained. "I should've stayed downstairs with Mar Mar and Kristoff. But . . . then all these *pé'bos* showed up and I . . . I didn't want any of them to touch me."

Putting his glass down, he stood and leaned over the dresser until his forehead rested against the cold surface of the mirror. He questioned his reflection. "Why are you ignoring me? Why did you push me out? Are you listening?" His eyes stung and he made no attempt to hold in his tears. After all, he was alone in the room.

Alone.

Angry at the thought, he whipped the fresh tears away and screamed his anguish. *"WHY AREN'T YOU ANSWERING? WHY!"* He slapped his hands hard against the mirror's surface, hoping that it would shatter and cut him, hurt him, so that he did not have to think about how he felt. But it did not. His voice was a desperate plea as he pulled away from the mirror.

"I didn't mean to hurt you. I didn't mean to be selfish. I didn't mean to make things worse."

The unexpected sound of clapping pulled him away from the mirror and his thoughts. A hooded figure stood by the door, clapping slowly, mockingly. "Well done! Quite the little actor, aren't we?"

"Whoever you are, leave me alone," E'sinea said bitterly. "I'm tired and am in no mood to play." Distantly, he thought, *I must've forgotten to lock the door.*

"Is that what this is to you? A game?" Whoever the man was, there was now no mistaking the fury behind his words. But to E'sinea it mattered little.

"I said 'leave.'"

"Leave? *Leave!* I will leave once I have my due."

The man threw back his hood and it took E'sinea a moment to remember the face, for it was gaunt and covered in boils, many of which had ruptured. It was the face of the man who had stolen his candy, now ravaged as if by some terrible disease.

"Oh, it's you."

The man strode forward, and E'sinea saw that he held a sword in his hand.

"Look at what you did to me! I know you did something to those candies that made me ill. You fancy yourself to be important because you are friends with those Sanctifiers, but you're nothing but shit!"

"Ill? Obviously not ill enough," E'sinea quipped. The man's fist struck out, crashing into his face and sending him to the floor.

The man gloated over him, his voice a sickly rasp. "Have something cheeky to say now?"

The taste of blood, hot, metallic, and . . . familiar . . . filled E'sinea's mouth. He swallowed the blood and then faced the man with a red-toothed smile. "We're going to play a game."

Anger twisted the man's face and he brought his sword down in an overhead slash. There was a loud *thunk* as it connected with the floor, scarring the wood. The man gasped, dumbstruck.

"Where . . . how did he—"

"I'm over here." The voice had come from the far corner of the room.

Sweat dripped down the man's ruined face as wary eyes found E'sinea. "H–how did you . . ."

"I told you I didn't want to play, but since you won't leave me alone, I'll play, but only if I get to pick the game. That's only fair. So, the goal of this game is to be as quiet as possible. If you scream or make any noise, you lose. After all, we are in an inn, and it would be rude to bother the other patrons. Oh yes, it would! Now" — a trickle of black tears flowed down E'sinea's cheeks and onto the wooden floor, from which plumes of gray smoke began to steadily rise, gradually concealing him — "let's begin."

The black tears that had fallen twitched fiercely. Then they began reaching upward and outward, forming hideous pulsing shadows that dissolved and reformed, but not without first casting whatever they touched into complete darkness. It was as if the room and the air were being visibly devoured by a living void.

The shadows slowly moved toward the man, who bolted to the door. He yanked at the handle over and over again but, despite the lock being undone, it would not budge. And yet he did not let go of the handle, nor did he ever stop pulling.

A dead voice called from the darkness, and the last light vanished. "Don't you want to play? Oh, I see. You're volunteering to go first."

There was a soft, fluidic sound, and then silence.

CONFLICT

KIRA RECOILED AT the sudden onslaught of sunlight. The land beyond the Gods' Spears was a sea of light that seared his skin and stung his eyes, blinding him. Shielding his eyes with his hands, he took a few steps past the last great trunk and then cursed heatedly as the ankle-deep sludge he had been trudging through for the last league suddenly gave way to deeper water that sloshed up to his knees. The water reflected the light like some grand mirror, and he squinted his eyes and blinked several times, waiting for his vision to adjust. Gradually, the world around him came into focus and he slowly turned his sight upward, eager to behold the sky.

It was a painfully beautiful sight.

His thoughts roiled. *Sun. Warm, scalding, bright. Sky. Blue, filled with clouds. Air. Crisp, damp, rousing.* He ran his fingers through the water surrounding him and marveled at its feel, cleaner and less murky than the dank water in the forest. He laughed, but even to him it sounded pathetic. He thought of his uncle and bit his tongue.

When will this need to call out your name, to hear your voice, subside? At that moment, he wished deeply, painfully, that Eutau had lived to see something other than darkness. But wishes and reality were two entirely separate things. It was an agonizing truth he was becoming too familiar with.

A loud splash drew him back to the present. A flock of wading birds nearby took flight, circled fully about, and then returned to the waters. He tried his best to repress a smile but was certain he had failed.

The girl Daemeon had sent as his guide was waist-deep in the water, and she was not pleased. "I am sick of always being wet!" She smacked her hands angrily across the water's surface, sending droplets flying into the air. She was very petite, and Kira suspected he could carry her without effort. So, he offered.

"I could carry you. At least for a while." The girl shot daggers at him with her eyes and began wading her way south, through the open water.

"Suit yourself," Kira said to no one in particular, and began following in her wake.

The land beyond the Spears was a vast collection of wetlands mantled with duckweed and yellow and blue water lilies spattered across the water's surface like confetti. Clusters of cattails, many of them spotted with small yellow-green birds with black masks, swayed in time with the gentle breeze, while the sound of frogs *croaking* and insects *buzzing* rang throughout in a deafening choir. Waterbirds waded on long legs or stood silently, occasionally spearing a fish with their harpoon-like bills.

Some of the birds Kira recognized, for many frequented the banks of the Silver River, while others were foreign and strange and seemed capable of spearing more than just a fish. He thought back to the maps he and Eutau would pour over on idle days back home and recalled that a great open marsh lay southwest of the Gods' Spears, a marsh known as the Winged Serpents' Dirge. It was said to be the final resting place for the last of its namesake, though the stories said little about when the last of the winged serpents had perished, or why, or how.

They waded through the wetlands for a full day, the girl fussing and cursing at the slightest annoyance, Kira reveling in the feel of the sun burning his face and in the array of colors surrounding him. Finally, after many miles, the water began to recede as the ground rose higher and dry land at last greeted them.

Halting only yards away from the last of the pools, Kira removed his boots and turned them over, allowing them to drain. He looked over at the girl. She had already removed her boots and was busy ringing the water from the ends of her gored skirts. His eyes fell on her legs—petite, shapely legs that were smooth and hairless, as if she had just taken a razor to them—and he realized his glance was traveling ever upward. Abashed, he focused his attention away from the girl, southward.

From where he stood he could not see far, hardly more than half a league, for the land south of the Dirge was flat, with only occasional rises, and in the light of the setting sun it was shrouded in a haze. He knew from his uncle's maps that the southern end of the Dirge was not far from an area known as the Labyrinth of the Cursed, but whether it was a league or a day's march away he did not know. He decided it would be best to make camp, and when he said as much to the girl she wholeheartedly agreed with him.

By the time darkness fell, Kira had managed to get a steady fire going using cattails as kindle and set to roasting a large fish that he had caught. The air was cold, and their clothes had not yet dried. For a long time they sat around the fire, each eating their share, neither speaking a word. Yet, from time to time, Kira found himself staring at the girl. He had never seen anyone like her and found her to be very beautiful, despite her prickly attitude.

"When are you going to tell me your name?" he asked, picking away at the last bit of fish with his dagger.

She looked at him with tired eyes, the *atche* running down her cheeks like wax running down a candle. "Tell you my name? What for? Once I'm done babysitting your stupid ass I don't intend to ever see you again."

"If I decide to accept Daemeon's offer you might end up seeing a lot of me." The truth was, he was curious to know more about her.

Her top lip curled mockingly. "You have a pretty face, but not enough for her to want to keep you. She'll probably feed you to one of her pets once she's done fucking you."

He ran his fingers through his hair and took a deep breath, trying his best not to let her words get to him. But the memory of the woman's strong fingers touching his face unnerved him, and he wondered if the girl's words were true. At last he said, "Just tell me your name. Otherwise, I am going to name you after one of the sows back at my uncle's parlor."

"Name me after a pig and I'll make you a eunuch."

"On second thought, I think I'd feel sorry for the poor sow."

Neither said another word for the remainder of the long night.

As he lay silent, trying to sleep, Kira wondered, not for the first time, why Daemeon had chosen someone as unbearable as the strange girl for his traveling companion. *She won't even tell me if she's a Doll*, he thought bitterly. If she was, the girl was nothing like the Dolls he had read about or heard of in stories—stories that he had heard whispered by folk in Opulancae, since his uncle had always skirted the subject.

For starters, there was the rich, dark-olive hue to her skin, while a Doll's flesh—no matter how fresh the corpse it was made from had been—was supposed to be blotchy and pale. Then there was the fact that she ate, drank, pissed, and even shitted. A Doll was supposed to need only the blood of the master to survive, no more and no less.

She even sweats! And Dolls aren't supposed to sweat! In one of the many old, flaking books Eutau had kept in his room—a book that he had used to level one of the legs of his bed—Kira had read dreadful stories of the horrors people suspected of being Dolls had been submitted to just to prove that they did in fact sweat. Toward the end of the Purging, some Deadbringers had become so adept at making such lifelike Dolls that the Ascendancy had approved certain . . . practices.

Kira clicked his tongue in annoyance. *If uncle was here I bet he'd be able to tell if she is a Doll.*

He fell asleep eventually and awoke early, while it was still cold and dark, to find the girl already awake and sitting quietly. They continued south, breaking camp before the sun had risen. Kira remembered from the maps that a waterway called the Silent River wound through the Labyrinth of the Cursed, and he hoped to find it and follow it east.

Florinia was located in the far southeast of the Land, a journey of many weeks by foot. Yet Eutau's books had said that the South was a land of many rivers, and that the rivers were connected by ancient canals used by traders and travelers alike. Kira vaguely thought that perhaps once they found one of the southern rivers they could find passage on a trader's boat, and so arrive in Florinia by water and shorten their journey. Even so, he wondered to himself if he would be able to tolerate the girl's company for that long.

The sun was far to the west when they finally reached the Labyrinth of the Cursed. Tall, stony towers suddenly loomed out of the haze less than a mile away as they approached. Kira beheld them with awe, for he had often daydreamed about the Labyrinth. Unlike the Dirge, of which little was known, the Labyrinth was said to be the site of one of the pivotal battles of the First War, a battle that had turned the tide against the Ro'Erden. He had read many stories of it, and Eutau would sometimes speak of it as well.

The towers were thick, between twenty and forty yards in diameter, and tall, many reaching almost a hundred yards high. Though they were rocky, Kira could see as he approached that they were lined by a foliage so lush and vibrant that it seemed to be challenging the oncoming grip of winter to do its worst. He halted then and turned to look behind, and shuddered. Despite having traveled for almost two whole days, and despite the haze that obscured much of the horizon, the Gods' Spears still stood clearly visible to the north, an ugly shadow, ever present, like a nightmare that would not fade. The Labyrinth seemed out of place and otherworldly and was in no way homely, but compared to the Spears it was a warm and welcoming sight.

Kira and the girl turned and entered the Labyrinth.

The towers were scattered thickly about, but there was enough space between them that a company of horsemen could have ridden abreast, albeit weaving their way through. Soon after passing the first of the towers, the outside world was lost to view, and Kira's sense of direction became confused. A low mist clung in the air, casting the world into a haze of grays and blues.

They had not gone far, only twenty minutes in, when they came across an unnaturally shaped stone that was starkly out of place: a dark obelisk, roughly fourteen feet high and five feet wide at the base, that tapered to a fine point at its apex. Its surface was akin to anthracite, and it reflected its surroundings, distorting them into pernicious shadows.

The obelisk was strangely unsettling, and as they stood looking at it the girl began muttering and cursing nervously to herself. Yet it put Kira in mind of the sardonyx mirror he had used to recall the souls of the dead, and he found himself filled with the sudden, tantalizing urge to touch its surface. But even as he began to lift his hand he thought better of it. The memory of the incident with the ancient tree in the Spears lay heavily on him, and he had no desire to repeat it.

They continued on, leaving the obelisk behind, though it soon became apparent that there were others like it, littered like weeds among the stone towers. There was no pattern to how the obelisks were spread, for some stood solitary while others were piled close together, almost on top of each other.

A morose thought crept into Kira's mind. *They're almost like headstones.* He shuddered, and from time to time as he walked he looked around to see if he was being watched. The air was chilly yet oppressive, as if the mist was full of some angry consciousness and not merely air, light, and water.

Without warning, a primeval, guttural scream echoed throughout the Labyrinth, and just as suddenly stopped. Overhead came first the sound of numerous wings hidden in the mist, followed by the calls of a murder of ravens, reverberating in time with the terrible cry's fading echoes. Kira and the girl stood stock still, listening, looking. Then from somewhere nearby came the furious voices of two men yelling at each other. The quarrel continued for some seconds, and then there was the sound of hooves galloping, a pained shriek, and then . . . silence.

Kira glanced at the girl and to his surprise saw that she already had a dagger in hand and was scanning their surroundings for potential threats. Kira's own hands were empty, for in his surprise he had not even thought of arming himself. Embarrassed, he drew his dagger and for the first time realized that Daemeon might indeed have chosen his guide well.

Several minutes passed in silence. Eventually, the two resumed their journey as quietly as possible, hoping to avoid whoever or whatever had made the sound. However, they had not gone far when they turned a corner and stumbled upon a man lying crumpled against a large stone slab at the base of one of the rocky towers. Despite the mist, a thin trail of blood could be seen running down his face from his scalp.

Dagger in hand, Kira carefully approached the man.

The girl hissed at him. "What are you doing?"

"Checking to see if he's alive."

"Leave him."

Kira gently prodded the man's leg with his dagger, but the man did not move. Then he placed his free hand over the man's chest. It rose and fell ever so slightly.

The girl's voice came again. "I said, *leave him.*"

He rose and strode back to where she stood. "We should at least wait until he awakens."

"He's not my problem."

"I will not abandon someone who is hurt," Kira responded defiantly.

A mocking fire burned in the girl's eyes, and he understood that whatever she was about to say next was meant to wound him. "Such a stupid, fucking bleeding heart," she began, and paused. "No wonder your uncle is dead."

He had expected anything but that. His brow twitched furiously and he struggled against the urge to lash out at her. He glared down at her with a dreadful loathing.

"We are staying. And *you* are going to help me tend to this man's wounds until he awakens."

The girl pursed her lips and then let out a barking laugh. "I do not fear a *boy.*"

He thought of the agents back in Opulancae and of the Kataru at Corpse Hill, and all of a sudden he envisioned the girl splayed out across the ground like a broken thing. The thought frightened him, but not enough for him to relinquish it.

"You should," he said finally.

Perhaps it was the tone in his voice or the look on his face, but the girl's mirth abruptly subsided. She took a step back, her small fingers fidgeting angrily.

"You want to play the hero?" she asked, with barely contained fury. "Then *you* do the work." And with those words she marched off, vanishing into the mist. For a moment, he considered calling out to her so he could apologize. But he did not. Instead, Kira turned his attention back to the man.

The man's appearance was striking. That much was clear despite the blood that was beginning to dry on his face like two forked rivers. Though his face was lined, he looked strong, a powerful man in his prime. But his skin was soiled with dirt, and his dark clothes were ashen from dust and wear as if he had been traveling in them for a very long time. His dark hair was tangled and matted like an abandoned bird's nest.

Kira took a deep breath, let it out slowly, and fervently hoped that he would not come to regret helping the man. He wanted nothing more than to prove to the girl that his choice had been the correct one. And yet, had Eutau lived, he too would have left the man to die. The thought nagged at him.

Donning his gloves, he took a piece of cloth from his travel bag, poured some water onto it, and began wiping away the blood and dirt on the man's face. Streaks of fair skin began to appear underneath the dirt, as did a series of faded, crisscrossing scars that covered his brow above the right eye.

Unexpectedly, the man's eyes shot open and danced crazily around in their sockets as if he was having a seizure. His body remained deathly still. Quickly but lightly, Kira pressed the point of his dagger against the man's throat. At last, after several seemingly everlasting seconds, his eyes stilled and Kira found himself resisting the urge to balk as burning amber eyes like those of a cat settled on his face. The man's breath caught as he perceived Kira, and his body tensed.

Kira eased his blade, desperately hoping that the man would turn his gaze away. "I won't hurt you. I found you unconscious. Hurt," he said quickly. He held up the cloth, showing the man the blood. "I was merely tending to your wound."

For the first time since opening his eyes, the man blinked and then slowly began moving his limbs, bracing his back against the stone slab, his body moving as if he had not used it in a very long time. Kira withdrew his dagger and stepped back, putting sufficient room between himself and the man. The man took his time to study his surroundings, looked down at his clothes and body, and finally lifted his arms to feel the disheveled tangle of hair that ran down to his chest.

"Were you attacked?" asked Kira.

The man's head shot up, and he looked at Kira, scrutinizing him, as if seeing him for the first time. A brief, ironic smile danced across the man's lips, followed by a bark of a laugh.

"I suppose I am in your debt for your kindness?" he asked. His voice held a vexed tone, and his question seemed to ask more than it said.

"Of course not," said Kira. "Only interest masked as kindness seeks payment."

An indecipherable look filled the man's eyes, but gradually the muscles in his face relaxed and his severity faded. He looked tired then, tired beyond measure. After stifling a yawn with the back of his hand, he said, "Then I thank you for watching over me until I fully awoke."

"Who attacked you?" asked Kira. The man did not answer and instead cast down his eyes. Kira saw a deep crease furrow his brow. *He doesn't want people asking him questions, just as I don't want people to ask me questions.* He felt a bit abashed.

"I'm sorry. I didn't mean to intrude."

The man laughed quietly. "You have no reason to apologize." He reached for his bag, which lay within arm's reach on the ground beside him, and began rummaging through it, pulling out an ivory gourd with a thin blue ribbon tied around its waist. He popped the stopper and took a long drink. Once done, he let out a long sigh of satisfaction and refocused his attention on Kira. Despite the mist, a strange light seemed to illuminate his eyes.

"Your eyes," he began, startling Kira, who had been focused on the man's own. Then with his pointer finger the man made an upward slashing movement. "Are you a Ro'Erden or from the Western Mountains?"

"Western Mountains," said Kira automatically, for it had been what Eutau had drilled him to say whenever anyone asked about his eyes, that his father must have been from the Western Mountains. It had also been what the girl had ordered him to say. Ro'Erden, or *Clots of Dirt*, as she had called them, *are common in the South, and even though they are tolerated they are not accepted. It is much safer if you are thought to be a westerner. Keep that in mind when you open that wide mouth of yours to answer nosy questions about your eyes.*

He had accepted her advice without question. Ro'Erden were hated in the North, another legacy of the First War, and he had never seen one in Opulancae. He had seen a drawing of several in a book long ago, and they had seemed a rather gray folk, with large horns and talons like those of a hawk on their fingertips. Other than the eyes, however, he had found no other resemblance between him and them.

The man grunted, sealed the gourd, and placed it back in his bag. "Yes. I suppose I see it, as you are quite tall and you wear your hair long, as they do. Though your hair is in the northern fashion as well."

Kira ran his fingers through his hair nervously and lied, poorly. "My mother was from the North, and she raised me to abide by those customs." The man began laughing again, though not in an unkindly way, and Kira wondered if he had seen through the pitiful deception.

"Northern woman are rather tall. And, as you can see" — he took hold of the end of his hair — "I hail from the North as well. Though I prefer to wear my hair in a braid, as it tends to have a life of its own."

"Ah," said Kira, deciding it was best not to give the man any reason to further the conversation.

The man stood, and Kira followed. He was surprised to see that the man was the same height as Eutau, only a bit shorter than he himself.

The man echoed Kira's thoughts. "It's not often that I meet someone taller than myself. It's rather . . . well, I rather enjoy having to look up at the sky instead of down at the dirt." He held out his hand. "My name is Lyse."

Kira noted that faint bite marks marred the side of the man's palm. "My name is Va'lel," he said, extending his own, gloved hand and accepting the greeting.

Lyse shook Kira's hand heartily and smiled broadly. "At least your name is typical of a westerner." Kira was surprised by the strength of the man's grasp. Already his injury, the blood running down his face, seemed forgotten, as if it had never been.

Lyse retrieved his pack and gathered his mess of hair into an awkward bun. "Night approaches, and I would like to reach the Silent River before the sun fully sets. I travel east, to Ghlande. You are welcome to join me, Va'lel of the Western Mountains. But it may be that you travel a different route?"

Before Kira could respond, a voice answered for him from behind one of the stone towers. It was the girl. "*That* is none of your concern." She marched over to Kira, gave him an eyeful, and turned to glare furiously at Lyse.

The man took her appearance in stride. "And now we have a southern islander," he said with amusement. "Who knows who you will meet these days in the Labyrinth of the Cursed?"

Kira interjected before the girl could say anything further. "Ghlande, you said? I have never seen a town by that name on any map."

"If it appeared on one I would be surprised. Ghlande is cut off from the main roads, has no rivers of importance that run through it, and has no precious metals. To the north are the Dirge and the Spears, and all around it is the Labyrinth. It is a town of no value and utterly unworthy of a place on a map. But it is where my pledged brother and his daughter live, and thus it is where I must travel."

"Can the town spare food and drink?" asked Kira.

"A handful of travelers will be of no consequence to them."

"And how far is it?"

"The upper courses of the Silent River are not far from here. We should set camp once we reach its waters and then head out at first light tomorrow. At a steady pace, we should arrive by noon."

We're that close? thought Kira, surprised. It was hard for him to imagine that any people would try to create a life in the mists and standing obelisks of the Labyrinth. Nonetheless, he turned to the girl. "We need supplies."

Her eyes narrowed. "And you're just going to buy what he says? You yourself said that such a town does not even exist on the map. What is to assure us that he is not leading us back to a camp of thieves and murderers?"

Lyse smiled. "I do not need a camp of thieves and murderers to kill a young boy and a small girl. I'm quite capable of doing that without any help."

She glared at him. "You still have not told us. You were lying there, dead to the Land. There was someone else, someone with a horse. Perchance you were just an unfortunate soul who was robbed? Or do you have a companion lying in wait for us?"

"I was not robbed, and I have no companions."

"Then to *whom* did the other voice belong?"

For the first time, Lyse seemed troubled. He paused for a moment, and then answered, "To someone I had not spoken to in a very long time, someone I hope to never see again."

"Do you think he'll return?" asked Kira.

An odd look crossed the man's face. "I would hope not."

"Is he dangerous?"

"Yes." His tone made clear that he would answer no more questions.

Kira nodded and then turned to the girl. "I think it would be best if we travel to Ghlande."

The girl spit out her words. "Of course you do."

"The two of you are quite the pair," said Lyse, laughing openly at them. Then he turned on his heel and began making his way south, never looking back. Kira and the girl followed, though they kept some distance between themselves and the man.

"So, Va'lel," said the girl in a violent whisper. "How are you and your new friend doing? I see you are already acquainted with each other's names."

"*My* name you have always known," said Kira, with more force than he had meant.

"You want my name?"

"Yes!"

She stopped in her tracks. "Fine. I am Teemo-Na'dissima Reyde'Es."

He schooled his face to be passive, not wanting to ruin the moment by showing his relief and, if he was being honest, his victory. She had *finally* given her name.

"It's a nice name. A bit long, but nice."

"I wasn't asking for your approval."

He refused to rise to the bait. "I was merely trying to give you a compliment," he said gently.

To his surprise, the girl blushed.

GHLANDE

THEY REACHED THE Silent River late that night and made a rough camp by the bank of its narrow, rocky stream. There was no sound other than that of wind and splashing water, and no one spoke. Kira wondered why the river was called silent if it was so noisy. But though the water was not quiet his companions were, and so he did not ask.

They left before dawn the next day, Lyse taking point as they followed the river's winding bank eastward as it twisted around and past the stone towers of the Labyrinth. Overhead, the flickering light of stars half-obscured by cloud watched over their trek while the damp, chill air danced in circles around them.

Kira exhaled and watched his breath briefly cloud before it was swept away by the wind into the mists that clung tightly to the Labyrinth. He then looked down at Teemo, who was walking close beside him. She was burrowed under his coat and travel cloak, both comically large for her small frame. Covered as she was, she reminded him of a sack of potatoes that had grown short, stubby legs.

A concerned voice called to him. It was the first time Lyse had spoken since they had begun their journey the night before.

"Are you not cold?"

Kira let go of his thought and watched as Lyse slowed his pace to walk beside him, opposite Teemo. As he did so, Kira thought he heard the girl grumble.

"A little," he admitted, draping his long hair over his shoulders, which were bare but for his leather vest. It did nothing to shelter him from the cold, but at the very least it warded off the wind. Rubbing his gloved hands together, he said, "But the North must be a blanket of snow by now, so I'll manage."

Lyse gave a firm nod. "True." Digging through his bag, he brought out the ivory gourd he had drunk from when they had first met. "It's *urovu*, a spirit from the Western Mountains. But perhaps you are already familiar with it?"

Kira resisted the urge to clear his throat. "No."

"Then a sad day it must have been for your father to leave the mountains for the North and its small beer and shitty wine."

"I was raised by my mother and her brother, and he had a penchant for wine, though he preferred the rich wines imported from the South. My father is dead."

"Then let us drink to those who have gone before us. To my brother." He brought the rim of the gourd close to his lips and took a quick drink. Then he passed the gourd to Kira, who began raising it to his own lips but paused at the smell of smoke, burnt sugar, and eye-stinging alcohol that rose to greet him. He changed his mind.

"For now, I'll pass."

Lyse considered him. "Do you not mourn the dead?"

It should have stung, but to Kira it somehow seemed a fitting question given how heavily Eutau's memory had weighed on his mind ever since he had emerged from the Spears. "Every day," he said fervently.

For a moment Lyse appeared taken aback by his intensity, but then a raw sadness gripped the man's countenance and he looked away. He grasped Kira's shoulder with a gloved hand and in a low voice said, "To each their loss."

Lyse walked ahead from then on, drinking occasionally from the gourd, seemingly lost in memories that pressed down upon him. Kira felt sorry for the man, but he wondered if he would carry the loss of Eutau for as long and as hard as Lyse obviously carried the loss of his brother.

It hurt to think so.

Three hours they traveled east, following the bubbling of the river and the emerging life brought by daybreak. Then, after halting for a while in front of a smooth boulder that appeared to Kira no different from any of the other rocks that lay scattered throughout the Labyrinth,

Lyse turned away from the water and headed north. After another mile, the land, which had been flat, began to rise, sloping gently up and down.

For close to an hour, Lyse led them over soft, rolling hills whose crests never betrayed what lay beyond. As they went, the stone towers began to thin out and the mists to clear. Gradually, the hills gave way to flat ground again and then, finally, to small farms. They had at last reached Ghlande, and had managed to do so before midday. Teemo roughly handed Kira back his coat and cloak, as if annoyed that Lyse's words had proven true.

Ghlande lay close to the Labyrinth, and the nearest tower stood within the village itself, a solitary pillar of stone and greenery surrounded by small buildings. There were no dark obelisks in sight. The village itself was less a town than a scattering of small houses built of mud and stone, separated by short, crudely built stone walls and tilled fields of leafy greens and root vegetables. Pigs lay in pens, basking in the sun or rolling in the mud, while flocks of chickens ran about pecking and scratching at the ground. White smoke curled from many of the dwellings' tiny chimneys, perfuming the air with the smell of food and burning wood.

Hardly a person was to be seen, though occasionally they saw children peering cautiously at them from the dim entrances of the little houses. As they walked by one house, a solitary hen broke away from a nearby flock and charged up to Kira. Flapping its wings, it lifted momentarily off the ground, snatched a lock of his hair, and then began tugging voraciously at it. Kira yanked his hair free and, despite himself, felt his mouth water and heard his stomach loudly rumble. Teemo merely eyed the chicken with interest, but Lyse echoed Kira's own hunger.

"I agree," he said mildly, patting his stomach and shooing away the hen, which had now taken to pecking at his boot. "Most of the villagers will be out in the fields, bringing in the last harvest before winter," he continued, anticipating the question that was forming in Kira's thoughts. "We will see more of them as we go forward."

They continued northward through the village. After half a mile, the houses dropped away and the fields around the path changed. Unlike the others, these fields were muddy, and they grew ranks of plants that Kira did not recognize, plants that swayed gently in the wind like a golden veil. Clusters of people could be seen moving about, cutting and harvesting, gradually building piles of the strange crop.

Kira's curiosity got the better of him. "What are they growing here?"

"So the northern boy has never seen rice before," Teemo responded sarcastically. "Isn't it *amazing*?"

"Yes," said Lyse without irony, stopping at a fork in the path. "Ghlande sustains itself mostly with rice, fish from the river, and game. Occasionally they trade with Rhaemond for goods or with Silfria, far to the east between the marshes and the sea, for salt. But that trade is erratic, not enough for a merchant to make a living off of. And, in any case, the Koyohal are the only ones who know their wetlands well enough to reliably traverse them."

Teemo snorted and rolled her eyes as if disgusted by the lecture. But Kira was interested. He had read of rice, and Eutau had once told him that it was a common dish in the South, but he had never seen it, at least not when he had been old enough to remember. He decided to keep that fact to himself, for something else that Lyse said had caught his attention.

"I know of Silfria, but who are the Koyohal?" he asked.

"A reclusive lot. They are the last followers of the Serpent Rider and the Fire Brothers, though with each generation their beliefs have been shifting in favor of the new gods. The more worldly ones live in Silfria, but many more live in small clans in the great eastern marshes where the Silent River vanishes. Most people look down on the Koyohal as a primitive race, so few of them will speak with outsiders."

Kira eyed him with curiosity. "You talk as if you have been there and know them yourself."

Lyse's smile was one of pride. "I have, and I do."

"You get around quite a bit, don't you?" asked Kira, impressed.

"They are many joys to being a wanderer," Lyse replied, laughing quietly and looking pleased with himself. "Come." He took the fork to the left, away from the rice paddies. "Let us be off."

A mile further on, the path ended at a stout house made of stone and wood, one larger and sturdier looking than most of the buildings they had seen in Ghlande. To the west were several of the Labyrinth's stone towers and a cluster of the strange dark obelisks, the first they had seen in the village, while to the north lay a patch of short, spindly trees. No other building was in sight, though wisps of smoke rising over a low hill nearby betrayed the presence of other houses.

"This is it," said Lyse, halting in front of a perfectly round door. To Kira's surprise, the man took several deep breaths, as if he was nervous. Finally, after patting down his clothes and fussing with his hair, he knocked on the door and waited.

A strong voice called from behind the closed door.

"Name yourself."

Lyse rolled his eyes, but his unease seemingly disappeared. "Open the door, you stubborn ox."

"Lyse?"

"In all his glory," he replied with a smile.

The door swung open with such force that Kira was amazed the hinges did not come clean off. A bold, broad-shouldered man stood grandly in the door's entrance. Heavy lines wrinkled his thick brow and deep-set brown eyes. A mess of dark hair clung tightly to his head, and a full, dense beard flecked with gray lined his face. His skin was deeply tanned and weathered, yet somehow it managed to soften rather than harden his features. He was also taller than Kira had expected a southerner to be, certainly taller than the villagers they had seen earlier in the fields.

"You *dog*! I was certain you had forgotten us!" The man regarded Lyse from top to bottom, grinning. "And for once you look worse for wear."

Again Lyse rolled his eyes, as if he was not the least bit surprised by the man's reaction, and let out a low, resigned sigh. "It warms my heart to know that I have made your day."

The man let out a mighty bark of a laugh and gestured for them to enter. They passed through, and Kira noted as he did so that the doorway was high enough that he did not have to stoop.

The main room was small but not uncomfortably so. In its center a low fire burned in the hearth, its warmth accentuated by the rich wooden panels that lined the walls and floor. To either side of the hearth were doorways, round as well, that led to other rooms. The windows were lined with thick glass, further helping to keep in the warmth. The room would have been unremarkable in Opulancae, but Kira suspected that here it was considered luxurious.

His study of the room was diverted, however, for in front of the hearth was a large rectangular table surrounded by a group of people. Most were men, though some women and children were present as well. All were studying him intently, and their eyes were not kind. One of their number, a man with wiry brown hair, stood suddenly, and his lips moved as if he had meant to speak. The sudden attention disquieted Kira, and he tried his best to ignore them, though he was finding it difficult to do so. Lyse too did not seem pleased by the unexpected company.

"Well, well," he began coldly, "quite the jolly reunion we have here, Sa."

Despite Lyse's discourtesy, most of the people gathered at the table acknowledged him with a brief nod or wave. But, even as they did so, they kept their eyes fixed on Kira. The man with the wiry hair made no motion, but his glare betrayed anger. The room fell silent. Then the man who had greeted them shattered the quiet by bellowing over his shoulder.

"Telera! *Telera!* Come see who's here."

From the doorway to the right of the hearth a young girl stepped out, holding a clay pitcher. She was perhaps eleven or twelve years of age and wore a thick woolen dress that just passed her knees, with no shoes. Upon seeing Lyse she smiled gloriously, revealing dainty canines. Her skin was the palest of grays, changing to a rose hue at her fingertips, around her eyes, and on the rims of her slightly pointed ears. Snow-white hair was gathered and pinned on her head in elaborate spirals and twists.

But what caught Kira's attention were her eyes, pale yellow like the flesh of a white peach, uptilted, and accentuated by painted-on eyebrows, needle-thin and sharply arched. *A Ro'Erden!* he thought, amazed, even as he resisted the urge to reach up to touch his own eyes. Though their color was different, the girl's eyes otherwise could have been his own. He thought back to Eutau telling him that his father must have been from the Western Mountains, and for the first time in his life, Kira felt a pang of doubt. He had accepted Eutau's words about his parents without question, and now it was too late to ask further.

"Uncle!" the girl cried out, elated, and placed the pitcher down on the table. She ran over to Lyse and jumped, managing to get her arms around his neck.

"Careful," cried Lyse, even as he took her into his arms, embracing her tightly. "You've gotten taller! How old are you now?"

She beamed proudly. "Twelve."

His eyes widened as if he was genuinely stunned. He cleared his throat. "Keep this up and you'll be taller than your ox of a father."

Sa laughed warmly. "She takes after her mother, thank the gods."

Lyse snickered wickedly. "If she took after you I'd feel quite sorry for her."

The girl let go of Lyse's neck and landed on her feet with a loud *thud.* She then looked over at Kira with her peach-colored eyes and waved at him with claw-tipped fingers.

"Hi!" she said, scrunching up her face.

"Hi," he responded warily, unsure how to react.

The man with the wiry hair spoke up. "Aren't you going to introduce your friends, Lyse?" His voice held more than an edge of irritation.

Lyse shot a vexed look at the man, apparently displeased at having been interrupted. The tension between the two men made Kira feel uncomfortable, especially since the other people in the room had not stopped watching him.

"This is Va'lel," said Lyse, turning first to Kira and then to Telera. "He's of the Western Mountains, not a Ro'Erden."

"Oh, poo!" said the girl, visibly deflating.

Lyse waved a hand in Teemo's direction. "And this is — "

"No need," she said dismissively. "My name is Teemo-Na'dissima Reyde'Es, and Va'lel is my partner."

Lyse winced, his brows shooting up in surprise. "Is this true?"

Kira inwardly cursed the girl for not having run the lie by him before speaking. With all eyes on him, he had no choice but to agree with her. "Yes," he replied carefully, taking great pains to smother the anger he felt.

"I don't envy you," said Lyse, with heartfelt pity.

Sa laughed again. "I see you don't let my pledged brother get to you. Wise lad. As you've probably guessed, my name is Sa and this is my daughter, Telera." He turned to the people seated behind him, by the hearth. "And these good people are our neighbors."

The wiry-haired man spoke up. "We were discussing a rumor that Maelynda brought back from Rhaemond." He paused for a moment, his face impassive. "A rumor about Deadbringers emerging in different parts of the Land."

TURMOIL

$\mathcal{L}$IFE SEEMED TO stop. *This isn't happening,* thought Kira, struggling to appear calm. The sweat beaded uncomfortably under his clothes, and a painful knot settled in his stomach as dread overtook him.

The man continued. "In particular, there was a rumor about a Deadbringer from the North. Opulancae, I believe."

Distantly, Kira felt his stomach lurch.

"What an interesting rumor," Lyse said dryly. "I'm sure Maelynda was not pleased to hear something so"—he waved a hand in the air, pretending to search for the word—"distasteful."

The man ignored Lyse and continued, his sight never leaving Kira. "The Deadbringer is said to be tall even for a northerner, and he has long, dark hair and pale skin." He paused, his face severe. "And he is said to have uptilted, fair-colored eyes."

Kira was dumbstruck. *How could the rumors have reached the South— let alone a town as isolated as this—so quickly?*

Lyse made a chiding sound with his tongue, waving away the man's words. "You have just described most northerners, not merely Va'lel and myself." He took a few steps toward the table, putting himself between Kira and the man. A rude smile touched the corners of his lips, and he looked directly at the man, holding his gaze. "Maybe you should be

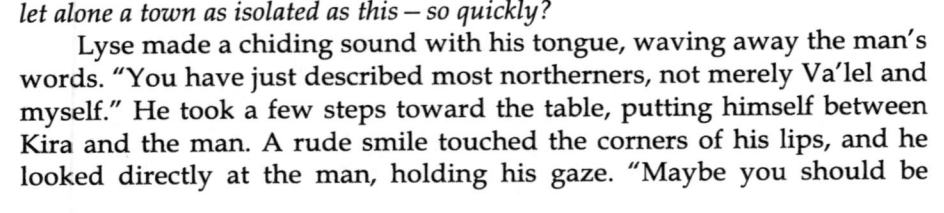

suspicious of me as well, and perhaps even call the Ascendancy to Ghlande. Why don't you, Osette?"

The man stood furiously, almost knocking his seat over. "True I have described a northerner, but what of his eyes?" He pointed an accusing finger at Kira. "Ro'Erden are despised in the North and—"

"Ro'Erden, yes, but not the westerners, you fool. They are the only ones who keep the few roads that run through the mountains in shape, and they have no quarrel with anyone."

Sa, who had been observing the men with apparent patience, finally reached his limit. "That is enough, Osette." His voice was dangerously low. Telera watched her father, wrinkling her face in worry.

Osette clicked his tongue in frustration. "I meant no disrespect to your house, Sa." He ran his hand over his face and let out a quick sigh. "We'll talk another day." He turned back to Lyse. "How long do you intend to stay?"

"Long enough to annoy you."

Osette scowled. "We should get going," he said, defeated. One by one the people excused themselves, the children among them promising Telera they would come back to play on another day. After shepherding the people out, Osette made his way to Kira and looked up at him, scrutinizing his every feature. Kira studied the man in turn and found more than suspicion in his eyes. He found fear.

"Perhaps Lyse is right," said Osette at last, slowly, "and you are not this Deadbringer from Opulancae. Still, try not to remain in Ghlande for too long. During the Purging this town managed to avoid the Ascendancy's wrath. Don't ruin that for us."

Nothing I say will ease this man's mind, thought Kira, and he remained silent, waiting for Osette to reach his own conclusions. But Osette merely sighed and then stepped back with an almost pained look on his face. He left, gently closing the main door behind him, and his footsteps faded away down the path. Kira looked around at the others who remained and experienced a moment's doubt. *Can I stay, after all this?*

Then, shock.

Kira's vision momentarily darkened and he felt the wind knocked from him. Then the sharp, unyielding swordpoint resting under his collarbone drew him back to his senses. His back was forced up against the wall, and the sound of Teemo's wails filled his ears. He could do nothing but stare at the man holding the sword, the man and his burning amber eyes.

"What are you doing!" cried Telera, confused.

Sa unsheathed his own sword and took a position behind Lyse. He called sternly to his daughter. "Go to your room, and do not interfere." The girl, peach eyes trembling, nodded and began making her way out of the room. She moved slowly, for she could not help but look back at the unfolding scene.

"I want to know the truth!" growled Lyse. "And just so you know, lie to me again and I will deliver your corpse to the Ascendancy myself."

All eyes now on Kira, Teemo made her move. As quick as a fox, she darted behind Telera, bringing a dagger to her throat and another just under her left eye.

Sa whirled around, but it was too late. "*BITCH!*" he roared, his hand nearly crushing his sword's grip in desperation.

Lyse shifted slightly so he could see both Kira and Teemo, but his blade did not move.

"What are you doing?" shouted Kira, more alarmed for the young girl than for himself, though the feel of the swordpoint did nothing to calm his nerves.

Teemo was livid. "Shut up! This is your fault!" she screamed, and inched her daggers closer until the point of the one in her left hand touched Telera's lashes. Telera gasped, trying her best not to flinch. Teemo ignored the girl, her eyes never leaving Lyse and Sa.

She hissed knowingly. "Ro'Erden might be able to use dirt as a shield on their body, but they cannot use it to protect their eyes. I'm sure we have an understanding now."

Kira felt Lyse's swordpoint break his skin, and he stiffened. Blood began to trickle down his chest, under his vest.

Lyse's voice carried death in it. "If she dies, neither of you will leave here in one piece."

"Then step away from him, and I'll let the brat go."

"Do not play me for a fool. I know you have no intention of letting her live." Lyse pushed the point further in, tearing muscle. Kira gnashed his teeth, not wanting to cry out, but more than that not wanting to see the girl hurt.

"Let her go, Teemo," he pleaded. "I will not have her blood on my hands."

She sneered at him disdainfully, her eyes tight, purple slits. "And this is why your kin is dead, Deadbringer. If you had truly cared for him you would have left a pile of bodies in your wake. Instead, you balked at every turn. Just as you're doing now."

He had not expected her to use Eutau against him, not again and not then. A deep anger overtook him.

"I will not see that girl harmed on my account," he rasped.

"Right back at you," she sneered. "I will not be harmed on hers."

Kira laughed mirthlessly as he recalled Daemeon's words back in the Spears. *Be what you yearn to be, and stop living for false ideals.* He looked at the girl and then at her father.

I'm so envious it makes me sick.

He pushed himself onto the blade, running it clean through his shoulder. Lyse let go of the hilt, and Kira fell to his knees. Yet even as he fell his eyes never turned away from Telera and Sa.

Teemo screamed her fury, and her daggers shifted just enough. Instantly, Telera dropped herself to the ground and Sa lunged with his sword, stabbing Teemo straight through the stomach and pinning her against the wall. Telera jumped up and ran to her father, tears streaming down her face. Then she turned to look at Teemo and let out a terrible cry.

"She's alive! How? How!"

Teemo kicked and screamed, desperately trying to pull the sword out, but to her rage and dismay she could not. Blood streamed from the wound, oozing down her gored skirts and onto the floor.

A knowing look passed between Lyse and Sa.

"She is not a girl," said Sa, placing a firm hand on his daughter's quivering shoulder. Telera bit her lip, trying her best to still her trembling even as she visibly struggled to take in her father's words. "She is a Doll. She will not die so easily, and she will do anything to protect her master."

Teemo shrieked, her face contorted in a mask of hatred. *"Master?* This trash is *nothing* to me. Go ahead, kill him! *Kill him! KILL HIM!"*

Lyse and Sa stared at her then, both shocked into silence. After a pause, Lyse walked to the hearth and retrieved a smoldering fire iron. Then he stood in front of Teemo and held it mere inches from her face. The iron's tip glowed red with the heat of the fire. His own face was unreadable. Fear filled her eyes and she sunk back against the wall, ripping the flesh around her wound, sending gushes of blood running down her skirts to the floor.

Telera at last found her voice. "Uncle, you can't!"

Lyse ignored her. "What did you say?" he asked Teemo quietly, implacably. "He is trash? He is nothing to you?" Teemo bit down on her lip, shaking her head frantically, her defiance extinguished.

"Telera," Lyse called firmly, "come here." He held out the iron to her. She looked at it and made a low whimpering sound in her throat.

"Telera," said Sa, stern but not unkind. "Do as your uncle says." Holding back tears, she took hold of the iron.

Lyse placed a huge, gloved hand over Telera's small, shaking hands. "Don't bother with remorse. She would have had none for you. I need you to stand guard and burn her if she tries to flail or escape. Can you do this for me?" She nodded her head up and down, trying to be brave. Lyse smiled warmly. "Thank you."

Kira had seen and heard enough. Lyse's words had come to him as if in a fog, but no pain could have masked the words Teemo had spoken. He lowered his head and slumped forward, just enough to rest the sword's pommel against the floor without driving the blade further through him. His long cascade of hair rushed forward, falling to the ground in time with the blood that dripped from his wound.

Oddly enough, as the dark red puddle spread slowly across the wooden floor, he found himself thinking of the hen that had grabbed onto his hair. He laughed inwardly, and then his thoughts shifted. *The wood will rot. I wonder who will be the one to step on it and have their foot go through the floorboards?*

Those same floorboards creaked as someone crouched next to him. Lyse.

"What am I supposed to do with you, hmm?"

Kira nearly lost consciousness then. He took several quick breaths to pull his mind away from the pain. Then he spoke, his voice strained but firm.

"I would not be surprised if there is a large bounty on my head."

Lyse sucked in air through his teeth and let it out slowly. "That girl is not your Doll, is she? No Doll would say of her master what she said of you."

"No."

"Then whose is she?"

Kira remained silent for some time and then said, "I can't say. I don't want to lie to you anymore." Again he heard the man suck in air through his teeth.

Lyse carefully laid his hand on the sword's pommel. "You won't die from this, will you?"

"No. But it hurts like a bitch."

Lyse nodded his head curtly, as if he had come to a decision. "Very well." Then he gripped the sword hilt and pulled out the blade in one smooth, brutal motion. Kira winced, his hand automatically cradling his collar even as he waited for the finishing blow.

But it never came.

"Sa," began Lyse, "I will not ask that you agree with me."

Kira forced himself to look up and focus through the haze, to see the men's faces. Both were deeply lined, Sa's with worry, Lyse's with a deep fatigue.

Sa spoke. "The boy's antics allowed an opening for my daughter to escape. I do not overlook such actions. As for the Doll—"

"Please!" pleaded Kira, though he did not understand why. "Don't kill her."

Lyse sneered. "From what I saw, that Doll treats you like trash and wanted to see you dead. I see no reason why you would spare her life, even if it were your decision."

"If it hadn't been for her I would never have found my way out of the Gods' Spears."

Sa snorted in disbelief. "You lie. No one who enters survives the Spears."

"The Sanctifiers were upon us. It was the only option we had left."

"We? You and the Doll?" asked Sa, seemingly surprised in spite of himself.

Kira shook his head, laughing bitterly as he recalled Teemo's words. "No. My uncle. My uncle died in the Spears, and I would have as well if not for her. It was she who guided me out of that wretched place."

"And what makes you think she will listen to you once she has been unpinned?" Lyse asked severely.

"Because she has to. And . . ." He stopped then and looked over at Teemo, who was staring at him with a blank expression on her face. She looked pitiful, and a part of him wanted to plead for her not to be further humiliated. But he was tired, so very tired. And the truth was that even though he wanted to have pity on the girl — the Doll — he could find none to give. Their eyes locked, and he said, "If she defies me again, *I* will end her. I give my word." Perhaps it was the light playing tricks on him, or perhaps he was just at his limit, but he thought he saw her flinch.

For some time Sa studied them both. Finally, his eyes rested on the sword that held Teemo to the wall and he nodded, satisfied. "It won't be going anywhere." He shot a quick glance at the blood on the floor. "I'll go fetch something to bind your wound."

"No need," said Kira, deciding it was pointless to continue hiding anything about himself. He slowly pushed himself to his feet. "I . . . I can heal this wound myself. Just . . . don't touch my skin directly. Ever." His eyes fell. "You might get hurt if you do."

Closing his eyes, he called upon Death. Despite the severity of the situation, he felt a sudden, unexpected ecstasy wash over him. It caused the pain he felt to morph into a pleasure that horrified him. *What's happening? Uncle, why aren't you here? I need you!*

A series of curses filled his ears, and he reluctantly opened his eyes, anticipating their fear and disgust. Sa's face had contorted in disbelief as curses spilled from his lips, while Lyse had risen and was slowly backing away, his mouth a grim line, his amber eyes stark and burning once again. Kira struggled not to laugh at their reactions.

Perhaps he will change his mind and kill me after all.

Pushing the thought aside, he focused his strength on the wound beneath his collar. Little by little it began to knit itself, and as it did his pleasure grew. Alarmed, Kira bit down hard on his tongue, drawing blood, distracting himself with the fresh pain. His mind cleared, and for several minutes he focused on healing himself. Slowly, he felt his neck and shoulder regain their use.

The others had not moved. Sa's disbelief now changed to amazement. "Incredible," he said. "Deadbringers are fast healers, and some Katarus even more so, but I have never seen anyone heal a wound in a matter of minutes."

Kira laughed, and then suddenly the room was a blur and he was on his knees again, vomiting profusely. When he was done, he found Lyse holding out a towel for him.

"Sa, do you have plans for dinner?" Lyse asked conversationally, as if nothing had happened.

"No," replied Sa, scratching his beard, his voice questioning.

"Could I trouble you for a pig, perhaps?"

Sa shook his head incredulously. "You *would* think of food. But I agree, let us feast tonight. I want to celebrate having you in our home, especially after so long. And" — his brown eyes regarded Kira — "we need to put meat on that boy."

Lyse turned his attention back to Kira, helped him to his feet, and then gestured toward Teemo. "I am going to trust that you will keep that thing in line and keep your word to end it if it strays. So, I will leave it to you, but for now it will remain pinned to the wall, and in the meantime I want you to sleep. Tonight, we will discuss what to do. Agreed?"

Kira could not find it in him to argue, nor did he want to. "Yes."

Lyse smiled warmly. "Then I suppose you should bathe before bed, or else you will ruin the sheets."

"I can show him to the watershed," chirped Telera quickly, obviously eager to yield her duties guarding Teemo.

For a moment, Kira wondered if everyone was just playing a game with him, to make him believe that everything was fine before delivering the fatal blow. *No, I won't think that way. I refuse to see shadows.* He pushed his hair out of his face and straightened up. He hoped he did not look as pathetic as he felt.

"My name is Kira Vidal." Satisfaction at being able to use his own name settled over him peacefully.

Sa chuckled, though grimly. "That name suits you better. Well then, Kira Vidal, welcome. I can be pleasant since no one of consequence was hurt." He turned to look at his daughter, and then at Teemo. There was no love in his eyes for the Doll.

An overwhelming knot gripped Kira's throat and he found himself unable to speak. *How can you allow me in your home after what happened?* he wanted to ask. *How now, after you know who and what I am?* But instead, when he at last found his voice, he merely said, "Thank you."

Not wanting anyone to clean up after him and afraid that someone could be hurt, Kira asked for rags and then wiped up the blood and vomit from the floor, warning Sa that the soiled boards were likely weakened and needed to be replaced.

"And why is that?" asked Lyse, glancing at him sideways and cleaning the blood from his sword.

"Because . . ." He took a deep breath. Even though they knew what he was, he could not help but fear that even now they would see him as a monster. "Because my touch rots, and my blood as well. I can control it somewhat, but, as I said before, it would be best if you did not touch me."

Lyse's face fell then, his sword slipping from his hand. Abashed, Kira quickly said, "But you have gloves on and you are using a cloth to wipe the blade, so you'll be fine. If it bothers you, I can wipe the blade clean."

"No," Lyse said flatly, as he leaned over to pick up his sword. "I'll be fine. It was just"—he looked at the floorboards and then at Kira—"unexpected."

Sa huffed loudly. "I will leave a rag to mark the area and we will walk around it. I have no desire to work on the floor right now. Besides, the pig will not slaughter itself." True to his word, he left a rag on the soiled boards and then left to prepare a pig for their dinner.

Telera led Kira outside to the watershed at the back of the house for his bath. Her shock now over, she seemed intrigued at Kira's ability to make things rot and began asking him all sorts of questions. *I wonder if I was this bad with my uncle when I was little,* he thought. He hoped not but had a feeling that it had been so.

Now only Lyse and Teemo remained behind in the main room.

Grabbing a pitcher from the table, Lyse brought the rim close to his lips and let its contents spill into his mouth. It was water. Satisfied, he drank, and then he poured a bit on his hands and splashed it on his face. He turned to look at the Doll and then strode up to her, seemingly fixated on the sword blade stuck within her. Numerous words were etched into its steel, each stained red from the blood that had settled into its grooves and ridges. A fond smile danced along the corners of his mouth as he ran a finger across the words.

"If I demand that you tell me your master's name, you won't say, will you?" he asked calmly.

Silence.

"So be it." Abandoning the blade, he wrapped his hand around the hilt and effortlessly pushed it into her gut up to the handguard as if it were a hot knife cutting through butter. Teemo's eyes bulged in agony, and she struggled not to cry out.

"Try as you might, you will never be able to pull this sword out." With those parting words, Lyse turned his back on the Doll and stepped outside.

Alone, Teemo wept.

REFLECTION

WHY AM I *here?* Kira had promised Lyse that after bathing he would retire to the room that had been set aside for him, but instead he had returned to the main room, where Teemo remained pinned to the wall.

Am I here to see her? Then why don't I speak to her?

Instead, Kira studied the Doll's every feature: the lines of her face, the texture of her hair, and the look in her eyes, fiery eyes that stared at him ruefully. She was perfect. Even the blood dried on her clothes was perfect.

Why should I care? he asked himself. *She would have seen me dead!* But that fact did nothing to quell his anxiety. Behind him, the westering sun shone through the window, its rays fracturing all around him and encasing the Doll in a faint halo.

Why?

It was such a short word, yet it carried more weight than the most verbose speech in the Land. Kira wanted an answer—no, that was a lie. He *needed* an answer.

"I trusted you."

"You never trusted me."

He resisted the urge to run his fingers through his hair. "I wanted to trust you," he began again. "I wanted to believe that you were a decent person."

Teemo laughed scornfully. "There is no such thing as a 'decent' person. Everyone, to one extent or another, always wants something, always schemes, or betrays, or is your friend until you are no longer of use."

"You're wrong. There are people who are not as you say."

"Who? That dog shit you met in the Labyrinth?"

"It's true that I can't vouch for someone I hardly know. But I have met people who are not afraid to put others before themselves." He thought of Elia and her unending kindness; of Sal and Kim, who had done their best to keep him away from the grip of the Ascendancy; and even of Daemeon, who had saved him from his own childishness, giving him the chance to reach Florinia, the goal that both he and Eutau had decided on.

Her lip curled up in an angry snarl. "How many?"

He saw no point in lying. "Not many."

"And how many have you met that seek to use you, or to end you if they cannot use you themselves, either because they fear what you are or what others could do with you?"

He thought of the Sanctifiers bent on his death, of Kim's entreaties to join the Bastion, and of the Kataru that had attacked him at Corpse Hill.

"Too many," he admitted.

"Then tell me, *why*? Why do you continue to try to see the good in people? Do you enjoy making yourself feel like shit? Do you like playing the victim? Do you crave pity?"

"Because I have tried living my life the way my uncle lived his: me against the Land. But I can't live that way. I don't want to push people away. I don't want to live my life waiting for a knife to stab me in the back." A part of Kira felt guilty for giving voice to what he felt, but it was the truth. With Eutau gone, he could finally acknowledge it.

Teemo laughed again, but her eyes were tight. "The longer you live, the more people you meet and befriend, the harder it will become for you *not* to see the knives that have always been in their hands."

He wanted to rebut her attack, but the agony in her eyes was too raw, too painfully familiar. With a wrenching feeling, he realized that it was the very same agony that had been on Eutau's face in the tree hollow in the Gods' Spears. He shrank back as if burned and turned away from the Doll, not wanting her to see the pain on his own face, not after what he had so boldly told her.

The peace I had found at her side. It was what Eutau had confessed to him. *You were a mercenary, but what was your life like before you stayed with my mother? Who really were you?*

Teemo's voice, quiet now, trembling faintly with every word, drew him from his thoughts.

"I'm sorry . . . for what I said about your uncle. I'm sorry, for everything."

He turned to face her and their eyes locked. Fresh *atche* was running down her cheeks. *She's crying!* Kira reached out to touch her face, but then stopped.

"Can — can I touch you?" he asked softly.

She smiled weakly. "Yes."

Kira walked to the table in the center of the room. There he wet a small cloth with water from the pitcher that Telera had brought out earlier in the day, what now seemed like years ago. Then he returned to Teemo, removed his gloves, and began gently wiping the black stains from her face. Her skin was soft and cool against his fingers. Teemo kept her eyes cast downward. Her lips twitched as if she was struggling to restrain some emotion, though what emotion that might have been Kira could not say.

His eyes fell on her midriff, where the sword had pierced her. The light from the window reflected on the handguard, illuminating the blood that even now seeped from the wound to spread slowly through her clothes. In dismay, Kira searched her face again and realized that her dark olive skin was waxen, the hollows of her eyes deep, the pain plain to see for anyone who cared to look.

How didn't I notice before? He cursed himself for treating her so cruelly, for treating her . . . *like a Doll.* He seized the sword hilt and, in one smooth motion, pulled it out. Teemo gasped and fell like a petal from a rose, but Kira caught her in his arms and then lifted her up, cradling her against him.

"Does it hurt?" he asked tenderly.

Her voice was a whisper, barely audible. "Not anymore."

We should leave, thought Kira, unsure how Lyse and Sa would react to his freeing her, to disobeying Lyse's orders.

He looked down at the sword that he now held in his right hand and saw that there was a strange series of words etched into the blade. He looked closer, expecting it to be in the Ro'Erden letters Eutau had taught him, since Sa's daughter was at least part Ro'Erden. But the letters and words were completely unfamiliar to him. He stared at them, unable to suppress his curiosity. *What language is this?*

The sound of floorboards creaking caught his ear and he turned quickly, his heart pounding. Lyse stood in the doorway. His expression was unreadable, but Kira thought he saw amber eyes flash.

Working moisture into his mouth, Kira said, "I am going to give Sa his sword back and thank him for his generosity. For your generosity."

Lyse's eyes flickered to the girl in Kira's arms. Kira wondered if he should apologize to the man for going against his orders. But he knew that doing so would be just another betrayal to Teemo, and that he would not do.

"I will not see her suffer further," he said slowly, taking pains to articulate the words without any inflection that could give away his emotions.

Lyse nodded as if he had been thinking or listening to someone else, and then he stepped out into the main room. Kira saw that he appeared freshly bathed and had changed into new clothes that flattered his frame yet looked comfortable and practical all the same. His long, dark hair, before a tangled ball of yarn, was now braided in such a way that it resembled a spine encased by a ribcage. His eyes fell on the sword in Kira's hands, and at last he spoke.

"I see you managed to draw out the sword." There was an odd cadence in his voice that Kira could not decipher, a harsh tone that seemed new but, Kira realized, must have always been there. He wondered how he had not noticed it before.

"Yeah," Kira said uncomfortably, trying to figure out what the man was getting at.

Lyse nodded at a snail's pace, as if deep in thought. Finally, he said, "Sa is particular about who touches his sword." He held his hand out. "I will tell him that it was I who pulled the sword and freed the Doll." Kira began to hand it to him, then paused ever so slightly as he felt Teemo tense in his arms, afraid of what Lyse would do with the sword once it was in his hands. Nonetheless, Kira handed it over and then stepped back, out of easy reach.

Lyse cocked his head to one side. "'To place your faith in those you do not know is death.' It is what my brother used to say." He laid the sword on the table and turned away.

"Your brother had a way with words," said Kira, surprised at the sudden revelation.

"Yes, my brother was quite fond of hearing himself talk. Well, my half brother, really." A heavy sadness overtook Lyse's face. "He did not heed his own advice and was killed."

"I'm sorry," said Kira, with sincerity.

Lyse waved the apology away and with it the memory. "So, you're leaving?"

"I think it would be best."

"What of food and water?"

"I'll manage."

Lyse sniffed, an arrogant, indignant look forming on his face, a look that somehow suited him. "Yes, I daresay you'll manage becoming carrion for the ravens." He waved at Kira from head to toe. "In the state you are in you will never reach wherever it is you are headed."

"Then I will die trying."

"I do not believe you came this far just to 'die trying.' And really," said Lyse, coldly but with a wicked smile creeping onto his face, "the sacrificial antics do not become you. Do you throw yourself on a sword every time you find your breakfast porridge to be cold?" Kira reddened and opened his mouth but found himself speechless. Lyse made a chiding sound with his tongue, shook his head, and then continued.

"I agree that it would probably be best to leave before Osette and the others take further interest in you. But, at least for this night, rest and eat. A lot. Now go to the watershed and wash yourself up."

"I've already bathed."

"Maybe so, but you do realize that you just covered yourself in the Doll's blood, don't you?"

Kira looked down at himself and realized that Lyse was right. Again he was filthy. Teemo tugged slightly at his shirt, and he had a feeling that if she could have she would have chided him. "If it's alright," he began, "I would like to take Teemo with me to the watershed, so she can wash up as well."

"As you wish," said Lyse, a slight edge in his voice. Kira did not hold Lyse's anger against him. After all, Teemo had threatened the people closest to him. And yet, despite it all, the man was still willing to help them.

"Thank you. For everything."

Lyse grunted. "Go on, and this time make sure you do get some sleep thereafter." A tight smile twisted his lips. "In the meantime, I will talk to Sa about the Doll."

Kira nodded, and then left the man and the strange sword behind.

SA SAT ATOP a smooth boulder, puffing out clouds of smoke from his pipe. Directly in front of him was a pig, its hind legs spread asunder and hung with ropes. The ropes were secured with hooks to a high, rectangular ramp of metal and wood that looked like some menacing doorway. Blood flowed out of the pig's slashed neck into a bucket that had been set directly underneath the ramp. A thin cloth that was stained the color of rust had been placed over the bucket and tied in place, allowing the blood to seep through but keeping the dirt out.

Lyse strolled up to Sa and held out the sword. Sa looked down at it and then up at him through narrowed eyes.

"You let her go. Why?"

Lyse raised a brow in disappointment. "I had hoped you would ask me if I had killed her."

"That would mean killing the boy, and from what I have gathered you seem unwilling to do so. Pity for a Deadbringer? That seems so unlike you." The sound of straining wood and metal creaked through the air as the pig briefly jerked. Neither man noticed.

"It doesn't matter." Lyse leaned the sword against the rock on which Sa sat and then sat on the ground, leaning his own back against the rock as well. "Kira is in the watershed with the Doll. Bathing it, fucking it, it matters little to me what he does with it as long as he keeps it on a tight leash." He picked a few pebbles from the dirt and began rolling them around in his hand.

"Stop trying to change the subject. The boy obviously affects you in some way. But why? You have forever been adamant about your distaste for Deadbringers. So why *this* boy?" Sa looked on, waiting for the answer, but Lyse sat as silent and as still as the dead pig hanging from the hooks. After a few minutes, when it became evident to Sa that he would receive no answer, he snuffed out his pipe and rose.

"It's getting late," he began. "If you could, please take the blood to the kitchen so Telera can start making the gravy. But make sure to come back in a few minutes so I can hand over the cuts for tonight's dinner. As for the rest" — he took in a deep breath, his chest puffing out, and then exhaled with great satisfaction — "it's the perfect temperature for curing."

"Perhaps . . ." Lyse began softly, so softly that it took Sa a moment to realize that the other man had spoken. He halted in his tracks, listening intently.

"It was after another sleeping fit that Kira appeared, a fit that came on in the Labyrinth yesterday as I was on my way to see you. Before I awoke, I was dreaming of my brother. I dreamed that he was by my side watching over me, as he used to."

A deep pain settled on his face, and he continued as if out of desperation. "Yet, as he did so, I realized in panic that I had forgotten what my brother looked like. What he sounded like. I saw him in my dream and I knew, in my dream I knew, that I was close to banishing his existence to a memory. Then, he pressed a finger against my forehead and told me to wake up, and I did. And when I awoke, I found Kira cleaning a wound on my head. Kira, a stranger I'd never met before, helping me without concern for his own safety and with no expectation of payment."

Lyse rose and looked straight up at the sky. "Why this boy, you ask? Because I don't want to forget again."

He went over to the bucket of pig's blood, lifting it as effortlessly as if it had been one of the pebbles he had been rolling around in his hand, and began making his way back to the house.

Sa called out to him. "Will you tell the boy?"

Lyse stopped walking, but he did not turn. "Tell him what, exactly?"
"About Osette."

Putting the bucket down, Lyse stalked up to Sa and glared at him through angry eyes. "You wish Kira to know about Osette? That they would see him dead without so much as a gesture of help? Is *that* what you want me to tell him?"

"Do not mock me, my brother. If the boy knows, he may tell us more, perhaps even reveal the master of that Doll. He certainly did not make it, and its master must be truly powerful to make a Doll so lifelike that not even Osette and the others recognized it as one. Also . . . his claim that he can rot with just his touch is an ability that I have never heard of before in a Deadbringer. It worries me."

Lyse waved Sa off. "Then go ahead and tell Kira. I won't stop you. So, go on and break the boy."

Sa reached for one of the water buckets and, taking a large bowl, began washing the dead pig down. "You've made your point. Still, I pray to the gods that the boy never learns how to craft a Doll like that wretched thing or decides to take up with a Deadbringer of such skill."

"Well then," said Lyse, even as he began walking back to the house, "it's a good thing I will be traveling with him."

INNOCENCE LOST

ᛕIRA HAD AWOKEN that morning in the Labyrinth of the Cursed with a Doll who hated him and a strange man he barely knew. Before the sun had traveled to the middle of the sky, he had found himself in a town that the day before he had not known existed. By evening, he had been faced with his death, found kindness from strangers, and even come to terms, of a sort, with Teemo. All this had happened in the span of one day.

That day was not yet over.

The sun had given way to the moon, and Kira found himself standing beside the very man whom a few hours before had nearly taken his life. Together they stood side by side in a dell set amid the rocky towers not far to the west of Sa's home. It seemed fitting, considering that he had first met Lyse among the towers of the Labyrinth.

"Were you able to sleep?" Lyse asked lazily, blowing a puff of smoke from his pipe. The tobacco smell reminded Kira of cinnamon, and unexpectedly the memory of Elia's little kitchen appeared vividly in his mind's eye. He saw her sitting at the table, holding onto her cup of coffee with frail hands that had never ceased to surprise him with what they were capable of. He wondered how she was doing.

"No," Kira answered. "Every time I closed my eyes, I would dream that my uncle was alive and that we were back in the parlor. In the dream I kept telling myself that it was a dream, because I remembered the anguish I felt upon realizing that I had lost him. Yet, despite that, the first thing I did when I woke up was to look for him."

Lyse drew deeply from his pipe and looked all around, as if searching for someone. Then, after a long moment, he exhaled, and his features became lost in a haze of smoke.

"You never had a chance to mourn, did you?"

"No. And now that I can, I don't know how." Kira laughed then, bitterly. "How pathetic I must seem to you."

Lyse shook his head in disagreement. A few strands of dark hair pulled free from his braid, coming to rest on the right side of his face. "You evaded the Sanctifiers, you survived the Spears, and you survived me. I'm surprised by how well you handled this day's events. Not many would have."

"Maybe it's because I don't have a choice. If I allow myself to fall apart now, I'm not sure if I'll be able to get back up." Kira regretted the words almost instantly and felt his heart ache, as if they had somehow bound him and were squeezing his throat tightly. Not wanting Lyse to sense his discomfort, he turned and moved away from the man.

All around him, the Labyrinth's towers obscured the night sky, plunging the dell into deep darkness. Yet, among the many towers, alone and out of place, a single one of the dark obelisks that had so unsettled Kira earlier stood gleaming in the moonlight. It seemed almost as if it wanted to be found. Almost unconsciously, he made his way toward it, then stopped a few yards away.

His desire to touch it, to feel its texture and temperature, was so strong that his fingers ached, but he did not trust himself to go any closer. As foolish as the thought was, it came to him that if the lone obelisk could move, it would go out to search for its companions—for its friends.

Then Eutau's face flashed in front of his, and the land lurched. *To search for its friends . . .*

Vaguely, Kira smelled the cinnamon smoke and felt his shoulder being shaken gently from behind.

"Kira?" asked Lyse, his voice concerned.

He turned to face the man. "I swore I would keep my uncle safe, but I failed."

"Do you blame yourself?"

A memory surfaced then, of Eutau warning him about revealing his true nature to Sal back when he had first assisted the Bastion. And though he could not remember the exact words that had been spoken that day, he remembered Eutau's anxiety and the turmoil etched on his face—the look of a man who knew what was to come.

If I had listened to him that day none of this would have happened, and he would still be alive! Kira's aching heart broke as the next words crept into his mind. *It's all my fault.*

"Wallowing in regrets will only hurt you and keep you from moving forward," said Lyse, filling the silence, as if somehow reading Kira's mind.

Kira pounded his fist against his chest, digging his gloved fingers into his coat. "Then how do I stop this pain?" he cried. "How do I stop blaming myself?"

Lyse took a step back, as if surprised by the sudden outburst. Then a deep sorrow marred his countenance, and he turned away. In that instant, Kira remembered what Lyse had said about his own loss, and shame washed over him. *I'm not the only one who has lost someone dear to them,* he thought miserably.

"I'm sorry," he said.

"For what?" Lyse asked quietly.

"For being selfish, weak."

Lyse laughed softly, sadly. "You are not weak."

"If I were strong, I wouldn't have gone on like this." As Kira spoke, he heard Lyse suck in air through his teeth and then slowly breathe it out. It was an odd habit.

"Kira," began Lyse, still looking away, "what do you plan to do once you leave Ghlande?"

"Plan?" asked Kira, surprised by the change of subject. It hurt to recall the plans he and Eutau had made within that great trunk in the Spears, the last time they had really spoken to each other. "Our goal was to reach Florinia."

"Does *your* goal remain the same?"

My goal? Kira thought about this for a moment. With Eutau gone, his decisions had now become his own to make, and he could do anything, go wherever he wanted.

Wherever I want . . .

He threw the thought aside. "*My* goal is to reach Florinia."

Lyse turned back and faced Kira, a warm smile touching not only his full lips but also his eyes. "And you say you are weak? Foolish boy. If I were your uncle, I would be proud of you."

Tears unbeckoned began to stream down Kira's face, and with his palm he wiped them away, telling himself, willing himself not to cry. But the tears continued to flow and he slunk away, feeling ashamed. His face felt numb, his chest tight, and he suddenly found himself struggling to remember how to breathe. But then a hand, foreign yet familiar, settled gently on his shoulder, and in a strange way he felt as if he had been granted permission to let go of the knot of pain and guilt that had been consuming him since Eutau had died.

Kira cried for some time, unaware of his surroundings, unaware that he had curled into a ball on the ground and that Lyse was kneeling beside him with eyes downturned, his mouth a tight line. Finally, when the well of tears had dried up and the ache in his heart had quieted, Kira broke the silence.

"When I was a boy, my uncle told me about the Labyrinth and the story of the Battle of the Cursed. The story fascinated me, and I used to daydream about it, and even entertained the idea that I would one day cross the Great Knife to see it. From there I would wander my way south to one of the port towns, maybe even charter a ship to the Southern Islands."

"You can still wander the Land," said Lyse.

Kira laughed harshly and sat up. "I don't have a choice now, do I? But it will be more fleeing and hiding, and less wandering and exploring."

"The best place to hide is in plain sight."

"That makes no sense," said Kira, shaking his head and laughing in earnest this time. It felt good to laugh.

Lyse took a seat next to him, unruffled. "Live long enough and it will. Besides, the alternative — living in fear, living as the victim — is far worse. In that case, I should have lopped your head off and saved you the misery of your existence."

Kira ran his hand around his neck and shot Lyse a sideways glance. "I'm starting to get the impression you might regret not having done so."

"I rarely regret my decisions," said Lyse, with a knowing smile. "So, what do you think of the Labyrinth now that you have seen it?"

"I think, 'why would anyone want to live here?'" A sudden thought came to Kira then, one that he could not resist asking. "Lyse, do you know anything about the Battle of the Cursed?"

The man smiled as if he had been given a challenge that he could not refuse. Pursing his lips, he began tapping his fingers along them, visibly pondering the question. Then, after a few seconds, his eyes lit up and he stopped. Clearing his throat, he took a deep breath and began speaking in an almost lyrical tone.

"The Battle of the Cursed: it was one of the battles that turned the tide of the First War in favor of the people of the Land. For before the Great Knife had been thrown up and the face of the Western Mountains altered, there lay a wide country between the Spears and the mountains, a land of rolling plains and towns, a great nation filled with people. I forget its name now, but they were friendly with all, and through them the North and South were connected, made one. Back then, the Land was truly one land. Traders and travelers had no need to resort to the Sea or to brave the hair-raising paths of the Western Mountains. Ghlande lies at the southern edge of what was once that country."

He paused for a moment before continuing. "But the Ro'Erden realized that this nation was the key to separating North and South. In their long war they often sought to fracture the people and the Land, and so they attacked, claiming the country for themselves. It was to be their doom. For the people of that nation had a long and proud history to maintain, and so they resisted, and they fought, and they died, but not before they had killed many Ro'Erden.

"The Ro'Erden were weakened, and they were destroyed when the armies of North and South came at them, too late to save this country, though not too late for revenge. But in the process" — he waved a hand toward the towers and the lone obelisk, a grim look settling upon his face — "the memory the people had fought and died to preserve was forgotten, and nothing was ever the same."

Kira looked on, mesmerized. He had heard a version of the story from Eutau, but never had he heard it told in such a fashion or with such familiarity. Indeed, he was about to ask how Lyse knew so much, but then his thoughts were swept away.

"And," cried Lyse and stood up, suddenly and dramatically, as if knowing that his version of the story was unlike any other and wishing to do it justice, "there is a greater reason why this area is referred to as 'cursed.' For the Battle of the Cursed was the final battle of that wretched campaign, and here the Ro'Erden forces made their last stand. Either the Land has forgotten it or has chosen to ignore it, but encased within each obelisk is the body of one of those long-dead Ro'Erden."

Reality slapped Kira hard on the face, and he found his eyes seeking the lonesome obelisk. He scrambled to his feet and stared at it as if he were seeing it for the first time, and suddenly the sensation of being watched gripped him, and he recognized it as the sense of oppression that had weighed on him upon seeing the first obelisk the day before. He wanted to blame his imagination but knew better than to dismiss the dead so lightly. He felt again the urge to touch the obelisks, and he shuddered.

"How can you be sure of this?" he asked, desperate to know how Lyse had come by such knowledge.

"Sa learned this lore from his partner and he told me of it, though I had already heard it from someone else. To the Ro'Erden, the history of the Battle of the Cursed is seen with very different eyes, and their interpretation of history is not the same as ours. To them, this area is sacred — for many of their kin died here — but it is also tainted, for so often in that war those very same kin were brought back by

Deadbringers and used against them. It is for this last reason that they avoid this area."

"But then why did Sa and Telera's mother come to live here?" asked Kira. "She was Ro'Erden, wasn't she?" Unexpectedly, as if realizing he had said too much, Lyse fell silent. A sudden understanding dawned on Kira. *They're hiding! But why?* And then another thought occurred to him, one that he could not ignore.

"Lyse," he began, "who were those people we met earlier?"

"Who?"

"Osette, and the others in Sa's house."

"Ah. What about *him*?"

"Well, it's just that, they seemed scared — almost panicked — even before we arrived, and then even more so after Osette wanted to accuse me of being the Deadbringer from Opulancae."

"Deadbringers are loathed and feared. You of all people should be very familiar with this." Lyse seemed annoyed, and Kira was suddenly reminded of how Kim Lafont acted toward people he did not like, especially when he wanted to skirt an issue.

Kira pushed on. "Of course I am. But that man, Osette, when our eyes locked I saw a fear in them that I had only ever seen in—" He faltered then, aware that he had been about to say that he had only ever seen that kind of fear in the dying eyes of the agents he and Eutau had been forced to kill. He pushed the thought aside and instead said, "Osette was terrified of the Ascendancy. But why?"

Lyse made a chiding sound with his tongue. "That man and his lot are spineless and not worth your consideration. I will not waste my time speaking of him. Instead, I want to ask you something."

Kira hesitated, surprised at having been so rudely cut off but also unsure if he was saying too much. "Sure," he said.

"I have wanted to ask you this question since discovering that you are a Deadbringer. Standing here — among these obelisks, among the long-dead Ro'Erden — do you *feel* anything?"

The question blindsided Kira. *How could he have known?* But even as the question formed in his mind, the answer formed along with it. *The man is a wanderer, and not young. He has learned things about Deadbringers that not even my uncle knew.* He thought back to Lyse's familiarity with northern and southern customs, to his knowledge of Ghlande and the people of the Koyohal, and to his recognition of Teemo as a Doll. The man was unquestionably learned.

Kira looked down at the tips of his worn-out boots. *I want someone to confide in even if it's only until I leave Ghlande. And I — I want to trust Lyse.* He knew the thought sounded foolish given that he had just barely met the man, but Lyse made him feel at ease. And, unlike Teemo, Lyse did not mock him at every turn. He made his decision.

"Yes. Ever since entering the Labyrinth I have felt as if someone is watching me."

Lyse nodded slowly, as if digesting what Kira had said. "I suppose your uncle was the one who guided you?"

"Sort of."

"Sort of? Was he not a Deadbringer?"

"No. He was a *moma*, and I suppose the same is true of my mother, his sister. It was my father who was the Deadbringer. He was the one who was from the Western Mountains."

"You make it sound as if you never met your parents."

"I didn't. He died before I was born, and then she died giving birth to me. I never knew either of them."

Lyse sighed then, a slow, bitter sigh. "I did not know my mother either, and was raised by my mother's younger sister. But then she died as well, and everything changed."

Kira had not expected Lyse to tell him such a personal secret. In a strange way, it made him feel closer to the man. "I'm sorry. How old were you?"

"Twelve. As old as Telera is now." Lyse turned so as to get a better look at Kira. "And you? How old *are* you, anyway?"

"Fifteen. But people tend to think I'm older because of how tall I am."

"Then you were born during the height of the Purging? The task of caring for a child such as you must have been daunting. I suppose that your uncle was able to touch your skin without fear of injury?"

"Yes." Kira smiled fondly at the memory.

"Why was he taking you to Florinia? You do know it is the stronghold of the Ascendancy?"

"Of course. You know, I had forgotten, but I was the one to suggest it to him in the first place. But I did so because we had friends who lived there." Kira's brow furrowed in contemplation. "Now that I think about it, I think uncle might have agreed with me for very different reasons."

"Indeed, perhaps your uncle understood the concept of hiding in plain sight. And now," said Lyse, "we should head back. To speak honestly, I am not comfortable leaving Telera alone for so long with that Doll."

"Teemo said she would not leave the bedroom."

"And you believed it?"

"I think *she* will keep her promise to me," said Kira with all the confidence he could muster, which was not as much as he had hoped. Lyse shot him an incredulous glance but said nothing more.

They began making their way back, leaving the obelisk behind and slowly passing one dark tower after another. The moonlight seemed to brighten, but the night was getting very cold. Lyse said nothing for some time, and to Kira the man's silence seemed awkward, though he could not tell why. It was several more minutes before Lyse spoke again.

"Earlier you mentioned that you have friends in Florinia. Are they originally from the North as well?"

"No. But I was actually born in the South and lived my first years in Florinia, though I was too young to remember it clearly."

Lyse pursed his lips. "I spent some time in Florinia," he began, "perhaps ten or a dozen years ago. The city is large, but perhaps I met your uncle? What was his name?"

Kira exhaled slowly and said Eutau's full name for the first time since his death. "Eutau Vidal. And I would prefer not to talk about him. Not yet."

"Very well," said Lyse, falling silent again.

They had left the last of the Labyrinth's towers behind and Sa's home had at last come into view, a solid dot of light that grew ever larger as they walked. A low wind greeted them, bringing with it the aroma of savory food. Kira's mouth watered and he placed a hand over his stomach, eager to eat and drink until he burst. He looked over at Lyse, expecting to see him as excited as Kira himself felt, but Lyse was fixated on filling his pipe with tobacco, oblivious to the wonderful smell.

It was at that moment that Kira caught the sound of voices. At first the words were broken and incoherent, but as he strained to listen to what was being said, one of the voices became familiar. It was the man from earlier, Osette. And, suddenly, the words became unmistakably clear.

". . . should become aware of who we are! I find it hard to believe that Lyse did not bring him here on purpose." At the mention of his name, Lyse stopped dead in his tracks, his pipe falling from his mouth to the ground.

"Are you there, Sa?" called out Lyse in a strong, loud voice.

A moment passed and then, "Brother?" It was Sa.

"Yes," he called back, "and Va'lel is with me." Lyse emptied the tobacco back into its pouch and then placed it and the pipe, which he quickly scooped from the ground where it fell, into a pocket sewn in the interior of his coat. He ran his fingers along the base of his hairline, pushing back a few rogue strands that were sticking forward haphazardly.

"Let's go," he said to Kira, not at all pleased. "By the sounds of it, I will have my chance to personally warn Osette to stop getting in my way."

Kira nodded in agreement, but his mind was uneasy. *Is something wrong? Lyse called out to Sa and Osette to warn them. Why?* The thought he had had earlier crept back into his mind and seized him. *Why is Osette so obsessed with the appearance of Deadbringers?*

Sa, Osette, and a third, unfamiliar man were standing outside the house, their faces bathed in the light that shone from inside. Sa and Osette appeared calm and indifferent to Kira and Lyse's sudden appearance, but the other man appeared ready to snap.

"Brother," said Sa, his smile apologetic, "forgive me for having kept you waiting."

Lyse shot Sa an eyeful and then turned his attention to Osette. "Stay out of my sight." His tone was venomous, and the words sent a chill up Kira's spine.

Osette's eyes tightened angrily. "With pleasure. My business with Sa is done. We're leaving." He touched the other man lightly on the shoulder. "Let's go home, Victor." They turned, and Kira realized that both men were doing their best to ignore him. It struck him as odd, particularly after the way Osette had treated him.

"Wait," called Kira, but neither Osette nor his companion turned to look at him. Instead—and Kira was certain that it was not his imagination—they quickened their pace.

"Let's head inside," Sa said eagerly. "My poor daughter must be famished. It took too long for me to prepare our meal. I must warn you that she is quite a sight to behold when it comes to eating."

Lyse came to her defense. "There is nothing wrong with eating with your hands."

"You only say that because you do as much yourself," Sa shot back.

Everyone's trying to distract me! Why? Why! Kira began walking after the two departing men.

Lyse called to him. "Va'lel. Let's go."

I can't. I can't! Kira broke into a run and stopped only when he had come close enough for Osette and the other man, Victor, to hear his words. From behind, he heard Lyse and Sa charging headlong after him. But it was too late.

"You and everyone who was here earlier are Deadbringers, aren't you?"

Osette halted, his back stiffening, his shoulders visibly tensing. Quickly, his hand reached out to grab Victor, but Victor was no longer there. The man had pulled a dagger from his belt and was charging at Kira, his face misshapen by fear.

Perhaps because his body still remembered the wound it had suffered earlier that day, Kira found himself instinctively reaching for the dagger sheathed within his boot. But, before he could draw it, Osette had tackled Victor from behind. Both men fell the ground.

"You idiot! What are you doing?" yelled Osette, his face contorted with rage.

"He heard us! He knows!" shrieked Victor, struggling to break free.

"If the boy was unsure, your antics have dispelled all doubts!"

Victor's strength left him as the truth of Osette's words sunk in. "I— I didn't . . ." He sunk to his knees, the fight gone from him.

Osette let Victor go and stood to face Kira.

"Please," he began, his voice angry yet sad, "he wished you no harm. None of us wish you harm. We just want to be left alone."

"Then," Kira said slowly, "you, he, *are* Deadbringers?"

"*Don't.*" Lyse's voice came in a violent whisper. Osette looked at Lyse and then back to Kira.

"You are strangely calm for someone who is face to face with a Deadbringer." Then his eyes widened in realization. "So it is true"—he pointed a finger at Kira—"that you are indeed one yourself, like we suspected earlier. The Deadbringer from Opulancae."

Kira had dreamed of this moment, of meeting his own kind, for his entire life. But now that the moment had arrived, he found himself terrified beyond comprehension. Still, he had dared to come this far, and he felt his heart rise in a kind of trembling joy.

"Yes. I'm a Deadbringer as well. Like you."

"*No!*" Victor said desperately, staring furiously at Kira as he rose to his feet. "You're *the* Deadbringer from Opulancae. You're the one everyone is looking for. You, not us! *You.*"

"Victor," Osette said sharply, moving quickly to put himself between the man and Kira. A terrible madness had filed Victor's eyes, and for a moment it seemed that he would charge again.

"How can you be so cruel?" said Victor. "Don't you have any feelings?"

Kira's mouth hung open in dismay. He tried to respond, but could only gasp, "What?"

"'What,' he asks. 'What!' I saw you in that room, with that girl. They say you fled the North with your kin, a man, but that was no man standing beside you. Did you leave him behind for a pretty face or did you use him to buy yourself time?"

"No!" said Kira, outraged.

With a sneer, Victor eyed him from head to toe and then let out a disgusted laugh. "Now that you know who we are, do you intend to use us to barter for your life?"

"I did *not* betray my uncle, and I would *never* betray a fellow Deadbringer!"

"Pretty words are just pretty words, boy."

Kira had endured enough. "You have no *idea* what I have been through," he hissed.

"Then why are you here? Do you wish to take us down with you?"

"I didn't even know there were Deadbringers here!"

"Victor!" shouted Osette, pulling the man back. "That's enough!"

But Victor would not listen. "Why did you have to come? WHY!" He screamed like a wounded animal, spittle flying from his mouth, his eyes wild with a despair that struck Kira deeper than anything the man had said.

"I won't let you take my family away from me! I won't let you ruin our lives!"

Osette grabbed Victor roughly by the shoulders and pulled him away from Kira. "Victor!" he called, but the man would not stop turning his head to stare at Kira. Osette called again, his voice trembling now with fear of his own. "Please, Victor," he pleaded. "Look at me. Please, look at me!" As if from afar, Kira watched as the madness in Victor's eyes faded and tears began running down his cheeks. Osette pulled Victor toward him then, embracing him tightly.

"It's alright," he said. "If Sa trusts him, then we should put our trust in him as well. This boy will not give us to the Sanctifiers."

"But what if he is caught?" Victor whimpered. "We have nowhere to go! I don't want to run again. Not again."

"We won't. This is our home and it will remain that way."

"How can you be so sure? How!"

Osette shook his head and let out a short, sad laugh. Then he took in a deep breath as if he also was struggling not to fall apart. He let go of Victor and turned to face Kira.

"I can imagine what you have been through. I can." His voice cracked, and he fought not to look away. "I wish we could help, but please understand that we cannot take that risk. We have managed to build a life here. Please, I'm begging you, please let us be."

Lyse was suddenly there in front of Osette, furious. "You expect this boy to have pity on you and yours, yet you have none to show for him." He spat at Osette's feet. "Whether Kira—yes, Kira, that's his real name— stays or leaves is *not* up to you. If Sa is willing—"

"Sa must speak on his behalf," said Osette. "Even if I speak in this boy's favor, the others would only listen to Sa."

Before anyone could say another word, Kira swallowed the knot that had lodged itself in his throat, and then he spoke.

"I"—his voice quivered, and he breathed in deeply to steady it— "you have nothing to fear. I promise I will keep your existence secret. And I promise I will leave come sunrise, and will never return."

Osette let out a long-held sigh of relief. He managed a weak smile. "Thank you. You have our gratitude."

And it was over. The wind had stopped, and the sounds of the night had disappeared. Everything was still save the sound of the footfalls slowly walking away forever. Kira watched in despair as Osette and Victor walked together back to their homes, back to their kin.

For as long as Kira could remember, he had dreamed of meeting other Deadbringers. In his fancies, the moment was always one of utmost joy and freedom, for it would mean that he would no longer be alone and would no longer have to hide. But it had only been a fantasy, a dream that he had awoken from and would dream no more.

THE NEXT MORNING, Kira bid farewell to Sa and Telera. Sa had offered to take Kira in regardless of Osette's wishes, but Kira had refused. He had already given his word. Seeing that Kira could not be deterred, Sa had told him of dangers he might meet along the way and of the paths that he should travel to avoid possible checkpoints set up by the Ascendancy. When Kira asked him how he was aware of such things, Sa's face filled with such sorrow that Kira did not have the heart to inquire further.

Telera also seemed saddened by Kira's departure, but there was a glimmer in her peach eyes that he did not quite understand, as if she was keeping a secret. But she would not speak to him, except to wish him luck and to tell him that she hoped they would meet again.

Kira thanked them for their kindness and for giving him a place in their home and at their table. In turn, they gave him their blessing, calling on names of gods he had never heard of and which he would not remember after leaving. And though he did not believe in the gods, he graciously accepted the blessing, for Sa and Telera had filled his bag and Teemo's with rice, dried meat, and rice wine. Then he and Teemo left, the two of them walking south across open fields, following Sa's directions so that they could return straight to the Silent River while avoiding Ghlande itself.

Of Lyse there had been no sign.

Kira's heart was heavy, and he regretted being unable to say farewell to Lyse and thank him for his aid. Teemo, on the other hand, had been relieved that the man was nowhere in sight. Once they were out of earshot of Sa's house, she reassured Kira that Lyse's missing companionship was no loss. He thought of her words to him the night before and said nothing. But a couple hours later, as they finally neared the Silent River, he saw a man crouching along its banks. A long braid that resembled a spine encased by a ribcage trailed down his back. Beside him were two wineskins and a travel pack.

Somewhere in the distance Kira thought he heard Teemo protesting, but his attention was solely on the man, who had turned to face him with smiling amber eyes.

A DIFFERENT KIND OF GAME

E'SINEA HAD AWOKEN miserable and ill—his stomach distended, the color of his skin paler than usual, his mood dour and sensitive. In short, he felt like shit. It was a terrible way to begin a voyage at sea, but there was not much he could do about it except lean over the timber rails of the ship's stern and throw up again, and again, and again.

From the moment the ship had departed the calm waters of the Idle Bay to begin its journey south toward Florinia, Kristoff had remained with him, holding onto his waist so he could lean over the rails without a care. But now, now he was alone, sitting slumped against those very same rails, watching Kristoff make his way to the main deck. E'sinea wrapped his arms around his stomach and rested his hands on the sides of his waist where Kristoff's hands had been just moments before. Even through his gloves he could feel the warmth.

Kristoff could have hurt him, could have flung him over the stern and into the Eastern Sea, and no one would have noticed or cared. But instead, Kristoff had asked him how he was doing and had refused to leave until he was feeling better. Kristoff had said and done all the right things. He had made E'sinea feel not alone.

Only you, he thought, dispirited. *I have only ever trusted you. But if I trust Kristoff now, then why didn't I answer him when he asked about the room?*

His thoughts wandered back to his room at the Unbroken Spar. Its walls had been blackened in places as if scorched and blanched in others as if the color had been drained. There had been an unpleasant smell like raw meat that had been left out on a hot summer day. He had gotten carried away. The innkeeper had demanded an explanation, but E'sinea had responded by swiping a finger across his neck. After that, the innkeeper had quickly excused himself and left E'sinea alone.

As for Kristoff . . . once aboard the ship, he had inquired about the room, and so E'sinea had given him an answer. It had not been the response Kristoff had expected, but he had not asked E'sinea again.

If I tell Kristoff and Mar Mar the truth, they will see me as a monster! I can't tell them, I can't! But if I stay with them, it will only be a matter of time before they see. He raised a finger up to the midday sun, blocking it from view. *You can only hide the sun for so long.*

The thought depressed him, for he did not want the siblings to hate him. He made to rise, longing to get away from the salty sea air and lie down on the bed in their cabin, but his stomach protested and he quickly sat back down, clasping his hands over his eyes, desperately hoping that the wave of nausea would pass and that he would not have to throw up again. Then the sound of footfalls caught his ears, and he wondered if Kristoff had returned. But the voice that spoke to him was a girl's.

"I brought you aerated salt dissolved in water to help calm your stomach."

Curious to see who had come to pester him, E'sinea hastily looked up. The strong sea wind beat at him, pushing his bangs aside and exposing his whole face. Instinctively, he snapped his head toward the deck and began combing his bangs back down with his fingers. *Stay in place!* he thought fiercely.

He looked up at the girl, expecting her to be repulsed—everyone who had ever caught a glimpse of his full face seemed unable to let it be—but the girl had been staring at the sea and had not noticed. E'sinea counted his blessings and used the opportunity to study her.

The girl was young, with mousy, unkempt hair that moved about wildly in the wind. She had ears that were too large for her face and her cheeks, lips, and nose were chapped and flaking from the chill sea wind. Her pants were rolled up to her knees, exposing pale, skinny calves, while the long sleeves of her thick cotton blouse and woolen short-coat were held in place over her elbows with a string. Both were as unkempt as her hair. She could not have been older than thirteen, but E'sinea knew that age was nothing more than a lie.

"What do you want?" he asked sourly.

The girl stirred, as if she had awoken from a deep trance, and then turned to face him.

Her eyes! thought E'sinea, startled, as he looked upon blue irises so crystal-clear that he felt as if he could drown in them. She had no pupils.

The girl held up a green goblet of pressed glass. "It's aerated salt in water. Here"—she brought the glass to her cracked lips and took a short drink—"I know it's the same stuff used to scrub teeth, sails, floors, and about everything else, but a little bit in water does help. It's always helped me, especially on days when the gales are nasty."

E'sinea cocked his head to one side, unsure whether to accept the girl's aid. But then his stomach protested again, and the feeling of sickness returned.

"Fine," he grumbled, as he accepted the glass and took a sip. At first he was certain he would be unable to keep the water down, but then the moment passed and he took another slow sip.

"I knew it would help!" the girl said gleefully. He said nothing, expecting her to leave. But she did not. Instead, she continued talking. "It must be rough being a servant for a Sanctifier."

E'sinea almost choked on the water and felt a bit come up unpleasantly through his nose. *Servant?* he thought. A part of him wanted to laugh until his sides burst; another wanted to snap the girl's neck and roll her severed head across the deck. He took several sips, waiting to answer until he was certain there would be no hint of anger in his voice.

"If the master is kind," he began, deciding that he would play along, "then the life of a servant is not that bad."

The girl shook her head in disbelief. "If you say so. The big Kataru seemed concerned about your health."

He said nothing. *Why is she still here? I answered your stupid question. Shoo, shoo, go away!* But the girl did not go away. Instead, she sat down next to him. E'sinea scooted away, putting some distance between them. He did not want someone so close.

"Are they kind?" she asked, either unaware of his agitation or simply too stupid to notice. "Sanctifiers have a reputation of being nasty, and Katarus are known to have bad tempers. Seems lose-lose to me."

E'sinea was outraged. *What does she know? This girl knows nothing about me or Kristoff and Mar Mar!*

"Says a girl from the swamp!" he spat, and then bit the inside of his lower lip. *Shit on a stick. That's not what I meant to say!*

The girl looked at him, her eyes becoming large pools of water. "How did you know?"

What am I supposed to say now? That I guessed? He pulled at his braid hard enough to make himself wince. *Oh, why isn't Amonos here to keep people away from me!*

"I've been to Silfria," he said at last, "and seen those very same eyes." His voice became low then, almost a whisper. "They were the beggars on the corners. Adults, children . . . small children staring off with vacant, hungry eyes. None of them spoke Moendan, but they begged nonetheless."

The girl looked away and brought her legs close to her chest. "Most people think I'm a *moma*. The few that figure out I'm Koyohal either laugh at me by asking if I can read or then just ignore my race. Out of pity, I guess."

"And *can* you read?" asked E'sinea, suddenly wanting to wound her, though he knew not why.

"I've gotten good at reading, but writing . . . why aren't these words spelled the way they sound? But I speak it good enough. And I don't have much of an accent anymore, right?"

E'sinea let go of his braid and began fidgeting with the laces of his boots. To his surprise, his stomach was feeling better. "You shouldn't feel bad," he began reluctantly. He had forgotten how hard it had been to learn Moendan. "The Leodians are treated badly as well. But at least the Koyohal don't sell their own. They keep their children next to them and beg or work jobs no one else wants to do just so they can stay alive *together*. And I think that's very nice."

Why did I say that? he wondered. *Why do I now want to make her feel better?*

The girl looked at him thoughtfully. "While the ship was docked in the Idle Bay, back in Jané, I saw a Leodian. Older woman, with a long, white braid."

"Oh, really! Where?" he asked, suspecting it was the same servant woman that he had met at the Unbroken Spar.

"My boot needed patching." She pointed to the underside of her left boot. "That's where I saw her. We sat next to each other, waiting our turn, or so I thought."

"What do you mean?" he asked, curious.

"The shoemaker was busy measuring this little girl's feet. She was really young, no more than five, I'd say. Everything about her — her dress, her coat — was new and nice, but not puff-puff. And she spoke Moendan, no problems at all. When the shoemaker was done, the girl walked back to the Leodian woman and that's when I saw it — her hair! The girl's hair was dyed, but the roots were as white as a flower's petals. Just like the woman's. The resemblance was obvious too. They were mother and daughter, but the woman had said she was the girl's nana."

E'sinea suppressed a smile, for the woman had told him the truth in Jané, and this strange girl's words confirmed it. It had not been a lie as he had feared, and he no longer felt the fool for having given her so much of his money. A strange feeling settled over him. It was warm and comforting but, above all, sad.

"I met her as well," he said. "We were staying at the Unbroken Spar and she works there, and servants like to talk to each other and all that. She told me she had fled the caravans because she did not want her daughter to be a *pé'bos*. Or sold."

"Sold? The Leodians don't sell their own unless they are orphans," the girl said matter-of-factly.

E'sinea stopped pulling at his laces. The woman had been so nice, so very nice. "She's dying. A wasting illness from her years as a *pé'bos*."

They both remained quiet after that revelation, almost as if their pity alone could reach out and save her. But E'sinea was not arrogant enough to believe that he could save anyone.

If Amonos had been with me, I would've never been able to speak with her. I would've never known. He felt an immense guilt at thinking of Amonos in such a way, especially since Amonos thought only of him. But in the time since Amonos had left he had come to know the siblings in a way that he knew would not otherwise have been possible. He had spent time talking with a Leodian woman, and he had even supped and toasted with Ro'Erden. And now he had spent the last half hour speaking with a new girl he had just met.

He downed the last of the remedy and then used his coat to wipe clean the rim of the glass. "Thank you," he said sincerely, "it really helped."

The girl accepted the glass. "Would you be interested in playing a game with me?" she asked.

E'sinea felt the corners of his lips twitch. "What kind of game?"

"A board game. Nobody on the ship likes to play with me because they say it's a child's game. But I don't like card games." A deep red tinged her cheeks. "I have a hard time counting unless I can use my fingers."

"It's been a while since I've played a board game. Paper and rocks, or an actual board with pieces?"

"A board with *wooden* carved pieces," she said with pride.

I think I would like to play. He nodded quickly, afraid that if he hesitated he would come up with an excuse. "Okay, but not today. Maybe tomorrow?"

A large smile lit up her face. "Ohhkay! I have a few chores and can't do much until the Captain says I'm done. Also, I help in the kitchen. But, after, can I knock on your cabin?" She stiffened. "If it's okay with your masters, the Sanctifiers, that is?"

He laughed softly. "They won't mind."

"If all goes well on the ship I'll come by tomorrow," said the girl, beaming. "But if you can't sleep, or want to talk, or need anything, just ask for Lan."

"That's not a normal Koyohal name."

The girl gave a bashful laugh. "It's actually Huaslan, but nobody ever calls me that."

"You give your real name, then?"

"Of course! I'm very proud of who I am and don't care what others think. But that doesn't mean I don't know when and when not to rub it in people's faces. What should I call you by?"

He considered giving her a false name but then thought better of it. He too was rather fond of his name — after all, it was the name his mother had given him — and he was unexpectedly excited at the prospect of seeing the girl again. "It's E'sinea. And you may come bother me whenever you wish."

"Ohhkay!" Huaslan stood, waved goodbye, and then broke into a run, darting toward the main deck and then the bow. E'sinea smiled sadly and buried his head in his arms, though he no longer felt ill. His thoughts wandered back to Amonos.

"So this is what a life without you would be like."

HOW IS E'SINEA doing?" asked Marya. She was sitting on one of the three narrow bunks in the passenger cabin, brushing out her long, curly hair. She wore red trousers that were cut close to her legs and a long-sleeved tunic the color of honey. The tunic was of sturdy wool and was draped loosely over her knees. A wide leather belt decorated her waist.

Kristoff closed the door behind him and crossed over to the small square of propped-up wood that served as the table. The smell of wax caught his nose and he cast his eyes down, toward the floor. To the right of the table he found their swords gleaming in the lantern light. He had spent only a few hours with E'sinea, yet Marya had managed to clean, sharpen, and wax not only their swords but their daggers as well. Her skill and speed with a whetstone had always impressed him. It had even impressed Amonos, who had initially been reluctant to let anyone touch his blades, though they were nothing special.

"Not well," he said, removing his heavy Sanctifier's cloak and draping it across the room's sole chair. He wore goatskin pants and a tanned leather vest that was lined with thick fur. His wavy hair hung down his back and around his pointed ears. He sat on the bed next to his sister. "I left him vomiting over the stern."

He scratched the sides of his beard as he spoke, annoyed at how much it still itched and how long he would have to wait until it grew past the scratchy stage. "I asked if he would confide in me what had happened in his room at the Unbroken Spar in Jané, but he threw my own words from before back at me."

"And what words were those?" she asked, putting the brush down.

"Only Fortune need know one's life from birth till death."

"We are accustomed to E'sinea apologizing for Amonos's actions, not us having to apologize to ourselves for his rudeness."

Kristoff glowered. "He still does not trust us."

"No. But trust takes time, and with Amonos gone E'sinea is hurt, maybe even scared." She crossed her arms under her breasts. "Despite how long we have ridden alongside them, we know very little about either E'sinea or Amonos. We do not know where they go when our campaigns are over, and they have always been cautious of their words, though E'sinea has been less so now that Amonos is gone. Still, I have never seen him this distraught before. Perhaps in his despair he lashed out at the room with those strange tears of his." Her gaze became distant. "I have never before seen an ability such as that, not from him or anyone."

Kristoff recalled how E'sinea's tears had caused the dirt to fume and tried to bore into his sword as if they were alive. It had been difficult to keep an impassive face. "E'sinea is unique. It is what I told Vas'tu at the Unbroken Spar. I thought I understood the measure of my words."

"We have always suspected that he is more powerful than he has let on and far older than he has been willing to admit. Otherwise, why would a self-absorbed ass like Amonos follow him?"

"Because Amonos is obsessed with E'sinea belonging to no one else but him, and E'sinea has allowed it even though he will tolerate no other Deadbringer. I must admit, their relationship troubles me. E'sinea is a mighty warrior; it has always sickened me to see Amonos shame him for enjoying the company of others."

"But now the possessive dog has abandoned E'sinea."

"I am sure it is only because Amonos is certain that when he returns E'sinea will forgive him, that E'sinea will push aside all he has gained just for him."

"I cannot believe that E'sinea would humiliate himself in such a way," said Marya, yet there was no mistaking the uncertainty in her voice.

"It depends how strong a hold Amonos has over him, and I fear that hold is great even though I have never been able to understand why. We have observed that E'sinea does not like to be alone, but his attachment to someone like Amonos cannot be due to simple loneliness."

Marya pondered Kristoff's words for several minutes before finally nodding to herself as if having reached a decision. She rose from the bed and went to the chair, straddling it and crossing her arms over her brother's cloak where it hung on the back of the chair. "Maybe," she began slowly, as if tasting each word, "we can give him a new apprentice. A new 'dog.'"

His eyes narrowed. "Go on."

"The Deadbringer from Opulancae."

Kristoff laughed, believing Marya had meant it as a joke. But then he saw the look on her face and knew that she meant what she said. His laughter morphed into a harsh snort. "Despite being a Deadbringer himself, E'sinea despises other Deadbringers. You know this. Else, why would he have become a Sanctifier?" Even as he spoke, the memory came to him. *I'm bored, Amonos.* That had been the reason E'sinea had given years before for why he was willing to aid in the genocide of his own. It had been a selfish and dishonorable reason.

"But with Amonos gone," Marya began anew, "E'sinea may be willing to talk to the boy. They are both scared, lost." She leaned forward in the chair, rocking it back and forth on its hind legs. "This is, of course, assuming that the boy did not meet his end within the Spears. And that Amonos has not decided to find the boy and kill him."

Kristoff felt as if the very room had darkened. *Fortune strike me blind for not having thought of this myself. Could Amonos have known about the Ten's orders?* He slapped his hand on his thigh, angry with himself for having overlooked something so obvious, and then instantly regretted doing so. Marya had risen from the chair, almost knocking it over, and was staring at him with knowing eyes.

"You have a secret. You're going to tell me." Her voice was iron. She was far too familiar with his habits. He hesitated, then barked a laugh and gestured for her to sit beside him again. She did as he bid and leaned in. "Well?" she asked quietly.

Kristoff studied his sister. *With Amonos absent and E'sinea in an unpredictable state, I may need help if I am to successfully carry out my mission.* Finally, he spoke. "You know our orders."

"Yes, yes," she said, frustrated, "find the Deadbringer in Opulancae and his kin and kill them both. But you received other orders, didn't you?"

He nodded and lowered his voice so that no hidden eavesdroppers could hear his words. "Later that same day, I was summoned and brought before the Ten."

She shot him a doubting look. "No one sees the Ten."

"I did not say that I *saw* the Ten, only that I was brought before them. Are you going to let me finish?" Abashed, the tips of her ears turned a deep red. He chuckled, making no attempt to mask his amusement. Continuing, he said, "The Ten want the boy for themselves.

I was ordered to take him aside upon finding him, to try to convince him that the Ascendancy means him no harm, that the Ten are willing to offer him sanctuary, and that he should join us. Only if my overtures failed were we to kill him."

Marya blinked a few times as if finding the order to be absurd. "E'sinea and Amonos—especially Amonos—would never have agreed to this."

"Then you understand why I alone was tasked with this mission."

"But why our band and not another? The Ten must have known that E'sinea and Amonos would seek to kill the boy, orders be damned."

"I can only guess the Ten gambled that our rebellious companions would obey my commands out of personal loyalty, while their power would be useful if combat became necessary. As for why our band was chosen in the first place, only you and I have traveled and fought together with Deadbringers. We alone among Sanctifiers are able to speak with the boy as a potential ally and friend." Kristoff sighed with frustration. "But Amonos is gone, and I fear that your words may come to pass. The Ten gambled too heavily on Amonos's loyalty to me."

"The gamble may not have been unreasonable. Ever since we met the two of them in that wretched cave years ago, they have never defied you. Even now, E'sinea continues with us. But, did the Ten at least tell you why they wanted the Opulancae brat over all the other Deadbringers that have emerged this past year?"

"No," Kristoff said flatly. "They were adamant about bringing this boy back alive, but they did not say why."

Marya studied him with the dark orbs that were her eyes—their mother's eyes. He watched as a vein on her forehead slowly grew and throbbed. She was angry. "The Ten are keeping us in the dark about this boy, just as they have kept us in the dark about affairs back home."

"I have not forgotten Meddo's words," he said gravely, for he felt the same anger as her. "But we have a mission to complete."

She laughed harshly. "Of course. A single lamb is to be plucked out of the flock being sent to slaughter, a single lamb that on the whim of the Ten will not meet the same end as the rest of its kind." There was a strange, sharp bitterness to her words that pricked uncomfortably at him.

Unable to shake the sensation, Kristoff rose from the bed and walked to where the swords lay on the floor. His eyes sought out his sword for comfort, but instead he saw a vision of E'sinea run through, dead. Dead, like so many other Deadbringers before him.

"We may be forced to engage Amonos," he said coldly. He heard Marya take a deep breath. She was fully aware of what that would mean.

"Then I suggest we sharpen not only our blades but also our skills. It won't be easy taking him down, but his death will be no great loss, if it comes to it."

He turned to face his sister. "And what of E'sinea?" He had tried his best to hold onto the cold, emotionless void, but he felt it slip painfully away.

Her words were fierce, desperate. "It will *not* come to that!"

Fortune hear your plea, little sister, Kristoff thought. *Fortune hear both our pleas.*

TO KILL A DEADBRINGER

THEY HAD BEEN at sea for almost a full week. As the days had passed, E'sinea had grown closer to the siblings, hearing stories of their youth and learning simple things about them—like that Marya used to enjoy hiding her father's belongings just to annoy him, or that Kristoff was skilled at weaving baskets and shearing sheep. He had also become closer to Huaslan, a stranger in comparison to the siblings, and had found himself spending most of his nights with her when he was not on watch or sleeping.

The first two days of the voyage had been painstakingly slow, and the daylight had seemed to last forever even though winter had long since driven summer away. E'sinea had spent the time in the passenger cabin talking with the Katarus. On the third day, however, Kristoff and Marya decided to break the monotony by rising with the sun, going up on deck, and alternating between swordplay and a form of hand-to-hand combat that involved swift footwork and a series of punches and strikes. E'sinea watched them for a while, though he did not join in.

On the morning of the fourth day, E'sinea had abruptly woken up from his sleep, drenched in a cold sweat that had soaked the bedsheets. He had been dreaming of Amonos, and yet it had not been Amonos. In the dream, E'sinea had been standing at a crossroads, and at the end of each path was the person who was and was not Amonos. E'sinea had racked his brain upon waking, trying to remember if he had made a choice, but to no avail. The vision of Amonos bothered him, and he had tried his best to forget the dream altogether.

The remainder of that day had come and gone like the rest—the siblings sparring, E'sinea staring at the sky and spending time with Pretty Mare—but after returning to his bunk from a long night of gaming with Huaslan, E'sinea had found that he could not sleep.

And so passed the fifth day, and the sixth day.

"Did you sleep last night?" asked Huaslan, on the evening of the sixth day, as she tried to muss her stiff hair. A ruckus of laughter and curses bellowed through the air, spilling over to the far corner of the cramped sailors' quarters. E'sinea did his best to ignore the rowdy sailors.

"No. I took watch instead, so the others could rest," he said, once the clamor had lessoned. He hated being down here. It was overcrowded and smelled of old piss and rancid beer. Above all, he hated when the sailors would crash into him as he made his way toward the corner where Huaslan had chosen to lay out the game. But Huaslan was here, so he was here as well. At first she had seemed fine playing the game in the Sanctifiers' cabin, as they had done for the first two nights. *No, that was a lie*, E'sinea reflected. She had never been comfortable with the Katarus around.

"The tea I made for you didn't help? Not even a little?" she asked, almost desperately.

He studied the cards in his hand, yearning to use one to his advantage, but all of them were useless. "Nope."

Huaslan's face fell. "Oh."

He looked up from his hand. "Try making it stronger. Disgustingly strong." Her bony shoulders slumped, and she reminded E'sinea of a reed wavering in the wind. "It's no big deal. I feel fine, honest!"

Gathering the bone dice, she placed them in the wooden dice cup and began shaking it. "I'll try that," she said, in a near-whisper. Her large, pupil-less eyes were glassy and her mouth was a tight line, as if she was thinking of something unpleasant.

E'sinea tugged at his braid. He wanted to know what was bothering her, but he was not in the habit of asking people how they felt. Still . . .

"Is something wrong?" he asked quietly.

At that moment, Huaslan slammed the dice cup on the floor, causing the pieces on the board to rattle. She lifted the cup, looked at the dice—a five and a three—and then began counting the carved holes one by one. "Eight," she said at last, and began moving her piece—a winged serpent with outstretched wings—eight spaces, leaving E'sinea three spaces behind.

"I'm in the lead now," she teased, and drew a new card from the game deck. Her face scrunched up in disappointment. "Not fair! I lost a turn."

He considered asking again what was bothering her but decided to let it be. If she wanted to pretend that nothing was wrong, then he would not take that away from her. He focused on the game.

"'bout time! Maybe now I can catch up."

She handed him the cup with the dice. "I hope not."

"You won last time. And the time before that and before that. I want to win for once."

"But I like winning!"

"And I don't like losing!" he responded. He shook the dice cup fiercely, eager for a number that would put him far in the lead. He slammed it on the floor and lifted it cautiously. "Yes!" he shouted, seeing the pair of sixes. But E'sinea felt victory slip away as he watched Huaslan pull a card from her hand.

"I play this card," she said, holding it up to his face. "Instead of moving forward all those number of holes you move back."

"No! You can't do that!"

She smiled with the utmost delight. "Go on, move your piece back."

He scanned his hand, hoping that he held a card that would negate hers. Nothing. Grabbing his piece—another winged serpent, but with its wings at rest—he grudgingly moved it back. Huaslan was now fifteen spaces ahead of him.

"I still have one more turn," he said, expecting her to say something clever. Instead, she remained quiet. "You have another card to use against me, don't you?" he asked. But she shook her head back and forth, her mousy, salt-crusted hair hardly moving.

E'sinea sighed and gathered the dice.

The game ended with Huaslan winning, though E'sinea had been only two spaces away from victory. It was the closest he had ever come to beating her.

"Are you mad?" she asked, after the game was over. Her voice held no mockery.

"Of course not, but I'd like to win for once. Well, we're still a week away from Florinia, so that still gives us time. Also, if you have time tomorrow, stop by and see my horse. Pretty Mare likes you and wants to see you again."

Huaslan's face suddenly crumbled, and again she looked almost on the verge of tears. "You've been all sad and forcing yourself to smile since I first saw you today," said E'sinea. "Did something happen?" he asked, breaking his promise to himself that he would not pry.

"No." Her eyes were traitorous, wavering pools. "I just wish the tea had worked. I really wanted you to sleep."

"I'm fine. Really." He stood, and Huaslan stood as well. She was an inch taller than him. He had not paid attention to such detail before, but he noticed it now.

"What are you gonna do now, E'sinea?" she asked. "Want to stay down here with me tonight? I can sleep on the floor and you take the bunk, since I know you don't like touching. We can talk and keep each other company. Maybe you'll fall asleep."

"I don't like it down here. And besides, Kristoff is waiting for me so I can keep watch. Why don't you come stay with me in the cabin?"

"I'm sorry. They're Sanctifiers. It's not seen with kind eyes to be with them so much."

He cocked his head. "And what of me?" he asked, far too coldly. Her words had irked him.

"You're just their pageboy," she laughed, "and a rather lazy one at that!"

"And if I were a Sanctifier, would you stop talking to me? Would you turn your back on me, so that you could continue to be seen with 'kind eyes'?"

Huaslan's laugh suddenly soured. "You'll come by tomorrow night, right?"

E'sinea struggled to contain his anger. "You didn't answer my question. But, yeah, *sure*, I'll come by."

Unexpectedly, Huaslan began cursing in her native tongue and stomping around in a circle as if she were having a fit. She huffed and swore to what E'sinea recognized as the name of the Koyohal god—the Serpent Rider—and then, without warning, she stepped over the game, closing the gap between them. She was close enough that he could feel her breath on his face. He forced himself not to step back or strike out at her. He was not used to having people so close to him, but he liked Huaslan, so he did not move.

"I wouldn't care if you were a Sanctifier because I like you for you, E'sinea. Please remember that."

He studied her face. There was a deep sincerity etched into the crease of her brow—and a layer of dirt. "You need a bath," he said bluntly.

A deep red washed over her face. "But it hasn't even been a month!"

"Ah. Well, you need a bath. There's dirt caked on your face. But your breath's nice."

"It's too cold to take a bath! Fine, fine, I'll splash some water on me. But you will come by tomorrow, yeah?"

He grinned. "I suppose." She shot him a dirty look and then stepped away. Crouching, she began gathering the game pieces and packing them away in a battered wooden box.

He had kept Kristoff waiting long enough. He made to go, but then Huaslan called out to him.

"E'sinea."

He turned to look at her. She was sitting on the floor. "Yes?"

"I'll come stay with you, if that's okay?"

"You said they wouldn't like that," he said, glancing at the sailors.

She looked up at him. "I don't care what they think. I want to spend time with you."

E'sinea did his best to hold back his joy but failed. Like a fool he grinned from ear to ear. He walked back to where she sat, stooped down, and began helping her pack away the game. "Let's go together, yes?"

Huaslan smiled. "Let's."

ON THE SEVENTH day, E'sinea sat leaning against the wooden rails at the stern, nibbling on a piece of bread glazed with crystallized honey, watching Kristoff and Marya spar. Despite the chill wind, the Katarus were stripped down to their waists, Marya with only an *atar* to bind her breasts. New welts from the morning and old bruises from days prior decorated their shoulders, arms, and the sides of their waists. Sweat dripped down their bronze skin, matting their hair to their pointed ears. The sun reflected off their polished gold earrings. Though their faces were cold, their eyes burned with a fierce passion as they effortlessly flowed from one strike to the next.

Stuffing the last of the bread in his mouth, E'sinea stretched out across the deck and then rolled onto his side so he could keep watching the Katarus. Then the wind carried the sound of a door closing, and he quickly looked up to see Huaslan running across the main deck toward the bow, where she began talking to three sailors. She had emerged from the Captain's cabin. E'sinea suppressed a giggle at the memory of her fast asleep on his bunk the night before, her mouth wide open and drool creeping down her chin.

Chink, clank, clink.

The sound of swords clashing drew his attention back to the Katarus. They had each bled themselves to forge blood-swords to spar with, an exercise that E'sinea recognized as an ancient tradition of the Herzmmen Clan, one designed to maintain its warriors' unique skills in forging blood-weapons while strengthening their endurance. For a few minutes he watched, and then he found himself predicting the next blow, and the next, and the next. He had begun to memorize their movements. That realization both comforted and bothered him. Deciding that he would no longer watch them fight, he rolled onto his back and instead focused on the cloudless blue sky and the sounds of the masts creaking, the waves roaring, the fabric of the sails stretching, the deck hands calling to the topmen . . . the sound of clashing blades.

Night came quickly, and Marya offered to take first watch so that E'sinea could meet Huaslan in the sailors' quarters. Kristoff and Marya were very different from Amonos. So very different.

Dawdling, he made his way down to the lower decks of the ship. He saw no need to rush, especially if Huaslan was still in the kitchen cleaning up. She had a tendency to linger so that she could gather the scraps and bring them down to share, but E'sinea had always refused to eat. He had long ago made a promise to himself never to eat food discarded by others.

Having arrived at the sailors' quarters, E'sinea pushed open the door and stepped in. What he found left him momentarily dumbfounded. The sailors, normally engrossed in their games of cards and drinking, were asleep. The room was quiet, quiet enough for him to hear his heart pounding in his ears. E'sinea made to leave, but then he caught sight of the board game set up in its usual corner, and he wondered if Huaslan lay on the floor sleeping as well, just out of view.

Despite his better judgment, he entered. He scanned the room for intruders, but there was no one save the sleeping sailors and the shadows clinging to the walls. Huaslan was nowhere to be seen.

He halted inches away from the game and crouched down to get a better look. The pieces had been laid out as if someone had been playing. Huaslan's piece was placed in the corner reserved for players 'lost at sea,' while his piece sat in the center of the board, the place players had to reach to win the game. An unnerving feeling ran up his spine. Not wanting to see Huaslan 'lost at sea,' he reached for her piece.

The moment he touched it, a ripple ran up his arm like a swarm of crawling insects. Recoiling, he stood swiftly, only to fall to the ground like a brick. He tried to move his legs, but they had become leaden weights.

A curse! he thought angrily. The sound of glass shattering echoed sharply throughout the room, followed shortly thereafter by the smell of oil and smoke. The sailors' quarters would soon be aflame.

Again E'sinea fought to rise, but his vision was beginning to blur and it was becoming increasingly difficult to stay awake. As if from a great distance, there came a loud *bang*, and he understood that he had either been locked in or that someone — an enemy, perhaps the spellcaster responsible for his plight — had stepped in.

Realizing that time was precious, he reached for the small dagger he kept in the pocket of his coat and then, clenching his teeth, rammed it into his left thigh. The pain was excruciating, but it jerked him awake. Once more he tried to move his legs and found that he could control them, though slowly and jerkily. He stood, warm blood seeping down his leg and into his boot, and found a room of smoke and flames. The fire was unnaturally bright and consumed what it touched with a voracious ferocity. One by one the sailors' sleeping bodies were bursting into flames. The stench of burning flesh filled the room.

Hurrying, he stumbled his way around the flames to the door and yanked hard at the handle, but it would not budge. The fire was closing in. He needed time.

Cupping his hands over his eyes, he bowed his head forward. Black tears seeped out from between his fingers. Hastily, he spread the tears behind him, enclosing himself in a half circle, his back to the door. The flames drew closer and the tears came to life, weaving themselves into the flames as a barrier. It was a battle of shadow against light.

A sudden thought occurred to him. *What if Kristoff and Mar Mar are also under a cursed sleep?* The thought of them burning tormented him, and he realized that if he did not act quickly he would lose them. Removing his tear-stained gloves, he gripped his dagger with both hands and then took in a deep breath.

In that instant, from behind the door, a deep, booming voice called out to him. It was Kristoff.

"Move away from the door!"

E'sinea did as told, relief washing over him that the Katarus were alive. He pressed his back against the wall and watched as his tears struggled against the flames. There were only a few tendrils left, and they were not faring well.

A throbbing pain gripped his left thigh and ran down his leg and up his hip. He had managed to forget the pain, but he noticed it now, especially since the wound should have begun to heal. *You've been away too long,* he thought to himself hazily. He was starting to feel tired again, but whether it was due to blood loss or the curse was impossible to tell.

The door splintered. Seconds later it shattered, sending bits of wood flying into the approaching flames where they, along with the last of E'sinea's tears, were quickly consumed. E'sinea clambered over the remains of the door, stepping out and into the hall. The siblings stood before him, apparently unharmed. There was no sign of Huaslan.

"This fire is cursed! There's a caster aboard!" he announced frantically. "Huaslan should be in the kitchen. We need to find her and then get to the ship's bo—" The hall spun, and E'sinea stumbled back, barely managing to keep his footing.

"You're hurt!" said Marya, shocked. E'sinea wanted to protest but found that he did not have the strength to speak. Without warning, Kristoff picked E'sinea up and draped him over his shoulder as if he were a rag. The Katarus ran up to the main deck only to discover that it too was aflame.

The sails glowed against the night like trees on fire while black clouds of smoke spiraled upwards, becoming lost in the darkness. The air, blistering and suffocating, wavered like distorted glass. There was not a single life moving aboard the ship.

Through falling debris and ash the three made their way to the davit at the stern, only to find the ship's boat gone. The fire was becoming larger and wider, as if it were a giant winged beast eager to take off into the sky. Then the ship groaned and the wood on the deck began to rapidly expand.

"Travail be damned!" cursed Marya, and even as she did so she took hold of Kristoff's arm and leapt, pulling him and E'sinea over the rails to tumble toward the water. "*JUMP!*" she screamed.

The ship exploded in a ball of searing fire.

STRANGERS

THE MORNING SUN glared cold and bright. Kira regarded the landscape from the crest of a tall hill a dozen miles southwest of the town of Rhaemond. Fields of dry brown separated by rows of leafless trees surrounded the hill like the squares on a great chessboard. To the south, five miles away, rose another hill, its crest adorned by a fence of short, crooked trees. To the east, the canal that met the Silent River at Rhaemond cut southward like a long, sinuous snake.

Kira heard Teemo swear under her breath behind him, and he understood that Lyse had at last returned from Rhaemond, where he had gone the night before.

"Mark my words," said Teemo in a false whisper as Lyse drew near, "dog shit is going to fuck you over worse than an animal. You're a fool to trust him."

"I prefer a bit more meat on my prey," called out Lyse. He shot Teemo a measured glare. "And I have no love for soured meat."

"No one gives a shit what you think," Teemo said angrily, her nostrils flaring, and then stormed off down the hill.

"Such a foul and senseless creature," Lyse muttered to himself as she left.

Kira clenched his teeth to keep himself from intervening. In the days since leaving Ghlande, he had learned that trying to keep the peace only made the bickering between his two companions worse. *I wonder how uncle would deal with this*, he thought to himself. *He would probably tell them to shut the fuck up or he would cut their tongues out.*

Kira cleared his throat. "Were you able to find a narrowboat to purchase our passage to Suelosa?"

"No," said Lyse, his mouth twisting. "We will have to go overland. There is no trade on the canal this winter. Rumors of Deadbringers hiding in Rhaemond have lured too many soldiers and Sanctifiers." He spat to the ground. "The town square reeks of burned flesh and treachery. The people are too scared to even shit, let alone do business with a stranger. If the Sanctifiers manage to find their way to Ghlande, Sa will have his hands full."

"You mean they are burning corpses, right?" Kira recalled reading that during the Purging the practice of burning the dead had been announced by the Ascendancy as a way to limit the number of bodies available to Deadbringers. The North had resisted. *They were not pleased with the decree*, Eutau had once told him. *The compromise they made to satisfy the Ascendancy was to sever or crush the head and rip out the heart.*

"What do you think?" asked Lyse, far too softly.

Kira felt sick. "Should you go back to Ghlande?"

Lyse turned away and looked northward. In the far distance, the Gods' Spears tainted the sky like ink spilled on the edge of a sheet of virgin paper. After a long pause, he said, "I have made my choice, and Sa has made his. Come, we've lingered long enough." Kira nodded, trying not to let his unease show.

They found Teemo sitting at the foot of the hill, her woolen-clad legs stretched out, her elbows leaning on her thighs, her chin resting in her hands. She looked up at them as they approached, her eyes lingering on Kira, but said nothing. The three set out southward toward Suelosa. They did not look at the pillar of smoke that rose from the direction of Rhaemond toward the graying winter sky.

Kira discovered that Lyse could be a quiet man, walking for hours or even days with only the most necessary of words spoken. But when the mood struck, he could be incredibly talkative.

At such times, Lyse would carry on about the people he had met in his travels: a Kataru woman with hair the color of the setting sun and the ability to manipulate fire; a child who had been cast aside by his people and would have starved to death had their paths not crossed; innkeepers and farmers he had befriended and would frequent; his younger brother, who—from what Kira could gather—had been vain and eccentric, yet had died protecting the woman he loved; a sister he spoke of with adoration. And, one evening at the end of a particularly long day of travel, Lyse chose to speak of Sa.

"Did Sa counsel you on the roads and checkpoints to avoid?" he asked, picking away at the last bits of meat from a duck he had shot with a shortbow brought with him from Ghlande. A gentle mist of rain swirled about them, threatening to snuff out the little warmth from the campfire.

"He did," said Kira, swallowing a spoonful of rice porridge. He had placed the metal pot filled with uncooked rice and water beneath the roasting duck to catch the dripping fat and blood. It had transformed the rice into a satisfying meal that even Teemo had been pleased with. After eating her share, she had curled up beside the fire and buried herself beneath her cloak. She would be taking second watch.

"Did he seem," continued Lyse, "for lack of a better word, unhappy?"

"He did, yes, but I dismissed it as him being tired from the ordeal with Osette."

"So the ox of a man could not bring himself to say it."

"Say what?" asked Kira, bringing his woolen travel cloak closer around him. The mist had picked up, and he wanted to keep his coat and the soft fur that lined it as dry as possible.

Lyse threw the duck carcass into the fire. Sparks sputtered into the air. "Sa is a former Sanctifier. Telera's mother was one as well."

Kira's stomach lurched. The dinner had suddenly spoiled. "A joke, right?" Lyse remained silent, and Kira felt a deep dread grip him. "He told you as much himself?"

"He had no choice."

"But, *why?*"

Lyse made a face. "I have never been able to understand why Sa fell prey to the horseshit spouted by the Ascendancy. From what he told me, his reasons were never personal, only idealistic." He stared intently at the fire as if seeking an answer. "You must understand that the Sanctifiers are not just the Ascendancy's elite, they are its *believers*, adherents to the cause of banishing Death and uniting the Land. They are hand-picked for loyalty, often from the Kataru clans or the Ro'Erden, who are well-known to hate Deadbringers, and there have never been more than a few hundred of them at a time, even during the height of the Purging. It is unheard of for a Sanctifier to betray the Ascendancy.

"But that is exactly what Sa and Telera's mother did. Sa has never told me why, but they eventually turned against their companions and slew the rest of their hunting band. Not only that—instead of hunting Deadbringers, they began saving them, bringing them to refuge in Ghlande. Osette and his kin are among those they saved."

Lyse paused, a faint ghost of a smile taking shape on his lips. "The first time I saw Telera, she was crying beside the fallen body of her mother." He barked a laugh, his eyes squinting as if he was seeing the memory. "When she saw me, this sprig of a child no longer than my arm glared at me with such ferocity that I laughed. Not far from them lay two dead bodies, each clad in the deep black worn by Sanctifiers. The woman herself was a bloodied mess, yet she clung to life."

His brow began to knit together, his eyes becoming distant with confusion and a bit of anger. "And then a Ro'Erden begged me—me!—to take her daughter home . . . and I did." He stood then, drinking gourd in hand, and turning up his hood fell into silence.

That night, as Kira took the first watch, he wondered how a man as generous and kind as Sa could have been a Sanctifier, and if he had ever condemned innocents to burn. He also wondered if Lyse had at one time hated the Ro'Erden. Perhaps he still did. Until meeting Telera, Kira had never seen a Ro'Erden, save in books or as crude caricatures on posters warning that Ro'Erden were not welcome in Opulancae. Growing up in the North, he had often heard people advocating a return to the purity of blood that had existed in the Land before the First War. The irony had not escaped him that a true return to those times could only be accomplished by including and accepting Deadbringers.

The morning came quickly. Lyse did not speak of the prior night's revelation, and Kira decided that some truths were not meant to be dwelled upon. Following a quick meal of dried meat, they began their journey anew.

After a week of slow, hard travel across uneven terrain, they arrived in Suelosa, the largest city he had seen since leaving Opulancae. Stucco-walled buildings were piled one on top of another, and red clay roofs stood like dark sentinels against the fast-approaching night sky. It was a clean city, a city that was still fresh and new and had yet to feel the passage of time. The streets were busy, but the people seemed unafraid and unconcerned.

Lyse halted in the market square. All around them vendors were busily dismantling their stalls as people hurried home to their dinners. "Not until we pass through the Foreign Hills are we likely to come across another inn," he said. His breath fogged in the air. "In the heart of the city there is an inn owned by a charming woman. We shall spend the night there and be off the next day." He leaned over and flicked the edge of Kira's hood with his finger. "The rumors of death and bloodshed that haunt Rhaemond have not made it this far south. Suelosa is the perfect place to practice 'hiding in plain sight.'"

Teemo smiled cheekily and in a singsong voice said, "Mark my words—worse than an animal!" Lyse rolled his eyes. Kira just laughed.

Lyse guided them down a broad cobblestone street that eventually met a wide waterway, one of the many tributaries that flowed into the

Forged River. Crossing over a high, arched bridge made of stone and timber, Kira noticed a lone narrowboat docked along the floodwalls. On one side of the boat a paper lantern, round and as large as a man's head, hung at the end of a pole. Its light shone on the surface of the dark water like the full moon against the night sky. The sight was strangely nostalgic.

The inn was crowded, yet it was large enough to keep from being unpleasantly cramped. It was warm and welcoming, and the savory smells of food and smoke lingered pleasantly in the air. Still, after so long on the run, Kira had to swallow his anxiety and try to ignore the urge to find a dark, isolated corner in which to hide. He yearned to sit at a table and have a decent meal just like everyone else. And besides, he wanted to prove that Teemo's warnings of Lyse's inevitable betrayal were wrong.

An elderly woman wobbled her way toward them, a kind smile gracing her thin lips. "Lyse? Is it really you?"

Lyse looked down at the old woman, clearly surprised by her familiarity. She stood before him, smiling and waiting. "Mori," he said at last, the shock clearly etched on his face.

"Just say it. I'm old, I am. No need for false modesty with me."

"Of course not," he said, smiling in turn, though the sadness in his eyes was palpable.

What's wrong? thought Kira. But his concern was short-lived, for the old woman walked straight up to him and leaned in to peek up under his hood. He blinked a few times at her boldness and then smiled nervously at her.

"By chance, this the younger brother you speak of?" she asked, pulling away.

"No, he passed away some time ago. This is a friend, Va'lel. The islander is Teemo."

"I'm sorry to hear that, but it's good you came, Lyse. I had started to believe I would never see you again."

"I'm here now."

Mori beamed at him. "Yes, yes you are."

A room was provided for each of them, along with hot water for a bath. Kira reveled in the near-scalding water as he scrubbed every inch of his body. Stepping out of the bath, he toweled himself dry and then stood before a mirror. He had become dreadfully thin. His ribs and spine pushed against his skin, and his arms and shoulders had become far less pronounced since he no longer worked with heavy stone. The muscles in his legs, however, had remained strong and well-defined.

His fingers began tracing the edge of the scar that covered his torso where he had been wounded. It was red and thick and raised in certain areas, forming distinctive nodules that were either numb or sensitive to the touch. He tried bending his spine all the way back, but the scar tissue along his waist pulled uncomfortably when he did so. He leaned forward then, his legs straight, and managed to at least place his hands flat on the floor. The scar made his skin tight, and the movement in his waist was no longer as good as it had once been. Resigned, he dressed and brushed his hair.

He found Lyse waiting for him in the hallway, a cloud of spiced smoke encircling him. Teemo emerged a few seconds later, and the three made their way down to the common room. Yet no sooner had they found a seat when a *pé'bos* caught Lyse's eye. Calling her over, he whispered into her ear. She nodded, and moments later the two retired back to his room. Kira had tried his best not to stare, but the sight had set off his desire to bed someone, to hold a lover in his arms and taste and touch every inch of their body. His blood boiled. His eyes fell on Teemo, and the image of her small body pressed beneath his filled his mind.

Teemo smiled. "The lust in your eyes is rather becoming." She dipped her finger into her cup of wine and placed it in her mouth, her tongue licking its length, her lips kissing the tip. Kira felt his breath catch, and he brought his hood further over his face, afraid that his desire was plain for all to see. His cock was hot and throbbing against his leg.

"All you have to do," said Teemo, inching closer to him, her hand searching for his, "is send dog shit away."

Kira grabbed her hand and squeezed it in his until she winced. "Lyse is staying. Get used to it."

"Fine, fine," she said, yanking her hand away. Kira considered going back to his room to relieve his frustration, but he knew that if he did so Teemo would never let him hear the end of it. At that moment, the serving boy brought out the food: a pie filled with freshwater fish, turnips, and mashed potatoes; rice dumplings stuffed with peas and doused in salted lard; and a creamy pudding baked with dried fruit. To wash everything down, a flagon of piping hot spiced wine.

Kira threw himself into eating and soon found that his desire to fill his stomach was even greater than his longing to bed a lover. Teemo kept up with him, and they ate as if to burst, each trying to out-do the other. As they finished, a silence fell over the crowd, and Kira's gaze turned toward the low stage in the center of the common room. A Ro'Erden woman sat on a plain chair, a simple lyre propped upon her thigh. With a gentle nod of her head, she acknowledged the crowd and began playing. The music was strangely offbeat yet beautiful. It held the attention of all in the room.

She had flowing dark hair that brushed the floor. Ivory horns that started above her temples and behind the hairline swept back, curving upward at the end like spearpoints. Only her talon-tipped fingers betrayed life as she plucked away at the lyre's strings. In that instant, Kira decided she was a statue come to life. He watched enthralled, unsure if it was the song or her beauty that had captivated him. Or, perhaps, he had simply had one too many drinks.

The song ended, and the common room came to life once again. To Kira's surprise, very few people applauded and even fewer deigned to leave coins at her feet. He scanned the crowd — even seated he was taller than many in the room — and noticed that perhaps half a dozen Ro'Erden were present, and that it had been they who had left the coins.

The woman sat for a few moments, and when it became clear that no one else would pay she packed her lyre in a red-stained wooden case and rose, making her way down from the stage.

Kira reached for his purse, but as he rose with it in hand Teemo flashed him a cruel smile. "Maybe if you leave her enough she'll let you fuck her. Oh, wait! I forgot, you can't touch her." Kira swallowed down his anger, though with great difficulty. He wondered if Teemo would ever forgive him for allowing Lyse to travel with them.

Leaving Teemo behind, he wove his way through the crowd toward the statuesque woman. As if realizing he was seeking her out, she stopped and turned to face him. To Kira's great surprise, she was only a few inches shorter than him.

"That was a very beautiful song," he said, hoping he did not sound a smitten fool.

Jade eyes lined by luscious lashes looked at him. "I'm glad you liked it."

"You!" called a strong voice behind him. "Lower your hood!"

Kira swallowed down the knot in his throat and turned to greet the voice. A Ro'Erden man stood before him, clad in the gray of a common soldier of the Ascendancy. He was a bit shorter than the woman, with a single dark horn that curved outward from the left side of his forehead. A harsh stump was all that remained of his right horn. He wore his dark hair in a high tail, the end of which brushed his shoulders.

His heart racing, Kira lowered his hood and hoped for the best.

"What's wrong, Jun?" asked the woman, startled. "This boy came to compliment my playing. It has been the kindest gesture I have received all night."

The Ro'Erden man ignored her and closely studied Kira's features, focusing on his eyes.

"Jun?" she called again.

"Where are you from, boy?"

Kira's mind raced back to Eutau's old maps as he desperately tried to remember the name of a city or town close to the Western Mountains but far enough from Opulancae not to raise suspicions. "Kessrennt," he said with all the confidence he could muster. The Ro'Erden's eyes momentarily narrowed, and then he nodded as if satisfied.

"You're a half-breed, yes?"

Kira was about to ask if by half-breed the man had meant *moma*, but then he thought better of it and just answered, "Yes."

The woman scoffed. "'Half-breed' sounds so unbecoming. It always makes me think of animals rutting."

The soldier rolled his eyes. "*Moma*, half-breed, whatever. There is no difference between them, A'ka."

The woman, A'ka, strode up to Kira. "Of course there is. This boy did not ignore his parentage. I see quite a few *momas* in the crowd who clearly have Ro'Erden blood in their veins, and they won't so much as even look at me."

They think I'm a Ro'Erden! thought Kira, stunned and oddly bothered. He spoke up, not wanting to linger. "I wanted to give you a gold piece. For your song." He held his gloved hand out to A'ka.

A dreamy glint filled the woman's eyes. Before Kira could react, she leaned in and pressed her lips against his, her breasts pushing against his chest, her fingers entwining in his hair. Her lips were soft and smelled like roses. His entire body burned, and he found himself struggling against the intense, conflicting desires to wrap his arms around her waist and kiss her fully, and to push her away before she was harmed.

Gently — regretfully — he pushed her away.

A deep, rich laugher spilled from A'ka's throat as she took the gold piece from his hand. She then went over to the Ro'Erden man and wrapped her arm around his.

"Such a sweet boy," she said, smiling. "I'm glad we met."

The man shot him a measured look and scoffed. "You're not bad, boy, but without horns you're simply nothing more than a *boy*. A shame, really."

Arm in arm, the two Ro'Erden walked away, leaving a bewildered and frustrated Kira behind.

A MEMORY DISSOLVED BY PAIN

E'SINEA HELD HIS breath. His eyes stung painfully and he closed them, hoping to find relief. But relief was not to be had. There was only terror. He wanted to bring his hands over his face, to somehow keep the vile water away from him, but his arms were tightly bound, the rope digging into the raw flesh of his wrists. He felt a sudden shift, and the chair he had been tied to delivered him from his agony as it was lifted out of the water.

He gasped, and he coughed, and he filled his lungs with rank air. His eyes pulsed and he tried to open them, then screamed as he felt his eyelids tear. There came a voice—the words inaudible—and then the chair shifted. He breathed in deeply, desperately trying to take in as much air as possible. But his body crashed back into the water mid-breath, and he felt it violate him from the inside. The taste of blood—of his own blood—scalded his tongue, and he wished he could just die.

The chair shifted, and he was once again out of the horrible water. He began vomiting, his chest feeling as if it would cave in. The water that spilled from his mouth and nose was cold and acrid. But then he began vomiting something *else*—it stuck to his chin and trailed down his neck. It was warm and tasted like metal.

The sound of voices danced all around him. He braced himself for the immeasurable pain he would feel by forcing his eyes open, because he needed to *see*. But there was no pain. There was nothing save the same wet, warm feeling trickling down his cheeks now, and darkness. He opened his eyes again, believing that perhaps he had not done so properly the first time.

The darkness was still there. A terrible knot gripped his chest, and for a moment he forgot how to breathe.

He was blind.

"*Why?*" he managed to ask, loudly, so he could be sure that someone would hear him.

No one answered him; everyone ignored him.

He caught the sound of something being poured into the awful water beneath him. He wondered what it was and if it would finally kill him. He hoped so. The chair shifted, and the second the water touched his skin he wailed hysterically, like an animal being slowly lowered into hot tar.

His torment was swallowed by the pitiless water.

He did not want to die with misery as his companion; he did not want to die alone. Frantically, his mind sought a peaceful memory, but the effort only served to remind him of all the people he had met who had hurt him. Despair gripped him, and he felt himself slip away. But then the memory of a tall man with amber eyes embraced him, and E'sinea found the peace he had longed for.

He imagined the tall man reaching out to him, and then . . .

E'SINEA OPENED HIS eyes. On the left side of his face he felt the stinging warmth of the sun and a chill wind; on the right he felt the bitter cold, wet sand. He dragged a fingernail along the surface of the sand and then rubbed the wet grains between his bare fingers.

He had been dreaming. He hated dreaming.

Refusing to acknowledge the dream, he rolled over onto his back and began taking in his surroundings. He was on a narrow beach of dark, course sand. Overhead loomed wind-blasted, twisted pines carpeting steep, rocky cliffs that plunged onto the beach or into the sea like huge walls. The clearest of blues washed a sky that had only the white light of the sun to stain it.

He made to rise and felt as if his entire body had been used as a kick ball. The sea had had its way with him. After a few tries he managed to stand, and, though at first he was certain his legs would betray him, he remained standing. The wound in his thigh had at last healed. He gazed at the endless sea and the thundering waves crashing against the cliffs. A deep fear gripped him as he wondered aloud whether Marya and Kristoff had survived the explosion and the merciless sea.

"They're alive. They have to be," he said to himself in a near-whisper. Huaslan's crystal-clear blue eyes came to mind and he felt a terrible stab in his heart. He recalled the board game on the ship and how Huaslan's piece had been 'lost at sea.' *An omen,* he thought, pained. He hoped that her death had at least been swift and painless.

He walked along the shore, flies buzzing all around him as he passed indistinct masses of flesh and debris. He did not feel either the Katarus or Huaslan among them, and he kept going.

Five minutes later, he reached the end of the beach, where the course sand was replaced by a bed of pebbles worn smooth by the tide at the base of a sheer cliff. Boulders that had fallen from the cliff into the sea formed a small pool of calmer water, protecting the shore there from the worst of the waves. A huge sea cave, its chamber wide enough for a merchant ship, yawned from the cliffside a hundred yards further on.

He turned his attention away from the sea and toward the cliff, eager to begin making his way to Florinia. He did not know exactly where he was, but he knew that it had to be somewhere north of Ulivi, in the wild country south of the Forged River. Nowhere else in the South did the Eastern Sea meet such huge, stony cliffs.

He had only walked a few paces away when he suddenly felt a familiar itch between his shoulder blades. Smiling, he ran into the water and carefully began wading his way toward two closely wedged boulders near the mouth of the sea cave. The ground dropped off a few steps out, and he was forced to swim against a current that threatened to carry him back to sea. But he made his way to the boulders and grabbed onto them as best he could. A mane the same color as E'sinea's hair wavered on the water's surface near the crevice between the two boulders.

"Oh, my poor horsey!" he said, wrapping his arms around her neck. Squeezing her tight, he said, "Wake up, Pretty Mare," and the thing wedged between the two boulders came to life. The horse opened its eyes and made to rise, but the water was too deep. E'sinea carefully pushed her toward the shore and helped her find her footing once they were in shallow water.

Once they reached the beach he examined her. Chunks of flesh were missing from her hindquarters and rump, and the bone along her right cannon was exposed. Her flesh was swollen from her time in the salty water. Yet, overall, she was in better shape than he had expected.

"Those gaping wounds don't look very good," he said, "but the flesh along the shore is icky and maggoty, and I'm too tired to make it look pretty. Do you mind waiting?" The horse neighed, an unnerving sound, and then began bobbing its head.

"Oh, I'm sorry! I didn't mean to forget, really."

Pretty Mare lowered her head to his height and E'sinea promptly gouged out her eyes with his fingers. A dark slurry of water trickled out of the empty sockets. Using the end of his disheveled braid, E'sinea wiped the mare's eyes clean and then held them up to the daylight. They shone like finely polished glass. Satisfied, he carefully reinserted them. Pretty Mare nickered happily.

E'sinea mounted, pulling himself up by her mane, and together they went back down the beach, trying to find a suitable path up the cliff. The going was slow, but after several hours they found a rough path and reached the top. Using the sun as a guide, he oriented himself and then turned his mount southward.

If the siblings had survived, they would go to Florinia.

Renewed determination surged through E'sinea and, though he was immensely tired, he channeled a small bit of his energy into Pretty Mare. Neighing with delight, she broke into a gallop that would have left the swiftest of living horses behind.

The game is over, he thought. He felt guilty, as he had known he would, but to his surprise that feeling was washed away by a flood of relief. His high, joyous laughter rang along the cliffs as Pretty Mare charged south, toward Florinia.

KRISTOFF FELT AS if he had been lying on the shore for months. He opened his eyes and tried to move, but his body was a lumbering weight that would not respond to his will. A feeling of utmost weariness washed over him, and he wondered how Fortune could possibly have kept him alive when so many of his friends were long dead.

Centuries seemed to pass before he found the strength to move. He had washed ashore on an inlet the length of which was enclosed by stone hills dotted with stunted trees and low grass. Gentle waves caressed the sandy shoreline. There was no sign of Marya or E'sinea. He was alone, with only the seabirds flying above him for company. And as hard as it was for him to believe, he was certain that he was somewhere along the shores of the South Basin. His mother's face flashed before him, and he wondered if she had had a hand in his good luck. If so, then there was a chance that Marya was alive as well.

His clothes were tattered and his skin was raw and chapped as if it had been almost burned, though whether from the heat of the fire or the sun's rays he could not tell. More painfully though, his mouth felt parched, and so he made his way to where the waves lapped at the shore. Going down on his knees, he lowered his head to the surface and satiated his thirst. The ability to consume seawater was a useful trait he had inherited from his mother, but it was not a perfect one. He knew he would pay for his drink with fiery pain when he next pissed. The water was salty and cold, just like the wind beating at his skin.

He stood and looked out past the mouth of the inlet, toward the breaking waves. Fortune had indeed been on his side. He hoped that it had been the same for the others, and that the luck would continue until he reached Florinia.

Florinia.

The attack aboard the ship had been premeditated, the work of a powerful spellcaster. Kristoff wondered if it could have been the cabin girl who had befriended E'sinea, but seeing no hard evidence either way he pushed her out of mind. He thought of the rumors he had heard in Jané, the whispers of turmoil and approaching warfare. He had dismissed them as baseless, but now he was no longer certain.

"Perhaps rumor has indeed become fact," he voiced darkly, wondering if other Sanctifiers had met fates similar to the one the unknown spellcaster had planned for him and his band.

A low rumble of thunder murmured in the sky. It seemed fitting.

Gathering his wits he set out, but he had not gone far when he heard a shout from above. Unable to believe his ears, he stepped back in haste, almost fell over, and looked up. It was Marya, standing on the crest of the nearest hill. Her clothes and hair were a mess, but otherwise she appeared unharmed. The sky rumbled once more, and it began to rain. It pattered against his face, washing away the knot of worry and pain that he had felt but refused to acknowledge.

"Praise be Fortune!" he shouted back to her with heartfelt vigor. "Praise be the Twin God!"

THE LAUGHING MAN

THE WINTER MORNING dawned chill in Suelosa. After a breakfast of fermented goat's milk, bacon, and larded bread, Kira and his companions found the innkeeper waiting outside with three bay geldings.

"Thank you, Mori," Lyse said sincerely. Kira and Teemo thanked her as well.

The woman smiled with joy, the lines on her face coming together. "My parting gifts to you and your friends."

"I . . . have nothing to give you," Lyse replied gently, his words hoarse.

"There you go again with your false modesty." Her smile wavered and she licked her lips nervously. "The Ascendancy has set its hounds loose on the Land again. Gods know it's a good time to be old."

"It will not come to that," said Lyse, seemingly torn, a strange light in his amber eyes.

Why do I get the impression that I am missing something important? thought Kira, feeling like a child who had stumbled upon the serious conversation of adults.

"Farewell, Lyse. Bring me some pretty flowers next time."

"Goodbye, Mori." Lyse bent down and kissed the old woman on her head. The gesture reminded Kira of Elia, and suddenly he felt very sad.

Mori stood under her inn's portico and watched them ride out from Suelosa, into the mist of the cold rain that drizzled down.

They rode south for a day on a wide road of hard-packed dirt, the first true road that Kira had seen since leaving Opulancae. The road was well-traveled with the carts of merchants and other travelers, and on the morning of the second day Lyse led them off to a small fishing village on the main branch of the Forged River, where they could hire a boat to take them across. It would not do to cross on the road, he explained, for the great bridge across the river was tolled, and the Ascendancy had a checkpoint there to keep a watchful eye on the traffic out of Suelosa. Teemo was suspicious of the detour, but Kira remembered that Sa had warned him not to cross on the bridge, and so they followed Lyse.

They crossed that day while the sun was high and then left the road again to travel through the open woodlands that lay south of the Forged River. The geldings Mori had given them were fresh and healthy, and they made good time.

For eight days they journeyed south across smooth, slowly rising terrain, accompanied by trees with gnarled branches that reached outward and upward, and yellow and red leaves that veiled the ground, setting it aflame. It was a gorgeous sight, but Kira found himself missing the North's austere grasslands and its proud green pines and rolling hills. He wondered if he would ever be able to return.

On the ninth day, the smooth ground began to rise quickly, giving way to rugged terrain dotted with loose rocks that forced them to slow their mounts to a walk. A ridge of tall, jagged hills came into view.

"These are the Foreign Hills," said Lyse, the first words he had spoken in days. "The road goes around them to the west, toward the towns and cities that follow the River of Veins. The journey to Florinia will be faster if we travel though them, and we are unlikely to see other travelers." He gently kicked his gelding's sides and headed off in the direction of the tall hills. Kira and Teemo followed.

The path through the Foreign Hills was narrow and covered in gravelly soil that crunched beneath the horses' hooves. Small thickets of brush dotted the sides of the hills. True to Lyse's word, they saw no one else.

As darkness fell, they came across a wide lake, surrounded by the hills, its water calm and beautifully clear, its banks lined with reeds. A row of trees stood near the base of the nearest hill, their branches bowed with bright orange, tear-shaped fruit. The three dismounted and the horses began walking eagerly toward the trees. Lyse took hold of the reins of his horse, pulling it back.

"Do not let the horses eat the fruit," he warned, guiding his gelding toward the reeds.

"Why not?" asked Kira, following suit.

"Kira the Deadbringer? More like Kira the ignorant," Teemo said sarcastically.

Lyse shot her a dirty look, and she glared back at him but then fell silent. He handed Kira the reins to his gelding. "Tether the horses near the reeds." He then walked over to the trees and began picking the fruit, returning with a hefty stack in his arms.

"Try this," he said, tossing a fruit to Kira, "but do not eat the seeds." He turned to Teemo. "Did you want one as well?" he asked, raising a brow at her mockingly.

She glared at him. "Choke."

"Here," said Kira, cutting his fruit in half with his dagger and offering one piece to her. "We can share it."

A deep red tinged her cheeks as she accepted it.

Kira studied the fruit. It was as big as his hand and had flesh as vivid as its skin. Two round black seeds decorated its core. He sniffed it. A warm, almost perfume-like scent swarmed over his senses. "Smells like cloves," he commented.

"Cloves?" asked Teemo, seemingly surprised. She popped the last bit of fruit into her mouth. "I take it back, you're not ignorant."

"You must have been well-off in Opulancae to be familiar with a spice as costly as cloves," said Lyse, though not in an unkindly way.

"Our parlor was rather popular, and business was good," said Kira, feeling unexpectedly embarrassed. He continued, eager to change the subject. "But you mentioned not eating the seeds. Why?"

"Because," began Lyse, as he picked away at the seeds with the tip of his dagger, "the seeds are poison. What you hold in your hand is in large part responsible for the demise of the winged serpents after the First War."

"You're joking, right?" asked Kira, unable to believe that a mere fruit could cause so much damage.

"Not at all. The tree was one of the many *gifts* the first Ro'Erden brought with them. To their peril, the winged serpents enjoyed the fruit too much, seeds and all."

Kira looked at the fruit in his hand and said, "I'll pass."

Lyse held out his hand. "Then I will eat it for you."

"Is it really that good?" he asked, passing along his half.

"Too good."

They made camp near the banks of the lake, where only soft grass and reeds grew. The horses, unable to reach the fruit, resigned themselves to nibbling away at the grass, while Kira and the others shared a bowl of rice porridge and dried meat.

It was early morning when they set out the next day, and at the end of the day after they came out of the Foreign Hills. The land beyond was a mix of tall, crooked trees and open fields that seemed to go on forever. Lyse had been in one of his quiet spells, and so Kira hesitantly asked Teemo what country they were in and what to expect.

He had expected something biting and sarcastic in response, but to his surprise Teemo smiled and answered him directly, looking pleased. "These are the uplands that lie north of the River of Veins. Shepherds run flocks here, but the soil is poor and there are few villages." She cast a hostile eye at Lyse's back. "Trader's Road lies to the south and west. But unless dog shit chooses this moment to betray you, he means to travel through the uplands until we are closer to Florinia." Lyse grunted, and Teemo nodded, seemingly satisfied.

They continued on. The weather had become strangely warm, so much so that Kira had been forced to remove not only his cloak and coat, but his gloves as well. The sun blared relentlessly in the sky, and as the days passed it was joined by puffy white clouds that resembled never-ending rows of sheep. Lyse warned that it meant a terrible storm was on its way, though he could not predict when it would arrive.

On the tenth day after leaving the Foreign Hills, the air began to grow steadily colder and the sun disappeared behind an overcast. At first Kira was relieved, but then the air became far colder, somehow more piercing than any cold he had ever experienced in the North. He looked skyward. A blanket of ominous clouds trembled like an ill-washed sheet hung out to dry on a windy day.

Lyse studied the darkening sky, his every breath fogging in the air. "We need to find shelter before this storm hits." His gelding danced side to side as if it was aware of what was to come. "We're not far from Trader's Road now, and there should be an inn only a few miles from here, The Laughing Man. I suggest we ride hard." The three kicked the horses into a gallop. Moments later, a skin-tingling rumble erupted from the sky, followed by a bitter waterfall that engulfed them.

As they fled, Kira noticed that his cloak was beginning to feel strangely weighted. He tugged at it and watched in disbelief as miniature icicles, no longer than the quill of a pen, dislodged from his hood. His eyes fell on the horse's dark mane, and he noticed that strands of it had become encased in ice. The rain was beginning to freeze. In a panic, he looked down at the ground and saw that it, too, was steadily becoming a thin sheet of ice. Lyse spurred his horse to run faster. Kira followed suit, half-expecting the horses to slip and send them all reeling to the ground. But the horses never lost their footing, and they arrived at the inn just as the rain turned into solid balls of ice the size of glowbugs.

The rank smells of old sweat and drink greeted them as they pushed open the door. The inn was ancient, cramped, and had an air of never once having been cleaned. Cold air whistled through the poorly plastered walls, and the fire in the hearth struggled against a mound of soot. Had the falling rocks of ice been any larger, Kira doubted the inn would have held up.

The small common room was full of a mix of rough-looking travelers of different races, including a few Ro'Erden with hoods altered to accommodate their horns. The innkeeper, a leering reed of a man with rotten teeth, greeted them, and Kira could not help but wonder if he was the laughing man that the inn was named after. Kira was uneasy under the man's gaze, and he certainly felt like he was being laughed at.

"One room left," croaked the innkeeper as he craned his head up, the bones in his neck cracking. "If you're fine with sharing, that is."

Lyse removed his cloak, water dripping down from its ends and pooling on the mud-covered floor. A few heads turned in his direction. "It will do," he said, ignoring the attention. "What of food and drink?"

The man waved to the common room. "Serving boy will tend to you." He then took hold of a key from his belt. "Up the stairs, last one down the hallway, to the right." Not until Lyse had placed the gold in the innkeeper's hand and he had checked it with his rotten teeth did he loosen his grip on the key.

The staircase leading to the second floor was obscenely narrow and listed heavily. The wood creaked with each step they took.

"If I fall through these stairs," Teemo said heatedly, "I will skin that innkeeper!"

"Then we agree for once!" said Lyse.

Kira, who was following at the end, looked past the others and saw two people standing at the top of the stairs, waiting to descend. Both had their hoods pulled over their faces, but black, lyre-shaped horns betrayed one of them as Ro'Erden, while the other was a short man. *But almost everyone in the south is rather short,* he reflected.

"Excuse us," said Lyse as he and Teemo reached the top and passed them by. As Kira approached the last steps, he noticed that the shorter man had begun to sniff the air. *I wonder what that's about?* he thought, and then looked up at the man more closely. Their eyes locked, and Kira felt the color drain from his face. He hurried up the last step and after Lyse, his hand opening and closing, unsure whether to draw his dagger or not.

He halted in mid-step as a familiar voice called to him. "My eyes do not deceive me, yet I am finding it difficult to believe them."

Lyse stiffened, his hand discreetly reaching for his sword.

Kira worked moisture back into his mouth. "Do you have business with me?"

"It depends if you still view a face from the past as a friend."

"A friend in the past, but what of now?" There was nothing else Kira could do. He turned to face his questioner.

"Nothing has changed," the man said smoothly. His eyes openly scrutinized Lyse and Teemo.

"Who are you?" asked Lyse.

"A friend," said the man once more. Kira nodded, and Lyse withdrew his hand from his sword. "But you" — the man shook his head — "I thought you were dead. Eutau certainly believes that you are."

Kira stood there for a long moment, his mind slowly processing what he had just heard.

"My uncle is dead." The words felt distant, unreal.

"No, Kira," said Kim Lafont, taking a step forward. "Eutau lives, and he is in Florinia."

HEART IN TWO

"TELL ME OF my uncle," said Kira, taking a spot beside the hearth. The storm outside roared against the inn's roof, but the fire's warmth felt pleasant against his bare chest. His wet clothes and cloak hung from pegs wedged between the brick and mortar of the small room's makeshift mantle. A puddle had already begun to gather on the floor.

After some reassurances, both Lyse and Teemo had agreed to wait in the common room, leaving Kira alone with Kim. Kim's Ro'Erden—a young man, only a few years older than Kira, with fierce ruby-red eyes—had also let them be.

Kim brought a stool in front of the hearth and took a seat. Then, taking hold of the fire iron, he began stoking the wood as if hoping to breathe more life into the weak flames. "Eutau blames himself for your death." He barked a harsh laugh. "He also blames me."

"Don't hold it against him. Uncle's just like that. Once he sees me he'll slip back into his amicable attitude toward you."

Kim stopped fussing with the fire and turned to look up at Kira. The shadow of a beard lingered on his face. "Yes, he is like that." There was a strange look in his eyes that Kira could not help but feel was surprise. "That wound," he began again, intently eyeing Kira's scars. "It must have given you trouble throughout your journey."

Certainly Kira's side had bothered him, especially after a long day's ride. Yet not since the Gods' Spears had it truly bothered him as it had in Opulancae. *Not since I tried taking the tree's life for my own.* Feeling suddenly very exposed, he moved away from the hearth and began rummaging through his pack for a dry shirt. Sensing that Kim was waiting for him to say something, he said, "It gave me trouble, yeah. But what choice did I have? I didn't have the leisure of staying still."

"No, you did not," agreed Kim.

Kira pulled out the only article of clothing he had left that had not been completely ruined by his touch: a soft, blackened-leather vest with ivory buttons and grommets on the shoulders that he had used to hold his long gloves in place. Slipping it on, he began fastening the buttons even as he retook his spot near the hearth.

"You still have not told me how you came across my uncle."

Kim's face turned sour. "He was obscenely drunk at an inn near Florinia. To be honest, with the way he was carrying on I had mistaken him for a *pé'bos*. He was ragged, filthy, and not until one of my men decided to get involved with him did I get a better look at his face and realize who he was."

Kira shifted his weight, disturbed. He knew Eutau had frequented the pleasure houses in Opulancae and that he had even gone as far as *comforting* a few of their parlor's clients, but he had always been very discrete about it. What Kim had just described was anything but discrete.

"Surprised?" Kim asked impassively. "Yes, well, he was even more surprised than you when he saw me."

"Do you know where in Florinia he is staying?"

"With a Florinese named J'kara."

J'kara. Kira took a deep breath and clenched his hands to keep them from shaking. Eutau had gone on ahead as he had planned — as they had planned. It was almost too much to keep his emotions contained. But something else Kim had said caught his attention.

"Florinese?" asked Kira. It was the first time he had heard the word.

Kim nodded. "It is a local term. I never told you, but I am from Florinia. We who hail from the city call its original people the Florinese, the race that was there before people from all over the Land went to live there."

Kira was surprised at the revelation. That surprise brought him back to the present, the strange coincidence of meeting Kim in a run-down inn near Florinia, and something else. "And why are *you* here?" he asked, suddenly suspicious. "And for that matter, why are you still speaking to me, to uncle, as friends? We killed your men."

"You were desperate, fleeing the Sanctifiers, and that only came to pass because of my own failure to realize the danger you were in. I cannot hold that against either of you. As for your first question, I have business in the South. I trust I have your discretion? I am not hunted by the Sanctifiers like you are, but they are no more my friends than they are yours."

"Yes, of course," said Kira, satisfied. He suddenly recalled what had happened on the stairs. "Kim, why were you sniffing so intently when you first saw me?"

Kim laughed. "Has Eutau ever mentioned that you have a peculiar musty leather smell, especially when you sweat or are drenched? It is not unpleasant, but it is unique. It is a scent I have come to associate specifically with you."

"Ah," said Kira, shuffling uncomfortably at the unexpected disclosure. "Leather is one of the few materials I can wear that will not deteriorate quickly when it touches my skin. I guess it's from that. Believe me when I say that I have tried every material possible."

"I believe you," said Kim. Then, "I saw that you managed to make some allies on your journey."

"I met them in Rhaemond. Both have been invaluable companions, especially Lyse."

"The tall man with the amber eyes, correct?"

"Yes. The girl's name is Teemo."

"And they are aware of what and who you are?" asked Kim, with obvious interest.

Kira wondered what he should say. *Teemo is really a Doll who belongs to a terrifying woman I met first in my dreams and then again in the Gods' Spears. And Lyse ran me through with a sword, and we have been friends ever since.* Finally, he settled on, "Without them, I would not have gotten this far. I trust them both and look forward to introducing them to my uncle."

The notion caused him to smile like a fool. "My uncle lives, Kim! He's alive! Your news has brought purpose back to my life. Before" — he thought of Daemeon and her offer — "before, I wasn't sure what exactly to do when I arrived in Florinia."

An odd look washed over Kim's face. "He didn't tell you, did he?"

"Who didn't tell me what?"

"Eutau."

"What about uncle? You look as if he did something wrong."

Kim stood and walked over to the foot of the room's decrepit bed, looking away. "There is no love between Eutau and myself," he began, and then turned to face Kira. "So thus there is nothing to be lost. More to the point, I think you have the right to know."

"Know what?"

"Eutau is not your uncle. He is a Doll."

Kira felt the corners of his lips twitch, but if he wanted to laugh or cry he was not sure which. "My uncle is not a Doll," he said, too calmly.

"Ask him yourself. He will most likely deny it, but if you persist I am certain he will tell you. When it comes to you, Eutau weakens."

"My uncle is *not* a Doll!" said Kira, through gritted teeth.

"There is no blood relation between the two of you. Eutau is not a man, he is a Doll. I am sorry."

"My mother was his sister!"

"Another lie, though it appears that he did know your mother."

Kira felt hot tears rim his eyes, but he held them back, refusing to give the man the satisfaction of a single tear. The sound of the storm hitting the roof thundered in his ears, and he felt as if the room was caving in. He took a step forward and the floorboards cracked beneath his bare feet. Without realizing it, he had called upon Death.

"Why are you doing this?"

Kim stepped back, his eyes flickering between Kira and the slowly rotting wooden planks, yet he did not reach for his sword. "I am telling you this because you must know. Because Eutau is alive, it means that his master lives as well and his allegiance cannot be to you. Understand that I do not doubt the love he has for you, but you must accept my word as truth."

Kira's face contorted with fury. "You're just upset because you don't *own* me anymore. Your pet Deadbringer is going to Florinia, the very heart of the Ascendancy, and it burns you to think that I could turn against the Bastion. Your *pet* is gone, Kim, and your lies are not going to turn me against my uncle!"

Somehow he had managed to stay near the hearth and not stride up to Kim and choke the truth out of him, though in that moment he longed for nothing more than to feel his fingers piercing Kim's thick neck. Their eyes locked and he waited, waited to hear Kim argue with him, to give him a reason to come to blows, but Kim only stood there, the pity in his eyes agonizingly real.

Memories surfaced then, and with each one Kira felt his anger stolen from him: Eutau's fanatical hatred of Dolls; his reluctance to aid Kira in becoming a more adept Deadbringer; that they looked so little alike; that Eutau refused to speak of Kira's mother and father; that Kira was able to touch his uncle, just as he was able to touch Teemo.

NO!

His uncle was alive; his uncle was not his uncle.

As the words spilled from his lips, a pain surpassing comprehension overtook him. "Why didn't you trust me?"

WHAT DO YOU want?" asked Teemo as she watched Lyse close the stable doors behind him. "You know, you really are not my type, but if you want me to bite your cock off, I think I'd enjoy that."

Lyse ignored her and instead checked the stable stalls. The horses danced nervously as he passed each one by. Satisfied that they were alone, he turned his attention to Teemo, who was smiling scornfully at him.

He smiled back at her, an insolent, knowing smile. "What does Daemeon want with Kira?"

"What are you on about?"

"Summon your master," he said. "I would much rather speak with her than someone as unpleasant as you."

A curt laugh escaped Teemo's lips and she turned on her heel. "Have fun waiting around for your imaginary friend." With unmasked haste, she began walking quickly to the stable doors.

Lyse called out to her, his tone commanding. "Summon her now, *Doll*, or I will summon her for you."

Teemo halted in her tracks and turned to face him. "You want to talk to *her*? Then *you* summon her. Go ahead, do it. With any luck you'll succeed and then maybe I can finally be rid of you!"

Lyse shook his head in disbelief and laughed, but the laugh held no amusement. "You really are a rather lively *pet*. Even after what you did in Ghlande, I had held out some hope for you. But now . . ." He began walking toward her. As he did, he spoke a series of strange words that flowed one into the other, his voice becoming harsh and cruel.

Fear etched itself in every corner of Teemo's face. "*No!*" she shouted. "I didn't know. I—" Her neck arched abruptly back and her eyes rolled in their sockets. A final, desperate moan escaped her parted lips as she fell to her knees with a loud thud.

The sound of horses slamming against stable walls filled the air.

Lyse halted in front of the kneeling Teemo. Blood trickled from her eyes and down the sides of her face, becoming lost in her red hair. Gradually, like a marionette whose strings were being teased, Teemo's head and limbs began to twitch. Then, as if those very same strings were now being yanked, her eyes rolled back in place and she stood in one smooth, fluid motion. Her head jerked forward toward Lyse and then dropped to one side as if the strings were no longer being pulled taut. The horses retreated as far back into their stalls as possible.

Lyse took a step back and cleared his throat. "I want to know how you met Kira and why you're interested in him."

A terrible smile slowly shaped Teemo's lips, and a voice spoke that was her own and yet not.

"Long has it been since I have seen this face."

BLOOD OF MY BLOOD

YOU ARE NOT my uncle.

But it doesn't matter.

You're alive; you're here.

Kira was not sure when it had happened, when he had stopped doubting Kim and finally taken his words as truth. Nor could he place the moment he had stopped tormenting himself about Eutau's lack of trust in him, that Eutau had never trusted him. But none of that mattered now.

We will start over again.

This desire had now become his obsession.

Kim had insisted that Kira stay with him or at least travel slowly for fear of discovery, but Kira, determined to reach Eutau immediately, had refused. Since leaving The Laughing Man three days before, he had ridden toward Florinia like one possessed, throwing caution to the wind as he hurtled down Trader's Road into the delta country of the River of Veins.

Now, with Lyse, Teemo, and their exhausted horses behind him, he stood before a grand house not a mile away from the high ivory walls of Florinia. The house was large and low to the ground, surrounded by walls covered with vines. Beyond its heavy wooden gates was the future that Kira sought to claim.

He took a firm hold of the worn rope that hung to one side of the gates and pulled it. The chimes of bells filled the air, sending a flock of songbirds that had been resting in a nearby tree to the clear blue sky.

After a few minutes, a muffled voice called from behind the gate.

"Can I help you?" asked a woman.

Kira looked to Lyse, who nodded his approval. "I am looking for J'kara. Does she still live here?"

A moment's pause, and then, "Yes, she does. Who are you and what business do you have with her?"

"I am sorry, but my business is with her alone."

"That's not good enough."

"Please, just tell her . . . tell her it's Kira, and that I am here to see my uncle, Eutau Vidal."

Lyse raised a skeptical brow. "Was giving your name necessary?" He rested his hand on the pommel of his sword. "Friend or foe, who will it be?" he murmured. For a second, Kira felt deeply embarrassed, but then the door opened and drove all thought away.

An olive-skinned woman wearing a long coat embroidered with purple roses along the hem stood at the open gate. A thick shawl was draped around her shoulders. Her brown hair was tied back into three long tails, two of which rested on her flat chest. Luminescent feathers curved outward like an ocean wave from the nape of her neck. Golden-brown feathers lined her bottom lashes, accentuating the honey-brown of her eyes.

"Your pranks are wasted here," she said dispassionately, even as her eyes locked on his.

"It is no joke," said Kira. "Are you J'kara?"

"I am," she said in a stony tone, though a steady frown had begun to mar her brow.

"J'kara, it's me, Kira. I know the last time you saw me I was a baby and Eutau believes I am dead, but it really is me." He was babbling and he knew it, but he could not stop himself. "Please, I need to see him. I need to confirm with my own eyes that he is really alive."

Frustration crept into her voice. "I *know* you."

Kira recalled a memory that only he and J'kara knew. It was a memory easily overlooked but impossible to forget. "I would sneak out at night, following the full moon because I believed it would lead me to my uncle. I never made it past the little bridge over the stream, because I would always fall asleep. And when I woke up, you were always there by my side, assuring me that he would return one day. That he had not forgotten me."

J'kara blinked, and tears spilled from her honey-brown eyes. "And he did come back. Just as you have." Taking hold of the shawl, she wrapped her hands many times over and then reached up to touch his face. She was short—far shorter than he had remembered—and Kira hunched down so that she did not have to strain to reach.

She caressed his cheek and tenderly brushed his brow. The look on her face was the same that Kira had always imagined his mother would have given him. "Praise be His name, it is you!" she whispered, looking him over and smiling. "You have grown into such a handsome and tall man. Just like your uncle."

Just like my uncle . . . He ignored the sting her words caused him. "Is he well?"

She pulled away from him then, a grim line replacing her smile. "Eutau has been inconsolable. I have done what I can for him, but what he needs is you, not me." Her gaze drifted to the two standing quietly behind him. "Your companions, Kira?"

"Yes. I met them shortly after leaving the Spears. This is Lyse, and this is Teemo," he said, pointing to each in turn. "They are the reason I was able to make it here." Lyse half-laughed and shook his head, as if the compliment was more than he deserved, while Teemo simply nodded without looking up.

What's wrong with her? thought Kira. It was true that they had had little enough time to speak on the wild ride from The Laughing Man, but even on their brief rest periods Teemo had been unusually distant. *Is she afraid that Daemeon will be displeased with her if I choose to stay with uncle?* He ran his fingers through his hair. *I'll speak with her privately afterward. And if need be, I will speak with the woman herself. I will not see Teemo harmed on my account.*

"Eutau told me you had passed through the Spears," said J'kara. "The very idea that you were in that dreadful place makes my skin crawl. Please"—she waved for them to enter—"come in."

Kira stepped through the gate and instantly beheld a memory both familiar and foreign: a rectangular courtyard with a roof that was the very sky itself, a cobblestone floor as black as his hair, a maze of pillars and doors beyond the courtyard that he had never been able to figure out, large clay pots scattered about and overflowing with flowers. The vague memories of his early childhood washed over him at the sight, as did the memory of his uncle playing with him in the very same courtyard—the memory of the man who had always smiled at him.

A hand touched his shoulder, bringing him back to the present.

"Nothing has changed, has it?" J'kara asked quietly, as if knowing what he was thinking.

"No." Reaching for her shawl-wrapped hand, he brought it up to his lips and kissed it. Strands of gray were spread throughout her brown hair, and the passing of time had written itself around her eyes. "It's all the same. Even you," he said, lying. Then, "I want to see him."

She nodded and turned to address Lyse and Teemo. "I know you must be tired after your journey, but would you mind waiting here while I show Kira to his uncle?"

"Of course not," said Lyse. Teemo said nothing.

"Thank you for all that you have done for my Kira. When Eutau brought me the news that he had perished . . ." J'kara licked her lips and then took in a deep breath that she quickly let out. "You have my eternal gratitude. By His name the door to this house will always be open to both of you."

Lyse spoke up in surprise. "By 'His' do you mean the Faceless God? I was of the belief that Florinia had traded in the old for the new."

A strange defiance overtook J'kara. "The new gods have no place in my life."

A half laugh escaped Lyse's lips. There was an odd glint in his eyes. "You must know that Kira is being hunted by the Ascendancy."

"Of course."

"And it does not frighten you?"

"No."

"Why?" Lyse pressed her, his voice severe.

"Lyse, what are you doing?" Kira called out to him, taken aback by his rudeness.

J'kara was not a tall woman, but as she took a step closer to Lyse she appeared just as tall and proud as him.

"I suppose I could say that my love of Kira stems from me viewing him as a gift sent by the God of the South to ease my solitude. But that would be a lie. To me, Kira is my son. I cared for him when he was nothing more than a babe and watched him grow before my eyes until Eutau decided it was best to leave." She paused as if the memory was something that was still tangibly painful. "My happiest memories are with this child, and I will protect him even if it means spilling my blood or the blood of others."

A completely different look washed over Lyse then, a look that Kira was certain was admiration. "He is precious to me as well. And I too would see the Land burn before giving him up."

Startled, Kira felt his face burn. "Lyse?" he asked, embarrassed. He had not realized just how much the man had come to care for him.

"Go on," said Lyse, a visible exhaustion washing over him. "Go to your uncle. When you are both ready, Teemo and I will be waiting. I am happy for you, but I must confess that I am also saddened. I was going to ask if you wanted to stay and travel with me." He barked an almost desperate laugh, and a deep, raw sadness gripped his countenance. "The time we spent together has made me feel as if my dead brother were alive. You remind me so much of him that it hurts. But you are not blood of my blood, you cannot be, though I wish it were otherwise."

Lyse fell momentarily silent as he ran his gloved fingers across his scarred brow. "Go. Afterward, when your heart is whole once again, we will talk. There are matters we must speak of." He turned away from Kira then and did not look back.

Kira stared at Lyse's back, stunned, not sure what to say or do. After Eutau, Lyse was the person he had come to care for and trust the most. The last thing he wanted to do was hurt him. He looked to Teemo, hoping that she would say something, anything, but she too had turned her back on him.

"Let's go, Kira," said J'kara, wrapping her arm around his. "Eutau needs you. Afterward, you can speak with your friends."

"Yeah." *Afterward . . .* Afterward, he would try to make things right. But for now, he needed to be with Eutau.

There had, perhaps, always been a tiny voice in his head whispering that his uncle was more than what he claimed to be. And though Kira had never given credence to that voice, he was now prepared to see things through to the end. He was tired of lies, most of all from the person dearest to him. The truth would mark the beginning of a new life.

WE'RE HERE," SAID J'kara. She shot him a worried look. "Are you alright?"

Kira had been so engrossed in his thoughts that he had paid no mind where she had led him. He looked around to find that they were in a long, brick-lined passageway. Thin columns lined with the remnants of rose vines held in place an awning overhead. On the ground beside each pillar were rosebuds, long-withered and blackened. They had halted in front of a door, pale-blue and arched, with paint that had begun to curl off.

He turned to face the door. "I'm fine. Just nervous," he said.

"Are you ready?"

He nodded, and she knocked. No one answered. "Eutau, there is someone here to see you. Someone who I think you would be happy to see."

A long silence followed, and then, "Tell them to fuck off."

She turned to look up at him as if saying, "You try." Kira took a shuddering breath and called out.

"Uncle? It's me. Kira. Please answer the door."

There was a commotion from behind the door, as if someone had stumbled, and then . . .

Eutau stood in the open doorway.

Kira's stomach lurched and his heart crawled up his throat. His knees were suddenly weak, and his entire body ached as if he had been beaten. In that moment, he realized that he was afraid, afraid that he was dreaming and that he would awaken to a reality where Eutau was dead.

"Uncle?" he asked.

Eutau embraced him so fiercely that his back popped. "I dreamed of this," Eutau said, sobbing hysterically. "I dreamed that you would come back to me, but I dared not believe."

Kira engulfed his uncle in his arms. All the grief he had felt poured out like a flood. "I thought you were dead! I swore I would keep you safe and when you died—" He stopped, not wanting to relive that nightmare. "I have missed you so much!"

At some point J'kara had quietly left, though Kira had not been aware of it. He followed Eutau into the room and watched as the door closed slowly behind him.

The room was spacious and well-furnished. Woolen rugs of various patterns covered the floor, and veils of delicate fabric covered the walls. Decorative oil lanterns hung from the ceiling, casting all in a soft, warm glow. A small cage was propped near the bed. In it were Belle and Leto, huddled next to each other, sleeping. Pen was nowhere in sight. Kira's heart sank, but he dared not ask what had happened.

Eutau was shirtless and barefoot, his scars accentuated by the flickering light. He wore only trousers and smelled heavily of wine and tobacco. He took a seat on a corner of the bed and motioned for Kira to sit next to him. Kira began to follow but stopped upon noticing a handful of *nologis* sitting atop the nightstand alongside a bottle of wine and a sheathed dagger. He recalled Kim's words back at The Laughing Man— that Eutau had been acting like a *pé'bos*—and wondered how long his uncle had been using the *nologis* and if it had had a role in his behavior.

Whatever had happened before, Eutau was no longer filthy as Kim had described him. Aside from the worn look on his face, he looked exactly as he had in Opulancae—his hair was no longer, his body was no thinner, everything was physically the same. Kira decided to hold his tongue about the *nologis* and instead sat on the floor next to Eutau, resting his head on his uncle's thigh. Eutau's fingers began stroking his hair.

Kira was home. They sat there in silence for some time, for he did not want to talk. He did not want to say anything that would change the bond between them. But, for the sake of a new beginning, he knew that he needed to put all the lies behind him.

"I ran into Kim several days ago. It was he who told me that you were alive."

"The water was far deeper than I had expected. When I at last surfaced there was no trace of you, and I began searching the Spears." Eutau sighed wearily. "I had lost both you and Pen. But you are here now. With me."

Pen is dead, Kira thought sadly, and he wrapped his arms tightly around Eutau's leg so he could not flee. It was now or never.

"Kim also told me that you are a Doll. Is it true?" Eutau went deathly still. "Uncle, please tell me the truth. I don't care if you are a Doll, but I need to know. Please, trust me!"

Eutau's hand twitched and the muscles in his thigh tensed. For a brief second, Kira was certain his uncle would push him away, but then Eutau's body relaxed and he began stroking Kira's hair again.

"When you were a little boy," Eutau said quietly, "you had the grating habit of regularly asking how I received so many scars. One day, after listening to you guess for an entire morning how I had gotten them, I gave you an answer. Do you remember what I told you?"

Kira clearly remembered that day. The answer had kept him awake for an entire week. "You said that you were a Doll who had left his cruel master. That the scars on your body were because your master had sewn together the flesh of different men to form your own." An uncomfortable feeling settled in the pit of his stomach. "I thought it was just a story, but it wasn't, was it?"

"If I could be your uncle . . ." Eutau's voice faltered, and Kira looked up at him. Tears were streaming down his cheeks. "All I wanted to be was your uncle. But I cannot be, because I am a Doll."

"But you *are* my uncle. My feelings for you have not changed. If anything, I think I understand now why you always passionately opposed me making a Doll of my own. If you had *trusted* me from the beginning we could have avoided so many conflicts and misunderstandings. I would never have tried to make a Doll, and I would certainly not have nagged you about it."

Eutau looked down at him, his very soul pouring through his eyes. "And can you live without ever realizing your potential?"

Kira pushed away from Eutau, though he remained seated on the floor. "I don't know. I'm not going to lie to you, but for now" — he looked straight into his uncle's storm-gray, pupil-less eyes — "I can live without making a Doll. But what I do want is to become stronger. Strong enough to keep us both safe."

Eutau gave an unusual look and then nodded slowly. "Do you hate me for not having trusted you?"

"Of course not! But promise me that there are no more lies."

"I promise."

Kira let out a sigh of relief. "Honestly, I would rather have learned the truth from you, not Kim."

"Ah yes, Kim. How is he?" Eutau asked, far too coldly.

Kira looked at him sternly. "Kim's fine, and you are going to let him be."

Eutau's eyes widened in dismay as if Kira had cursed at him. "Very well," he said, visibly displeased. Standing, he walked over to the nightstand and drew the dagger from its sheath. The blade was long, and it curved inward ever so slightly.

"Come sit," he said, pointing to the bed. "Your hair is far too long. How you managed not to strangle yourself with it is a mystery."

Kira shot him a dirty look but sat on the edge of the bed. His eyes fell on the *nologis* again. "Are you in pain?"

"I am a Doll, Kira. What pain would I feel?"

Kira picked up the smallest nub of *nologis* and rolled it around in his palm. "Please, don't be this way with me."

Eutau let out a trembling sigh. "Forgive me." He cut Kira's hair halfway down the back, the blade slicing through it as if it were air. Once done, he gathered the locks, placed them in the porcelain washbowl, and sat down beside Kira.

"My heart was" —he spat the word—"*damaged* by the Kataru at Corpse Hill. It has been bothering me since that night, but this past month has been particularly unpleasant."

"Do you need to see your maker?" Kira asked delicately, taking pains to avoid the word "master."

Eutau's response was chokingly bitter. "I will *never* go back."

An unexpected knot settled in Kira's stomach as more of Kim's words came back to him: *Eutau's allegiance cannot be to you.* "I thought a Doll needed its maker's blood in order to survive?"

Eutau leaned forward, arms resting on his knees, his body tense. "I am different from other Dolls in the sense that my life belongs solely to me. My maker has no power over me. I control my life, but I cannot mend my own body. I was careless in the cemetery."

A surge of relief washed over Kira at hearing Eutau refute Kim's warning. "Do you think I could heal you?" he asked carefully, trying his best to mask his excitement.

"Irony is quite the fucker. I forbid you from making a Doll, and yet I have wondered if you can fix me."

"You are not a Doll. You are my uncle."

Eutau patted Kira's hand. "If you feel that way, then I suppose I still am. But tell me, how did you manage to get this far?"

"I made some friends along the way. I was hoping to introduce you to them."

"Friends?" asked Eutau, concerned. "Do they know who and what you are?"

"You know, that is exactly what Kim asked me as well," said Kira. Eutau sneered at the comparison. "They know who I am and, please, try not to judge them until you have met them. Okay?"

"Very well," said Eutau, smiling at him as if he were still a foolish child. "Did you and your friends travel the back roads, at least?"

"For most of the way, yes. But there was no need. The people in the South believe I am a Ro'Erden. Even the Ro'Erden I have met believe I am one of them, though they have looked down on me as a *moma*." To Kira's surprise, Eutau fell silent, and he felt that there was something else. "Uncle, was my mother Ro'Erden? Or maybe my father? Remember, no more lies."

Eutau grabbed the wine bottle from the nightstand and took a long drink before answering. "Your mother was Ro'Erden. She was the most beautiful woman I have ever seen, with long silver hair and emerald-gold eyes just like yours."

A thrill of excitement rushed through Kira, for it was the first time Eutau had truly spoken of his mother. "And my father. Did you know him as well? He must have been the Deadbringer, then? And if my mother was Ro'Erden, does this mean my father wasn't from the Western Mountains after all?"

Eutau took another drink, this one far shorter. "No, I did not know him."

Kira's heart sank. "Oh. Well, do I at least look like my mother?"

"You bear some resemblance to her, yes. Certainly the eyes."

"I guess I must look more like my father?"

"I suppose so. Kira, did you not say you wanted me to meet your friends? Did they come with you?"

"Yes. They should be waiting in the courtyard."

Eutau put the wine down and stood. He walked over to a wooden chest lined with thin sheets of brightly painted metal. Throwing the top open, he pulled out a loose-fitting blue shirt that covered his scars. "Let us be off. I am eager to meet these friends you speak so fondly of."

"You're making fun of me," said Kira, only half-joking.

"*Nit*, my dear nephew. I am merely curious."

Together, they left the room and began making their way to the courtyard.

"Uncle, do you know what happened in the Spears?"

"What do you mean?"

"Well, when the attack happened and I first fell into the water, it seemed to have no end. But when I tried going back into it to search for you, it was only ankle-deep. Is that what happened to you?"

Eutau ran his fingers through his uneven hair and cursed. "I will be damned if I know what happened in that accursed forest. All I know is that when I surfaced you were nowhere in sight and the water was as you described it. One day, I will torch that shit-stain of a place and watch with pleasure as it burns."

Kira laughed. "Wouldn't you burn half the Land along with it?"

Eutau shrugged and then stopped in his tracks. They had just entered the courtyard.

"Lyse, Teemo!" called Kira, excited to see them there.

"Kira, do you trust me?" Eutau asked urgently.

"Of course I do, why?"

"Then go! Please, go now!"

"Wait, why?"

"GO!"

What's going on? Kira thought in confusion, but before he could gather his wits Lyse stalked up to them, his voice a howl of fury and anguish, his amber eyes ablaze with a surreal light.

"*YOU! YOU KEPT HIM FROM US!*"

Kira rounded on him. "What's wrong with you? Why are you so upset?"

"Ask him!" shouted Lyse, pointing at Eutau. "He knows damn well why!"

In a flash, Eutau drew a hidden dagger from his shirt and lanced himself at Lyse, who deftly moved away and drew his sword.

"*STOP IT!*" shouted Kira, grabbing onto Eutau's arms and forcing him to drop the dagger. Eutau struggled to free himself and Kira had to fight with all his strength just to barely keep hold of him. Lyse closed in and Kira turned to him. "Don't do this, please!"

At his plea, Lyse wavered and sheathed his sword. "I had my suspicions, but I could not believe, I dared *not* believe it possible that you were blood of my blood." His voice was thick with emotion.

"What do you mean?"

"Kira, you are my dead brother's son. Of this I no longer have any doubt because *he*" — he pointed to Eutau — "he knows it as well."

"That's a lie!" screamed Kira. "He never knew my father. And how do you even know him?"

"Your so-called uncle's name is not 'Eutau.' He is a Doll, and he knows exactly who your father was. He knows all of us, especially his master, my sister, Daemeon."

Eutau snarled back, shaking himself free from Kira's grasp. "You would have made Kira as vile as *him!*"

Kira could not believe his ears. He stared at Eutau. "Wait, you *did* know my father? Are saying that you lied to me? Didn't you just swear that you would *not* lie to me anymore? And you!" He rounded on Lyse. "You know Daemeon? She's your *sister*? And what of you, Teemo?" he asked, turning to her. "Did you know about all of this? Did you enjoy laughing behind my back?"

For the first time since leaving The Laughing Man she looked him in the eyes. Terror was on her face. "I didn't know! I didn't know that you and *he*—" She flinched and looked away. "I want no part in this," she whispered, and ran off out the front gate, vanishing.

"Kira, please listen to me!" Eutau implored him.

"Listen to you?" sneered Lyse. "Why? So you can tell him more lies?" He laughed in disgust. "You told him he was a Deadbringer. A fucking *Deadbringer* of all things!"

Eutau ignored him. "Kira, hate me all you want but please, I am begging you, stay away from Daemeon. She is a monster. They all are."

Kira felt numb and cold, and more than anything else he was suddenly possessed with an overwhelming urge to hurt Eutau. "Then I suppose I am a monster as well. Maybe this is why you have never been able to trust me."

"*No*! You are nothing like them!"

Kira turned his attention back to Lyse. "And what's your excuse for lying to me?"

"I never lied to you. Yes, you resemble my brother, but without solid proof I could not allow myself to believe that you were my brother's son."

"Why? You couldn't stomach the idea of a *fucking Deadbringer* as your blood?"

Lyse flinched. "Because I wanted you to be his son so badly that every time I looked at you it hurt. Your features, your abilities, everything resembled him—us!—but if I allowed myself to believe that you were his son I might have let my guard down and hurt you. It was better for me to believe that you were a Deadbringer, a friend, someone I cared deeply for but would forever need to keep at arm's length."

"Am I not a Deadbringer, uncle?" Kira asked Eutau, yearning for this not to be another lie.

"All I have done has been to keep you safe."

"Safe from what? Him?" Kira pointed to Lyse. "From Daemeon? Do you know that it was she who rescued me from the Spears? That it was she who made it possible for *ME TO EVEN BE HERE!*" He was shouting now, and it tore at him. He laughed then, he laughed wildly because it was the only thing he could do to keep himself from screaming.

"And I suppose us meeting"—he pointed at Lyse—"was just a grand coincidence?"

"Yes, it was," said Lyse in a tone that dared Kira to doubt him. "Our meeting in the Labyrinth only happened because *you* chose not to ignore me. Had you continued on your way with Teemo, we would never have met and I would most likely still be with Sa and Telera in Ghlande. As for Daemeon, my sister's affairs are not my business. But once I heard that your . . . *uncle* was alive I confronted her, because I wanted to make certain that she did not want you as one of her pets."

"And I suppose I'm not privy to what was discussed between you because it was being done to keep me *safe*."

"You're being dramatic," snapped Lyse. Then, less harshly, he said, "If you will recall, I said I wanted to speak with you after your business with this Doll was done. I was going to tell you of my sister. Unlike your *uncle*" —again he sneered the word—"I had no intention of keeping you forever in the dark."

Kira's gaze traveled to Eutau, who seemed somehow small and, above all, resigned. Their eyes locked, and he felt the fool for not being able to hold back his tears. But it hurt; it hurt to learn that the man he had trusted the most had lied to him over, and over, and over again. As if he were a spectator watching a play, Kira watched as Eutau's hand, which had moments ago comforted him, reached out to do so once more. But he did not want this man's comfort.

"Don't touch me," he said heatedly. Eutau made an agonized sound in his throat and looked away, stumbling, his hand clutching at his heart. Kira wavered, for in his own heart he longed to be at his uncle's side, assuring him that everything was going to be all right, that the lies did not matter. But Eutau had broken his trust, and Kira's desire to know the truth was stronger than his heart's yearning.

To no one in particular, he asked mildly, "Then what is the truth?"

Lyse removed his gloves and closed the gap between them. As he spoke, his skin became ashen, his amber eyes lusterless and milky white, his pupils thin, piercing slits. A deep black like *atche* fiercely bordered the shape of his eyes, turning them truly into those of a cat. He rested his hand on Kira's cheek, bidding him to call upon Death as well. The sensation was cold and pleasant, but above all it was familiar, familiar and intoxicating.

"You are the son of my younger half brother Shonnell, and you are blood of my blood and of Daemeon's, my sister. In your veins courses not the blood of Deadbringers but that of a race extinct for millennia. You are Ellderet."

SUMMONS

THE TEN'S CHAMBERS were filled with the odor of wet earth and mold. Kristoff and Marya were deep beneath the Citadel of the Ascendancy, and there were no windows to allow Florinia's ocean winds to spirit away the stench. In place of daylight, a lone chandelier, forged of twisted metals and larger than a horse, hung overhead in the center of the room, casting all in a false sunset.

Marya cleared her throat. The sound bounced menacingly off the stone walls. From the corner of his eye Kristoff saw her turn her head toward him, as if wanting to say something. He remained silent, his face betraying nothing, his eyes ever forward. She took note of his reaction and from then on kept her sights on the large metal mesh screen that had been erected a dozen paces beyond the chandelier. Kristoff could see nothing through the screen, but he suspected that the light overhead illuminated his silhouette for anyone on the other side.

Behind the screen sat the Ten.

This was Marya's first time in the room, a room that lay ten floors down a wide descent of stone-carved spiral stairs. Kristoff had counted them on his first visit, many years before. Normally, the Ten did not bother themselves with giving orders in person. They would instead send a tall woman whose face was always hidden behind a veil so dark that Kristoff had wondered how she could see. Her name was Han, a word Kristoff had learned meant "ten" in the Ro'Erden tongue. He had almost laughed upon learning that fact, for she *was* the Ten as far as most of the Ascendancy was concerned. Ever since the end of the Purging, when the reclusive Ten had vanished entirely from the public eye, it had been she who commanded the Ascendancy's generals, and the Sanctifier bands answered only to her.

Han's quarters were on the ground floor of the Citadel. From an oak desk with high stacks of papers, with thickly bound books of dried leather at her feet, she dispensed the Ten's orders and saw to the city's needs. Nailed to the wall directly behind her desk was a grand map detailing not only the Land of Moenda and the Southern Islands but also Vi'ame—the island to which many of the surviving Ro'Erden had fled after the Great Dance of the Dead and the Land—and other continents Kristoff had only heard rumor of.

A strong, husky voice called out from behind the metal screen, and Kristoff instinctively shut down his thoughts and focused only on the now. At first he had believed that the voice belonged to a man, but over the years he had picked up on certain nuances that betrayed the voice as female.

"The Deadbringer of Opulancae. You were unsuccessful in his capture, correct?"

The stone room had been built in such a way that any sound greater than a whisper carried. In dealing with the Ten, Kristoff had learned that it was best to speak only with certainty. There could be no doubt. Never.

"Yes. The Deadbringer and his kin escaped into the Gods' Spears." The siblings had been two weeks in Florinia, recuperating from their ordeal and searching for word of their quarry. Though Kristoff had submitted his report soon after arrival, the Ten had summoned them only that morning. Marya had not been pleased at the delay.

A high voice snorted, "Who cares about his kin!"

Silence, and then, "You sought passage on a merchant ship to Florinia. Why?" It was the husky voice again. There was no way of knowing if all of the Ten were present, or if they were even watching him. But, somehow, Kristoff knew that they were all there.

"E'sinea and Amonos discovered that the Deadbringer had strong ties to Florinia. We acted under the assumption that if the Deadbringer survived the Spears he would then make his way to Florinia." He waited for their response. The summons had been for all in his band, yet only he and Marya were present. That dangerous fact hung heavy on him.

"In your report to Han, you stated that you believe the attack on your ship was premeditated, and that it was carried out by a spellcaster.

Care to explain?" It had been a neutral, forever-skeptical voice that had asked the question.

Kristoff resisted the urge to take a deep breath. What he wanted to say was, *How often do ships with Sanctifiers on board suddenly go up in flames while the sailors sleep through their own fiery deaths?* But what he said instead was, "In Jané, there were rumors that the Bastion was preparing for conflict with the Ascendancy."

"Are you implying that the puny Bastion has risen up against us?" said the high voice, at once both dismissive and demanding. Kristoff hated that voice.

"Not necessarily," he said calmly. "That is a possibility, but the attack could have been organized by a Deadbringer or another of our enemies, or even one of our erstwhile allies. What I mean is that there are rumors of movement in the Land, and I believe someone powerful arranged that attack."

"Maybe it was a spellcaster–Deadbringer, yes?" asked a shy, quiet voice. "But such a creature is unheard of. I think, *mmm*, Kristoff's theory may have merit, though I concede other possibilities are viable."

Inwardly, Kristoff praised Fortune, grateful for not the first time to this member of the Ten. "The attack may have been from an organized group of Deadbringers," he said. "Yet the Bastion must not be overlooked."

"But in any case," asked the shy voice again, "if you are right, this means that a spellcaster greater than any of ours is running amok."

There was a murmur among the group, and then a solemn male voice spoke. "It would be foolish for us not to concede that the Bastion wishes to expand its power. Such is the nature of any organization. Kristoff, what course of action would you recommend to us?"

He had always felt a peculiar uneasiness, a mix of fear and admiration, when before the Ten. Part of it was the feeling that he needed to do everything he could to prove his devotion to their cause, the cause of unifying the Land as one people. He had never wavered from that devotion. Yet there had always been another feeling present as well, one that he could never place.

"I would advise sending a formal envoy to the Bastion," he responded. "In light of our forces' encroachment in the North—"

"It is our *right* to do as we please," said the high voice. "The Bastion is only in power in the North because we allow it."

"You're such an idiot," said a voice like silk. "Please, Kristoff, continue."

He swallowed. "I would also advise that we recall my fellow Sanctifiers from the North, at least until we ascertain that the Bastion is not plotting against us. I would not take them lightly, not after the incident in Opulancae, which, in hindsight, I confess was regrettable."

Silence. And then the question Kristoff had dreaded was asked.

"Kristoff, Marya," began the neutral voice, "where are E'sinea and Amonos?"

Kristoff hesitated, considering how to respond. The Ten knew all about Amonos's disappearance and exactly what had happened to E'sinea, for he had omitted nothing from his report save for the details of E'sinea's strange black tears and emotional outbursts. Those he had decided were better left unmentioned.

"E'sinea may have been lost to the sea," he said finally, hoping it was not true. "We are uncertain if he survived."

"And how did you both survive, while E'sinea did not?"

"Fortune," answered Kristoff, with characteristic reverence.

A prolonged silence followed. Finally, "Marya. Do you think E'sinea really died?" It was the shy voice.

She responded immediately. "It is unclear."

"Then what of Amonos?"

"He too will return to Florinia, if he spoke truth in the note he left behind," said Kristoff.

"Do you have this note?" asked the neutral voice, its normally mild tones inflected with unmasked cynicism.

"No. E'sinea fed it to his horse."

"A Deadbringer looking after another Deadbringer," tittered the high voice. Murmurs of agreement rose in the air, and in truth even Kristoff had to agree that E'sinea likely knew more than he had let on. Only Marya believed E'sinea's word without any doubts.

Kristoff cautiously continued. "We suspect that Amonos may have taken it upon himself to find and eliminate the Deadbringer."

"We?" asked the neutral voice.

Travail strike me, they already know the answer! Why this show of ignorance? He gritted his teeth. "Amonos is a formidable warrior. In light of his disappearance, I believed it prudent to reveal my orders to Marya."

"Did you, now," whispered the solemn voice. Something in the tone made the hair on Kristoff's neck stand on end.

The silken voice spoke up. "Amonos has ever been a problem. And slaughtering two agents in front of Lafont, of all people, was hardly prudent."

"Do you think E'sinea will betray us?" asked the shy voice.

"No," Kristoff answered immediately. "He was surprised by Amonos's disappearance."

"*Tsk,* don't tell me you believed his act?" said the high voice.

"He has given us no reason to distrust him."

"Kristoff," said the silken voice, "E'sinea trusts you, doesn't he." It was not a question.

"Yes."

"And do you trust E'sinea?"

"Yes." He had waited a fraction of a second too long to answer. He prayed to Fortune that the Ten had not noticed.

"If E'sinea has survived and seeks you out, you will inform Han immediately," said the silken voice. It was impossible to tell from her inflection if she had believed him.

"What of Amonos?" he asked.

It was the high voice that answered. "E'sinea may just have to learn to live without his dog."

The words hung in the air.

"What are our orders?" Kristoff asked stiffly.

"You and Marya are to remain in Florinia and continue searching for the Deadbringer from Opulancae. If your suspicion is correct and he has come here, he will not be hard to find. But if he has not been found in a month's time, we will speak again."

"It will be as the Ten commands."

"Kristoff, Marya," said the solemn voice. "We have high hopes for you. For the good of the Land, I pray that you will not disappoint us."

"For the good of the Land and its people, I will not falter," said Kristoff, echoed by Marya.

"See that it is so," said the silken voice. "Rest assured that your advice has not been in vain. We will speak with Han and choose an envoy to send to the North. You are dismissed."

For the first time since entering, Kristoff bowed his head low to the ground. "You honor me." Then he and Marya left the room and the Ten behind.

Neither spoke a word on the long way up, though Marya's obvious displeasure became more pronounced with each step they took. *The walls have ears,* Kristoff had told her upon receiving the summons. *Whatever you may wish to say, wait until we are beyond the gates of the Citadel.*

I know this, Marya had retorted, annoyed.

Then I trust I will not have to repeat myself.

Daylight blinded them as they exited the stairwell. The sun had begun its journey west, toward the highlands and the clans.

"The Ten would probably be right at home in the Gods' Spears."

"Marya," Kristoff said severely.

"What?" She spat. "I meant it as a compliment." The smile that played across her lips was anything but complimenting. Had E'sinea and

Amonos been present, he knew they would not only have agreed with her but would have taken the jab a step further.

"Let us return to the inn," he said, his voice sharp.

She sneered at him. "Let's, dear brother."

She's angry, thought Kristoff, unsurprised. He was on edge as well. *The Ten made no mention of our clan, nor of the letter sent by father.* Moreover, the words of the high, grating voice echoed in his mind: *E'sinea may just have to learn to live without his dog.*

If it were only that easy, reflected Kristoff. *Do they mean to hunt Amonos down? If so, what of E'sinea?*

As they made their way to the gates, Kristoff scanned the Citadel's activity like he always did. The Citadel was located in the inmost part of the city, on the shoreline a stone's throw away from the port. It was enclosed within an inner wall built of the same white stone as the Waning Wall that surrounded the entire city. The Citadel itself was composed of two rectangular stone buildings connected by elevated walkways, surrounded by a courtyard of setts and hard-packed earth. Four watchtowers stood about the courtyard, forming a larger rectangle around the main buildings. There were a good number of soldiers about, but no other Sanctifiers that he could see.

They had just entered the outer courtyard, heading to the Citadel's gates, when they passed a Ro'Erden that Kristoff had not seen in years.

"Jun," whispered Marya, her voice barely audible. And yet that whisper had been enough. He turned and looked at them, a flash of surprise and nostalgia showing on his face.

"Marya," he said, approaching them with a warm smile. "You look well."

Marya pursed her lips. "As do you."

"Kristoff." Jun inclined his head in a show of respect. "It has been a while."

Jun was striking for a Ro'Erden, several inches taller than Kristoff, lean yet powerful and strongly built. He had grown out his once oiled-back, shoulder-length hair and set it in a high tail, as was the norm for his kin. He wore a gray soldier's uniform, which showed from beneath a long brigandine, and plated leather greaves. His feet were bare, though Kristoff knew better than to mistake that for a vulnerability.

"Six years," answered Kristoff.

"Your band was tasked with apprehending a Deadbringer in the North. Opulancae, if I am not mistaken."

"That is correct."

"I thought you were stationed in Suelosa?" asked Marya. "Is the Lady A'ka with you?"

"We arrived this morning. The news of Deadbringers emerging found its way to Suelosa. An old woman whose inn we frequented was accused of harboring them."

"And what do you think? Were the accusations true?" asked Kristoff, now curious, for Jun had always been a practical man, one of the few Ro'Erden who had viewed Deadbringers as a threat to be respected, rather than an ancient enemy to be despised. He had been an honorable warrior, and yet . . .

"It was envy that lay under the charges, nothing more. But the damage to her reputation had already been done. A'ka took pity on the woman and convinced her to come to Florinia for her own safety, to clear her name before the Ten. The woman's heart gave out soon after we left."

So he is still A'ka's guard, observed Kristoff, running a finger across one of his hooped earrings. After the loss of his right horn, Jun had given up the Sanctifier's black and his rank of Captain for the gray of a common soldier. He now settled for being A'ka's shadow, wandering from town to town and reporting what he saw back to the Ten. Kristoff had been unable to understand how a warrior such as Jun could shame himself by stepping down from a position of command to that of a servant, even if the master was the daughter of one of the Ten.

As if he had summoned her by thought, the scent of roses caught his nose, and he turned to see A'ka striding up to them. She gave a knowing smile. "I heard everything."

The siblings shot quick glances at each other.

"You know what I mean," she said with a practiced sigh. "Mother said it was time I sat in on those tiresome meetings, but yours was anything but boring."

A'ka was an extraordinarily tall woman, at least two inches taller than Jun. Her skin was gloomy, and the slightest tinge of gray and palest of pinks surrounding her eyes and lips only added to the dreariness of her appearance. To Kristoff, she resembled a piece of chalk that had sprouted ivory horns and black hair. She wore a thick woolen coat and a long black dress that dragged across the courtyard's setts as she walked.

Jun looked at her reproachfully. "A'ka, how many times have I advised you not to speak so boldly?"

"Far too many times. But there is no need to be shy in front of our friends, is there?" She openly studied them with her jade eyes, which reminded Kristoff of those of a *tezca* snake. He wondered which member of the Ten was her mother, though he suspected it was the woman with the silken voice.

"No," said Kristoff at last. "You honor my sister and myself with such trust."

"Jun," said Marya. "Finish your story. What happened in Suelosa?"

"The same as what happened in every town during the Purging. The people are turning against each other. But the Ten have an interest in Suelosa, so the Ascendancy cannot idly sit back and let it burn. Our soldiers have reestablished order, but the head of the merchants' guild was angered by our protection of the accused innkeeper."

"Jun threatened to level the guild members' homes if they kept defying him. It was quite the show," said A'ka, pleased. "Even better, he threatened to take back the head merchant's land holdings and sell his children as slaves to the southern islanders. It was all justly deserved. Sadly, the old innkeeper did not survive to clear her name. Poor thing, I did like her."

"The Land has embraced her. Had she remained in Suelosa, her death would have been far less kind," Jun said matter-of-factly. But A'ka was not satisfied.

"The people of this land are unruly, undisciplined. Mother says the Land was a mess before the Ascendancy came into power, but, frankly, I see little progress."

"The Land has come far," said Kristoff, failing to restrain his irritation.

"Has it? Then why is Moenda divided into North and South? Why is the Bastion allowed to do as it pleases, as if it was the one responsible for bringing unity? The people act according to their own selfish interests, using tragedy and pity and religion as weapons and shields. And why is that? I say it is because this land did not learn proper fear and respect during the Purging. The people of this land have been allowed to do as they please for far too long."

Kristoff was speechless. Everything he had ever done as a Sanctifier had been to bring peace to the Land, to unite its people. To suggest the Land was in chaos was an insult to his honor and to the memory of those who had fallen before him. Only the quick hand of Marya squeezing his wrist restrained him from some action that he would have regretted.

"Marya," began Jun, seemingly unfazed, as if he was accustomed to such insults, "will you be in Florinia long?"

"For a month, perhaps longer," she said, clearing her throat and smoothing out the fabric of her Sanctifier's cloak.

A ghost of a smile played across Jun's lips as if saying, *I know that gesture.* "Perhaps we will see each other again, then. I am staying at the inn near the new port, should you wish to catch up. A'ka?"

A'ka pushed a strand of black hair behind an ivory horn. Her eyes flickered to Marya, and then she smiled. "I have to speak with Han. Do as you please, Jun."

Her words were followed by a cascade of explosions.

THE FACELESS GOD

THE **CRENELATED WALL** ringing Florinia was known in the South as the Waning Wall. It was set in a semi-circle that began and ended on the shores of the Eastern Sea, and its face was as luminous as the full moon itself, its top capped with elaborate merlons dotted with ornate arrowslits. In its northwestern face the city's main gate opened onto Trader's Road where it ran in from the delta country. A huge, fortified watchtower stood guard on each side of the gate, as if proclaiming Florinia's power to all comers.

Kira stood before a different gate, a small one too narrow for a merchant's cart but just wide enough for a single rider and his horse. It opened discreetly on the wall's southwestern side, not far from the Eastern Sea but far enough from the main gate to be unobtrusive. A few people passed in and out, but there were none of the merchant convoys and crowds that streamed through on Trader's Road. It was through this second gate that Kira had decided to enter.

Up close, the stark whiteness of the Waning Wall reminded him of bone porcelain, a material that had always felt pleasant against his bare skin, like the smooth, cold flesh of the recently deceased. He found himself possessed with the urge to run his hands over the wall, to revel in its coolness. But soldiers clad in light armor and the gray cloaks of the Ascendancy stood guard on the battlements overhead, silently studying him. He ignored them. After all, he was no longer the Deadbringer from Opulancae.

Still, he threw back his hood to show he had nothing to hide and walked through the gate, into the city. He held his breath, waiting to hear the sounds of swift footfalls pounding after him, but none came. Kira let out a sigh of relief and merged with the flow of traffic.

From the roof of J'kara's house, he had marveled at the size of the city. He had watched until the sun completed its journey westward and twilight had brushed the approaching night in violent purples and melancholic blues. Kira had sat alone, wondering when Eutau would unlock the door to his room, when Lyse would awaken from the sudden sleep that had incapacitated him.

That sleep had been a terrible thing to behold. One moment, Lyse was before him, exhausted yet standing. The next, Lyse's legs had buckled and he was twisting his body as he fell to avoid hitting his face in the dirt. Kira had expected Lyse to be as shocked as Kira was himself, but what he had found instead was annoyance. He understood then that it had not been the first time it had happened.

Shit, why now! Lyse had cursed. *I'm fine. Just . . . need to sleep.* His eyes had closed then, and nothing Kira did to rouse him had worked. Kira had carried him to one of the rooms J'kara had set aside for them. It was only seconds after Lyse's body touched the bed that the wooden frame began to creak. Kira knew from experience that the bed would not last long. The truth was strangely comforting.

As for Teemo, he had considered searching for her to see if she would accompany him to the city, but after looking for some time without success he had decided to let her be. If she wanted to be left alone, he would respect that.

A stab of guilt jabbed at Kira as the memory of his conversation with J'kara surfaced. He had revealed everything about Eutau, yet he had still omitted much of what Lyse had told him, especially the parts about his father. He had been afraid that J'kara would become frightened of him, especially since Kira himself was having trouble believing what he had learned.

It did not seem real. It could not be real.

And so this morning Kira ventured into Florinia alone, hoping to at once distract and order his thoughts. Pushing aside the memories of the day before, he focused on the today that was before him. He had promised J'kara that he would return before nightfall, and he meant to keep that promise.

Closely built structures covered in white stucco and reaching nearly thirty yards high dominated the city. The low morning sun cast long shadows on many of the streets, which were cobbled with red and black setts. Kira avoided the shadow-laden streets as much as he could, seeking the sun's warmth as he wandered. As he walked the streets of Florinia he stared, nearly forgetting his own cares in wonder at the architecture surrounding him and the multitude of different races living within the city — southerners, northerners, Katarus, Florinese, islanders, Ro'Erden, and *momas* of every kind. The people around him were bundled up as if for the coldest of winters, and he smiled, idly wondering how they would handle the North's snows.

The diversity around him was striking, for he had never realized how similar everyone in Opulancae had been. Kira's height and pale skin had allowed him to blend in well in the North, but the few southerners like Kim who lived in Opulancae had been instantly visible. He had only seen Katarus on rare occasions, and it was easy to forget that they were even there. And, of course, there had been no Ro'Erden.

As Kira leaned against a wall, resting, a Ro'Erden man carrying a basket full of root vegetables and slender batons of bread walked by with his young daughter skipping in tow. The man wore his dark hair in a high tail and had modest horns that curved up, away from his forehead. Both he and his little girl, who looked much like him without the horns, wore thick pelt coats and boots that were open at the toes, exposing talons just as sharp as those that peeked out through the ends of their gloves.

Suddenly, the little girl lost her footing and tripped, falling hard on her knees. Tears quickly filled her eyes, and she began crying. The man stopped walking and, using his free hand, gingerly lifted her back to her feet. He spoke to her in the Ro'Erden tongue.

"You have to listen as you walk. Now, stop crying."

The girl nodded, her face a snotty, tear-stained mess as she clenched her teeth, trying her best not to cry. The man began walking again, but the girl did not follow. Instead she looked straight at Kira, who had not realized that he was staring. Embarrassed, he turned away and began pretending that he was searching for something in his bag.

"A thief," said the man in a whisper, again using the Ro'Erden tongue, but Kira had overheard.

"I am no thief," he said, irritated, replying in the same language, which Eutau had taught him what now seemed like ages before.

The man's eyes narrowed in surprise. "You are Ro'Erden? I have shamed the Land, forgive me."

Shamed the Land? thought Kira, just managing not to make a face. *What does that even mean?*

The man came closer with his daughter following after, his curious eyes searching Kira's face.

"Your skin is plain and your accent strange," began the man. "You are not from around here, are you? Where are you from?" He spoke fast, and Kira found himself having to listen very carefully to make out the words.

"Sorry, I have only ever spoken in this tongue with my uncle. And yeah, I'm not from Florinia, I just arrived from the North."

The Ro'Erden man's posture stiffened, his tone becoming defiant. "You are welcome in the South, though even here the Land has not forgiven us. You are plain enough to deceive most northerners, but I'm surprised the Land there did not harm you. It is dangerous. Your uncle was either a stubborn man or a foolish oaf."

Kira was taken aback. *I'm plain? And what does he mean that the Land is dangerous?*

"You have no idea what I'm talking about, do you?"

"No, I don't," responded Kira, his face reddening.

"You speak our tongue poorly, so I am not surprised. From whose blood do you come?"

Kira was unsure what the man was getting at, but he took a guess. "My mother. But I was raised by my uncle on my father's side. He was not Ro'Erden."

"That much is obvious," said the man. "A small thing knowing your mother tongue may seem to you, but be proud of it."

Thanks for nothing, thought Kira, forcing a smile. A part of him found it amusing that this man, this stranger, felt the need to berate him for not being Ro'Erden enough. The other part was irritated, especially since until yesterday he had believed himself a Deadbringer. He was done with this conversation.

"It was a pleasure meeting you," he began, "but I'm trying to find the Rose Market and should be on my way." J'kara had told him to visit the market should he enter Florinia.

"I know where it is!" said the little girl. "See?" She pointed to the basket of goods. Her smile was contagious.

Kira squatted down to her level, his annoyance gone. "Is that so? Could you point me in the right direction?"

The little girl looked to her father, who nodded his approval. Then, unexpectedly, she grabbed Kira's hand. He was wearing his gloves, but even so he had to fight the urge to recoil and pull away.

"Umm"—she looked up at the sun and then pointed—"northeast there's this *huge* building in the middle of a *huge* plaza with lots and lots of people going in and out like ants! There's so much to see and eat in there! Right, Papa?"

"Yes, there is."

"Thanks for that," said Kira, slipping his hand out of hers. He stood to his full height and found the man studying him again.

"As a northerner, I am certain you are familiar with scorn. I tell you now, do not think this city exempt from such hatred. It is here, both hidden and in clear sight."

"I wasn't expecting anything else, but that doesn't mean I have to accept it," said Kira, surprising himself with the fervor in his own voice.

The man's eyes narrowed, and then he nodded. "May the Land be solid under your feet and reunite us as friends."

"Yeah, same here."

The man laughed, though in a kindly way, and Kira had a feeling that he was supposed to have responded with some other formality. But it did not matter anymore, for the man and his daughter had left, and Kira was eager to find the Rose Market and quell his hunger.

Eventually, he came upon a large, open square bustling with people. At its center, just as the little girl had promised, was a building unlike any he had ever seen. It stretched for several blocks, its stone walls worked to mimic huge, false-arched windows, its every surface lined with oxidized copper and lattices overgrown with ancient rose vines. Rosebuds reached skyward from the vines like butterflies ready to take flight, yet not a single one was in bloom, and many lay withered and smeared on the ground. Luminous red tiles that resembled fish scales graced the building's peaked roof. The impossible curves and lines that the builders had coaxed out of the intricately worked stone enthralled him.

Curious to behold what lay inside, Kira followed a stream of people through the enormous doors and soon found himself standing like a fool, his eyes wide, his head turning every which way in an effort to absorb all he saw. He was in a great hall, a bustling marketplace filled with people and vendors whose stalls were pitched with vibrant fabrics that invoked the colors of spring. Huge colonnades lined either side of the hall, supporting tall arches upon which windows were set just below the ceiling. Looking up, he recognized the ceiling as a kind of barrel vault, a design that had always fascinated him. But, unlike the small barrel-vaulted ceilings he had seen in Opulancae, this curved ceiling had two parallel vaults joined by a thick seam of masonry that was itself supported by pillars running to the floor. The resulting effect made it appear like the ceiling was a colossal ribcage, with the seam its spine.

As much as he loved the North, Kira was starting to understand why Florinians like Kim never renounced their home, even though they had settled elsewhere in the Land.

The sudden sensation of something settling on the back of his neck yanked him from his reverie. He looked around in alarm but found no one, and then the sensation moved down toward his spine. *An insect,* thought Kira. He ignored it and moved on. After all, whatever unfortunate creature had found its way to his skin would not survive long.

The market's smells and sights were overwhelming. He walked by a stall packed with fruits so strange and ugly that he at first believed them to be fake. But then the merchant waved him over and presented him with a black, oval rock that she claimed was a fruit. No bigger than his hand, its skin was shiny, warty, and reminded Kira of a toad. But when the merchant cut it open, on the inside was a vibrant green flesh that was both creamy and refreshing. Kira's eyes widened in amazement, and to the merchant's delight he purchased half a dozen of the fruit to take back to J'kara's, along with a warm stack of thin flatbreads made from ground corn. These too were quite tasty, and the merchant had been kind enough to show him how to roll the flatbreads in his palms to form cylinders capable of holding other foods.

From another stall he purchased some tea, its leaves tightly bound to resemble pearls, its taste similar to what Eutau had imported at great cost in Opulancae. He wanted to give it to Eutau and hopefully convince him to stay away from the wine for a bit, and in particular from the *nologis.* For Teemo, he purchased a fiery red shawl to match her red hair. He wanted to see her again and hoped that she would emerge from whatever hiding place she had disappeared into.

Having explored every inch of the market, he stepped outside and noticed for the first time a large mural made of small tiles set high above the exterior doors. The image was of a man with his arms outstretched and his long hair curving around him like a veil caught in the wind. He was dressed in a white robe, with a shawl embossed with purple roses wrapped around his waist. At his back was a wasteland, the land barren, the sky gray. In front of him was a grand city that seemed to be emerging from the sea itself, rising toward a blazing sky as if by his command. Small letters set beneath the mural proclaimed the image to be of the Faceless God.

Going up on his toes, Kira scrutinized the God's image, hoping to gather some idea of what he truly looked like. Yet the God's face was turned at an angle away from the viewer, and only the slightest glimpse of his cheek and nose was visible. Kira dismissed the mural and turned away, wondering in frustration if the city contained a single image that actually depicted the countenance of the Faceless God. The deity's name, at least, suggested a search would be futile.

Kira looked to the sky and saw to his surprise that the sun had already begun its journey west. *I have a few more hours until twilight,* he thought. *I'll look around a bit more and then head back.*

He had not wandered far from the market when the sensation of something crawling along his skin returned. Annoyed, he removed his travel bag and then his coat and cloak, which he immediately set to swatting against a wall. *If I were alone,* he thought to himself in annoyance, *I would call upon Death and rot the damn insect where it crawls!* The feel of something touching his skin continued and irritated him, and he swore he would have to go through all his clothes when he returned to J'kara's and find the thing that was plaguing him.

He put his coat and cloak back on and patted down his clothes to smooth them, but stopped as his fingers touched a round lump in one of the hidden pockets sewn into the sleeveless doublet he wore. *It's the jaave Daemeon gave me! I had forgotten I even had it.* The thought was oddly disconcerting, and he left the *jaave* in his pocket and kept walking. He wandered aimlessly through the city, passing row upon row of houses, shops, and well-tended parks that breathed life into the stone and brick surrounding them. It was all very pleasing to the eye, but it failed to assuage the rising frustration he felt.

Suddenly, he heard the roar of the sea, and coming to his senses he saw that he was in a wide avenue leading to a large plaza. The sound of ocean waves echoed along the avenue from the plaza, and he hurried forward, excited to gaze on the sea for the first time. But he reached the plaza and then stopped, distracted. No one else was about, and zigzagging red and black setts gave the illusion of the plaza being deep, like a pool of dark, tainted water. At the center of the plaza, upon a colonnade centered in the middle of a public fountain, was a towering marble statue of the Faceless God.

Standing forty feet high, the Faceless God stood tall, a narrow sword in his right hand, its point resting in the fountain beneath him. His hair was separated into sections by a spiked supportasse fastened to a long robe that opened at the chest, exposing armor. A featureless mask concealed his face. Trailing beneath his robe were the carved bodies of Ro'Erden. Their faces were crushed, their heads severed from their bodies, their hands reaching upward, fingers contorted in agony. A shiver ran up Kira's spine as he stood before the fountain, gazing up at the statue.

Ca-clop, ca-clop, ca-clop.

Startled, Kira whipped around, his hand already reaching for his dagger. A handsome golden, buckskinned stallion was lazily approaching him. It bore no saddle and was unaccompanied by any rider. *It probably wants a drink,* thought Kira, swallowing down his sudden panic and releasing his grip on the dagger. He moved around the fountain to give it room, but the stallion followed.

"Listen," he said. It halted paces from him, its ears moving to and fro. "I don't have anything to give you." The stallion shook its head and scraped a front hoof across the setts as if calling him a liar. Sighing, Kira rummaged through his bag and pulled a corn flatbread from its packet. He tossed it at the stallion, which sniffed it and then quickly ate it.

"That's it. Go away. I don't have any more."

The stallion snorted, apparently displeased at having been dismissed. It made to go, but then in a heartbeat it turned back and charged at Kira, bashing him with its head and knocking him against the fountain. Kira fell back and just managed to keep from falling in by using his left hand to brace himself against the fountain's shallow bottom. He winced as something sharp pierced through his glove and into his palm. The horse nickered with delight and pranced across the plaza and into a nearby street, disappearing from view.

"Fucking animal!" shouted Kira, enraged.

A familiar scent wafted up from the disturbed water as Kira dislodged his bleeding hand. Instinctively, he turned and looked in. He felt his skin tingle as his eyes registered what lay beneath.

A terrible anxiety gripped him then, and he looked up at the statue of the Faceless God. "I shouldn't be here," he muttered to himself. With a reluctance he was unaware of, he pushed away from the fountain, his hand clutching at the water as if he could carry some of it back with him. Kira turned away from the fountain, eager to make his way back to J'kara's, to be with his uncle and talk to Lyse and Teemo, and found himself inches away from the Faceless God.

His presence was heinous, overbearing. Reality trembled around the Faceless God as if afraid to touch him, and a harsh noise like metal tearing against metal, distant yet close, echoed through the plaza.

A memory pricked at Kira then, of a man in a mask surrounded by red boulders, and of an emotion: hatred. "I *know* you," he said, staring up at the Faceless God. "I have *seen* you."

In response, the Faceless God lifted his arm and then gestured with his open palm toward the ground. His hand was veined and strong, the hand of a man who had spent countless hours laboring. "My gift," he said, his voice smooth and rich, "to you."

Kira reluctantly tore his gaze away and looked down. The plaza had become a rippling pool of blood.

"I don't want this!" he said fiercely, his head jerking up in defiance. But the Faceless God was gone, and Kira was not alone. From the streets surrounding the plaza, human-shaped shadows began to amble in. Most bore no face, though a few wore animal heads or sacks with richly painted faces.

Kira looked up at the sky, hoping to dispel the images before him, but the sky and the buildings had become breathing shells. *It's just my imagination,* he thought, and felt himself become oddly calm. From behind, a cold, damp hand clasped his. He looked down and found that it belonged to a formless shadow that could have been that of a child. The shadow-child tugged at his hand, and Kira found himself being led out of the plaza and through the city.

The streets had all become serene rivers of blood, and the sky burned with melting colors so vivid that it could have been a painting. The buildings vibrated in the wind like stone trees, while from the windows and the streets more and more shadows emerged to silently greet him.

Kira sighed, and the city itself seemed to sigh with him. It was enthralling.

A shocking noise *boomed* through the air, causing the rivers of blood to churn violently. Seconds later, debris and flesh rained down from the sky, and the shadows lifted up their arms with vigor. It was a breathtakingly beautiful sight, and yet . . .

A choir of voices called to him. They cried, and they screamed, and they sang, and they begged for one singular thing. Not far from him, metal clashed against metal until it at last tore through flesh, sending blood dancing through the air like flower petals. The familiar stench of spilled bowels and the sweet aroma of decay and disturbed earth filled his nostrils. Above, the hissing of arrows sailed though the air like diving birds.

Eye for an eye, life for a life.

Thoughts crept into Kira's mind as he stared up at the pulsing sky and the ascending plumes of smoke: that he would never again feel the warmth of the sun on his face, the passionate touch of a lover against his skin, the joy of the ocean's waves lapping at his feet. As if in a dream, Kira recognized that these thoughts were not his, but it did not matter. His eyes settled on the chaos before him, and a single desire overtook his mind.

Kill.

SHATTERED WALLS

THE EXPLOSIONS HAD been deafening, and now the frantic blare of the trumpets calling the garrison to arms was no less so. Plumes of smoke rose from the ruined watchtowers. Kristoff pushed himself up from the ground and drew his sword, looking for the enemy. Marya was already up, scanning her surroundings.

"The gates!" she shouted.

The gates to the Citadel had burst open, and the soldiers that had been guarding them lay sprawled out across the dirt and setts, their limbs either twisted or missing. The wall itself was intact, but its fresh-snow color was stained red with swathes of blood. Yells of confusion and agony began to supplement the trumpets.

Jun rose, helping A'ka rise in turn from where he had shielded her with his own body, and briefly he and Kristoff locked eyes in mutual understanding of what was to come. Somehow, an enemy had managed to infiltrate the Ascendancy itself, and this was only the prelude to the song.

"A'ka," said Jun, "inform the Ten." She nodded and darted off to the inner courtyard, back to the Citadel's main buildings. Jun then ran over to the gates, took hold of their warped metal bars, and began pulling them shut. The metal *creaked* and shifted and then, as if he were pulling shut a drapery, Jun began reforming and sealing the gate. As he finished, armed soldiers and Captains emerged from the main buildings shouting curses and orders, while along the top of the wall archers scurried to take up positions on the battlement.

"Marya!" shouted Kristoff. "Command these soldiers here while I look up above! We must determine what we are up against." She nodded and began roaring orders to the common soldiers and officers, all of whom jumped to obey the commands of a Sanctifier. Kristoff turned and charged up to the battlement.

As soon as he reached the top, a war horn sounded ominously over the blare of the Ascendancy's trumpets, and he heard the thunder of an advancing army. Through the crenels, Kristoff made out a green and silver banner rippling in the cold wind. A bowman standing next to him screamed out an echo of Kristoff's own thoughts.

"THE BASTION! IT'S THE BASTION!"

From below he heard shouts of dismay rise up.

"The Waning Wall has been taken!"

"A traitor, there must be a traitor!"

The bowmen nocked their arrows, and a few of them raised their bows to fire. Kristoff's eyes narrowed, and he bellowed his wrath. "Release those arrows before I give the word and I will throw you over the battlement so their horses may trample your bodies!" He studied the soldiers gathered under Marya's command and winced, for Marya was the only black-clad figure present. *The enemy has caught us with our finest absent, and they have already succeeded in revealing the cowards among our numbers,* he thought grimly. He looked out at the approaching force.

A large avenue fifty yards across ran along the outside of the Citadel's walls. In peacetime it was a grand, scenic promenade, but now it served as a moat of open space through which enemies would have to cross to reach the walls. It was still largely empty. Kristoff saw hundreds of enemy soldiers gathered at the entrances of the cross streets that opened onto the avenue, staying under cover as if waiting for something.

A dozen enemy riders on horseback appeared at the opening of the nearest cross street, led by a rider with lyre-shaped horns. The leader looked around as if surveying the scene and then yelled some indecipherable war cry. He spurred forward, and the hundreds of enemy soldiers poured after him into the avenue, charging the gates.

"MARYA!" screamed Jun from below, his eyes wide with surprise and anger. "I FEEL A RO'ERDEN-JA IS AMONG THEM! THEY HAVE A RO'ERDEN-JA!"

Kristoff felt his skin crawl with shock. "Ready your arrows!" he shouted. The bowmen complied, fear and intensity written on their faces. *At last they understand what is at stake,* he thought.

The enemy leader was halfway to the gates.

"LOOSE!"

A *hiss* of arrows rained down from the battlement, and the enemy leader brought up a long shield. Not a single arrow connected with him, but several hit and bounced off his horse. "Focus your attack on the infantry!" ordered Kristoff, even as he took hold of a bow and nocked his own arrow.

The horse is shielded with dirt, he thought in dismay. Rare indeed was the Ro'Erden powerful enough to manipulate the Land to such an extent. *Their leader is the Ro'Erden-ja. But the eyes,* he recalled from his clan's sagas, *the eyes are its weak point.* He aimed, pulled, and released in one expert motion. The horse reared back on its hind legs in agony, an arrow jutting from its left eye, but the Ro'Erden-ja expertly slipped off before the horse could fall, bringing his shield up over him as he ran the last steps to the gates. Once there, he lodged a strange sword between the two gates where they met, and then he turned the sword as if it were a key.

The gates burst inward and ripped from their hinges, crushing some of Marya's gathered soldiers where they stood. The Ro'Erden-ja slipped back into the ranks of his oncoming troops and vanished. Marya yelled for her troops to charge to defend the opening where the gates had stood, but then an enemy unit carrying a dozen battering rams of metal and wood ran to the opening and stopped. In a smooth, practiced motion, the unit brought the rams down on the ground, positioned them as if aiming at Marya's oncoming soldiers, and touched the backs of the rams with smoldering coals.

In the next moment, a scene of utter devastation lay all around the courtyard, and half of Marya's soldiers and horses lay torn in pieces on the setts. Those who still stood were motionless, stunned, confusion covering them like a shield. Smoke fumed from the front of the enemy's rams, and a terrible realization dawned on Kristoff.

Black powder! But only the clan Amistrites know the secret to such a weapon! Truly we have been betrayed.

But there was no time to think, for enemy spearman were already pushing into the courtyard. Kristoff ran down to join the fight while his bowmen redirected their aim, sending waves of arrows upon the enemy that had penetrated the Citadel. The enemy faltered, and Jun advanced with a squadron of cavalry hastily rousted from the stables.

As Kristoff leapt off the last step, he saw an enemy spearman charge at Jun's horse, but suddenly Marya was there, deflecting it with a blood-forged war scythe. Four spearmen rushed her. Dodging a thrust to her neck, she jabbed the war scythe into a spearman in front of her. The remaining enemy fell on her then, confident of their victory, but let go of their spears as multiple blood-forged blades punctured their chests. Blood and foam poured from their mouths. The blades retracted and the men fell dead. Marya was unharmed, her skin now splattered with her enemies' blood, her war scythe sweating as it made itself whole once more.

Then Kristoff was in the melee and all was chaos. A double-sided axe swung down on him and he brought his shield forward, blocking it. The moment he felt the axe bite into the shield and stick, he pulled it down to throw his enemy off-balance, bringing them face-to-face. He brought his mailed fist forward, smashing into the axe-man's face and sending him reeling back before stabbing him in the neck, where his helmet and cuirass met. And then . . .

Kristoff was in the air. A chunk of snow-white stone connected with his head and everything went black. Then he was on the ground, though he did not remember falling, and blood was running down his face from his ears. Everything was quiet and unfocused, and it was a while before hearing and vision returned. He sat up, trying not to vomit. Pushing aside his disbelief, he studied the scene before him.

The Citadel's wall, the wall that no Ro'Erden could affect, had been shattered. The gates were entirely gone, and the walls were down for a hundred yards on each side. Enemy and friendly soldiers fought weakly or wandered around stunned, catching their bearings. Fierce explosions rumbled through the air from the rest of the city, and multiple plumes of smoke begun to darken the late afternoon sky. Whatever weapon the Bastion had managed to create with its black powder was more powerful than any that the Amistrites' lore had yielded.

Kristoff pushed himself to his feet just in time to dodge an incoming blow. His broadsword was gone, and in desperation he bit into his wrist to bleed himself so he could form a blood-forged weapon. He was about to attack when a stake of stone shot from the ground, impaling the enemy soldier through the groin and out the chest, suspending him in the air.

Jun! thought Kristoff, shocked by the strange power, but it was not Jun. A woman, her face covered by a boiled-leather mask similar to that Amonos wore, stood a few feet from him. Dainty brown horns graced her head, her hair was cut in a short bob, and her curvy body was covered in a high-necked gown with tight, long sleeves upon which she wore dark green vambraces. The wrinkled hem of her gown dragged across the dirt.

"HEAR ME!"

Her voice carried through the chaos with unrelenting force. "The Ten stands with you, soldiers and Sanctifiers of the Ascendancy. The

Bastion has dared to rise up against us, but they will advance no further!"

The burning force in her voice had prevented Kristoff from recognizing her, but now he realized it was the member of the Ten whose voice was normally so shy. He had never realized that she too was a Ro'Erden. *How many of the Ten are Ro'Erden?* he thought, oddly bothered by the revelation.

From all around him, relieved shouts swelled throughout the courtyard.

"The Ten!"

"The Ten have come to aid us!"

"For the Ten, for the Ascendancy!"

Lifting a crescent-shaped blade of stone high in the air, the Ten shouted, *"DESTROY!"* and the soldiers pushed forward with renewed vigor.

The false eyes painted on her leather mask turned to Kristoff. "You were right," she said, "but the Bastion will not win." With those parting words she advanced, stone stakes rising from the ground to silence anyone who dared approach her.

Kristoff advanced as well, his blood-forged sword laying waste to armor and flesh. A mounted enemy tried to run him down, and he lengthened his blade into a lance that he drove into the horse's shoulder as he dodged. The rider fell, and Kristoff reshaped his sword as he circled around, bringing it down on the rider's head.

Then there were no more enemies around him. All the Bastion's soldiers within the courtyard had been slain, but the battle was not yet over. The enemy Ro'Erden-ja appeared on the rubble of the ruined wall with hundreds more soldiers behind him.

The Ten swiped her hand across a fallen brick from one of the destroyed watchtowers. Without ever grasping it in her hand, she hurled it at the enemy as if shooting it from a bow. The Ro'Erden-ja deflected it with his strange sword, but the impact flung him to the ground. The Ten wrapped her arms around her body as the hem of her gown jabbed into the dirt. As she did so, the Ro'Erden-ja slapped his hands against the ground and swept them in a strange circular motion. The Ten's stone stakes shot from the ground all around him, yet none managed to connect.

Soldiers on both sides rushed together, obscuring the fight between the Ten and the Ro'Erden-ja. *Where is Marya?* thought Kristoff, pushing his way forward. And then the damnedest thing caught his eye, and he found himself unable to look away.

A tall youth with long black hair had wandered onto the battlefield from the gap in the Citadel's wall. His gaze was fixed on the sky above him, and his left hand was outstretched and clutched, as if he was holding onto something. Oddly, even though the battle revolved around him, it never touched him. It was as if he was not there.

An explosion of dirt and flesh momentarily obstructed Kristoff's view, and then Travail unleashed his fury.

The youth with black hair was on all fours, ripping into a dead soldier with his bare hands and teeth. His skin had become like that of a days-old corpse. He looked up, his lips a wide, hideous grin from which fresh blood spilled forth. Bits of gore slid down his face and neck, back onto the body from which they had come. He had to be a Deadbringer, but it was like no Deadbringer Kristoff had ever seen. It was a monster that had stepped out from a nightmare to taste the flesh of those it played with in dreams.

A soldier came up from behind, seeking to slay it. Without ever looking back, the monster slid off the dead man's body. In that very instant, the body gave a violent twitch and, in one smooth motion as if it had been propelled from behind, it threw itself upon the surprised soldier, its teeth tearing viciously at his face.

The monster had risen—a tall beast that was at once obscene and powerful. His hair writhed about him like venomous snakes. Looking up at the sky, he threw his arms into the air and then smiled with such greed and raw lust that Kristoff felt sick. But Kristoff soon forgot his disgust, for the bodies of all those who had fallen began to rise. Thereafter, the battle ceased to be one of warring factions and instead became one of survival.

The Ten turned her attention to the monster and stabbed her crescent blade into the ground, but nothing happened. She staggered back as if surprised, and then she drove the hem of her dress into the ground as well. Still nothing happened, and she screamed as if in despair. Directly behind her came two Risen, one with a knife and an arm hanging loosely, the other with a battleaxe and no head.

Kristoff charged forward. Bringing his blood-forged sword around, he cleanly lopped off the first Risen's head and then pierced its heart. He withdrew his sword, expecting it to fall—as so many had done during the Purging—but it did not.

The head is severed and the heart pierced! Why is it still standing?

Something grabbed at Kristoff's ankle. His head snapped down to see a dead enemy soldier with no legs dragging herself closer, her mouth opening and closing in anticipation. Severing the hand at the wrist, Kristoff jumped away only to find that the hand was still latched onto his ankle, its fleshy fingers digging into the leather of his boot.

His mind screamed. *Travail be damned, this is not possible!*

The axe-wielding Risen lurched itself at Kristoff, and though it was headless it swung its axe true. Kristoff cried out as the bit connected with his armored shoulder, sending both of them to the ground. Congealed blood poured from the Risen's neck, bathing Kristoff's face in the foul stench of rot.

"I will not die this day!" he shouted. With those words, he rammed his hand into the Risen's gaping neck and gave a furious yell. The Risen twitched violently and then split in half, further drenching Kristoff in viscera. Lurching to his feet, he pulled the axe from his shoulder with his left hand and used it to pry the wretched corpse-hand off his ankle. His right arm was useless now, and he had lost too much blood to forge a weapon without peril.

At that moment, the order to retreat cut through the chaos. "FALL BACK! FALL BACK TO THE END!" The Ten was yelling, trying to preserve some semblance of order. She took the front line as the remnants of the Ascendancy's soldiers scattered, fleeing back to the Citadel's main buildings.

Seconds later, the enemy Ro'Erden-ja echoed the Ten's words. "FALL BACK! REGROUP ALONGSIDE LAN!"

From the madness the monster advanced, a shield of rotting soldiers from both factions surrounding him. Kristoff fell back, and then the sound of someone coming up from behind made him whirl about, raising the axe in one arm as the pain in his wounded shoulder screamed.

"Marya!" he said, relieved. Blood was seeping from a wound on her head, and her left ear was missing a chunk around the lobe as if it had been bitten off.

She opened her mouth to speak, but then her eyes widened in dismay at something behind him. Kristoff turned around and felt surprise etch itself on his face.

"Pretty Mare," he whispered, stunned. E'sinea's horse was trotting through the melee without a care in the land. She had no rider.

"Brother," cried Marya in despair, "where's E'sinea?" The Risen ignored Pretty Mare as she made her way toward the Deadbringer, toward the monster. Suddenly, Marya began yelling at the top of her lungs. "PRETTY MARE! APPLES! I HAVE APPLES!" The mare's ears twitched and its head turned in their direction. Then, giving a terrible cry, she charged at them.

"Shit!" said Kristoff, unsure whether he should use the axe. Marya appeared nervous as well but stood her ground, though Kristoff realized that her thumb was atop a wound on her wrist, ready to forge a weapon.

Pretty Mare halted paces away, her black eyes studying them, her chestnut tail swishing to and fro as if she herself was uncertain how to proceed.

Her wounds! thought Kristoff, taken aback. Chunks of flesh were missing from the mare's hide in gaping wounds that no living horse could bear.

It was Marya who voiced his thoughts. "She . . . *she's a Doll!*"

Pretty Mare snorted and took a few steps back.

"Wait, don't go," pleaded Marya. "E'sinea. Where is he?"

Pretty Mare stared at her and let out something that resembled a death grunt, though Kristoff assumed it was meant to be a whinny. She then trotted over to Marya and began nibbling on her hair.

"Good girl," Kristoff said urgently. All around them, dead soldiers were rising and steadily closing in. They had lingered long enough. "If E'sinea lives, you must take us to him. Can you do that?"

Pretty Mare bobbed her head, and the siblings mounted, hoping that her hindquarters would not give out from the wounds.

The three fought their way out of the courtyard—Marya with a blood-forged sword, Kristoff with the axe, Pretty Mare with her hooves and teeth—and into the open street. Soldiers from both factions were fighting their way through the living and the dead. Paces behind the monster, the enemy Ro'Erden-ja was steadily advancing through a wall of Risen, his strange sword rendering them truly dead as if it had some power over them.

As Pretty Mare broke into a gallop, the last thing Kristoff saw before they disappeared into the city was the enemy leader bringing his sword down upon the monster.

Kristoff prayed to Fortune that the Ro'Erden-ja struck true.

REUNION

𝕬 **MAN, A** soldier of the Bastion, stood with his back to the alley wall, a swordpoint pressed against the nape of his neck. The muscles in his hands were strained, his arms stretched out before him in terror. He was oblivious to the wetness running down his legs to pool beneath him.

Lyse stood just out of arm's reach, his mouth a dour line, the pupils of his amber eyes the fierce slits of a cat. He took a step forward, coming close enough that he could smell the hot piss steaming in the cold air.

"The Deadbringer from Opulancae, has he or has he *not* been captured?"

"Maybe. No, I mean, I don't know. But," the soldier began anew, "if he is here, I can be of use to you in catching him."

"Is that so?" said Lyse. He smiled, but his voice was cold.

"Yes! Yes, I can!" the man said desperately, a frantic hope lighting his face.

"Such an amusing thing you are," hissed Lyse, "offering me aid when you cannot even save yourself." The man's face fell. He attempted to speak, but his words were drowned out by the blade stabbing up through his throat and into his skull. He collapsed in the pool of his own piss.

Lyse rammed his fist into the alley wall, cracking the stucco. "I have not found you just to lose you!"

Leaving the alley behind, he entered the chaos of the streets and kept heading northeast, toward the Citadel. The sensation of death was strongest in that direction, and he was beginning to think he could feel someone calling upon Death itself. It had to be Kira.

In the distance, pillars of smoke had begun to rise into the air. The sound of battle echoed against the buildings, its origin indecipherable and ominous. All around him, people fled in alarm or milled in the open streets, uncertain of what was happening. In their midst were human-shaped shadows, many of which wore thin veils of fabric that bore the painted semblance of a human face. They stood motionless amid the chaos, ignoring the people and ignored by them, turning only to watch Lyse as he pushed his way forward through the crowds.

The street opened onto a small plaza where it intersected with two other streets. The plaza was plain and unremarkable, with empty vendors' stalls at the sharp corners of the surrounding stucco buildings. The sound of battle was closer here, and the few people in sight were fleeing back in the direction from which Lyse had come.

He hurried on and had just entered the northeastern cross street when his back twisted sharply in on itself. His knees buckled, and he fell to the hard street in pain.

"It can't be," he whispered to himself in disbelief, even as he turned and pushed himself up, his eyes scanning the plaza.

A dun mare galloped out from the northern cross street, and time slowed.

A boy urged the mare on, his long, chestnut braid trailing in his wake. The shaft of an arrow protruded from his back. At his heels were three riders with the green and silver sashes of the Bastion strapped on their arms. The lead rider thrust a long spear, hitting the mare's croup and sending it and the boy crashing to the ground. The boy landed on his back, crying out as the arrow was pushed through his torso and out from his chest, and then he went still.

Snarling, sword in hand, Lyse charged forward and with uncanny precision sliced deeply at the horses' hocks, sending the unsuspecting riders tumbling. He ran over to the struggling mare and pulled the spear out of its croup where it had lodged. Now unhindered, the mare charged one of the fallen riders, toppling him back to the street and trampling him to death.

Lyse wheeled about in time to counter an overhead strike. He then shifted his hip and swung his right leg out and around, connecting with his attacker's head. The agent's face caved in and his jaw dislocated, robbing him of his cry.

From behind, the last agent closed in, swinging her sword. In that instant, Lyse ducked and turned, and then he swung his left leg, crushing it into the agent's armored chest. A brief sound of crunching metal was swallowed by the wetness of shattering bone. Horror pulled the agent's face taut as she fell to the ground convulsing, gasping for air.

The sound of more riders approaching echoed through the plaza. Lyse scooped the boy into his arms, careful not to disturb the arrow, and then turned to the mare.

"I need time. Distract them, and then return to us." The mare's ears momentarily flicked back and forth, and then she galloped back up the northern cross street. Lyse hurried over to the dead agents where they lay and called out to them, his eyes becoming milky white orbs lined with deep black. "Rip apart any soldier that comes this way," he ordered. Then he pulled the hood of his cloak over his head and fled across the plaza and down the street to the south, away from the Citadel, toward the sea.

"Forgive me, Kira," he whispered over and over again, cradling the boy's body to protect it as he ran.

For almost twenty minutes he ran through a maze of side streets toward the far southern corner of Florinia, where the Waning Wall met the sea on the far side of the port away from the Citadel. The buildings closed in, becoming older and more decrepit. Children watched with staring eyes from open alleyways, and beggars and the elderly, many of them native Florinese, called to him as he ran. Echoes of the far-off battle could still be heard, but no one paid them any mind.

Eventually the ground began to rise steeply, and he slowed, breathing heavily. The last buildings fell away as he pushed up a weed-covered path on a cliffside that was strangely out of place in the flat city. The sound of waves surrounded him as he reached the top, coming to a rusted, wrought-iron gate fifteen feet high. Whatever wall the gate was set in was not visible, for ancient rose vines strangled it, concealing what lay beneath. Years of rust coated the door's hinges.

Lyse pushed against the door and with great effort managed to break it open. He was greeted by a large garden of overgrown roses, their thorns sharp and waiting, their dark green leaves dancing in the chill sea wind. There were many buds but no blossoms, and tall grasses grew wild between the flowerbeds, with small saplings and shrubs rising where once had been carefully manicured lawns. At the garden's center, at its highest point, stood an octagonal temple with stained glass windows depicting images of the First War. The garden echoed with the *booms* of waves lapping against rocky cliffs.

He walked through the temple's door and then stopped, looking back over the city below him. Columns of smoke rose all about, and the

Citadel itself was invisible under a pall of blackness. He could feel the death that was going on there, and agony gripped him. "You are blood of my blood, Kira. You will live. You *must* live."

Lyse took a shuddering breath and, turning his back on Florinia, entered the temple.

Inside there was but a single room that was quiet as a tomb. Gold reliefs outlined paneled walls of black lacquer, and the floor was of veined marble covered with a thick layer of dust. Bodies long decayed and draped in tattered clothes dangled like puppets from the domed ceiling. A wooden table, the room's sole furnishing, was set in its center. It was stained a deep rust color.

Lyse laid the boy on the table. Drawing a dagger from his belt, he cut away at the boy's tattered leather doublet and found that the arrow had pierced perilously close to the heart. Bracing his left forearm against the boy's chest, he grabbed onto the shaft of the arrow with his right hand and, counting to three, swiftly pulled it out. The boy came to life, his hand clutching at Lyse's arm.

"Lyse?" he asked weakly, uncertainly.

"Yes, E'sinea. Now hold still." Removing his gloves, Lyse gingerly pressed a finger against the exit wound and said, "The pain will only be momentary." Then he lodged his finger deep into the cavity. Blood flowed out of the wound and onto the table, enlivening the rusty stains.

E'sinea winced, his fingers digging into Lyse's wrist as he fought not to writhe. "*Aye, aye,* Lyse, it hurts!" he cried out through clenched teeth. After several minutes, Lyse pulled his finger out of the wound, which began to knit shut.

"I have given you some of my strength, but you must rest," said Lyse, brushing E'sinea's bangs aside. Vacant eye sockets surrounded by disfigured flesh stared up at him. "Why are you in this state?" he asked, worry gathering on his brow.

"He left me," said E'sinea, whimpering, as black tears trailed out of his vacant sockets. "Amonos abandoned me! I'm alone now."

Lyse cradled E'sinea in his arms and sat on the floor, resting his back against one of the table's legs. He gently sat E'sinea on his lap as a father would his sick child.

"You are abandoned?" he asked, his voice heavy with grief. "And what of me? Am I of so little importance? Is that why you chose Amonos over me?"

E'sinea's breath wavered, and he rested his head against Lyse's chest. "Please don't say that. You know why I made the choice I did, but now . . . maybe it's better this way. I miss Amonos, but . . ." His hand tightened around his braid. It was shaking. "I don't think I want to play this game anymore. And I'm afraid Amonos wouldn't agree with me."

Lyse brought his cloak around them. "Sleep. I won't leave your side."

"I'm sorry."

"*Shhhh.*"

"Lyse?"

"Yes?"

"Please, don't let me dream."

"Is the dream so awful?"

E'sinea's breathing had slowed, his voice almost inaudible. "Yes, except the end. Because that's when I see . . . you."

He had fallen asleep at last.

Lyse brushed E'sinea's bangs aside once more and gently ran his fingers across the boy's ruined eyes. "Forgive me for not arriving sooner, my poor E'sinea."

HONEY AND SPICE

IT WAS DARK. Then, from that darkness, snow began to fall. *Feathers,* thought Kira as he watched, *they're just like feathers.* A flurry landed on his cheek, where it quickly melted and slid down like a tear.

A sudden torrent of laughter ripped through the darkness. It was joyous and welcoming, and Kira found himself wanting very much to be a part of it. He began walking toward the laughter, but he had not gone far, only a dozen steps, when a crowd came into view. They were dressed in flowing cottons and rich velvets threaded with blinding gold. Their hands, feet, and heads were dark shadows, and a thin layer of snow had settled on the tops of their heads, which had been cleanly severed just above where their noses would have been. Wide, curving mouths full of sharp teeth adorned their faces.

A pitiful whimper was trickling from the center of the crowd of shadows, accompanied by the sweet smell of honey and warm spice. Curious, Kira stepped forward, and the crowd parted for him like a gentle ripple.

A man lay naked in the snow, his limbs bound behind his back, chained to a collar that had been fastened around his skinned neck. The man's eyelids had been torn off, his genitals were crushed, and bite marks marred his entire body. Yet, there was no blood. Beside him, a triangular piece of meat flopped about like a fish out of water. Upon seeing Kira the man tried to speak, but his words were incomprehensible. He had no tongue. The circle of laughing mouths with their sharp teeth inched closer, and the man cowered into a ball.

The shadows began to strip away Kira's clothes then with their strange hands, and he allowed it, though his gaze never wavered from the pristine snow beneath the mutilated man. Once Kira was fully naked, they began to clean his body with the fallen snow and comb out his hair until it flowed like oil, and they dressed him in clothes that seemed to be woven from the darkness itself. In his right hand they placed a narrow sword; over his face, a featureless mask. Then they pulled back, their sharp teeth sheathed behind pale lips.

The man's head jerked up, and Kira felt an inexplicable sense of guilt surge through him. But when he opened his mouth to speak—to apologize, for some reason—his right hand thrust forward with the sword, piercing the man through the throat. Blood poured forth as from an overflowing well, marring the virgin snow. The shadows smiled, and the sweet smell of honey and spice, of blood and rot, engulfed him.

Kira woke up.

His body was stiff and raw all over, and he was finding it difficult to move his hands. The sound of metal *clanked*, and something unyielding dug into his wrist. He lurched into awareness.

"No," he whispered in shock, beholding the heavy shackles that bound his hands. His eyes instantly scoured his surroundings. He was alone in a small room that, save for the ceiling, was entirely of stone. A door of iron and wood lay far from reach, mocking him. A lantern stood on a high post opposite him, suffusing the room in a gentle light that cast flickering shadows on the walls.

His limbs protested as he stood, and for the first time his mind registered that his coat and cloak were gone. He struggled not to flinch at the sight of his hands and forearms, which were stained dark crimson. His clothes stuck uncomfortably against his skin.

"Whatever happened, happened," he said, lying to himself, even as a voice inside his head screamed, *WHAT DID I DO? WHY AM I LIKE THIS!* Refusing to acknowledge that thought, he took hold of the chain linking the shackles and followed it to its base.

I can't rot this, he thought, dismayed, as he ran his hands against the stone wall where the chain's pin was secured. *But this chain.* His fingers slid from one link to the next. *Yes, yes, I can rust it. I know I can. I have to!* He squeezed the chain between his hands until they ached, trying to rust and break the metal. But metal was not flesh, and it did not give way. *Rust, damn you!* Panic gripped him then, and he began yanking at the chain and trying to force his hands through the shackles.

The sound of approaching voices and footfalls saved him from losing control.

Swallowing down his panic, Kira backed up against the wall. He wondered fearfully what the Sanctifiers would do to him and if he could somehow free himself to escape. Another thought crept into his mind then, one that drove away all fear for his own safety. *What of my uncle and Lyse? What of Teemo? What of J'kara? Will they burn her as a traitor?* Newly determined, he took hold of the chain once more and waited.

The door swung inward and two soldiers walked in. One was a Ro'Erden with lyre-shaped horns who looked strangely familiar, and the other appeared to be a northerner. Each soldier held a sword in one hand and a lantern in the other, further illuminating the small room and dispelling the shadows.

Then Kim Lafont walked through the door. In his shock, Kira let go of the chain, which clanked noisily on the stone floor.

Kim wasted no time. "The Citadel has fallen to the Bastion, and the rest of Florinia will soon be ours. But thanks to your antics, the southwestern quarter of the city has yet to fall."

Kira tried his best to appear calm as he tried to process the information. "You must be pleased. I'd applaud if I could, but I seem not to have the use of my hands," he said sarcastically.

"Why did you attack my agents?"

"Attack?" Kira blurted out, confused, his facade shattered. "What are you on about?"

The blood . . .

His eyes cast down, seeking his crimson-stained hands, but the sight of something moving in the corner of his vision jerked his head back to where Kim and the agents stood. They had not moved, but Kira was certain he had seen something else in the room.

Kim's fury was visible on his face. "Natsu'es," he spoke, his voice commanding.

The Ro'Erden spoke up, his words heavily accented. "You wandered into the battle and raised the dead to attack the soldiers of the Ascendancy—mostly theirs, but also some of ours. You felled many soldiers yourself. You"—he paused as if reluctant to speak—"you *ripped* at the living with your hands and teeth, and then you raised the dead and directed them to attack the living, just as you had."

Kira's legs wavered underneath him and he fell back against the wall. His lips suddenly tasted of salty tears. "Lie. It's a lie. Kim, please say this is a lie!"

The second agent snapped. "How dare you mock my fallen brethren? How dare you say you have no idea what kind of monster—"

"Hold your tongue, agent," Kim barked harshly. Kira watched as Kim's questioning eyes examined him. "You really have no idea what happened, do you?"

Kira's mind raced. *It's not my fault. It's . . . no. No. It is my fault. It is all my fault.*

"H-how many," asked Kira, dreading the answer, yet needing to know. "How many did I kill?"

"Too many are dead, and too many are nursing *bite* wounds. Do you understand what I am saying to you, Kira? You had my men—*my men*— attack as if they were mindless beasts!" Kim took in a deep breath and let it out slowly, gathering his composure. "Despite our losses, Natsu'es is correct. For whatever reason, you focused your attacks mainly on the Ascendancy. Your appearance may have had a hand in our victory at the Citadel."

Kira said nothing, stunned, at a loss for words.

"In all my years as a soldier, I have never seen or heard of a Deadbringer accomplishing what you did." Kim's eyes narrowed, and for the first time Kira saw something that might have been fear.

"What are you?"

Kira remained silent.

"Then what of your friend, Lyse?"

"Lyse." Kira stirred at the name. "Is he safe?" *Did I hurt him?*

"He was spotted aiding a powerful enemy—one of the Sanctifiers who was tasked with capturing you in Opulancae, who must have been pursuing you. Lyse is not your friend."

Something in Kim's voice irked Kira. "What, and you are?"

"I am not your enemy."

"Then what are you? My friend? My savior? What should I call you? Tell me!"

"I am your friend. Otherwise, we would not be having this chat."

Kira recalled everything Kim had done for him, and he felt ashamed. "Kim, I . . . I don't know what happened. I saw my uncle. And then I wanted to see the city, and I was at a fountain that had a statue of the Faceless God." His breath caught in his throat, and for a moment he was certain he would vomit. "I saw the Faceless God—don't look at me that way!—I *saw* him, and these, these *shadows* with painted faces. They led me through the streets and then . . ."

His voice trailed off as patchy memories put the truth to their accusations.

"You remember, *vel?*" asked Natsu'es. There was a strange pity in his eyes. Kira nodded, not trusting himself to speak.

Kim continued. "You're not my prisoner, but you will have to remain here until we have eliminated the last of the Ascendancy's soldiers in the city — for your protection, and for ours. Then we can speak of what comes next."

"What of my uncle?"

"That *thing* is not your uncle."

The cold edge in Kim's voice pulled Kira from his shock. A strange madness possessed him.

"If you hurt either my uncle or Lyse, I *will* kill you."

Kim's face had become an impassive mask. "I will have water and food brought to you. Try to sleep, and tomorrow we will speak again." He turned and left, the two agents following him.

Not long after, several other agents walked in, one carrying a tray with food, another holding a porcelain pitcher. They stared at him with venomous eyes. Then one of them was on Kira before he could react, bringing the pitcher around into the side of his head. Everything went black.

Kira awoke face down, the side of his head throbbing. He tried to move and cried out as a paralyzing pain shot through his torso. A coughing fit seized him and did not let up until he had spit up blood and a broken molar. Carefully, slowly, he pushed himself up. The pitcher lay on the floor, shattered. He was alone.

Why didn't they kill me? He dragged himself to the wall and propped his back against it. The pain shot through his side again, and he winced. *They didn't kill me because they want to hurt me for as long as they can. Or maybe Kim still thinks he can use me in his plans. Or both.* He stared at the wall across from him, his eyes unfocused as he fought off the pain. *They know about uncle and Lyse and . . . they know.*

The lantern's light flickered and the shadows briefly formed a tall figure. His mind wandered to the Faceless God.

"Fuck you."

Kira's thoughts roiled. *Kim doesn't trust either uncle or Lyse. If he succeeds in capturing them, what will he do to them? What will his agents do to them? Do his agents know that my uncle is a Doll? What will they do to Teemo and J'kara?*

The light began to flicker madly and the shadows began to dance, morphing into man and then beast and back again. His gaze fell on the porcelain shards. Their edges would be sharp enough to pierce flesh if he was forced to attack Kim's agents. The realization that he would have to kill to survive did not sit well with him, but neither did the prospect of losing his life and the lives of those precious to him.

I have to make a choice.

Kira tried to stand, to reach for the shards, but then the shadows began to laugh and the walls lurched inward. *An illusion,* he thought, remembering the bloody streets and the pulsing, breathing buildings. *It has to be!* Disoriented, he fell back and pressed his palms against his eyes, hoping that when he opened them everything would be in its normal place. But as he did so the unexpected smell of honey and spice filled his nostrils, and he remembered the blood on his hands, the blood of the people he had murdered without even realizing it. He uncovered his eyes and found the room alive with malice, the shadows taking visible form, their teeth grinning in their cropped heads.

A numb realization settled over him then, and he remembered Daemeon's words on that terrible night in the Gods' Spears, telling him to stop living for false ideals, to be what he yearned to be. He clutched at his doublet and felt the *jaave* still there, sitting safe in its hidden pocket.

"She gave me the choice to see the truth, but I held onto uncle's lies and refused to accept it, and now I can't control my powers," he whispered. "Everything that's happened has happened because I've been afraid of being something other than a Deadbringer! Even now, I'm afraid to change. But I can't continue like this. I won't!" His heart pounded and his voice rose, shouting his defiance to the gathering shadows.

"I ACCEPT WHO I AM, WHAT I AM. IF IT MEANS PROTECTING THOSE CLOSEST TO ME, I WILL BECOME THE VERY EMBODIMENT OF A NIGHTMARE LORD!"

The shouts echoed and faded away, and the shadows hissed, as if displeased with his proclamation. They began peeling from the walls, floor, and ceiling and flowed slowly toward him, their arms reaching and grasping.

Kira stiffened, his heart beating loudly in his ears. He quickly undid the buttons of his doublet and pulled out the *jaave*. Long shadow-arms with elongated fingers sprouted from behind the wall on which he had been leaning and wrapped around his arms. But he had already emptied the contents of the *jaave* into his mouth, and though the yew leaves were dry and pricked like broken glass he chewed, and swallowed, and hoped.

The shadow-hands had rendered him immobile, restraining him far more tightly than the metal shackles around his wrists. One set of hands reached for his groin and set to stroking his cock, and he shuddered, hating it. Another took hold of his chin, pointing it up toward the ceiling. A third caressed his lips and face.

A group of shadows stood over him, their heads nothing more than mouths set with sharp, glistening teeth. A choir of voices spoke to him, their call a binding, mesmerizing weight on his mind and very being.

Love us as we love you. Give us life, and we will worship you.

Then a deep, familiar voice cut through the darkness, a woman's voice laughing a rich, joyous laugh, and Kira found himself laughing wildly along. The shadows clawed at him desperately as if trying to pull him to them, but Kira continued laughing as Daemeon's words vibrated in the air, and the shadows screamed and melted away.

"Welcome home, blood of my blood."

EPILOGUE

ON THE WALLS, in the streets, and in the gardens of Florinia, amid the stink of death and sound of battle, the purple roses began to bloom.

The End

of

Book One

Author's Note

Thank you so very much for buying this book! You all have allowed me to do what I always wanted to do, and for that I am grateful. I hope you were able to connect with the characters, if even just a little bit. I'd love to hear your thoughts and would love to see images of you with my book. Also, it would be great to hear about which characters and chapters were your favorites. I can't help but be curious.

Send your thoughts to emmarkoff@ellderet.com

Tag your images on Instagram to @tomesandcoffee using the following hashtags: #emmarkoff #deadbringer #ellderetseries #thedeadbringer #ellderet

Or, if you just want to see what I'm up to (I promise I'm working hard on the second book!), swing by either my personal blog or book website.

Blog: www.tomesandcoffee.com

Website: www.ellderet.com

Fortune be praised (or maybe it's Travail), Kira and the rest are just beginning on their journey. I hope you will continue on the journey with them, and with me. Let's get together again in the next book!

-E. M. Markoff
With my cat, Kanoqui, in the sunless, concrete crevice of
my workroom, San Francisco
February 24, 2016

ACKNOWLEDGMENTS

To my friends who made time in their busy lives to read the story and give me feedback, I thank you. Being able to discuss the events and characters with you meant the world to me.

To my editor and partner-in-crime, Gabriel. You were the first to believe in me, even before I believed in myself. And, as a consequence, you are also the person who prods and rips apart everything I do because you know I can do better. No matter how busy you are, you always make time to read my drafts and discuss every scene with me. I could not have made it to the end without you by my side. ¡Besos!

To my #1 critical fan: Silva Frankian. Your thorough analysis of the book and willingness to suffer my every question at any hour of the day — I'm never going to let you rest. Travail has damned you — has been invaluable. You're the best and you're going to let me buy you a cocktail . . . or three.

To Gabriella Quiroz aka Pink Pigeon Studio. Thank you for reading the manuscript and for taking on the challenge of creating the cover art. I will never forget the exact moment I saw the completed drawing. It was magical. Your work was the final piece needed to bring *The Deadbringer* to life.

To all the bloggers and vloggers who took time to post about formatting, Photoshop, topography, Word issues, your experiences in self-publishing: thank you. You were the light at the end of many long, dark tunnels.

To Ioana Cosma: I value our long walks.

Lastly, I want to thank my cat, who always seems to know when I need him to be on my lap (including right now, I kid you not). He is my constant furry companion.

Te extraño.

CPSIA information can be obtained
at www.ICGtesting.com
Printed in the USA
LVOW08s1540270917
550281LV00003B/573/P